Beyond the Brink

D. R. Hill

ONE

A voice. A whisper. Something so subtle and undistinguishable it was barely perceptible, called from out of the darkness. The neophyte stirred suddenly beneath his blankets, panting frantically in the chilling air of the tent as he momentarily forgot his surroundings. What was it that had roused him from his troubled slumber? Was it a mere fading dream that had transformed into muddled reverie, or had the calling truly found him and awoken him? Still it beckoned, niggling at the deepest recesses of conscious thought. As the young man recollected where he was, and why he was there, realisation set in. He was being summoned.

The neophyte emerged from the tent pitched in knee-deep snow and gazed out across the planes of ice. The Aurora Norteius burned fierce shades of emerald and violet in the heavens above, weaving and twisting against a backdrop of speckled stars. To the southeast, the first glow of dusk had begun to seep upwards from the horizon. Shivering in the freezing wind, the young neophyte revolved to gaze up the slope of the hill, slowly raising his eyeline to the black shadows of the henge beyond the brow. It was time.

Plodding heavily through the snow, the young man steadily fought his way uphill, towards the Northern Circle, towards his fate—perhaps towards his end. He shuddered once more, though he suspected it was no longer the frigid winds chilling him to the bone. He was numb. Nauseas. Utterly terrified of what awaited him atop the slope; but there was no running now, no turning back. This was it. He had made his choice, and now he had no other option but to see it through, regardless of the outcome.

The snow shallowed as he reached the brow and the eleven sarsen standing stones illuminated beneath the glow of the northern lights overhead. Centred in the henge rose five triliths; beneath each stood a Circle magister, hooded in their crimson-hemmed white robes. Under the great trilithon stood the Archon himself, Zadkiel Al'Ilah, cloaked in ceremonial black vestments. Around the periphery of the Northern circle, beneath the lintels that stretched across the tops of the main menhirs, were a number of paladins and acolytes, there to bear witness to the ritual. Each of the magi's faces were concealed in shadow beneath their drooping cowls, yet despite this, the neophyte knew all eyes were upon him.

The voice of the archon tolled, transmogrified by the thaumaturgy of the Northern

Circle into deep and thunderous speech, both terrible and compelling. "Arlas Al'Asim," Zadkiel boomed, "cast off your garments."

Silence descended. Arlas could hear his heart drumming powerfully between his ears. Oblivious to the freezing temperatures, he stripped, letting his clothes fall to the snow.

"Step forward into the Circle," commanded Zadkiel.

Taking a final lungful of air, Arlas advanced between the two sarsen pillars ahead, across the threshold and onto the stone floor of the Northern Circle. The moment he crossed over the brink, his senses came alive to the Aether around him. He felt a heat beneath the soles of his bare feet, and as he glimpsed down at his toes, he witnessed the carved runes begin to glimmer with white energy.

"Repeat these words as you hear them, Arlas Al'Asim: Here dies the man I was, and from his ashes shall be forged an instrument of valour, justice, and virtue!"

Arlas gazed toward the central altar, upwards from which rose a length of elder oak planted in the stone. He turned his attention once more to the archon, and struggling through nerves to catch his breath, he repeated what he had heard. "Here dies the man I was, and from his ashes shall be forged an instrument of valour, justice, and virtue!"

"I accept my duty to serve and protect, and am willing to make any sacrifice in doing so," Zadkiel boomed.

"I accept my duty to serve and protect... and am willing to make any sacrifice in doing so."

"I hereby give myself; mind, body, and soul; to serve the Circle of Magi, now and forevermore."

"I hereby give myself; mind, body, and soul; to serve the Circle of Magi," Arlas declared. "Now and forevermore!"

"Approach the altar!" instructed the archon.

Apprehensively, Arlas stepped out across the stone, making his way towards the heart of the circle. At the foot of the steps, he hesitated, looking at the flawless grain of the elder oak before him.

"Ascend," commanded Zadkiel.

Arlas anxiously climbed, pausing atop the stone altar.

"Turn to face the dawn."

Arlas's teeth began to chatter. Slowly he revolved around the altar's circumference until he was facing southeast. The horizon was aflame with the blood of dawn, the sun mere moments from erupting. A whisper of ancient tongues wove their way into the neophyte's mind, growing steadily in volume until they were a deafening chorus. Light spilled from the runes into the carved channels of the ley lines, carrying the current of energy inwards until the powerful ancient magic converged upon the altar. The staff of elder oak began to heat until its surface shimmered with mystic energy. Above, the ripples of the aurora churned into violet rays and thunder tolled heavily out of emerging storm clouds, all the while, the horizon burned scarlet and amber with the impending sunrise.

"The time is now!" roared Zadkiel over the drowning chanting inside Arlas's mind. "Bind!"

Arlas extended his hands, slowly curling his fingers around the elder oak. Pain fired through every synapse. His heart throbbed and convulsed wildly. His mind was ablaze, his body dying. Arlas glimpsed out through a fading window of vision at the breaking dawn. The first rays of golden light pierced between the standing stones, colliding with the length of elder oak, and all went dark.

Rhys opened his eyes, bolting upright in his hammock as he gasped for breath. His heart pounded and his head throbbed as cold sweat trickled down his brow and soaked into his shirt. He steadied his breathing as the hammock rocked from side to side. He pressed shut his eyelids, willing the images of his dream to fade, and listened to the creeks and groans of the White Marlin. The crew quarters were otherwise empty; Rhys was alone. Clambering down from the hammock, he eased his feet into his boots and gulped a few mouthfuls from his waterskin, dwelling for a final few moments on his dream. The lingering sensations receded, and with a deep inhalation, the mage pushed open the doors and stepped out onto the main deck.

Overhead, the mainsails were billowing in a strong tailwind, the gales driving them steadily northwards across the open sea. The clear skies had darkened since Rhys had last been on deck; the heavens having grown thick with murk that descended from the clouds in great tendrils of smoky mist. A fat droplet of rain splattered on Rhys's brow; it was the first of many to come. Infrequent drips continued to splash across the top deck in the moments that followed, staining the bleached wood of the Marlin steadily grey. But the rainfall never quite broke into the storm that was threatening to impend, instead, it pelted the ship and her crew with sporadic squalls that broke as rapidly as they started.

Rhys climbed the steps to the aftcastle and greeted Sol and Arne. "Sol, Captain Anderssen," he nodded to them.

"Please," insisted the captain. "Arne will do just fine."

"Very well—Captain Arne," smirked Rhys.

"Is he always like this?" Arne asked, looking to Sol.

"Yes," nodded Sol deadpan. "Always."

Rhys chuckled and directed his gaze fore to the wall of gloom being run through by the bowsprit. "How do you navigate in this weather?" he questioned, struggling to even make out the tip of the spar.

"Memory, mostly," replied Arne.

"But I thought you had never sailed into the Wyrm's Triangle before?"

"I haven't."

"Then how do you know where we are going?"

"I don't," replied the captain straight-faced.

"I see," Rhys returned anxiously.

Arne shot him a coy smile.

"Is he always like this?" Rhys turned to Sol.

"Yes," nodded the mage. "Always."

"I suppose I had that coming," conceded

Rhys. "But in all seriousness, how do you know where we are going?"

"Wayfinding," replied Arne.

"Wayfinding?"

"I know where I am going because I know where I have been. I can read the stars, the sun, and the swell. I know our bearing, and I know the current and the winds. Because of this, I can find my way ahead."

"Okay," nodded Rhys. "But if you cannot see past the bowsprit, then how can you be sure we aren't seconds away from crashing into something?"

"There are breaks in the fog, places where you can see for a mile or so at a time that emerge every so often. Because of this, I know how far ahead is clear. When the way ahead is clouded for too long, we drop to half sail and slow her up until another break."

"Alright," yielded Rhys, deferring to Arne's lifetime of experience.

"I may not see the way ahead now, but I've caught glimpses of the waters before us. Fret not. We won't sail into unknown seas blindly. I promised to get you to the shores of Thule—I intend on doing so with the Marlin still afloat!"

"That's reassuring," remarked Rhys, rather unassured.

"Don't worry, Rhys," soothed Sol, "I trust him with my life."

Rhys shot his friend a smile and nodded to

them both before turning to descend back down to the main deck. "Vidar, Eirik," Rhys greeted Arne's sons, the tillermen.

"Good morning, sleepy head," teased Eirik.

"Is it a good morning?" questioned the mage looking up at the bleak skies.

"Compared to what is on the horizon…" responded Vidar.

"I see your point," agreed Rhys, as through a fleeting break in the mist, he glimpsed black anvil-shaped clouds up ahead.

"If the legends of the Wyrm's Sea are true, lad, this is the best weather we are going to see in a long while!" a gruff voice came from behind.

"Ever the optimist, Ulfgar," returned Rhys as he revolved to see the dwarf gazing over the ship's bulwark out into the mist. "It can't always be stormy in the Stormy Isles. There must surely be breaks in the weather?"

"You are assuming that the weather is just weather," put in Cade, moving across the deck to join the conversation.

"You reckon the storms are magical?" questioned Rhys.

"I don't know," shrugged Cade. "You are a greater authority on the subject than I."

Rhys pondered for a moment, listening to the distant gurgles of thunder echo across the shrouded horizon. "No, I don't think so," he declared finally. "Just plain old nonmagical thunder by my judgement!"

"But what about the Grey?" questioned Cade. "You know better than anyone what dark magic is capable of. Longford froze over in the middle of summer; it conjured a mist even more impenetrable than this."

"You are right," conceded Rhys, "magic— or at least blood magic, is more than capable of manipulating the weather and the elements. But the Grey was summoned by Indus, and my bet was that it was done so at great cost. From what I understand, magic, in all cases requires a caster and source of energy for the enchantment. To produce an eternal tempest... it would require an unprecedented source of energy to power, and an incredibly powerful being to invocate."

"So, what you are saying is: a god might be able to produce such a phenomenon?"

"No," chuckled Rhys. "That is not what I am saying."

"Just checking," grinned Cade.

"I wouldn't be so sure," put in Ulfgar.

"You're not telling me that you are a recent convert, Ulfgar?

The dwarf chortled. "Fat chance! But I have heard of things in this world that would make a forever-raging storm seem like a reasonable idea; things that even Thia would have trouble explaining!"

"We'll see then," smiled Rhys as a gust of wind drove inward a sudden squall. "If ever we make it to shore, that is."

Rhys turned from the huntsman and the dwarf and made his way over to the starboard gunwale where Alkis and Nathaniel were in conversation, the two men likewise peering off apprehensively into the murk.

"I don't like this," uttered Nathaniel.

"I'm not sure anyone does," returned Alkis.

"I don't know," interjected Rhys as he leant up against the bulwark beside them, "Sol seems quite at ease."

"And he was the most reluctant to come here!" remarked Alkis.

"I can be very persuasive when I want to be," smirked the mage.

"Yes," agreed Nathaniel, "worryingly so at times."

"The blood magic helps," jested the mage.

"I'd be careful making jokes like that!" returned Nathaniel.

"Someone might take you seriously," added Alkis.

"I'm just trying to lighten the mood," assured Rhys as he gazed about at the darkling gloom descending ever thicker around them. "I've got a feeling things might get pretty dire in the coming weeks," he added more sombrely.

"I reckon you are right," nodded Alkis.

"I hope you know what you're doing," sighed Nathaniel, turning back to look out over the black brine.

"You know..." confessed Rhys, "I'm not sure I have the faintest idea."

"Reef the main sail," Arne commanded his sons as he descended the steps of the aftcastle and manned the tiller himself. Vidar quickly dashed to the mainmast and began unfastening the rigging; Eirik meanwhile scurried up the post to the base of the lateen sail. Locking his powerful thighs in place around the mast so that he was held aloft by the grip of his legs alone, he began rolling up the base of the sail around the lower spar. When the sail was taken in to about half its area, Eirik slid back down the mast and aided his brother in re-securing the rigging. As the two brothers performed the well-practised routine, Arne put his burly mass to use, shifting the tiller sharply from side to side in a series of motions that rocked the Marlin in the waters. Rhys watched them in fascination, and before he had realised it, the ship had slowed to a crawl.

The mage approached the tiller as Eirik and Vidar took back the roles of helmsmen from their father, Arne returning to his position atop the aftcastle. Ascending to the stern, Rhys approached the captain

"What's wrong?" questioned the mage.

"It's as I said, lad," Arne replied. "We've ventured past the point I've last seen ahead. The mist is thickening. We are sailing blind."

TWO

Rhys peered down from the prow at the churning foam seething in the Marlin's bow wave. Rain was beginning to lash down more feverishly as the world continued to dim around them. Icy gusts swelled through the choking fogs. A flash of lightning lit up the gloom. Then another, and another, a drumroll of thunder peeling shortly after each explosion of white. Rhys pulled his leather cowl up over his head and listened to the loud patter of rain as it dashed against his hood.

"We're getting close," came the gentle voice of Thia from over his shoulder.

"Is that what Arne said?" questioned Rhys, turning to behold the witch as she approached. Silver tresses danced in the breeze as her cobalt gaze penetrated past Rhys into the fog.

"No," she replied. "Just my own intuition," she confessed.

"I imagine you are right," assured Rhys, "given the weather."

"I fear it will only worsen," she smiled, pulling up the hood of her woollen cloak as she sidled up beside Rhys.

The mage watched as the rain beaded across the fabric of her cloak, collecting in globules that streaked across the cloth as if it were impermeable to water. "That's clever," remarked Rhys, nodding to the cloak as he examined his own sodden tunic.

"You like it, do you?" the witch teased.

"Given the conditions, I think it looks rather cosy. Care to share your secret?"

"A reasonably simple enchantment," remarked the witch, "though time consuming to apply."

"Would you mind waterproofing my tunic for me?"

"Nope," she replied abruptly.

"Is that a *'No, you wouldn't mind,'* or *'No, you won't do it,'*?"

"No, I won't do it."

"Why not?"

"Because if I do it for you, then you'll never learn how to do it for yourself," she smirked.

Rhys sighed heavily. "Fine. Will you please teach me?"

"I'll think about it," she jibed.

"Well, in the meantime I'll just stand here like a drowned rat," conceded Rhys.

"You realise that there are non-magical means by which to waterproof clothing?"

"Like what?"

"Look at Ulfgar's coat, or Arne and his

sons' cloaks."

Rhys turned and gazed back at Ulfgar's duster jacket and likewise the oilskin hooded ponchos worn by the sailors. To his surprise, though to not the same extent as Thia's enchanted cloak, water was beading off the material and trickling downwards off the clothing worn by the four men.

"How does it work?" questioned the mage.

"Oil or waxes, obtained from flax mostly," replied the witch.

"The magical means seems more convenient," replied the mage.

"Perhaps," agreed Thia, "provided you have the aptitude."

"Which I do," smiled Rhys.

"Unfortunately, the material needs to be dry for the enchantment to be applied," responded Thia smugly. "Therefore, you'll have to dry out before I can teach you."

"If the weather continues like this, as I have been assured several times today it will do, then I'm not sure I'll ever dry out enough."

"You could always go below deck," proposed Thia.

"No," sighed Rhys. "I'm on look out."

"Look out?"

"I need to be up here—in case anything emerges out of the fog."

"Like what?" questioned Thia.

"Like that," responded the mage somewhat disbelievingly, his eyes widening as through the mist loomed a jagged shadow. "Up ahead!" cried Rhys, sounding the alarm of the encroaching obstacle that still had yet to take form from out of the veil of haze.

"Hard a starboard!" boomed Arne's voice as he caught his first glimpse of the silhouette.

Vidar and Eirik lunged against the tiller, forcing it over portside with all their might. The rudder cut through the waters, slowly turning the caravel. The bowsprit angled away as a jagged tooth of rock appeared through the gloom; it rose ten fathoms high, spiking raggedly from the foam as waves broke against its craggy surface. The Marlin continued to drift; though the prow was directed away from the spire of basalt, the ship was still careening towards it.

"We're not going to make it!" breathed Rhys as the stack clove steadily through the murk on track to scupper the Marlin.

"We need full sail!" roared Arne as he and Sol charged down the steps from the aftcastle towards the main mast. Together, Sol and the sea captain loosened various ropes and allowed the lateen sails to drop into their most open configuration. An immediate gust bulged the canvas and Rhys felt his weight shift as a surge of acceleration took hold of the caravel. The rigging snapped taught and the ship's momentum aligned with the direction of the prow. Rhys clenched the bulwark, digging his fingernails into the white wood as the jutting sea stack swam over larboard, mere moments before the bowsprit tip passed it. The hull skimmed passed the rock by little more than a few feet, narrowly avoiding a collision that could well have sunk the Marlin altogether.

"That was close," sighed Thia with relief.

"Too close," agreed Rhys.

"It just came out of nowhere!" remarked the witch.

"I've never seen nothing like that!" puffed Ulfgar as he jogged up the steps to the forecastle and took up a position beside Rhys as secondary lookout.

"What do you mean?" pressed Rhys.

"Stacks like that... they're normally off headlands, near the coast... not in the middle of the ocean!"

"It's not over yet!" uttered Rhys as another ragged pillar of stone cut through the haze. "Another. Dead ahead!" he shouted back to Arne.

"Take in the sails," ordered Arne as he dashed over to the tiller, relinquishing steering duties from his two sons.

Vidar and Eirik aided Sol, and between the three of them they hoisted the sails until they were almost closed entirely. Arne continued the hard starboard turn, his massive form straining as the Marlin's deck sloped in the tight manoeuvre. The caravel swerved away from the incoming pillar, coasting once more into open water as the ship gradually shed knots to the resistance of the swell.

"There are hundreds of them," called back Rhys as the mist thinned enough to grant a view out from the bow for several scores of yards. "They are everywhere!"

"I reckon we've passed it now," uttered Ulfgar.

"Passed what?" questioned Thia.

"The Brink of the World."

The waters were a mess of breaking foam and sharp fingers of basalt protruding up from the waves. Some stacks rose several hundred feet from out of the brine, whilst others formed spiny ridges that vanished beneath the swell. The rain streaked down, saturating the deck until it turned grey and slippery. Thunder continued to toll whilst snaking bolts of lightning lit up the murky heavens. The Marlin slowed to a gentle drift as both Arne and his sons now manned the tiller, heaving the giant lever to and fro as they anxiously navigated the fractured maze of waves and rock. Rhys and Sol continued to call back from the prow at each new sighting of an obstacle in their path.

"What's that?" questioned Cade as he peered out over the larboard gunwale.

Rhys's head swivelled left; he instantly sighted what Cade was looking at. A smooth and straight pole scudded past, shrouded in the seething mist; as the Marlin floated nearer, Rhys made out the horizontal yardarms of a square-rigged mast jutting out of the boiling waters.

"It's a wreck!" shouted Sol, realising that the entire hull of the ship was sunk beneath the waves.

"There are so many," uttered Thia, her eyes locked ahead.

The gloom thinned further, and Rhys directed his attention forward of the bowsprit. Dozens upon dozens of masts poked out of the waters at jaunty angles. Some still bore tattered fragments of rigging, and some even still flew shredded rags of sailcloth. All were sunk beneath the waters, and Rhys could not help but wonder how many others rested deeper on the ocean bed, concealed by the foaming seas.

"It's a graveyard," realised Rhys.

Still the mist parted before them, revealing scores of further wrecks. In places, fractured hulls were splayed open on jagged ridges, whilst others had run aground and buckled open on the shoals. Though Rhys knew little of the world of seafaring, he reckoned some of the wrecks to be recent, not yet rotten away by the waters and winds, whilst others, heavily disintegrated and almost fossilised, were perhaps centuries old. Many resembled the Marlin, and several wrecks Rhys could make out as modern knars and longships, but some of the skeletons were utterly unrecognisable, their ancient designs in advanced states of decay.

"We're going to die out here," lamented Nathaniel as he gazed out at the hundreds of ship carcasses, all too aware that most, if not all of the sailors onboard had probably drowned when their vessels went down.

"You can swim? Right?" Sol looked to Rhys apprehensively.

Rhys shook his head. "Not very well."

"I can't," added Ulfgar bluntly. "I swim like a stone… one that's been tied to an even heavier stone!"

"Then we had better pray to the gods that we don't run aground," breathed Sol, reminded all of a sudden why he had been so reluctant to sail beyond the edge of the known world.

THREE

The Marlin rocked and swayed across the white foam, weaving its way between skeletal shipwrecks and bony sea stacks. Spray swept off the waters as sudden barrages of wind surged from nothingness and subsided within moments back to eerie tranquillity. For now, the thunder had abated, yet noiseless lightning still flashed infrequently across the cloud ceiling. Fog hung in suspended layers that often wove together and once again came unstitched, adding to the overall impression that these seas were haunted.

"Welcome to the edge of the world," breathed Sol as he and Rhys looked onwards in ever-growing disbelief.

"Thousands must have lost their lives in these waters."

"I did warn you," smirked Sol uncomfortably.

"You did," agreed Rhys. "But we're not dead yet."

"*Yet*," emphasised Sol. "There's still plenty of time for that."

"I thought you trusted Arne's sailing?"

"I do," nodded Sol. "But even he does not know what we are in for."

"Some one must have made it back from here," reasoned Rhys, "else there would never be anyone to tell the tales."

"Some stories are merely invented to explain the unknown," replied Sol.

"I know," nodded Rhys, "that is how religions are started."

Sol shook his head disapprovingly, not wanting to spark another debate. "I know you saw the map of Cambria back in Ultair Castle, but have you seen any mariner charts of the Wyrm's Sea, Rhys?"

"No," confessed the mage, "I cannot say that I have."

"Most sailor maps of the region don't have imaginary charted coastlines, or depictions of the Stormy Isles. Most simply have four words scrawled across the parchment. Do you know what those four words, which I saw and heard time and time again when living in Westport, say?"

"A rather lovely place?" joked Rhys.

Sol looked coldly back at him.

"Its not that then, is it?"

"Here there be monsters," uttered Sol with an unflinching seriousness.

"Do you want to turn back?" pressed Rhys, no longer frivolous.

A long pause endured between the two.

"I never wanted to come here in the first place."

"Do you want to turn back!?" Rhys repeated, grilling Sol intently with his gaze.

Another bout of silence preceded Sol's response. "No. Not now."

"Good," nodded Rhys as he faced onward again.

Hours passed as the caravel skirted the turbulent waters, winding amidst the graveyard as it thinned, until all that was left of the masses of sunken ships were a few stray pieces of flotsam, forever being broken down into smaller and smaller smithereens as they were continually dashed against rocks and shoals. The fogs rarefied and lifted into the blanket of haze hanging above, and for a time, the swell calmed. The deluge of rain diminished to a fine drizzle, and even the winds seemed to die down.

Rhys's eyes fell to the wooden rail of the bulwark over which he was leant, and his attention was drawn suddenly to a single droplet of water nestled on the grain. It was quivering, vibrating back and forth in a manner he had never seen before. The mage lowered his head closer to inspect the bead, when suddenly and unexpectedly, the droplet lifted from the wood and floated upwards. The spherical dot of water hovered higher and higher until it was raised above Rhys's head, all the while the mage stared in mesmerised disbelief. The globule faded beyond the limits of Rhys's vision as it accelerated upward towards the clouds.

"What is it?" questioned Sol, straining his neck in an attempt to sight what had grabbed Rhys's attention.

"I..." stammered Rhys, when a second raindrop streaked upwards past the periphery of his sight. The mage's gaze lowered and glanced out across the water. There was another, and then another. Water was beading up off of the surface of the waves, collecting into drips and flying towards the clouds in a strange phenomenon that Rhys could only think to describe as the complete inverse of rainfall.

"What in the world?" breathed Sol as he and everyone else onboard had their attention drawn to the bizarre spectacle.

Rhys peered further ahead and caught sight of a helix of upwardly raining water coiling from out of the deep, then suddenly there were more. Spiralling bands of raindrops were all around them, steadily climbing upwards into the clouded skies in ever-growing globules until several of the larger helices resembled gushing torrents: rivers flowing from sea to sky.

"What is this?" despaired a disconcerted Nathaniel.

"I... I don't know," remarked an intrigued but uneasy Thia.

"It's magic," insisted Sol. "It must be."

"But how?" questioned Rhys.

"I'm not sure," replied the mage.

The crew and passengers continued to stare about them in disbelief as water poured up from the surface of the sea, feeding the clouds above until they turned from ashen grey to inky black. The skies, laden with the weight of a storm, began to swirl into a dark vortex, whilst up ahead, Rhys glimpsed an eddy of vapour steadily growing out of the waves.

"What is that?" questioned Rhys, looking now at what seemed a very different, but perhaps related event.

"Who the hel knows!" worried Sol as the two of them continued to observe the circle of mist as it began to shape into a column a mile or so ahead of the prow.

"Err... Father!" the distressed voice of Vidar called from the tiller behind the two mages.

"What is it?" called back Arne, but the captain had already seen what his son had alerted him to.

Arne's heavy boots trampled across the deck and the hulking man ascended to the forecastle, taking up position beside Sol and Rhys. For the first time in their voyage, the seaman's countenance was an expression of concern.

"What's wrong?" asked Rhys.

Arne shook his head in fear. "It's a waterspout," replied the captain coolly.

"A waterspout?" repeated Rhys, but Arne

did not stop to explain.

The captain darted back down the steps to the main deck and barked several urgent orders to his sons. Vidar and Eirik took to the mast and rigging once more, letting out the mainsail as Arne heaved powerfully on the tiller, forcing it as far over to the portside as it would go. The deck sloped to the right as the entire marlin tilted in the waves. The winds were suddenly picking up and began buffeting the sailcloth as the gusts tore around the Marlin.

Rhys revolved and gazed back towards the spiral of fog, this time seeing what Arne had anticipated fearfully. The ascending column of mist was just the precursor of what was to come; the real danger became apparent when Rhys's eyes returned upwards to the darkling clouds. The vortex had intensified and was funnelling downwards as a snaking black pillar that was mere seconds away from connecting with the maelstrom rising from the sea.

"That can't be good..." murmured Ulfgar.

Rhys looked on in horror as the two vortices of black vaporous winds connected, the waterspout completing its formation. Howling gales ripped outwards from the cyclone and spray whipped laterally off the water, mixing with the upwards rain, instantly saturating the decks of the Marlin. The tornado fattened and darkened as it snaked and coiled from cloud to sea, lifting gallons upon gallons of brine from the waves. The Marlin's deck continued to slope away to the starboard, the angle of the mast decreasing, whilst the boards beneath Rhys's feet gradually steepened. Rhys felt his weight begin to shift, and behind him, he heard Thia cry out as her boots lost traction against the slippery wood, causing her to slump hard against the deck.

"Arne!" Rhys called out, barely able to hear his own voice over the roaring squalls. Rhys peered back to see that the captain was fighting against the tiller as the winds and currents forced the ship onto its side, the waterline encroaching ever closer towards the gunnel. In spite of the captain's attempts to re-right the Marlin, it continued to list more and more heavily. The soaking gales persisted to wet the deck, and within seconds, Thia began to slide across the greasy wood. Rhys could feel his own feet about to give out against the tilt, as Ulfgar, Alkis, and Cade all tumbled over within moments of each other.

Rhys dove for Thia, flopping onto the wood ungracefully, sliding across the boards just in time to clasp a hand around the witch's wrist. The two of them were now skating down the slope together, accelerating towards the lower gunwale as frothy waves broke over the bulwark and swamped the forecastle. Flailing his free arm, Rhys snagged hold of a baluster from the steps down to the main deck. His shoulders popped taught as Thia's and his own weight lurched against his grip, and for a terrifying moment, Rhys feared the baluster would slip from his fingers.

"Hold on!" Rhys urged the witch as they dangled on the watery slope. He looked around and saw to his relief that no one had been lost overboard. Each of his friends, Arne, Vidar, and Eirik included, had clasped hold of either the bulwark or rigging, finding themselves in much the same predicament as Rhys.

"Rhys…" Sol cried faintly over the deafening crackles of thunder. "I think I want to turn back now!"

"Me too," replied Rhys weakly. "Me too."

The mast groaned under the strain, and the ropes of the rigging creaked in tension. The mainsail suddenly deflated and flapped loosely, causing the lower spar to swing downwards, its tip plunging into the waters. Suddenly, the lateral force on the Marlin diminished, the winds no longer forcing the caravel to capsize, and slowly but acceleratingly, the ship rocked back. The keel plunged back into the waves as the decks levelled, and for a short instant, Rhys and Thia were lying flat. The momentum of the mast continued however, swinging through like a pendulum, and before any of the crew had a chance to clamber to their feet, the Marlin began to tilt the opposite way.

Rhys felt himself sliding across the deck once more, this time head first towards the larboard gunnel with Thia in tow. He fumbled once again for a baluster, but this time his fingers flailed helplessly short. Thia reached out, snagging hold of the railing; the two of them swung into the forecastle banister, striking the posts hard. In the collision, Thia's grip of Rhys failed her and the mage slipped through her fingers, leaving her dangling.

Devoid of anything to grasp, Rhys felt himself reaching instinctively for the scabbard strapped to his boot. His hand coiled rapidly round the hilt of his father's blade, and in the blink of an eye, he had unsheathed it. Still careening over the greasy deck boards towards the black waters lapping over the bulwark, Rhys lunged with all his might, stabbing the point of his father's blade into the wood of the deck. The dagger bit into the boards and his weight snapped heavily about his arm. He had stopped barely a fathom above the breaking waters. The deck was near vertical and the mast near horizontal. The main lateen sail flapped violently up and down, and Rhys made out the twangs of snapping rigging over the hounding gales.

Rhys hung suspended from his knife and revolved slowly as the Marlin tipped gently backward to a less severe angle, but it remained too steep for anyone to stand. Rhys looked out at the raging waterspout; it had swollen further and the entire cyclone above appeared to be collapsing into it, but it was the sea itself that now seemed the greater danger. The waters were swirling inwards, banking down towards the heart of a gargantuan maelstrom that revolved in synchrony with the tornado at its heart. It was because of this whirlpool that the Marlin had swung back and remained at its current inclination. The mast pointed inwards towards the twister as the water continued to slope further and further away beneath the Marlin's keel.

"What is happening!?" roared Cade in terror.

"We're sailing off the edge of the world, that's what!" replied Nathaniel.

The prow descended over the crest of a wave and suddenly the sails filled with air once more. The ballooning of sailcloth caused the mast to lurch back towards a more upright angle and Rhys felt himself pressed back onto the deck. It was steep, but he was able to plant his feet on the slippery wood. He rent his knife from between the deck boards. The others were still clutching their respective anchor points, not daring to release their grip for fear that the Marlin would once more sway and finally tip over.

"Arne!" Rhys called back to the captain who had fought his way back over to the tiller. "How do we get out of this?"

The seaman, awestruck by the power of the raging tempest, glanced out at the descending maelstrom, the Marlin skirting its fringes at its slowest point. "We can't sail out of this," he boomed. "Not at our current speed!"

Rhys peered down at the seething brine to see that the Marlin was merely a piece of driftwood being swept up in the current. In order to escape the clutches of the vortex, they would need to be travelling faster than the water in which they were floating. The mage peered inwards towards the waterspout, which now was plunging deep into the throat of the whirlpool, where sooner or later the Marlin would likewise be swallowed. But nearer the heart of the vortex, the waters were swirling at dizzying speeds, gushing and boiling as surges of white foam; it looked in escapable, but Rhys suspected that was where the winds were at their strongest.

"What if we sailed in closer?" Rhys shouted back to Arne. "Could we pick up enough speed to get clear?"

Arne stared back at Rhys blankly as rain lashed both up and down.

"You want to get closer!? Are you mad?" shouted Sol.

"No..." replied Arne, "No... he's right. It's the only way."

"Father, are you sure?" pressed Vidar.

"Yes," Arne nodded as he surveyed the heart of the cyclone.

"If we get closer, we won't be able to escape it, Arne!" insisted Sol as everyone on deck gazed out to what was more than likely their doom.

"We can if we use the spinnaker," explained Arne, "but we have to time it right, or the sails will be shredded!"

"Okay," nodded Rhys. "What do we need to do?"

FOUR

"I hope you are right about this, Father!" shouted Vidar as he finished rigging up the spinnaker bag to the bow.

"If I'm not, you won't be able to blame me," remarked Arne as he tensioned various ropes.

"You are right," smirked Eirik, shuffling down the jaunty mainmast from where he had reefed the sail. "We'll be dead."

"So, this is it," uttered Rhys, as he took up position beside Sol near the prow, line in hand ready for Arne's signal.

"I trust Arne with my life," replied his friend.

"I trust him too," agreed Rhys. "But I prefer my life being in my own hands."

"You still have a part to play," insisted Sol as they both watched the waterspout continue to grow as it raged faster and faster.

"Hardly," Rhys remarked anxiously.

"Is everyone ready?" called Arne's booming voice over the howling tempest.

All on deck responded with a chorus of terrified silence.

"Now!" cried the captain, throwing his full weight against the tiller.

Both Arne and his two sons forced with all their might, shoving the tiller up the slant of the deck towards the larboard side of the Marlin. The rudder cut into the flow of the swirling whirlpool, and in the seconds that followed, the bowsprit aligned with the column of black descending from the clouds. The Marlin tipped forwards, riding the current and the surf created by the immense maelstrom, surging in towards the heart of the storm. The caravel's mainsail and jib were completely taken in, the ship powered now only by the torrential currents and the pull of gravity as the vessel dipped down over the precipice of water towards the depths of the briny abyss.

"Hold!" shouted Arne as spray and foam gushed over the gunnels, washing across the forecastle and flooding the main deck where the others were all huddled, tethered by lines to the mast and bulwark. "Hold!" Arne roared again as lightning flashed through the core of the waterspout and thunder drummed deafeningly through the hurricane. "Hold!" the Captain screamed as the hull of the Marlin groaned and shuddered.

The whole ship tilted sharply once more as the Marlin banked hard on the wall of water. The tornado was now impossibly close, its winds pummelled Rhys into submission, the rain stung as it pelted the deck furiously. Rhys squinted, his eyes tearing, and peered over the bow to see the constricting throat of the maelstrom as it swallowed the waterspout into the depths of oblivion. The Marlin was now truly horizontal, and Rhys was held only in place by his boots wedged into the bulwark's scuppers and the line around his waist.

"Hold!" Arne shouted one last time, his booming voice finally failing against the elements as the Marlin made its last approach. Suddenly, the caravel lurched, banking sharply in the opposite direction. The bowsprit lanced above the wall of water. The Marlin was climbing back out from beyond the precipice, regurgitated from the throat of the whirlpool by the grace of the speed it had garnered in the faster flowing waters; but as it tilted back to an almost horizontal plane, Rhys could feel the ship shedding its speed. The Marlin would not make it. In mere moments it would be halted by the staggering drag of the maelstrom, steered by the swirling foam back in towards the heart of the vortex, this time unable to return from the edge of the gulf where the abyss would swallow them whole.

"Now!" ordered Arne, his voice so loud it drowned out the rumbling thunder itself.

Vidar and Eirik released the tiller, leaving their father to shoulder its strain alone. The two of them darted across the greasy deck and cut the rigging across the mast reefing the mainsail. The spar dropped, dragging downwards the sailcloth, and the sail ballooned immediately. Rhys and Sol heaved and heaved, hand over hand, drawing in their respective lines, hoisting the spinnaker out from the bag, raising it across the bowsprit in front of the jib.

The new sail filled with wind, swelling and rattling in the apocalyptic air torrents. The mast groaned, the lines twanged, and the Marlin lurched forwards on a surge of speed that nearly sent Sol and Rhys toppling backwards. The caravel was now flying through the slower moving waters on the periphery of the maelstrom. The waterspout was at their backs, and though they were slowing, they had garnered a great enough kick from water and wind to clear the edge of the cataclysmic tempest.

The waters levelled out as the Marlin plunged over the circumference of the titanic whirlpool, racing out with air-flooded sails back into the suffocating haze that had descended beyond the limits of the storm. The winds abated and the regular swell return, the thunder drowned, and the lightning dwindled until all that was left was the steady upward drizzle of rain.

"Let's not do that again," smiled Rhys weakly as he staggered down the steps to the main deck.

"That was amazing!" laughed Eirik.

"No one will ever believe it back home,"

agreed Vidar.

"It was too close," remarked Arne.

"But we made it," put in Sol.

"We did," nodded the captain calmly.

"Is everyone okay?" asked Rhys, looking to the ghostly expressions of his companions as they still clung to the ship for dear life.

Thia and Alkis managed a nod each, but Rhys's attention was drawn away by the heavy footfalls of Ulfgar; the dwarf darted for the gunnels and vomited over the side of the Marlin.

"I'll take that as a *'yes,'*" Rhys jested shakily before slumping against the steps to the aftcastle. "Thank you," he directed to Arne and his sons.

"I have never seen the sea behave so violently before. We are fortunate that the Marlin held together."

"What did you expect, Father?" returned Eirik jovially. "We have sailed into the Wyrm's Sea. We are off the edge of the map!"

"No," retorted Vidar. "There *are* maps of this place... they are just mostly covered in drawings of giant sea serpents rather than anything useful!"

"My boys," returned Arne. "Having seen that storm up close, I am starting to believe those drawings may be of some importance after all."

"Father, you are the least superstitious sailor I have ever met," insisted Vidar. "You cannot tell me you are starting to believe in monsters!"

"I believe in monsters because Sol and Rhys both say they have fought them first hand," returned Arne gravely.

"He does have a point, Brother," smiled Eirik.

"Also, it is currently raining upwards," put in Rhys. "I don't think anyone would have believed in that happening before today, so…"

"Rhys is right," agreed Sol. "After what we just survived, we need to be on guard for anything and everything that could be looming out beyond the mists… sea serpents included!"

"I know we just had a close call," admitted Rhys, "but we cannot go losing our heads—"

"Umm…" murmured Ulfgar having finally finished heaving his guts overboard.

"The weather has calmed," Rhys continued. "We should expect it to worsen again before long—"

"Umm… guys!?" called Ulfgar.

"But until we have any cause to be suspicious of such, there is no reason why we should suspect a sea monster to erupt from beneath the waves at a second's notice—"

"Rhys!" cried Ulfgar in distress.

"What is it!?" snapped the mage, swivelling to look at Ulfgar.

The dwarf was stood rigidly gazing down at the waters lapping against the hull, his face, already pallor from nausea, was now bleached of all its colour as he gawked wide-eyed in terror.

"Ulfgar?" Rhys asked more sympathetically.

The dwarf extended an arm in stupefied silence and pointed mechanically towards the foaming saltwater. Nearing the gunnels in dread, Rhys and everyone else onboard peered over the railings, down at the undulating sea. The waters were black with shadow. An immense shape was gliding beneath the keel, its gargantuan silhouette extending a dozen metres either side of the ship. Something colossal was moving beneath the waves.

"What is that!?" demanded Nathaniel.

"A shoal, perhaps?" suggested Sol optimistically.

"That's no shoal," uttered Arne.

Rhys watched intently as the titanic silhouette scudded swiftly beneath the Marlin. The moment the lip of the shape vanished beneath the keel, everyone dashed across the sopping deck to the portside gunwale to watch as the shape continued to glide silently underwater. Seeing the profile now in full, Rhys made out its snaking form. Everyone watched on bated breath as the serpentine leviathan swam clear of the ship and continued onwards, vanishing into the obscurity of the mists.

"I would like to retract my last statement," uttered Rhys, finally breaking the silence that followed.

"You mean to say it's now no longer preposterous to assume a sea monster might erupt from the waves at any moment?" smiled Sol gravely.

"Indeed," nodded Rhys nervously. "Assume away."

FIVE

In the hours that followed, Rhys sat with his heart in his throat, clutching the gunwales as he scanned the hazy horizon ahead and the bubbling brine below. Jagged stacks of black basalt continually emerged from out of the mist with occasional remnants of shipwrecks protruding from the water. Rain continued to bead upwards from the surface of the sea in an unrelenting up-pour that grew steadily heavier with each mile they sailed deeper into the Wyrm's Triangle.

Rhys shivered as the grey light of day began to dwindle and the winds turned cold and biting, but he dared not move from his lookout post at the prow of the ship, nor even divert his eyes from the sea, for fear that whatever creature lurked in the deep would suddenly emerge the moment he did to capsize the Marlin. Night fell and a smothering blackness closed in around the ship as the caravel continued to drift slowly through the dark.

"Rhys," came the voice of Thia, startling him suddenly from his watch.

"Yes?" he asked, averting his gaze from the

waters for a fraction of a second before returning to scan the dark waves.

"You need to rest."

"No, I'm fine," replied the mage.

"No, you are not," she insisted. "You are soaked to the bone and look half frozen to death! You've been here for half the night. Let someone else take over."

Rhys bowed his head in concession and suddenly felt the weight on his neck and shoulders. He was tired, exhausted even. His eyes felt raw and his neck muscles were on the verge of spasming. Thia was right. If he remained stood there, he would soon fall asleep on his feet.

"Okay, you are right," he agreed.

"Come on," she beckoned warmly, "let's get you into some dry clothes.

Sol relieved Rhys as the mage went down into the crew quarters beneath the forecastle. He endured a disturbed sleep as his hammock swayed throughout what remained of the night, constantly waking to each groan and shudder of the Marlin and every toll of thunder to echo through the skies. Muddled images lingered throughout his dreams of raging tempests and sea serpents lurking beneath the ship, though these confused ideas never coalesced into any form of comprehendible dream. Instead, Rhys seemed to exist in a realm somewhere between waking and reverie, where he was never fully aware of what was occurring in his surroundings, yet where there was little recuperation. As dawn arrived, Rhys finally awoke in full, and unable to suffer disturbed sleep any longer, he donned his damp leather hood and overshirt and emerged back on deck.

Smoking fog draped over the top deck of the Marlin; beyond the bow it appeared so impenetrable that the tip of the bowsprit was almost invisible. The main sail and jib were largely reefed, and the caravel crawled along at a snail's pace.

"How long has it been like this?" Rhys asked Ulfgar as he accompanied the dwarf at the prow.

"Since before first light."

"Any sign of it lifting?"

"None yet."

"Curse this place," uttered Rhys.

Together they stood, watching the mist effervesce over the front of the ship as the bowsprit steadily plunged further and further towards the heart of the Wyrm's Triangle. Eventually, the gloom lifted and Vidar and Eirik let out the sails, allowing the Marlin to pick up speed. The morning trudged slowly along as everyone onboard continued to wait for something, be it sea monster or shoreline, to emerge from beyond the curtain of murk that surrounded them.

Rhys felt his stomach turn over in what he believed to be dread, but several minutes later it occurred again, and then again shortly thereafter; it was a queer sensation, one that he likened to jolting suddenly awake in the night due to the impression of dropping suddenly out of bed. After a fourth turn, the mage felt dizzy as if blood were collecting in his head; he grimaced as he tried to shake the feeling, but looking to his side he saw Ulfgar pinching the bridge of his nose as if he too were suffering from the same sensation.

"You all right?" questioned the mage.

"I must be seasick," Ulfgar insisted, "my ruddy head is spinning!"

Rhys peered around at his friends, most of whom leant over the bulwark peering into the fog with their backs to him. He caught sight of both Cade and Nathaniel shaking their heads and palming their faces as if they too were off kilter. Rhys moved to go speak to them, but as he did so, he almost fell over; only, falling was perhaps not the correct word for it. It was as if his muscles had moved more vigorously then he had expected; his slight step felt more like a sudden bound, and instead of worrying that he might topple over onto the deck, Rhys feared quite the opposite. The mage rocked about off balance, terrified for a moment that the deck might plunge away beneath him, sending him soaring upwards, plummeting towards the heavens above like the rain drops lashing off the surface of the sea.

Regaining his footing, Rhys tried another

step; this time the feeling was more subdued, but even still, there was a definite clumsiness to his gait. His entire body was plagued by a dizzying floating sensation. He felt incredibly light, as if somehow, in the hour he had been stood guard at the prow of the Marlin, he had shed half his body weight. He lurched forwards several steps, half expecting to bound clean into the air with each footfall. Nonetheless, he remained anchored to the deck, however weakly, his gait as lithe as if he were ten-pints-drunk.

"Sol? Thia?" Rhys called out to his companions, hoping to garner their attention.

Both the witch and the mage revolved to look at Rhys groggily, and as they did so, the two of them almost fell over in much the way Rhys had done. He watched as one by one everyone else on board became steadily aware of the unusual sense of weightlessness they had each contracted.

"Remarkable," Thia bemused.

"This does not bode well," added Sol.

"What is this?" questioned Rhys.

"It must be the same force drawing water up from the surface of the sea," hypothesised Thia.

"And now its acting on us?" asked Erik as he staggered over to the mainmast to adjust the rigging.

"It would seem so," confirmed Sol.

Rhys stumbled, though this time only in

part due to the strange sense of weightlessness. The ship's deck had listed suddenly as a gust inflated the sail. The boom swung across the deck and the Marlin tilted unexpectedly back. The whole ship began to groan as everyone looked to each other in confusion. Arne abruptly bolted to the gunnels and peered down over the side of the ship. The deck continued to rock steadily back and forth, the mast swaying like a pendulum from side to side.

"Reef the sails!" Arne shouted back to his sons.

"Father?" Vidar questioned.

"Now!"

As Vidar swiftly ascended the main mast, aided by the lack of heft to his brawny form, Rhys approached the captain.

"What is it?" questioned the mage.

"Take a look for yourself," replied the seaman.

Rhys peered over the gunwale down at the water. At first the mage struggled to see what exactly was awry, but as the mainsail's boom swung over the deck once more and the Marlin tilted again, he realised. The sea had receded down the hull of the caravel, the ship sitting incredibly high in the water, with the keel barely a few feet beneath the lapping waves. Whatever force was acting on Rhys and the others, was also acting on the Marlin.

"What can we do?" Rhys asked as the

others gazed down at the waterline and steadily came to the realisation Arne had first made.

"Without adding more ballast, there is nothing we can do. We just need to sure her up. Take in the sail before we are capsized!"

In the minutes that followed, Vidar and Eirik clumsily reefed the main sail and jib until there was nothing but a small fraction of canvas exposed to the wind. Arne manned the tiller, heaving it this way and that to negate the rocking of the Marlin. Water boiled from the surface of the sea, streaking upwards in torrential rain. The clouds steadily blackened, and before long, the sky was alight with sizzling forks of lightning, booming thunder rolling over the breaking waves. The winds picked up and the rains began falling as downpour in juxtaposition to the ascending squalls, all the while the Marlin seemed to be inching further and further out of the water.

"Shoals ahead!" cried Sol from the prow as a flash of lightning illuminated the outlines of jagged stacks and spines cutting out of the foam before them.

Arne rammed the tiller sideways, but to his despair, it now had little sway on the ship's bearing, the Marlin's rudder now sat too shallowly in the water to have a great enough effect on the caravel's course. Vidar rushed to his father's aid, and together, the two of them pivoted the tiller back towards the starboard side. The Marlin rocked gently but remain obstinately on its forward heading, the tiller now all but useless.

"It's no use!" cried Arne.

"It's like she's skating across ice!" shouted Vidar.

Rhys darted buoyantly up the steps of the forecastle. Thunder drummed again, and in the glare of the lightning bolt, Rhys saw a serrated spine of rock appear suddenly from out of the storm.

"Brace for impact!" shouted Arne.

All around, everyone snatched hold of the nearest anchorage points. Rhys darted for the gunnels, but his feet fell lightly against the sodden deck and slid out beneath him. The mage stumbled in slow motion, his weight shifting gently, giving him an abundance of time in which to replant his footing. Righting himself from a fall which under normal circumstances would have been inescapable, the mage once more attempted to make for the bulwark. Suddenly, his entire weight came crashing down, the upward force acting on the Marlin and its crew dissipating in an instant.

The full strength of gravity returned, and Rhys's knees almost buckled immediately. The Marlin's keel plunged suddenly back into the sea, the fore end tilting downwards. Water flooded over the prow as the bowsprit speared into the breaking waves. Rhys collapsed to a kneel as the buoyancy of the caravel forced its hull back out of the displaced water, floating it to its original waterline. Foam and brine drained through the scuppers as Rhys clambered back to his feet, his body lagging in its readjustments to his normal weight.

"Arne!" Sol screamed in terror as a final bolt of lightning clove through the storm, revealing a spine of basalt as it emerged from beneath the froth and swell mere yards ahead of the bow.

"Again!" ordered Arne to his son as both he and Vidar lunged with their full weight against the tiller spar.

This time the resistance was there. The rudder cut against the flow of water and the Marlin rolled over in the waves, tilting away from the shoal. But the sails were almost entirely reefed, closed against the drive of the wind. The Marlin careened forward, turning too little too late. Before the impact there was a sudden moment of calm, a split second where everyone aboard realised their incoming doom and came to understand there was no escape. The winds seemed to quieten, the rain seemed to slow, and the roaring thunder seemed but a distant whisper.

The keel struck rock, grinding against the portion of the shoal concealed beneath the waves. The Marlin almost stopped instantly as the hull ran aground. Rhys lurched forwards and was sent sliding across the slick deck on his front. Wood splintered and ropes frayed and twanged, but the rock remained undamaged. The hull crumpled and the Marlin groaned as the caravel's momentum forced it up the weathered face of stone. The ship twisted and the upper strakes slammed against the sea stack jutting above the waves. The Marlin continued to plough up the slope, before grinding finally to a halt.

The lashing torrents of rain resumed from all directions and the winds returned to their deafening shrieks. The Marlin creaked and cracked, but it was stationary. Heaving himself back onto his feet, Rhys realised the deck was now sloping away to the rear. The ship had not only mounted the shoal, but impaled itself utterly and completely; the keel was pinned to the angular sea stack, the spar of the mainsail now battering against it in the wind. Rhys approached the starboard bulwark; he peered over the side to see the rocky spine's serrations had punctured the hull. The entire ship was perched on the ridge, the aft end of the caravel still submerged, yet as a whole the Marlin was beached

"I think its safe to say we've run aground," muttered Rhys gravely.

"I see ground," remarked an even more solemn Sol, "but no land."

Sol was right. Rhys scanned the horizon in every direction and saw nothing but fog and sea. They were impaled and isolated, scuppered and secluded, deserted and perhaps very soon drowned.

"What do we do now?" Rhys questioned Arne as the mariner peered down at the white water and black rock as flotsam from the Marlin was bludgeoned between the two elements into smaller and smaller smithereens.

"There is nothing we can do…" croaked the captain weakly. "We are scuppered."

SIX

"How bad is it?" questioned Rhys. He stood below deck in the hold, ankle deep in bilge, staring in disquiet at the buckled and ruptured hull planks. Through the breeched strakes protruded a row of basalt tusks that had skewered the Marlin's hull.

"Bad," replied Arne.

"It's below the waterline," explained Vidar.

"At least it isn't at the moment," sighed Rhys in relief.

"If it were, we would be at the bottom of the sea by now," warned Arne.

"Can you fix it?"

"Not here," the sea captain shook his head. "Not now."

"But can you patch it?" pressed Sol.

"Aye," Arne affirmed after a time. "It'd take a few hours. We'd have to chisel the stone clear first... but yes."

"But this is the worst of it?" questioned Rhys as he peered about the dimly lit hold.

"The keel held out," Arne clarified with relief. "There are a few other splits and cracks in the strakes, but nothing we won't be able to seal with caulk and tar."

"Then there is just the matter of finding a way to get the Marlin back in the water," mused Sol.

"No," returned Arne. "There isn't"

"What do you mean?" returned Rhys.

"Come," the captain gestured, leading them up the ladder, out of the hold and back onto the main deck.

The storm had attenuated in the last hour; the winds subsiding to damp draughts and the rain to gentle up and down pattering. Across the deck stood the others, gazing drearily out into the mists, awaiting whatever deadly peril would appear next from the Wyrm's Triangle, this time perhaps to finish off the Marlin for good. There was an uneasy tension between everyone in the party, the likes of which Rhys had not previously seen; they had faced imminent dangers before, but none to which they had been so powerless as those they faced now.

"Look," pointed Arne, gesturing to the pillar of basalt against which the Marlin was pinned.

"What is it?" questioned Rhys, unsure what Arne was hinting at.

"Look at the rock," insisted the captain as he led Rhys and Sol closer.

"Mussels," breathed Sol with a sudden realisation.

Across the sea stack's surface grew a slimy layer of seaweed, nestled amidst were hundreds of shellfish mortared to the rock. Their smooth black shells were sealed against the air, but Rhys recognised them as the orange molluscs he had bought on several occasions from street vendors in Westport. Even seeing the mussels anchored amidst the kelp, Rhys had not yet come to the conclusion that Sol and Arne had arrived at.

"I don't understand," puzzled the mage.

"Look at the seaweed," replied Sol, gesturing then to a clear boundary on the stone where the growth abruptly ended, above which Rhys could not see a single mussel.

"Is that a water level?" questioned the mage, gradually piecing together what was obvious to Sol and Arne, both having spent most of the lives living beside the coast.

"It's the tide," confirmed Arne.

"You are saying the water will rise to there?" asked Rhys as he peered over the bulwark to see the white waves breaking against the rock nearly ten fathoms below the line of algae.

"I couldn't believe it myself at first," nodded Arne.

"The tidal range in Westport is what...? Little more than two fathoms?" Sol queried Arne.

"Fifteen feet on the spring tide," agreed the sailor.

"And you are telling me that it is nearer fifty feet here?" pressed Rhys.

"Aye," nodded Arne. "Else there would be no mussels."

"So, what then?" reasoned Rhys. "We just wait for the tide?"

"Yes," agreed the captain, "but I'm not sure we'll be waiting."

"What do you mean?" probed Sol.

"We've been beached an hour all ready, and in that time the water has already risen two fathoms."

"And how long before high tide?" quizzed Rhys.

"Five hours at the most," breathed Sol.

"Probably a lot less," stressed Arne.

"And how long do you reckon it will take to get the Marlin seaworthy?" asked the mage, fearing all too well that he might already know the answer.

"Longer than we have," replied Arne simply.

"Well, shit," hissed Rhys. "What do you need us to do?"

"Get overboard and start chiselling!" urged Vidar, emerging from the hold with various lump hammers and bolster chisels.

In the next few minutes, Rhys, Sol, Eirik, Ulfgar, Alkis, and Nathaniel all clambered over the bulwark, descending ropes to the shelf of rock on which the Marlin was perched. The constant clanging of iron against rock rang out over the roar of breaking waves as the six men hammered and chiselled away at the stone that had ruptured the Marlin's hull. Each strike sent flecks of stone flying from the rock, peppering Rhys's face; he squinted to avoid any shards flying into his eyes. Together they frantically whittled away at the black rock, stood ankle-deep in rock pools as the tide steadily rolled in, the white foaming waters gradually climbing higher and higher. Occasionally, a large seem would split through one of the various stone spears and a jagged point would be cleared from a puncture wound to the strakes, but overall, the work was slow and laborious, and time was quickly running out. Soon the water was regularly surging over the ground on which they stood.

As a precaution, they each tethered lines around their waists to prevent the wash from knocking them off the shoal. Not long later, a white breaker gushed clean over the rock, sweeping their feet out from under them. Rhys struck the stone as the white horse trampled him, the current dragging him across the jagged surface of the shoal; he felt the skin of his shoulder rip against the crags as pink water drained away. Brine stung the bleeding wound, and as he stood, he looked at the others to see they had all sustained similar injuries. But there was no time to be lost in tending to their wounds. As quickly as they could, bruised and bloodied, they pressingly resumed chipping away at the stone in one last desperate push to free the Marlin.

From inside the hold, Arne and Vidar, with the help of Cade and Thia, were shoring the various holes in the hull as the stone was dislodged. Boarding the breeched strakes, the sailors worked quickly with hammer and nail; the seams were then packed with caulk by Thia and sealed with hot tar by Cade. Together, they were patching the punctures almost as fast as they were exposed, but the process was still not quick enough.

Outside, the swell had risen to waist-height and Rhys feared that in mere moments the waves would be breaking over their heads. The Marlin had begun to groan and creak. The mage could hear the splintering of wood over the gales as the rising water levels began to float the Marlin. The ship's hull was under strain, the last tooth of basalt lanced through the Marlin's hull stressing the entire frame of the caravel.

"Get back on deck!" Rhys ordered Nathaniel, Ulfgar, and Alkis. "We'll take care of this. Just be ready to hoist us up when she's freed!"

The three of them scampered up their sodden lines and over the bulwark where they watched Sol, Vidar, and Rhys wade through the froth and swell towards the final point of stone. Rain lashed up and down. The thunderstorm began to flash and gurgle in the skies once more. Rhys swung his hammer repeatedly down against the basalt. A chunk sheered from the rock, but no fracture formed despite his efforts.

Vidar and Sol, stood on the opposite side of the stone tooth, had forgone their chisels, and were now swinging their lump hammers violently at the basalt, sending chips shooting off in every direction. A crack slowly began to appear across the stone and Rhys immediately saw they were in with a chance of freeing the Marlin from its impalement. The mage positioned his chisel across the fracture line and drew back the hammer to deliver a decisive blow, when suddenly a wall of brine enveloped him. Rhys tumbled in a torrent of white water. The rope snagged taught around his waist and suddenly his head struck rock. Everything went black and silent.

Submerged, Rhys opened his eyes as lightning flashed, its white glare diffusing through the murky water. His lungs were aflame. His eyes stung, his head throbbing. Flailing his arms, Rhys fought his way upright. He managed to plant his feet against the stone and righted himself. His head erupted above the waves and he gasped desperately for air. Sputtering and coughing, he span around on the spot. He had been unconscious for barely a minute, but in that time, everything had changed. The water was chest height, the waves breaking above his head as the mage bobbed up and down in the swell. Sol and Eirik were gone.

Rhys called out to them, his voice drowned by the raging storm. He swivelled about as the spray clouded his vision. To his relief, he saw Sol and Eirik being hoisted up over the gunnels; the two of them had been washed clean off the sea stack by the same wave that had struck Rhys. Though he could barely make out more than the silhouettes of the two men, Rhys could see them grappling the lines that were raising them. They were unharmed.

Rhys turned his attention now back to the basalt spire driven into the Marlin's hull. The entire caravel was groaning under the strain of its buoyancy, fighting against the point where it was skewered. The crack was still there, ready for Rhys to drive a chisel into the rock. One blow could well be enough to fracture the stone if it were struck right, but in his moment of unconsciousness, he had dropped the hammer and chisel, both of which were now lost beneath the water.

The wooden strakes continued cracking under stress. If the caravel were not freed soon, the entire hull could rupture open bow to stern. Looking about frantically, Rhys realised he had few options. He could hear Cade and Ulfgar calling down to him from over the bulwark, the two of them barely able to make him out in the seething brine. Rhys gasped for breath and dove beneath the waves. He fumbled blindly about on the craggy rock shelf, holding out all hope that he might find his hammer and chisel. His fingers groped over the sharp edges of basalt, but before long, his lungs were crying out to resurface. Rhys stood up once more, his head punching above the water, but in the moment he gasped for air, a wave broke over his head and he swallowed a mouthful of seawater. He coughed and wretched violently.

"Rhys!" Ulfgar roared down to him. "We are pulling you in!"

"No!" the mage sputtered. "You can't. Not yet!"

Forcing as much air into his chest as was possible, Rhys dunked himself back beneath the foam. His hands swept over the pitted rock again, searching once more for his tools to crack the stone. The swell picked him up and slammed him against the hull of the Marlin. Bubbles erupted from his mouth in the force of the impact. His stomach grated against the serrations of stone and he clawed against the current to pull himself back to the surface. As he planted his submerged boots back on the rock, his chin now barely above the water's surface, he felt his toe strike something hard and loose.

Recycling the air in his chest, Rhys plunged back under. He groped for his toes, and to his amazement his hand clutched the head of his lump hammer. He plucked it from the ground and emerged from the water once more.

"Rhys!" Cade cried out faintly.

"Not yet! Please!" the mage blubbered, scrabbling up the slanting spire of basalt.

The mage straddled the stone, clutching

its sharp edges with his thighs. He still was without his chisel, but if he could strike the rock hard enough, the hammer would potentially fracture the seam alone. Timing his strike, Rhys raised the hammer high above his head, clutching it tightly in both hands. The split in the stone was underwater, but as the swell dropped away, it resurfaced. The instant the crack in the basalt was exposed, he swung. The stone and metal chimed dimly and the hull boards creaked. Rhys raised his hammer again. The water dropped. He swung. The hammer rebounded from the stone. The crack expanded, but the rock had still not sheered. The Marlin lurched suddenly upwards and the hull began to splinter.

"Rhys!" cried Alkis from above. "She's going to go!"

"One more hit!" Rhys insisted. He raised his hammer as he felt the line tighten about his hips, his friends heaving him upwards against his will. "No!" he roared, gripping the rock tighter with his thighs. The water dropped away. The hammer swung down. It struck the seem perfectly. Rock splintered. Rhys shielded his eyes from the flecks of basalt. He heard cracking, but it was the cracking of wood, not stone.

Rhys had failed. The rock had resisted his swing, and now the hull of the Marlin was being rent open by the ship's own buoyancy. The basalt spear finally gave as it was ripped out of the Marlin's side. The caravel tipped sharply back. The ship was rapidly dislodged, but in being extricated, it had been scuttled. Rhys plunged into the sea. The rope slackened as he felt himself washed from the basalt ridge. He tumbled deep beneath the breaking waves and opened his eyes in the salty abyss. The glow of the storm illuminated the rippling surface overhead. Above, he made out the shadow of the Marlin freed from the rock.

He was sinking, slowly but surely. He fought against the weight of his clothes and the ripping current that sought to drag him down into the black depths below, but his open fingers snatched at the water in futility. The line, still somehow attached around his chest, tensioned. It constricted tightly, and to Rhys's relief, it began to hoist him back towards the water's surface. He was out of air. His lungs were empty. He was growing faint and his vision was beginning to fade, but in seconds, he broke through the waves and choked and gagged as he fought for breath.

Several hands clasped hold of Rhys and heaved him over the gunnels. The mage slumped and floundered on the deck as he vomited brine from his gut. He heaved, fighting against the spasms of his chest. He was out of the water, yet still he felt as if he were drowning. He coughed and coughed, and suddenly, to his relief, the water was dispelled from his lungs and windpipe, air inflating his chest once more.

He rolled over to look up at Thia, Alkis,

and Cade gathered around, gazing down on him in relief to see that the mage had once again somehow cheated death.

"You okay?" asked Alkis, placing a hand on the mage's chest.

Rhys nodded weakly, unable to speak through spluttering gasps. Eventually, the mage caught his breath and was able to sit up. Alkis and Cade eased him gradually to his feet. He looked around to see that the four of them were alone on the main deck. "Where are the other's?" Rhys rasped.

"In the hold," explained Cade. "They are trying to patch the hole."

Rhys nodded and began stumbling towards the steps to below deck.

"Rhys, don't you think you should rest for a moment!?" Thia scorned.

"I'll rest when I'm dead," Rhys returned stubbornly, staggering towards the open hatch to the hold.

"Which will be very soon if you aren't careful!" the witch called after him.

Rhys ignored her. He staggered towards the steps, nearly keeling over several times along the way, and clambered down into the hold. He splashed into knee deep bilge and waded his way over towards Arne, Vidar, Eirik, Sol, Ulfgar, and Nathaniel. Together, the six of them were pressing their weight against several boards in an attempt to hold them in place over the rupture in the hull. Arne himself was hastily hammering nails in to fix the boards, but water was spewing through the gaps. Rhys relieved Vidar from his position, allowing the sailor to aid his father in securing the timber. Together, the two men worked quickly, and before long, the boards were all fixed in place. Even still, water was gushing from between the cracks. They worked to plug the holes as best they could with caulking before smearing tar across the seams to seal against the water.

Once they were done, they all stepped back and stared in silence for a long while. The shoring had held, but it was obvious that the hull was still leaking. A flowing film of water glazed down the wood and tar and the bilge was steadily rising.

"What do we do now?" questioned Sol.

"There is only one thing we can do," replied Arne gravely. "We must find land. Or, by nightfall the Marlin will be on the sea floor…"

"And us along with it," croaked Rhys.

SEVEN

"Here," offered Cade, heaving a pail of water up the ladder and passing it to Rhys.

Rhys picked up the bucket and chucked its contents over the deck, watching for a moment as the bilge drained off through the scuppers. He passed the pail back down to Cade and accepted the next from Nathaniel, immediately dispensing the water overboard again. Abaft, Eirik and Alkis were operating the Marlin's bilge pump, ratcheting the handle around as quickly as they could. The chain mechanism clanked jarringly as the series of cups continuously descended into the hold where they scooped away the rising bilge water, lifting it up the hollowed elm trunk through which the chain pump passed, and discarding the water on the top deck where it drained through the scuppers. With the pump unceasingly operating and the others bailing water out from the hold by hand, the bilge level was rising by only a couple inches an hour. The Marlin was sinking, but it was doing so slowly. They were buying themselves as much time as they could manage as they sailed heedlessly in to the mist at full sail, but as of yet, no land had yet emerged from the stormy seas.

"I don't know how much longer we can keep this up," panted Cade as he lifted another bucket to Rhys.

"Do you need to swap with someone?" Rhys asked.

"Not yet," assured Cade. "I'm good for a few more minutes."

"Let me know the moment you need to," he insisted. "Sol?" Rhys called to the mage stood atop the forecastle, gazing ahead into the fog for any sign of land. "Any luck yet?"

The mage shook his head in frustration. "No. Just sea and mist!"

"How long do you reckon we have?" Rhys directed to Arne who was operating the tiller with Vidar.

"Its hard to say," replied the Captain. "None of my ships have ever sunk before."

"But if you had to guess?"

"An hour... maybe two."

"And then what?" pressed Rhys.

"Either we find land, or we drown."

Rhys returned to bucketing water overboard. After a short while he relieved Cade, clambering below deck to take a shift at filling the pails and lifting them up to Cade and Thia. After a half hour of bailing out the hold, Rhys was then relieved by Sol and took a shift atop the forecastle, peering through the all but impenetrable murk for any sign of land.

The pall of gloom constricted around the Marlin as the hull steadily descended deeper beneath the waves. The caravel began to drag slower and slower through the black brine of the Wyrm's Triangle. Deadly upward daggers of basalt continued to emerge from out of the haze. The bowsprit's tip faded from view. The ship was suffocating. Time was running out.

The din of the storm continued to hammer across the darkling heavens. Sparks of electricity flared through the veil of mist, the arcs of lightning bolts obscured from view. The thunder strikes were growing more regular, and though Rhys could not see the crackling forks, he feared the discharges from the storm were growing closer. If lightning were to strike the Marlin's mast, everything would be over. Another flash lit up the gloom, brighter than any other thus far, but its intensity was swiftly supplanted by its successor. Lightning struck again, somewhere not far beyond the bow, the jagged line of plasma now faintly perceptible in the otherwise hazy glare of white. But it was not the bolt of electricity that Rhys's eyes were drawn to. Instead of the light, it was darkness Rhys found faintly call to him on the fringes of his peripheral vision.

His head pivoted, his eyes scanning the ubiquitous shroud of gloom that enveloped him. There was something out there; he had seen it; it had been for merely a fraction of a moment, but he was certain he had not imagined it. He found himself waiting for another lightning strike. Until now, the bolts had seemed to be descending from the storm at rapid intervals, but suddenly there were none. There were no thunder tolls echoing through the clouds and no accompanying flare of white to illuminate the mists. He waited, unconsciously holding his breath in anticipation. Lightning. A glare of white. But his head was turned the wrong way. He swivelled his neck, but by that point, the flash had faded back to dreary murk. He continued to wait, straining his eyes through the smoky fog, not daring to call out to the others for fear that he was wrong. But there had been something. He knew he had seen it.

Lightning struck again, this time further off, towards the distant obscured horizon. The white flash was faint, but a momentary thinning of the gloom had synchronised with the bolt. Rhys saw it, dim and almost indistinguishable, but his arcanely attuned vision made it out nonetheless. He was certain now. He had seen the line of shadow. A ridge of mountains silhouetted against the white fire of the storm had revealed itself on the starboard side of the bow. That was what he had been searching for. That was all they needed, and it had come not a moment too soon.

"Land..." Rhys stammered, choking on his own words. "Land hoy!"

"What!?" cried Sol, rearing his head from the hold.

"Starboard!" shouted Rhys, dashing down the steps to the main deck.

Lightning glared against the backdrop of fog once more, this time revealing the spine of mountain peaks clearer than ever. Arne sighted the silhouette of the ridge, and with the help of Vidar, the two of them swung the tiller larboard. The Marlin began to turn heavily in the water, the ruptured hull groaning under the strain. The shoring creaked and cracked, and more water continued to seep through the gaps. The bilge below deck was now above waist-height and the caravel was sitting worryingly low in the swell.

"Do you think we can make it?" Rhys asked as the mountain tops flickered once more into view.

"It'll be close," warned Arne.

"Hopefully we won't have to swim the final leg," jested the mage anxiously.

Over the next half hour, Rhys stood at the bow watching as the peaks of the mountains gradually encroached through the spooling fog. The winds picked up, clearing away the low wisps of murk, and suddenly a smoky gale drew back the last veil of gloom obscuring the black and craggy sea cliffs of an isle. Steamy waters broke against the dark bluffs, washing up the jagged faces of the rock before being whipped away in the unrelenting onshore winds. The waves raged perilously at the foot of the cliffs, frequent pillars of spray erupting high from the surface of the water as the surging swell charged into the narrowing inlets.

"We need to find somewhere to make land," urged Arne.

"And in the next few minutes," declared Eirik as he emerged from the hold, sodden up to his shoulders, "or we will not make land at all."

"She's served us well," lamented Arne as he caringly ran his fingers across the grain of the Marlin's tiller. "She'll see us through to the end."

"Her last act," breathed Vidar, now suddenly aware that their family's beloved ship was nearing its final moments."

"Her body is broken," mourned her captain, "but she still has enough life in her to see that we make it."

"We can fix her," refused Eirik, planting a firm hand on his father's shoulder. "We have to… or we'll never make it home!"

"Maybe," supposed Arne. "But I fear this is where she meets her end!"

"There!" declared Rhys, his finger lancing beyond a receding face of dark rock.

"I don't believe it!" sighed Sol in relief.

As the Marlin continued to skirt the shoreline, a bay began to revolve into view. It was a sheltered alcove protected by an encompassing wall of broken cliffs that formed a natural anchorage. Inside the alcove, the white crashing waves settled into gentle breakers that rolled steadily towards the still obscured shore.

"It gets better," promised Rhys as the first glimpse of the grey sand appeared along the lapping shore. A narrow band of beach emerged as the sinking caravel drifted through the mouth of the bay.

"We need to careen her!" announced Arne with a sudden sense of urgency.

"You want to beach the Marlin?" pressed Sol.

"We could be stranded, Father!" warned Vidar.

"No, he's right," insisted Eirik. "It's the only way to save the Marlin. We have to run her aground."

"It's still high tide," insisted Arne. "We'll be able to get her afloat again."

"But Father," resisted Vidar again. "We are too heavy. She is brimming below deck. The bilge is up to our chins! We won't make it close enough to the shore before we run aground!"

"We have to try!" insisted Arne. "Or else she sinks... and like Eirik says, we'll never make it home."

Rhys walked over to the three sailors as the water-laden Marlin ploughed deeply through the bay. "You want to run the ship aground?" questioned Rhys.

"Aye," confirmed Arne. "If we beach her, then when the tide goes out we can heave her down and repair the damage to the hull."

Rhys peered out to the thin strip of silver sand dusted around the foot of the cliffs. "You reckon you can get her seaworthy again?"

"We have to," insisted Arne. "Or there is no way back to the mainland."

Rhys surveyed the shore one final time. "Do it!"

Arne heaved the tiller and the bowsprit aligned with the beach. Slowly, the Marlin crept towards the lapping shore. Ulfgar had long since emerged from below deck, the water level having risen above his head, now finally, Alkis and Nathaniel emerged, leaving no one in the hull. Still, everyone took turns bailing away bilge, now lowering buckets on ropes through the open hatches on the main deck.

"Steady," Arne breathed to himself, the shoreline now merely a furlong away.

Vidar and Eirik reefed the jib and began final preparations to take in the main sail.

"We're not going to make it!" despaired Sol, the waterline rising rapidly now.

Rhys dashed to the gunnels and peered over. The waves were lapping so high against the hull that they were spilling over the scuppers. In the seconds that followed, the main deck became quickly awash with seawater.

"Sol's right," Rhys warned Arne, "she's going down!"

"Not yet," insisted Arne.

The bilge within the hull started to effervesce. The Marlin was sinking; it had taken on too much water and now it was accelerating downwards beneath the waves. The main deck was steadily being swamped, but still the ship's captain remained firmly manning the tiller.

"Arne, we need to abandon ship!" warned Sol as the mage hastened about, gathering what little possessions he could as he readied to jump overboard and swim the final few hundred feet to the beach.

"Just a little further!" pleaded the Marlin's captain, the beach now well within a hundred yards.

"Father!" urged Vidar. "She's gone! We've lost her."

Vidar was right. The water had risen to knee-height on the main deck and was climbing the steps to the fore and aftcastle. In mere seconds, Rhys suspected he would be paddling above the sinking ship, and if they did not get clear of the Marlin, it threatened to drag them down with it into the dark and briny depths.

"Now!" cried Arne.

Vidar and Eirik drew in the sail. The caravel continued to drift forwards. Everyone besides Arne and his sons ascended the steps to the forecastle, as the water rose above waist height below. Rhys was the last to climb, and as he set foot on the upper deck, he lurched abruptly forwards. The keel of the Marlin had struck sand,

and over the course of the final ten yards of its voyage, the ship ground steadily to a halt. The Marlin groaned and swayed momentarily from side to side, before listing gently starboard where it came to rest.

"We made it…" uttered Rhys in disbelief as he glanced over the bow to see the shore barely more than two dozen yards away. Looking back, the mage saw that the water had dropped on the main deck as the Marlin had driven its way up the bank of the seabed. Now the slanting water level was just below Arne's knees at the tiller. "We made it!" he repeated with zeal.

Suddenly the mage found himself embracing Thia. She beamed at him as they parted before Alkis and Nathaniel each dealt the mage a celebratory pat on the back. Rhys shot Cade and Ulfgar a smile as he descended the steps of the forecastle to the main deck.

"Arne," the mage smirked, "you did it!"

The sea captain seemed dazed. He looked around, still tightly clasping the tiller of his grounded ship, hardly believing that they had made it to the beach without sinking.

"You got us here! Just like you promised you would!" Rhys insisted.

"Barely," the captain replied gravely.

"You've done something that all others said would be impossible—myself included," put in Sol as he too emerged from the bow. "Arne, you sailed us into the heart of the Wyrm's Triangle, and landed us on the shores of the Stormy Isles!

"We did it!" cackled Eirik, dropping down from the main mast to embrace his brother.

"I never doubted it for a moment," lied Vidar.

"What's next?" asked Cade, appearing at Rhys's side.

"Tide's on the way out," remarked Arne. "If the range is as great as it was out in open water, then soon the sea will retreat from the bay."

"And the Marlin should be left on dry ground," explained Vidar.

"We can begin repairs once her hull has been drained," insisted Arne.

"She'll be back out on the water in no time," added Eirik.

"Not immediately, I hope," remarked Rhys. "We came here for a reason."

"And we will not depart from these shores until it is done," insisted Arne.

"Thank you," responded the mage.

"You have a job to do," returned the seaman. "And we have ours. When the tide is out, we will set up a beach camp. We'll unload all of the supplies and begin repairs to the Marlin. You meanwhile, are to go searching for what we came here for."

"The conduit," breathed Rhys, rotating to scan the beach as his mind returned to his quest to reunify the network of stone circles across the continent and restore the Nexus at its heart.

"You don't need any help with the repairs?" quizzed Sol.

"No. That is for me and my sons," insisted Arne, placing a hand on Sol's shoulder. "You go with Rhys. Find the stone circle. With a little hope, the Marlin will be ready for the voyage home upon your return."

EIGHT

In the hours that followed, the tide receded rapidly from the bay, exposing an expansive beach of grey sand throughout the cove. As the water dropped swiftly down the hull of the Marlin, gallons upon gallons of bilge began to drain from the hold. Rhys and the others readied their sodden possessions from their quarters beneath the forecastle, and as the last lapping waves drew away from the keel of the beached caravel, they prepared to make their way off the slanting deck and descend to the expanding beach below.

Securing lines over the bulwark, they took turns to abseil overboard. Rhys was the first to vault the gunwale; with his pack slung over his back, he gripped the braided rope and steadily abseiled over the gunnels, kicking off from the damaged strakes of the hull on the short descent. His boots splashed into the foamy sea as the wash swept up the sand, and as the wave retreated back down the beach, Rhys found himself stood on true dry land for the first time in a fortnight. Stepping away from the hull of the Marlin, the mage strode several steps up the beach, collapsing to his knees in the sand. Suddenly overwhelmed with exhaustion and relief, Rhys felt the weight of the last few days begin to ease from his shoulders. They had well and truly made it; they had sailed beyond the edge of the known world, and landed on the beach of a place described only in myth and legend. They had sailed through the Wyrm's Sea. They had made it to the coasts of the Stormy Isles. And against all odds, they had landed on the shores of Thule, something that, if the stories of sailors were to be believed, had quite possibly never been done before.

Sol was the next to plant boots on the beach, followed presently by the others. Vidar and Eirik established a halyard to the top of the main mast and secured it up the beach via a system of stakes driven deep into the sand. Then, using various planks, pulleys, and ropes, they began the systematic process of unloading the sodden cargo and supplies from the Marlin's hold, lowering it keg by keg and crate by crate onto the beach.

Alkis and Nathaniel coordinated the erection of a campsite on the upper fringes of the beach, set against the base of the cliffs where only a springtide would hopefully be able to flood. Rhys and Sol Meanwhile took it upon themselves to scout the length of the ever-draining cove, together walking the mile-long extent of the sheltered bay.

"I can't believe we are here," remarked Sol aloud, more to himself, Rhys suspected, than for his friend's benefit.

"I trusted Arne to get us here," responded Rhys.

"But you hardly know him!?" returned Sol in bafflement. "Nor anything, save what I've told you, about his skill as a sailor! In fact–you don't know a thing about sailing at all for that matter!"

"Your point being?"

"You, more than anyone else I have ever known, rely solely on yourself, Rhys; you have trouble putting your faith in others and try to bear everything on your own two shoulders. How is it that you could so wholeheartedly put your faith in a man you did not know?"

"I trusted Arne to get us here, Sol, because I could tell that *you* trusted him to do so," replied Rhys, smiling weakly. "You are right. I have trouble placing stock in others, especially those I do not know. But I trust *you*, and it was clear to me, from the moment I first met Lena, that Arne, Vidar, and Eirik were like family to you. For that reason, I trust them; because I know that *you* do."

"Lena..." breathed Sol in a moment of reverie. "I wonder what she must be doing right now."

"She's probably sat wondering the same of us."

"Only, we know that she is safe in Westport. She must be worried half to death about

Arne, Vidar, and Eirik."

"I think you might have forgotten about someone else," alluded Rhys.

"What?" replied Sol, his musing suddenly dispelled by Rhys's comment. "Who?"

Rhys shot his fellow mage an intrigued glance, unsure whether Sol was genuinely as clueless as he was acting. But the mage's confusion seemed legitimate, and so he gave his friend the benefit of the doubt. "You, perhaps?"

"Me!?" replied the mage rapidly.

Rhys had been right, Sol really was oblivious. "Yes! You, you idiot!"

"You really think so?" questioned the mage, blushing subtly.

Rhys sighed laboriously. "I did see the two of you outside Arne's house–back in Westport, before we escaped."

Sol grinned both bashfully and smugly.

"It's not just me that's noticed, anyway," assured Rhys, returning his gaze to scanning the bases of the cliffs. "Everyone has."

"Everyone?" pressed Sol.

"I'm afraid so," returned Rhys jauntily.

"Even…?"

"Yes, even Arne, Eirik, and Vidar."

"Oh," returned Sol, suddenly aware that he had not been as sly as he had hoped.

A period of silence elapsed as Sol brooded in his embarrassment.

"If it's any consolation," added Rhys

finally, "everyone is rooting for the two of you."

"They are?" returned Sol after a time.

"Yes," replied Rhys vacantly, his attention almost entirely elsewhere. "What's that?"

"What?"

"That there," pointed Rhys as they neared the edge of the beach.

Ahead, where the black cliffs swept around to shoulder the silver sands of the bay, the rock descended from craggy natural faces into what appeared to be regular carved columns.

"I don't know," shrugged Sol, sighting now what Rhys was referring to.

The two magi approached the array of hexagonal basalt columns, all rising to random heights as they swept down from the cliff tops to the beach at their feet, forging a causeway of six-sided steps against which the sea was breaking.

"Are these man-made?" puzzled Rhys as he inspected the bizarre stone formation.

"I'm not sure," returned his friend.

"They don't look natural," pondered the mage. "But they are carved seemingly at random."

"They must be natural," Sol decided. "Look at the imperfections in the shapes. Some have seven–others eight sides, and many of the prisms are skewed and lopsided. Anyone or any people who would take the time and effort to carve these shapes from the stone would ensure they were at the very least symmetrical."

"You are probably right," agreed Rhys, "but I've not seen anything like it before!"

"Nor I."

Rhys bound up onto one of the columns and skipped across a series of raised stepping-stones to garner a better vantage. He revolved on the spot and directed his attention up the cliffside. His jaw fell agape in wonder as he suddenly realised the stone causeway climbed the black bluffs steadily through a channel carved in the rock, forming what seamed and almost perfect natural stone staircase that rose from the beach to the full height of the clifftops, and perhaps farther still.

"Looks like we've found our way up the mountains," commented Rhys as he drew his friends attention to the geological phenomenon.

"I think you are right," agreed Sol as he ascended the columns to stand beside his friend.

"Come on," urged Rhys after the two of them had spent a moment silently studying the various ways to climb the basalt staircase. "Let's head back to the others and let them know what we've found."

Together, the two magi backtracked along the beach, returning towards the encampment quickly taking shape. Several tents were now erected against the shelter of the cliff faces, whilst the majority of the Marlin's cargo had been stacked around the fringes of the campsite. The Marlin itself was a sight to behold from this distance; canted over on its side, its mast listed acutely away from the sand, the spar's tip tethered to the stakes positioned up the beach to prevent the ship from rocking back to upright in the gales. Though the tide had retreated far down the sands, leaving the caravel well and truly beached, bilge water was still spewing through the gaps in the shored strakes, and Rhys suspected that it would be several hours before the ship's hull was drained completely.

"Find anything?" questioned Alkis upon their return.

"Yes," returned Sol.

"It's probably something you should see, rather than us try to explain it to you," insisted Rhys, "but we have found a way up to the clifftops, and most probably further up the mountainside."

"Is that so?" remarked the intrigued knight.

Rhys nodded with a smile.

"Very well then," agreed Alkis. "We are just about done here. We've set up the larger of the tents, but we still have the smaller more portable ones to take with us in case we venture too far from here to return before night fall."

"Good thinking," praised Sol.

"Thia and Nathaniel have sorted out packs," added Alkis. "We should each have enough supplies for a few days—any longer and we'll have to return here to restock. But given the apparent size of this island, I can't imagine we'll be venturing too far."

"Just as well," reckoned Rhys. "We don't want to be hauling unnecessary weight uphill."

"What do you think, then?" asked Thia, approaching the three of them having already heard the first part of the conversation from afar. "Do you believe the conduit is here, on this isle?"

"I can't sense anything as of yet," returned Rhys, his vision returning to skirt the ledges of the cliffs above, "so, really it is impossible to say."

"We have no idea how many islands are scattered about these seas," reminded Sol. "As much as I dread having to head back out onto the water, I suspect we will be doing so soon enough. It cannot be that the conduit is on the first island we come across."

"You may be right," affirmed Rhys. "But so far, this is the only true island we have discovered. There may well be hundreds more concealed in the sea fog, but likewise, this isle might have many other wonders we have yet to discover. Perhaps it extends for quite some way on the far side of the mountain ridge—if the isle is elongated and we approached from the narrowest side..."

"Possible," supposed Sol, "if not wishful thinking."

"Or," continued the mage, "maybe there could be an elaborate system of caves in the mountainside; it wouldn't be the first time we discovered a stone circle underground."

"I'm not trying to be obstructive," insisted Sol, "I just think we need to be realistic about our chances of finding the conduit here."

"And I'm not naïve," emphasised Rhys, "I just don't think we should be so pessimistic."

"That's enough, you two," interjected Thia, sensing the disagreement could potentially escalate. "You both make valid points."

"In all likelihood, Sol, you are right," confessed Rhys. "The chances are that the conduit lies on some other undiscovered island. But for the time being, we are marooned here—at least until Arne finishes the repairs to the Marlin. So, we might as well use the time we have to scour the island top to bottom, shore to shore."

"Then let's make a start," nodded Sol.

Rhys peered about at the dying light. Though it was difficult to tell in the ever-present gloom that engulfed the Wyrm's triangle, night was definitely on rapid approach. "Its too late to set off today," conceded the mage. "We'll head out at first light tomorrow."

"I'll let the others know the plan," finalised Alkis, turning to head back to the rest of the party.

"Arne," Rhys called out to the hulking sea captain as he and his two sons were rolling a trio of kegs up the sand towards the camp. The three of them each heaved their respective barrel upright, standing them with the assortment of crates stacked in the sand, and made their way over to Rhys and the others.

"We are going to set out come morning," Sol informed the three seamen.

"Aye," agreed Arne, "it'll be dark soon."

"Do you need any help unloading?"

The sailor shook his head.

"This here's about it," explained Eirik.

"Everything else we need is onboard to carry out the repairs," chimed in Vidar.

"The tide will come back in after dark. But she should be back out beyond the mouth of the fjord by sunrise. We'll start work on the Marlin in the morning."

"Any idea how long the repairs will take?" asked Rhys.

Arne turned to look upon the careened vessel. "A week," he supposed, "maybe more."

"We'll make good use of that time," returned the mage.

Using various off-cuts of planks and splintered boards from the makeshift shoring carried out on the Marlin at sea, the party constructed a campfire and pitched a tarred pall out from the cliffside under which they took shelter from the persistent drizzle. The fire delivered some much-needed warmth and the shelter allowed Rhys to dry out fully for the first time in several days. Though the bay was shielded against the worst of the elements, gales swept down from over the mountains and swirled about the cove, buffeting the canvas of the tents and the pitched tarpaulin, causing the flames to quiver and dance frantically.

"At least it isn't raining upwards anymore," remarked Ulfgar as the dwarf hunkered down beneath a blanket.

"Why would you even say that!?" rebuked Cade.

"It won't happen just because I said it!" retorted Ulfgar gruffly.

"I bet it will now," sighed Nathaniel, as together they each noted the distant flash of lightning lost somewhere in the black blanket of storm clouds on the distant horizon.

"I have a surprise!" suddenly proclaimed Vidar.

"A surprise?" bemused his father sceptically.

"Yes!" perked Eirik, realising immediately what his brother was referring to.

"It is actually two surprises," insisted Vidar now, as both he and Eirik rose to their feet and disappeared into the stacks of supplies heaped up on the fringes of the camp. Moments later, the two of them emerged, each carrying a small keg in their arms. They sauntered back over and planted their respective firkins down in the sand.

"What is this?" questioned Arne sceptically.

"Sorry, Father," began Vidar, "but I knew if I asked you would say no."

"Why am I not surprised," bemused Arne. "Let us have it then; what is it you thought so important to transport across the Wyrm's Sea?"

"Well, this one here is nothing too special," explained Eirik. "It is just ale."

"Ale!?" Ulfgar reared his head excitedly.

"Yes," replied Eirik.

"You mean real ale…? Not grog?"

"Yes," returned Vidar.

"Okay," shrugged Arne amiably. "I see no problem with that. Tell me now, Vidar, what is in the other barrel?"

"This is the surprise," returned Vidar. "Something I brought to celebrate if we actually survived and manage to land on the shores of Thule!"

"You did not answer my question," Arne lowered his eyebrows.

"It is for us to eat… for dinner tonight."

"And what is it?"

"Well…" began Vidar. "It's a little early…. Midsummer isn't until next week."

"You brought surströmming?" asked Arne.

"Yes," smiled Vidar nervously.

Arne shook his head.

"Surströmming?" questioned Rhys.

"Wait…" started Sol in realisation. "Is that what I think it is? From the coastal towns north of Cape Tulva?"

"Yes," smirked Vidar excitedly.

"You have some of it? Here?" replied Sol. "Why!?"

"We've begun importing it to Westport," explained Arne begrudgingly. "There is actually quite a market for it, believe it or not."

"I don't believe it. You always said it was disgusting!"

"It grows on you," shrugged Eirik.

"You mean that you like it now!?" asked Sol in disbelief.

"Yeah," replied Eirik, "I think I do."

"You *think*?" the mage repeated, looking now to the other two seamen for their opinion. "Arne? Vidar?"

"It is nice with potatoes," Arne gesticulated.

"What is it?" pressed Rhys, eager for some explanation.

"Herring," replied Vidar.

"As in, the fish?" inquired the mage.

"Yes," responded Vidar.

"It's rotten herring!" interjected Sol.

"Fermented herring," corrected Arne. "It's not rotten."

"That doesn't sound so bad," put in Alkis.

"Yeah," agreed Rhys. "Ale is merely fermented grain, is it not?"

"You have no idea," muttered Sol.

"Have you tried it before, Sol?" asked Nathaniel.

"No," returned the mage. "I'm not that stupid."

"You never know," smiled Alkis, "you might like it."

"Trust me... I know," returned Sol flatly. "And *you'll* know soon enough once they open that barrel."

"What do you mean?" investigated Rhys.

"Just let them try it for themselves, Sol," insisted Vidar, discouraging the mage from giving too much away.

"Well, if we are going to eat it, we had better prepare some potatoes to go with it then," suggested Arne.

"You mean you'll let me open the barrel?" asked Vidar, somewhat in disbelief.

"We brought it all this way... past the brink of the world. We might as well eat it," replied his father.

"More importantly, can we please also tap the other barrel?" pressed Ulfgar impatiently as he salivated over the prospect of a pint of full-bodied ale.

"Yes," chuckled Arne.

"I'll need to find a spigot," warned Eirik rising to his feet.

"No need," replied the dwarf. "I've got one in my pack!"

"You carry a spigot with you in your pack?" questioned Cade in disbelief.

"Always," returned the dwarf as he began rifling through his knapsack.

"Why?" asked Nathaniel confusedly.

"For situations like these! I'm always prepared!"

"And how often is it you find yourself in situations like these?" pressed Alkis.

"More often than you would think," returned Ulfgar cryptically as he produced, as promised, a spigot from his pack.

The dwarf made his way promptly over to the firkin, picked up the small keg and placed it atop a supply crate. Without delay, he hammered his spigot into the barrel and swiftly filled his tankard to the brim. One by one, each of the party members helped themselves to a serving of the ale, whilst Vidar and Eirik began making preparations for supper. Before the hour was up, they were plating out servings of boiled potatoes and onions, accompanied by a slice of dry bread.

"Is everyone ready?" questioned Vidar as he gathered up a lump hammer, hoop driver, and crowbar to remove the barrel head.

"I guess," replied Ulfgar taking his plate over to the barrel.

"No," replied Sol, backing away to the fringes of the campsite where he began to eat his food, watching in morbid anticipation what was about to unfold.

"Everyone, gather round," smirked Vidar.

Everybody apprehensively rose to their

feet and made their way over to the keg as Vidar began hammering the chisel around the top hoops of the barrel. Rhys realised early on that neither Eirik nor Arne had approached, and, like Sol, were keeping their distance. But the mage was curious, and against his better judgment, he too moved inwards as the two upper hoops were removed from the firkin. Using the crowbar, Vidar popped off the barrel head and swiftly took several steps back.

Almost immediately, Rhys was overwhelmed by the noxious smell of putrefaction; his stomach turned and nausea boiled up in his gut. The others all recoiled at the noisome smell of rotten fish. Nathaniel, Cade, and Thia each wretched in disgust.

"Nope!" uttered Ulfgar decisively as he backpedalled in retreat and took up position next to Sol.

"That smells vile!" exclaimed Thia, smothering her face in her cloak.

"Easily the worse smell I have ever experienced," grimaced Alkis through tearing eyes.

"You like the taste of that stuff?" questioned Rhys in disbelief as he clasped his hand over his nose.

"It smells like piss and corpses!" shouted Ulfgar from down the beach.

"I can smell it from here!" gagged Sol. "And I'm up wind!"

Vidar and Eirik cackled with laughter

whilst Arne shook his head sporting a broad grin.

"It's a joke, right?" questioned Cade, recovering his senses as the winds went some way towards dispelling the worst of the repulsive odour. "You don't actually eat this stuff?"

"No," replied Vidar, "you do. I promise."

"Go on then," insisted Rhys sceptically.

"Okay," smiled Vidar as he approached the barrel. Using a knife, he fished out a scaled fillet of the herring and flopped it onto his plate with his vegetables. Taking several steps clear of the barrel upwind to avoid the worst of the smell, the sailor took a seat beside the fire, his brother following suit with a helping of his own. In dreaded anticipation, the others watched in horror as they sliced up the fish and spooned it into their mouths with a bite of the bread and vegetables. Several of the party members cried out in disgust as they took their first mouthful, and Rhys was sure he heard the sound of someone vomiting beyond the edge of the firelight.

"It tastes a lot better than it smells," promised Vidar, speaking with his mouth full.

Arne subsequently approached the keg of fermented fish and served himself a portion before taking a seat on the sand beside his sons. This was the deciding factor for Rhys. He bravely wandered over to the firkin, ensuring he breathed solely through his mouth as he did so, and delicately lifted a fillet of the surströmming with the flat of his blade, positioning it on his plate so that it did not touch the rest of his food for fear of spoiling it. Stepping clear of the barrel, Rhys made his way back to the fire and plonked himself down on the ground next to Arne.

"Go on," encouraged Eirik, who along with his sibling was now nearly halfway through his meal.

"It still smells repulsive," responded the mage as he peered down anxiously at his plate, not sure if he'd be able to stomach the toxic smelling fish.

"You probably won't like it," warned Arne. "Few do the first time they try it."

"So, it's an acquired taste?"

"One I hope never to acquire!" shouted Sol from beyond the camp perimeter.

"Well…" hesitated Rhys, loading a piece of the herring with some of the potato and onion onto his spoon. "Here goes nothing." Rhys raised the spoon to his lips and prepared himself for what was to come. If the smell was any indication, the fish would taste rancid and vile, but he understood that if it was as popular as Arne claimed it to be in both Westport and the Fjell foothill towns from where it originated, such was unlikely the case.

Rhys opened his mouth and pushed the morsel past his lips. At first he tasted nothing, but as he began to chew, his mouth was overwhelmed by potent sour and salty flavours; it was not as he had imagined, nor did it taste how it smelt. As he swallowed and grimaced slightly however, he knew he would be lying if he claimed to like it. Arne chuckled softly; Vidar and Eirik meanwhile cackled in hysterics. Rhys shuddered involuntarily as the taste lingered. He reached swiftly for his waterskin and downed several swigs to cleanse his palate.

"Well, how was it?" questioned Arne sombrely as his two sons wiped tears from their eyes.

"Better than I feared," replied Rhys. "But worse than I'd hoped."

"It takes a lot to convince most folk to eat it," remarked Arne.

"As is probably evident by those of us stood here without any of it on their plate," returned Alkis.

"This is not exactly how I would have imagined celebrating still being alive– but, you only live once," declared Nathaniel, throwing caution to the wind and helping himself to a portion of the surströmming.

Cade was next to serve himself a helping, followed swiftly by Thia. Alkis reluctantly took a portion, and then after so did Ulfgar, who up until this point had been inquisitively moving closer from beyond the fringes of the campsite. The dwarf leant over the firkin and peered down at the fillets of herring; his nostrils flared as he took a long whiff and finally reached into the keg with his knife and hooked out not one, but two of the fish fillets. One by one, they all took mouthfuls of the fermented fish, each agreeing in turn that it was far better than they had dreaded, however it was not to any of their liking. Ulfgar however, after much deliberation, took a meaty mouthful, chewing excessively as he wore an expression of deep cogitation, before finally nodding to himself in satisfaction, after which he wolfed down the remainder of the fish in several large bites.

"Good stuff this is!" Ulfgar announced, taking a large swig of ale as everyone stared at him. "Sol," he called out to the mage who was still stood beyond the limits of their camp, "you've got to try this!"

"No," responded the mage sharply, remaining out in the dark.

"Suit yourself."

NINE

Rhys awoke the next morning to mounds of thick foam blowing up the beach. The rain had ceased for a brief respite, but storms were once again brewing on every horizon. Their night's sleep had been broken and disturbed by tolling thunder and howling gales, but Rhys had been glad even still to spend the evening on land. After a hastily prepared breakfast, the party gathered together what they needed for their initial scouting expedition up the cliffsides.

"We'll have the camp ready for you when you return," assured Arne.

"We should only be gone a few days at the most," explained Sol.

"We just want to gauge the size of the island initially," expounded Rhys. "Beyond the extent of the mountain ridge we could see from offshore, we currently have no real indication as to its scope."

"We've got plenty to be getting on with here—the Marlin needs a lot of work," returned Arne. "Hopefully, the stone circle you seek is not far from here."

"Well, if the other circles we've visited so far are any indication, then there'll almost certainly be some complication in finding it!"

"Rhys is right," agreed Sol. "We won't just stumble across it. It'll either be near impossible to find, or nigh impossible to access"

"But nothing we shouldn't be able to overcome," winked Rhys.

"Then I wish you well," replied Arne.

"Make sure you take care of Sol," replied Eirik smirking.

"Or Lena will be furious with us when we return," chided Vidar.

Sol's cheeks flushed as he tried to ignore the remarks.

"See you in a couple days," bid Rhys, taking the first few steps on their journey up the mountainside.

Together, they marched out across the sands. The tide was once more receding from the cove, breaking waves now lapping as far out as the mouth of the bay, leaving behind a massive expanse of shore. Centred in the drained inlet, the Marlin reclined on its side, a sight to behold beached so far from the water's edge. As they neared the end of the bay, they turned back to see Arne and his sons distantly waving them off from the camp. Rhys and the others returned the gesture, before pressing on, soon after arriving at the foot of the natural stone staircase that led to the clifftops above.

"I see what you mean now," remarked Alkis as he observed the hexagonal columnar causeway that climbed up the inlet of the black cliffs.

"Who would make this?" questioned Cade. "It must have taken decades to carve!"

"No one carved this!" laughed Ulfgar mockingly.

"Well if no one carved it, then why don't you enlighten us as to how it got here?" responded an irked Nathaniel.

"It's natural. Basalt columns; they're formed from molten rock," explained the dwarf.

"How then do you explain their shape?" returned Cade.

"You ever seen mud dry once a puddle's evaporated?" asked Ulfgar.

"Yes…" responded Cade.

"Like that. The larva rises up, it cools, and it cracks."

"Makes sense," shrugged Rhys. "Though I'm no geologist."

"Well, I'm a dwarf," replied Ulfgar. "So as far as you are concerned, that more or less makes me an expert!"

"He has a point," agreed Sol.

"I suppose so," conceded Nathaniel.

"Come on," beckoned Rhys somewhat impatiently, taking the first step of their ascent. "We can debate geology as we climb. As interesting as this all is, it's not why we sailed beyond the edge of the world."

Following the mage's lead, the party began the climb, scaling the rise of basalt steppingstones up the inlet to the cliffs overhead. The silver sands of the bay receded beneath them, and before they knew it, peering down over the edge of the steps revealed a hundred-fathom drop to the beach below. The staircase continued to rise higher and higher, until after the better part of half an hour, they had reached the top of the bluffs, the sheer faces of black rock now softening to mossy slopes. The causeway of basalt continued upwards, having risen out of the corridor inlet to draw level with the mountainside, it persisted uphill, forming a stepped road that drove towards the summits ahead.

The ridge drew clearer now, though the peaks were still shrouded in low cloud. Green mosses and rusty lichens matted the rocky slopes, but as they climbed higher, brown sedges and windswept grass sprouted from the topsoil. Eventually, the hexagonal columns of volcanic rock began to sink below ground. The causeway broke down steadily, the steppingstones becoming gradually more and more sporadic, until finally, as the bay vanished back beyond the brow of the slope, the path of basalt disappeared altogether.

"Looks like it is cross-country from now on," remarked Rhys as they stepped down from the remnants of the natural causeway.

"In all honesty, I'm still amazed we found a path of any kind this far off the edge of the map, be it natural or otherwise," responded Sol.

"If this is indeed Thule, then you never know," replied Rhys. "We might yet find the ruins of an ancient civilisation."

"I wouldn't expect us to simply stumble upon the remnants of the holy city of Annwn, Rhys. This island is so far removed from the rest of the continent that I wouldn't be surprised if no one has ever set foot here before."

"If the conduit is here, then surely someone had to have built it," interjected Thia.

"Thia makes a good point," smirked Rhys.

"I'll believe it when I see it."

"I'd have said that about a great deal many things that we have borne witness to in the past fortnight," put in Alkis.

"Upwards rain, waterspouts, and ships rising out of the sea being chief amongst them, I suppose," beamed Rhys.

"I take your point," conceded Sol. "But as of yet, we've seen no indication of any human inhabitance, be it present day or historical."

"Who said anything about humans?" rebuked Ulfgar. "These mountains are the perfect stomping ground for dwarves!"

"I would say you make an excellent point, had dwarven civilisation not collapsed over three thousand years ago," contended Sol.

"There are still a good few of us around,"

protested Ulfgar.

"A good few who've integrated into human society," insisted Sol. "Beyond the few isolated hill clans scattered across the continent, modern dwarven settlements are near nonexistent."

"There's no need to be so insensitive about it!" snapped the dwarf.

"Ulfgar..." began Sol apologetically, "I'm sorry... I didn't—"

Ulfgar chortled. "I'm just yanking yer chain, lad!"

"Ulfgar—you're a real bastard sometimes," huffed Sol.

"Yep," he agreed as if it were a compliment. "We got what we had coming to us, if you ask me," Ulfgar went on to explain. "A hundred years of war against you lot, then another fifty squabbling among ourselves... heck, we were lucky any of us survived!"

"Its quite refreshing to meet a dwarf that doesn't hold me personally responsible for the genocide of his people," returned the mage.

"Yeah, most of my kind are a bit too touchy on it all. As far as dwarves go, I'm pretty laid back," Ulfgar chuckled. "Anyway, it was almost a hundred generations ago for us and nearer two hundred for you! Anyone who knows what really happened is long dead, and as far as I can tell, we attacked you first! A grudge that's lasted over three thousand years ain't worth holding onto if you ask me!"

"Very few of your race see it that way," remarked Alkis.

"They're just bitter; they know as well as I do that dwarves were as much to blame as humans for what happened."

"And what exactly *did* happen?" questioned Rhys, who until now had remained silent in his ignorance, as he suspected several other members of the group were likewise doing.

"That's a long story," replied Ulfgar.

"And one for another day, I suspect," added Sol.

"The point I was originally making was, Thule and Annwn... they are just plagiarised straight from dwarven folklore! If we discover any ruins here, I reckon they are more likely to be dwarven then human."

"Thule is not taken from dwarven folklore!" protested Sol. "It's a saga carved on to the tablets!"

"Based on dwarven lore!" insisted the dwarf.

"No!" refused Sol. "It is one of the oldest stories in the Titan mythos!"

"Come on, Sol," returned Ulfgar jovially. "Surely you've heard this before?"

"No," retorted Sol. "Thule and Annwn are a cornerstone of my religion. They have not been appropriated from dwarven mythology. Beyond a few carvings in abandoned mines, your people barely have any folklore left!"

"It all fits, Sol," persuaded the dwarf. "Annwn... a city in the mountains... advanced technology... it all sounds a bit familiar doesn't it?"

"For a start, Annwn is atop the mountain, not underneath it, and the saga says nothing about technology; the citizens of Thule possessed innate magic."

"Technology looks like magic to anyone who doesn't understand it," responded Ulfgar. "And the semantics change with each telling of the tale."

"Its not the same," refused the mage.

"All I know is, us dwarves have our own stories about an island and a city ripped apart by the sea."

"Well that's just a coincidence then," asserted Sol.

"Have you ever seen the tablets, Sol?" questioned Ulfgar.

"You know I haven't," growled the mage. "Only the high priests can see the tablets."

"So how do you know that your version of the story is correct and mine is not?"

"Right! That's enough!" snapped Thia, raising her voice. "I have had it with everyone arguing with each other!"

"We're not arguing, we're debating," quarrelled Ulfgar.

"Ulfgar, shut up!" threatened the witch.

Ulfgar fell meekly silent.

"Why is everyone at each other's throats? We are trying to work together here and achieve something of immense importance; and everyone is squabbling like children! I'm sick of it!"

"It's as if bundling us all into the confines of a ship for a fortnight and sailing off the edge of the known world has everyone on edge or something," mocked Nathaniel.

"Nathaniel!" hissed Thia sharply.

"Sorry," returned the guardsman.

"I know tempers are high, and everyone is frustrated, but a modicum of civility would go a long way," stressed Thia.

A long uncomfortable moment of silence elapsed as they stood motionless on the mountainside. Most of the party members were staring shamefully at their feet, no one daring question Thia, none of them having ever seen this side of her.

"Come on, everyone," urged Rhys finally as fat droplets of rain began to patter down from above. "Time is wasting."

With a few quiet mumbles, they set onwards again up the slope towards the veil of thickening murk.

Rhys waited for the others to overtake before sidling up alongside Thia at the rear. "You alright?"

"Yeah," nodded the witch, issuing Rhys a tired smile.

"I'm sorry," offered the mage. "I was one of the worst offenders."

"Yes, you were," agreed Thia teasingly. "But I can hardly blame you."

"What do you mean?"

"We all agreed to come here because we have faith in you," the witch explained, "but Sol has been fighting you every step of the way. I'm not sure he quite believes we'll find the conduit here."

"I'd be careful," whispered Rhys, glancing nearly a furlong up the slope to where Sol marched at the head of the party, "he can probably still hear us at this distance."

"Oh!?" replied Thia, horrified she'd been overheard. "That far away?"

Rhys nodded. "Its probably on the limit—but if his hearing is like mine... just, careful what you say."

"I just meant that we should be working with each other right now, otherwise we definitely won't find the conduit."

"I know," smiled the mage. "It's as you said: we are all under a lot of stress at the moment. As it stands, we are more or less marooned here; and I scarcely know where *here* is!"

"Up here!" called the voice of Sol suddenly from a way ahead. "I've found something!"

Rhys gazed up the mountainside to see the mage perched on the lip of a brow; by his reckoning, they were not far from the top of the spine, but the pitch of the slope made it difficult to tell for definite. Sol turned to face ahead once again and swiftly vanished over the curvature of the ridge.

"Come on," Rhys motioned to Thia as he hurried to catch up.

Jogging up the slope, overtaking Ulfgar, Alkis, and Nathaniel, Rhys crested the lip of the rise. As the mage caught sight of Sol once again, a din of cawing erupted, and dozens of crows flocked into the air. Rhys slowed the last few steps, and into view emerged the largest piece of carrion he had ever set eyes on. The rancid smell of decay wafted on the breeze. An enormous splayed rib cage curled upwards from the ground, each long white bone spar curving higher than Rhys was tall. A chain of hefty vertebrae linked the skeletal thorax, extending nearly two dozen yards before attaching to an elongated head with a colossal maw. The whole carcass had been ravaged and stripped, leaving now only the last rotting tendrils of flesh for maggots and scavengers to feast on. Swathes of leathery skin slumped on the ground surrounding the remains, too tough for the crows to tear at. The beast was unlike anything Rhys had ever seen, but even in its decaying state, the mage could see that it possessed fins and a tail.

"Is that... a fish?" questioned the mage.

"No," returned Sol in disbelief. "It's a whale."

"A whale?"

"Yes," replied the mage. "I've seen a few up close, but much smaller. There are whaling ships that set sail from Westport; they hunt these creatures with harpoons… wait for them to surface and riddle them with spears. I had heard some of them were huge… but this… this is larger than I had ever imagined!"

"How in the world did it get up here?" questioned Rhys.

"I have no idea…" uttered Sol under his breath.

A moment of silence elapsed before the others made their appearance.

"What is that thing?" asked Nathaniel as he emerged over the lip of the mountainside.

"That is massive," remarked Cade.

"Sol says it's a whale," answered Rhys.

"A whale?" puzzled Alkis. "One of those giant fish they hunt out of the Tulva?"

"It's not a fish," replied Sol.

"It bloody looks like one!" insisted Ulfgar.

"It breathes air, not water."

"If this thing lived in the water, as you say Sol, then what is it doing up here?" quizzed Nathaniel.

"Perhaps it was cast up here by the same forces that lifted the Marlin from the sea," suggested Thia.

"Maybe," doubted Rhys, "but the Marlin didn't even clear the water's surface. This thing is halfway up a mountain!"

Sol moved closer, covering his mouth against the noisome stench of the decaying creature, and inspected the carcass.

"What do you reckon killed it?" questioned Nathaniel.

"I'd have probably thought being pulled out of the sea and dropped onto the side of a mountain would have been enough to do it," ridiculed Ulfgar.

"Oh... right," chuckled the guardsman.

"I wouldn't be so sure," uttered Sol.

"What do you mean?" pressed Rhys.

"Something pretty big has had a go at these bones," remarked the mage, indicating to several furrows and puncture holes to the ribcage.

"Are those—"

"Bite marks?" finished Cade. "Yes. Definitely."

"It could be a shark," proposed Sol. "But that would mean the whale was dead before it left the water."

"That still doesn't explain how the carcass came to get here," insisted Rhys.

"Its been here a while," explained Cade. "I can't tell for certain, but by my reckoning, it's been dead a couple weeks."

"It would have had to have been for the crows to strip it this much," responded Sol.

"That's assuming the crows were what

stripped it," replied Rhys.

TEN

The rain intensified throughout the afternoon as they made their final push towards the summit of the ridge. The terrain had change to one of knee-high moor-grass that clumped together into tussocks lumped unevenly across the mountainside. The slopes were stubbled with sprouts of red bracken and small rills babbled out of the ground, trickling down gullies before soaking into pits of peat and sodden moss. The winds howled and whipped the rain in to horizontal streaks that lashed against the party as they struggled up the uneven and rude ground, but as they neared the pinnacle of the ridge, the storm suddenly yielded, and all fell eerily calm.

"Nearly there," assured Rhys at the head of their rank as he pulled back his hood and surveyed the oncoming crest.

In a matter of moments, his eyeline would surpass the height of the mountaintop and he would be granted a view beyond the ridge. He felt his heart twang in anticipation; currently, there was no sign as to what laid beyond the massif they had sighted from out at sea, but presently all would be revealed. What Rhys hoped for were rolling hills, where maybe on the distant horizon he might just spy the sarsen menhir of a stone circle waiting for him to approach. But he feared disappointment was imminent. He expected to summit the peak only to be granted a view of misty ocean, thereby indicating that they had landed on but one of possibly hundreds of isles located in the Wyrm's sea, and the wrong island at that.

Rhys had still not felt even the faintest whispers of a nearby conduit, indicating to him that he was still some way from its location. It was possible that the circle was located underground; he suspected that such was the reason he'd had difficulty locating the conduit in Orthios, however, thus far there had been no suggestion as to the existence of a cave system or the like across the mountain ridge. Consequently, the mage imagined the conduit was in fact, as Sol had assumed, more likely not located on this island at all. But until he peered beyond the summit, he would know nothing for sure.

A terrible sense of foreboding descended on Rhys as he plodded the final few yards. Each step he climbed, his view beyond the crest lowered. In mere seconds he would reach the top, and still he could see nothing but murky sky. Then, it appeared to him. The horizon was still smothered in gloom, but it did not matter. Beyond the peak, Rhys gazed out at an expanse of black foaming water.

"No..." he gasped in defeat.

This was it. There was nothing beyond the ridge. All the island consisted of, was a narrow spine of mountains rising out of the sea. Rhys took another step forwards as he peered out into the gloom in despair, before, looking down, he leapt suddenly backwards in distress. In a sickening moment of vertigo, Rhys realised he had been mere inches from a precipice. Without knowing it, he had wandered up to the very brink of a sheer-sided escarpment. This side of the mountain ridge, the massif plummeted as vertical cliff faces, the sea smashing against the rock hundreds of fathoms below.

"Careful!" Rhys warned, raising his hands in alarm, signalling his companions to go no further.

"What is it?" asked Cade before his eyes widened at the abyss only a couple feet in front of him.

With his head still spinning from the dizzying height, Rhys once more edged closer, braving a second look down over the vertiginous wall of craggy rock to the distant crashing white waters below. He swivelled his head left and right to see that the entire ridge was cleft in this same manner, as if the very mountains had been carved perfectly in half, the far side of the ridge seemingly having sunk beneath the waves.

"Stranger and stranger," remarked Thia as

she too inspected the seemingly missing half of the range.

"This place just makes no sense whatsoever!" grumbled Nathaniel in frustration.

"Now this...." puzzled Ulfgar, "is *not* natural!"

"No," agreed Sol. "No erosion could have formed this. Only some kind of cataclysm."

Rhys gazed out from the ledge across the ashen waters as the sea mist effervesced. A squall was picking up across the brine and the clouds of gloom were evaporating rapidly from the horizon. Suddenly, from out of the fog, across the expanse of sea, the silhouette of another ridge solidified into view.

"There!" blurted Rhys. "There across the water!" he pointed.

The others gazed on as the murk thinned even further, and sure enough, several miles in the distance, the shores of another isle loomed into view. Much like the island on which they had landed, the far range appeared to have been severed down the middle. However, on the distant isle, it was the nearside that descended as sheer cliffs.

"And over there too!" gestured Sol, indicating to their right.

Rhys swung his head in the direction Sol had gestured, sure enough sighting a third island as it emerged from the haze. Far closer than the isle ahead, it rose from the dark waters only a furlong from the shores of the isle they were on; but until now, it had been invisible, concealed within the ever-shifting veil of murk that suffocated the Wyrm's Triangle.

"And there!" exclaimed Cade, as looking west, he spied an additional cloven ridge that swept around the body of sea with eastward facing bluffs.

"There's a whole ring of islands," concluded Thia. "All with sheer cliffs facing inward to this central lagoon."

"Then, does that mean...?" mused Rhys, looking into the heart of the black lagoon as hundreds of questions raced through his mind.

"You reckon the main bulk of the island is sunk beneath the waves," predicted Sol, "don't you?"

"No," smirked Rhys, tilting his head upwards. "What I'm thinking seems even more impossible!"

"Pray tell," pressed an intrigued Thia.

"No," refused the mage. "You won't believe it. Not unless... well, not unless it turns out that I am right!"

"I might just," remarked Sol, his head facing east to the nearest of the isles they had spotted. "Rhys, look there."

Sol positioned himself beside his fellow mage and guided Rhys's eyeline with his outstretched finger. Sol traced the fringes of the broken shore of the island on which they stood.

It was steadily fading with an incoming pall of mist, yet still the faint features could be made out; subtly Sol's finger left the base of the cliffs and glided out onto the open water, where in the fleeting moments of visibility, Rhys made out a sagging line of shadow above the foaming waves. A second later, it had vanished completely.

"Is that a rope bridge?" questioned Rhys in disbelief.

"I think so," agreed Sol.

"Then that must mean..."

"We're not alone on these islands!"

They stood atop the ridge, staring into the mist where the shape had long since disappeared, awaiting another clearing in the gloom for it to reappear, but after several minutes, no such thinning of the veil came.

"We'll need to get closer to investigate," decided Rhys.

"It can't be a rope bridge," insisted Alkis. "In these weather conditions, a rope bridge would be lucky to survive..."

"A couple of years at the most?" interrupted Sol.

"If that," added Cade.

"We could be wrong," returned Rhys. "I only caught a fleeting glance of it."

"I can't say for definite, but I believe that is what I saw," affirmed Sol.

"Come on then," beckoned Rhys, setting off. "Let's go find out."

They bestrode the ridge as they made west across the undulating peaks of the island. Smoky clouds wafted swiftly across the grassy mountainside and drizzle soaked their cloaks. After nearly an hour, they had traversed the spine, descending the peaks to the eastern sea cliffs of the isle. The murk had congealed now into a smothering pall, and only the sound of waves breaking across the rocks a hundred feet below hinted at the precipice that lurked just out of view.

"Careful," warned Rhys. "Watch your footing."

Gingerly, they pressed closer. A surging gust buffeted Rhys, nearly upsetting his balance as he crept forward, watching his feet as the mist parted ahead of him. Then suddenly, the land vanished abruptly as the cliff edge materialised into view.

"What now?" questioned Nathaniel. "We can't see a thing in this!"

"Be patient," assured Sol gently as the billowing cloud continued to plume and swirl in the winds.

Sure enough, in the seconds that followed, several drooping lines appeared as silhouettes against the mist directly in front of Rhys. Thunder drummed, but the flash of lightning had been lost to the impenetrable gloom. Rhys took another step closer. The shadowy lines condensed into girthy ropes, anchored to two stone pillars carved from basalt set into the hillside. From the pillars, the parallel cords curved away, sagging down over the precipice, vanishing from sight into the murk. The two runs were lashed to a series of lower lines of equally thick cordage via a system of upright suspenders, forming the floor and sides of the bridge respectively. The lines swayed violently in the drafts and the whole bridge swung too and fro.

"That looks terrifying!" uttered Alkis as the gloom steadily parted.

"Will it support our weight?" questioned Thia.

"It should do," replied Cade as the hunter examined the fraying lines, each of which was thicker than a man's arm. "But I'm not sure I want to be the first person to try it."

"Any idea how old this is?" asked Rhys, turning to Sol for answers.

"As I said: it cannot be much older than a couple of years."

"Then someone is maintaining it," concluded Rhys.

"Several persons, by my reckoning," deduced Cade. "A lot of rope has gone into making this."

"Well..." hesitated Rhys, "who's first?" The mage turned back to the others, watching as in unison they all retreated several steps from him.

"Well volunteered, lad," returned Ulfgar.

"I suppose I had that coming," grumbled

Rhys, revolving in dread to face the swaying bridge.

Rhys's heart trembled in his chest as he edged closer. Approaching the precipice, he set his palms atop the two basalt anchoring piers and gawked at the murky gulf ahead as the ropes lashed violently about in the gales. Swallowing, his gaze descended to the fluttering footropes extending out from the brink of the cliffside, the fraying lines fading as they delved into the mist ahead.

"Just take it slow," urged Thia apprehensively.

"We'll go one at a time," suggested Rhys.

"Don't worry," jested Sol, "none of us are planning on following until you've tested the entire length across."

"If you hear a long scream and then a splash, followed by the lines falling slack, that means I'm safe across and that you should head straight over," quipped Rhys in return.

"Noted," returned Sol.

"Be careful," insisted Thia one last time.

"I always am," beamed Rhys back at her.

She rolled her eyes.

Turning his attention back to the rope bridge, Rhys lifted his foot and extended it out over the precipice; tentatively, he lowered it onto the tightropes and eased his weight forwards. The lines creaked gently underfoot, yet aside from this, his bodyweight seemed to have little bearing on the cords. Removing his second foot from solid ground, he stepped out onto the bridge in full, clenching both hand lines as tightly as he could.

"There," smirked Rhys apprehensively. "Simple enough."

He edged further out, taking the crossing one step at a time, and before long, the cliffs and his friends to the rear had vanished altogether in the swirling gloom. After what Rhys suspected was near a hundred yards or so, the downward slant of the bridge levelled out to the lowest point in the sagging lines, before steadily curving upwards beyond the halfway point. Rhys could hear the raging waves beneath him, but the briny waters were still concealed in the mist. Suddenly, a rogue squall struck the bridge and the ropes swayed violently. Rhys clasped the lines tighter and waited for the pendulum effect to subside, all the while his heart thumped loudly in his ears.

"How are you doing?" Rhys heard Alkis's voice call out to him from a way back.

"It's quite precarious!" shouted Rhys as the bridge started to swing under the influence of another powerful gust. "I'm about halfway!"

"Can you see the other side yet?" called Sol.

"No," responded Rhys, peering forth into the wall of gloom.

"Keep going!" encouraged Nathaniel.

"Well, I'm hardly going to turn back now," Rhys muttered to himself as the bridge's swing settled down once more.

The mage pressed forwards, watching his boots as he continued to balance on the tensioned lines, and after what seemed an eternity, the far cliff edge emerged into view. Hastily lurching the final few steps, Rhys landed his feet on the second isle. He bent over with his hands on his thighs and waited for his breathing to settle.

"I'm across!" Rhys shouted back at the top of his voice.

A pause elapsed before Sol faintly shouted a return to him. "I'm heading over to you."

"It's stronger than it looks," Rhys replied. "I think it can take several of us at a time without much trouble."

No response followed, so Rhys took a seat on a particularly large tussock and waited for Sol to emerge from out of the fog. After a short time, the mage loomed out of the haze, emphasizing to Rhys that his own crossing had unlikely endured as long as he had perceived it to. Once Sol stepped back onto solid ground, Cade's silhouette emerged, followed swiftly in turn by each of the others.

"Slightly unnerving in the middle, isn't it?" remarked Alkis.

"Just a little," agreed Rhys sarcastically.

"Where to now?" asked Sol, the mage

clearly rallied by having been proved wrong.

"Across this ridge," replied Rhys, turning his attention now up the slopes of the spine before them. "Maybe there'll be another bridge on the far side."

"It'll probably be about nightfall by the time we arrive," warned Cade, pointing out how long it had taken for them to get this far.

"We'll be on the look out for somewhere sheltered to make camp then," returned Rhys.

"If such a place exists here," responded Nathaniel.

"We'll find somewhere," assured the mage.

Throughout the afternoon, they negotiated the ridge, following the chain of mountains, keeping clear of the cliff ledges that plummeted hundreds of fathoms to the foaming seas below. The fog thinned steadily as evening drew in, and more and more isles became visible through the gloom across the lagoon.

"Thia's right: there's a whole archipelago encircling this patch of sea," Sol remarked as they paused briefly atop a peak, surveying the ring of broken mountains.

The murk spread thinner and thinner, granting clear views out across the black waters, yet overhead the ceiling of cloud hung stubbornly low, shrouding the mountain summits and blotting out every ray of sun. Rhys lingered a moment longer as the others set off once again, continuing to peer down into the cauldron of sea centred in the island rim. Just as he was about to turn away, he caught glance of a patch of shadow moving swiftly through the dark waters.

"There it is again," Rhys announced, pointing to the shape scudding ominously beneath the distant waves. "The sea monster!"

"Even from here it looks colossal," remarked Alkis.

"Is it me," hesitated Rhys, "or does it appear to be getting bigger?"

"Its surfacing!" uttered Sol in incredulity.

The party halted, watching in mesmerisation, as sure enough, the shadow beneath the sea began to swell as it glided steadily across the lagoon. Then, to everyone's disbelief, the water abruptly began to bulge. In a fraction of a second, the glassy surface of the sea shattered. White froth erupted in a misty column from the centre of the bay. Spearing from the foam, shot an enormous maw of razor teeth encased in a skull of white scales and ivory horns. Slithering rapidly up after the monstrous head, came a spiny neck, followed by a set of immense talons clawing their way from out of the deep. The hulking leviathan slithered up into the sky, unfurling a breadth of leathery wings that spread on the wind. Behind the wyrm's mass kicked a second set of balled talons followed swiftly by a serpentine tail that writhed as the creature effortlessly took flight. Water beaded and misted in the air as it rained down from its draconic form. The waters beneath it displaced into hollow ripples as it beat its mighty wings, and in a matter of seconds, the creature had surged from the depths of the ocean and climbed high above the surrounding mountain peaks. In the moment before it vanished into the cloud cover, Rhys sighted in its jaws the black and white body of an orca. The whale thrashed its tail helplessly between the dragon's teeth as it was carried high beyond the realm where it dwelt.

As the wyrm faded from view in the clouds above, Rhys peered around to see that the others, Sol included, had thrown themselves to the ground in an effort to escape the beast's notice. Now that the gargantuan creature had vanished high into the heavens, they slowly clambered back to their feet.

"That was a... a..." Cade stammered.

"A dragon!" lamented Sol, equally bewildered.

"It was immense..." mumbled Nathaniel.

"It had to be thirty—forty yards in length," declared Alkis. "Maybe more!"

"Is that usual?" Thia turned to Sol for answers.

"From the legends I've heard... no!" replied the mage, still flabbergasted. "But dragons are all but extinct on the continent... or so Arlas used to say. Few barely make it to reproductive age before they are hunted down; any that make it near to full-adulthood have huge bounties put on them. It is said that they never stop growing... but to reach that size..."

"It must be over a thousand years old!" insisted Ulfgar, speaking for the first time.

"Why are they hunted down?" asked Cade.

"They are too dangerous," answered Sol. "Our order has killed more than our fair share of them. We've been careful not to let them go extinct; ensuring to leave the clutches of young mothers, and sparing wyrmlings, so that they aren't wiped out completely... but before they become too dangerous, those that reach adulthood are killed. Otherwise they rampage across the countryside, slaughtering everything from livestock to entire towns of people. They eat and burn everything in their path if left unchecked. When that happens, kings and lords normally put up enormous bounties which more often than not leads to armies and mercenary groups taking it upon themselves to hunt the creatures.
"

"Why preserve them if they are so dangerous?" asked Nathaniel. "Why not let them go extinct?"

"What a travesty it would be, if man killed every last dragon in existence," scorned Cade as he disapproved of Nathaniel's suggestion.

"Cade is right," agreed Sol, "as dangerous as they are, it would be a great evil to wipe them from the world. After all, it is their nature to be as they are. The Order of Magi, though such cannot be said for other groups who have taken to hunting dragons, saw their efforts as a culling rather than an extermination."

"But how is it this one here has grown so massive?" questioned Thia.

"Its been isolated here," returned Ulfgar, "probably for millennia, with no humans to kill it, and no competition from other dragons. There's a name for a beast of this size... one that hasn't been used in hundreds of years, since the death of the last great wyrm."

Sol nodded. "Leviathan."

"Aye," confirmed Ulfgar.

"Can it be killed?" asked Nathaniel.

Sol laughed nervously. "Not by us," he assured.

"What now?" questioned Alkis, staring up at the distortion in the clouds through which the creature had punctured moments earlier.

"We turn back," replied Sol. "We hunker down on the beach and we make sail back for Westport the moment the Marlin is seaworthy."

"No!" refused Rhys. "We continue."

"Rhys!" challenged Sol. "I'm not making any jokes here. If we have a run in with that beast then we are dead for certain."

"We are not leaving," assured Rhys. "We came here for a purpose, and I don't intend to leave until I have accomplished what I set out to do."

"Rhys, I don't exactly want to give up either," put in Nathaniel, "but I think Sol has a point."

"We are not running," refused the mage.

"Circumstances have changed," insisted Sol. "Your plan made sense... but that was before a leviathan erupted from beneath the waves. We are in enough danger stood here out in the open. To continue on would be suicide; and for what? The off chance that we might find your stone circle on one of a hundred islands out here?"

"For a man of faith, Sol, you seem to have very little of it," argued Cade. "Rhys is not afraid of this thing... and neither am I."

"You should be," sneered Nathaniel, "otherwise you are more of a fool than you look!"

"I was game beforehand," put in Ulfgar, "but I'm with Sol on this one. We've survived a lot together... but a leviathan is something I am not willing to chance! I'll hedge my bets back out on the water again rather than risk facing that bloody thing!"

"Stop trying to undermine what we came here to do!" scalded an enraged Thia. "Sure, that dragon is dangerous, just like everything else we have encountered in these seas, but you are forgetting that back on the continent, Sol, you and Rhys are the most wanted men in all of Westverness and the Capital Realm! Unless your idea is to go into hiding immediately upon our return, we are in no less peril here in the territory of a leviathan than we are being hunted by Indus and everyone loyal to him across two kingdoms!"

"I know Westverness and the Capital realm!" retaliated Sol. "Well enough to evade capture from Indus! And in case you are forgetting, Thia, Indus has yet to conquer your home, Gwent! We know Lord Brandis; he is our best chance at stopping Indus. He already has amassed his armies, and he'll likely be preparing for Indus's imminent incursion. We should be there, helping him! Not off searching for a set of standing stones on some godforsaken island beyond the edge of the world!"

"Everyone, shut up!" roared Rhys so loud that all fell silent and nervously scanned the skies to see if Rhys's shouting had alerted the leviathan to their location. "In case anyone has forgotten, we deduced that the rope bridge we crossed earlier could not be more than a few years old. Some one is living here on these islands, and if the leviathan has been here as long as Ulfgar and Sol claim, then they have been surviving here in its presence.

"I believe you, Sol, when you warn just how dangerous a beast like that is, but I scarcely think that we'd be a mainstay of that dragon's diet! If you didn't see, it had an entire whale in its mouth; I imagine that's how that carcass made it halfway up the mountainside, and I'm willing to bet that whales are its staple. Why would a creature that immense go after such insignificant morsels as us?"

"It's got bigger fish to fry!" remarked Cade whimsically.

"Precisely!" nodded the mage.

"Rhys is right," agreed Alkis. "I'm sure that creature is about the most dangerous thing we've ever seen—but I don't think it will waste its time to come after us. Maybe if it stumbled upon our party by happenstance we'd be in immediate peril, but so long as we keep clear, I doubt its much of a threat to us."

"That's right," confirmed Cade. "Bears have little interest in hunting mice."

"Then it is settled then?" asked Thia. "We continue on?"

A long silence endured before Sol finally conceded. "Fine," the mage agreed. "But we need to head back now to at least warn Arne, Vidar, and Eirik."

"Definitely," agreed Rhys. "But we have probably little more than an hour's worth of good daylight left—it's too dangerous to make our way back along those clifftops after dark. What's more, I reckon we are not long off reaching the far shores of this isle. I want to scout the remainder of the way ahead before we turn back —see if there's another bridge to lead us further on."

"Fine," grumbled Sol reluctantly. "We head on until nightfall and return to the beach come morning."

ELEVEN

The light of day began to fade as they crested the final peak of the second island ridge, descending towards the sea cliffs. A storm rolled in, and heavy rain pelted the party. Lightning flared. Thunder crackled. Mist swirled around the vast cauldron of sea, condensing and evaporating, granting fleeting glimpses of isles looming across the water, but as of yet, the way ahead lay hidden. Soon enough however, the gloom began to draw back, and up ahead, the anchoring posts of a second rope bridge emerged through the haze.

"It continues on then," observed Sol.

"But where to?" wondered Rhys.

"We had better look for somewhere to make camp."

"I sighted an overhang some way down the slope a while back," announced Cade.

"I think I saw the one you mean," Nathaniel returned. "Set above a slight hollow?"

"Sounds as good as anywhere around here," replied Sol.

"How far back is it?" asked Rhys.

"Not far," responded Nathaniel.

"I think it was about ten minutes ago we passed it," Cade affirmed.

Rhys peered ahead to the effervescing wall of fog wafting across the rope bridge. "We must still have another half hour of light," he estimated. "I want to get a bit closer—see if we can make out the far island before we turn back."

"I'm not sure you'll see it with this storm blowing in," warned Sol.

"It's worth a try," insisted the mage, lowering his hood for a better look.

Lightning flashed through the gloom as another jagged bolt clove down from the heavens, preceding a grumbling peel of thunder that lingered low and drawn out before finally dying on the wind.

"You all can head to the campsite—begin setting up if you'd like," added the mage as he took note of Sol's reluctance. "I won't be long."

"No," Sol shook his head in refusal. "We stick together. We'll come with you."

"If we can't find that shelter in the dark, I'm blaming you Rhys," warned Ulfgar as he turned his collar up against the wind.

"We'll be fine," assured Sol.

Slanting rain hammered at them as they trudged down the tussock-covered slope. Rills gurgled through stony channels underfoot, the celestial battle of thunder and lightning raging overhead. Finally, as they reached the clifftop, wind surging up from the turbulent sea below, a towering mountain peak materialised fleetingly against the murky backdrop as a flare of electricity cut through the gloom. The angular summit loomed vaulting in the distance, the pinnacle rising double the height of any other peak thus far.

"Did you see that?" asked Alkis.

"Yeah—it was huge," replied Nathaniel.

"It must be a larger island," concluded Sol.

In the surging gales, the pall of fog ahead began to sweep away. Gazing onward, Rhys peered through the retreating haze, expecting to make out a distant shoreline, but as the mist cleared, all the mage could see was an expanse of breaking waves.

"Where is it?" questioned Rhys, shielding his eyes from the lashing rain.

"There," pointed Sol, another flash of lightning illuminating the mountain zenith against the sky.

Rhys once more lowered his gaze to see nothing. The veil of fog had receded further now, yielding a view out across the water as far as a mile, yet still no cliffs or beaches presented themselves out of the foaming brine.

"That's strange," remarked Sol. "The summit doesn't look that far away!?"

"You remember that idea I had..." began Rhys as the fog and clouds continued to recede. "The one I said was too impossible for you to believe?"

"...unless you were proved right," finished

Thia.

"Well—I reckon I'm about to be proved right."

The winds swelled and the mist continued to recede. No shoreline appeared. Waves rolled on endlessly as foaming horses across the water, not a single dark cliff or silver beach appearing for them to break against. The clouds lifted higher. The squall attenuated to fine drizzle. Together they stood, soaked to the bone, the frigid gales buffeting their sodden clothes, gathered close to the cliff ledge at the brink of the world, as from out of the haze, the strangest spectacle that the Wyrm's Triangle had yet presented steadily revealed itself. From out of the rising cloud emerged the underside of the mountain. An immense ceiling of stone hung suspended in the air, levitating several hundred feet above the surface of the sea. The gloom withdrew further, and the face of the mountain was exposed in full, floating still and silently in the darkling skies.

Outwards from the cliffside before them stretched the rope bridge; it drooped away from the ledge on which they stood, before, after a short distance, the thickly coiled lines levelled and began to climb, ascending higher and higher away from the sea, where eventually, shrouded by the final wisps of evaporating mist, they attached to the face of the hovering island. The bridge was a tether, offering the free-floating isle its single terrestrial connexion to the rest of the world.

"I don't believe it," muttered Sol.

"I can't believe it," returned Thia.

"And yet, here we are, staring at it nonetheless," finalised Rhys.

Silently, they stood gaping in awe as the residual glow of dusk surrendered to night. Bursts of lightning continued to reveal the outline of the suspended mountain long after the twilight had died, but as the storm swept further out to sea, the flashes petered out, leaving nothing but a veil of impenetrable darkness ahead.

"Best find that overhang—before the storm returns," mumbled Rhys, the first to speak in some time, his head still spinning after witnessing the world defying phenomenon.

"That mountain... was floating," uttered Nathaniel, terrified by the revelation.

"I know, right?" chuckled Rhys nervously.

"This just makes no sense..." refused Thia running her fingers agitatedly through her hair. "How!?"

"Beats me," replied Sol.

"It defies the very laws of nature... it defies everything I understand about magic!"

"Clearly, there's a lot more to magic than what we understand," returned Rhys unhelpfully.

"That mountain was floating!" repeated Nathaniel with greater emphasis.

"There must be more of them," insisted Sol.

"The mysteries of this place are starting to come together now," declared Rhys.

"How so?" asked Cade.

"Think about it," began the mage, "the upwards rain, the Marlin rising from the water, the halved mountain ranges which look like they've been ripped out the sea... I won't pretend to understand the forces at work here, but the normal laws of nature are at war with themselves. Gravity has been upended. Land and sea are being lifted into the sky; the elements are all blurring together. The rules that govern the rest of the world have broken down!"

"You think it is because we have passed beyond the edge of the world?" questioned Sol.

"We've moved beyond the edges of the material plane!" declared Cade, drawing ideas from his pagan beliefs. "We are outside the realms of the Elementals!"

"Let's not get ahead of ourselves," backtracked Rhys. "But there is something at work here that is tearing the forces of nature apart, and I am willing to bet that we'll find the conduit right at the heart of it all."

"Then what?" asked Thia. "You think the conduit is...?" she ended her question by directing her finger upwards.

"Quite possibly," nodded Rhys.

"Then how do we get to it?" asked Nathaniel.

"My guess…" returned Sol, "we follow the bridges."

"We have no idea how far it goes," cautioned Alkis. "We'll need all the supplies we can take with us if we are going to press on."

"Just as well we are heading back to the beach camp first thing in the morning," returned Sol.

"We need to get set up here for the night first," reminded Rhys. "Cade, I trust you will still be able to lead us to that hollow now it's dark?"

"It shouldn't be too difficult," returned the huntsman.

"Good," smiled Rhys.

They made their way back up the ridge under the shadow of night. The overcast skies grew laden with fog once again, turning the darkness as black as pitch. Yet despite the near absolute absence of light, they eventually managed to stumble their way along the slopes until they located a small sheltered alcove tucked into a nook in the mountainside lipped by a rocky overhang.

Blindly, they pitched their tents in the hollow and sparked a fire from the kindling they'd carried with them. Sleep came swiftly after the physically arduous climbs and mentally taxing revelations of the day, and as the first hazy light dawned the following morning, they rose, ate a meagre breakfast, and resumed their return journey to the Marlin.

To their relief, the leviathan made no appearance throughout the day, the party deducing that it was likely hunting beneath the waves or lurking in a lair, possibly located on some as of yet unseen floating peak. The murk and rain closed in as the morning endured, lingering late into the afternoon, only lifting shortly before nightfall as they began their descent of the basalt staircase back towards the beach.

As they dismounted the bottom steps onto the sodden grey sands, neither Arne nor his sons were anywhere to be seen. Their absence roused an uneasy silence with Sol in particular as they set off along the final stretch of beach, but when they drew nearer to the camp, the three sailors emerged from the hold, up onto the slanting top deck of the Marlin. Already, many of the ruptures to the ship's hull appeared to have been repaired, with a good portion of the damaged strakes replaced. Arne sighted Rhys and the others as he emerged on deck and called out to them from down the beach, waving his muscular arms in greeting. Descending lines overboard, the three merchant sailors planted boots on the ground as Rhys and the others arrived at the edge of camp.

"How goes it?" questioned Arne, embracing Sol, then Rhys, then the others each in turn. "Found any trace of the stone circle?"

"Not yet," began Rhys. "But we have seen

things you wouldn't believe."

"I've already seen plenty I wouldn't believe since coming here," smirked Eirik.

"We've had some excitement of our own whilst you were gone," declared Vidar.

"Really?" questioned Sol with some surprise.

"No," returned Vidar bluntly.

"Not unless you think shoring a ship is exciting," added Eirik.

"There's a lot we need to explain," insisted Rhys.

"Then you can tell us as we prepare supper," replied Arne.

"We are having mackerel," announced Eirik. "Vidar and I went fishing off those rocks this morning. And I caught nearly a dozen!"

"Well done, Brother," congratulated Vidar unappreciatively.

"Why don't you tell them how many you caught, Vidar?"

"I don't think they care much, Brother."

"How many did he catch?" Sol directed to Eirik.

"One," replied Vidar teasingly.

Sol chuckled.

"I was just unlucky, alright!" sulked Vidar.

"Don't worry, Brother, that is still one more than last time," Eirik snickered.

"Vidar, son," began Arne, putting a giant palm on his son's equally large shoulder, "you are an excellent sailor... but a terrible fisherman."

"And here I was, father, thinking you might try and make me feel better."

"You and I both know, Vidar, I am not that kind of father."

This time even Vidar laughed, as together, they all entered the campsite. Within the hour they were eating mackerel by the fire whilst Sol and Rhys took turns explaining what had happened the previous day.

"And this dragon..." paused Arne, once the account was finished, "you believe it will not come for us... attack the Marlin perhaps?"

"I believe if it had any desire to attack the Marlin, then it would probably have done so when we encountered it out at sea," Rhys speculated.

"Hopefully, it has very little interest in us whatsoever," Sol assured.

"Then we shall continue with the repairs as normal. With any luck, if it flies over, we will be hidden below deck."

"On a ship made out of wood!" returned Vidar.

"Did you not listen to what the mages said?" Eirik scolded his brother. "It eats whales... not sailors!"

"And so you plan to set off again at first light?" questioned Arne.

"Yes," confirmed Sol.

"But we don't know how long we'll be

gone this time," added Rhys.

"You needn't worry," assured Arne. "We will not sail home without you."

TWELVE

Arlas trudged through the quivering bronze grass beneath the blistering heat of the morning sun. Sweat beaded on his dark skin as he surveyed the sweeping inclines of the mountain ahead; it climbed gradually up from the savannah of Dessex, its domed peak standing high above the baked grasslands. Somewhere on Mlima's slopes, the creature dwelt, resting until its insatiable hunger roused it from its lair once more. If Arlas did not find it, another unsuspecting village on the southern plains would fall victim to the fiend's monstrous appetite.

The mage uncorked his waterskin and took a sip, allowing the tiny mouthful to wash across the inside of his mouth for a long moment before he finally swallowed. His skin had nearly run dry.

Across the slopes of the extinct volcano, countless babbling springs birthed fresh rills, but the mountain still hugged the horizon; he would not reach its foot until midday. For now, he needed to conserve every drop of water he had left.

The enduring images of the village still

haunted the edges of Arlas's mind. The bodies of the children troubled him most. Dismembered and ravaged, their bones had been stripped of meat. He had seen a great many corpses since his binding; with his life sworn to the Circle, he knew there would be countless more. But, never before had he seen the body of a child. The mutilation had been sickening.

What the massacre would have been like to behold, Arlas could scarcely imagine. The young girl's account had painted a harrowing depiction, but the trauma had left her little more than a babbling wreck. He discovered her buried beneath the ruins of her hut. At first, the mage believed he'd found the last piece of the puzzle: a survivor, a witness, a first-hand account of the brutal slaughter that might finally help him identify the beast. But the girl's testimony had only muddied the water, raising more questions than answers, and tarnishing the theory Arlas had formed over the last fortnight of his hunt.

Ultimately, it mattered little; the creature was deadly and needed to be stopped. He had hoped that by identifying the monster he might learn of some weakness, but the chances were, a beast such as this had none. By all accounts, it seemed unkillable. But everything could be killed, or so Arlas assured himself.

"What have you learnt, my student?" the familiar voice of Zadkiel Al'Ilah called out to him from under the shade of an umbrella thorn.

Arlas turned slowly to face the man, his preternatural senses having long ago alerted him to the nearby presence of another mage.

"Have you identified your quarry?"

"I have tried, Archon," insisted Arlas, stepping beneath the canopy to shelter from the blistering sun.

"Trying is not the same as succeeding, Arlas," Zadkiel scorned. "You must study your target and learn its nature to complete the Rite of Ascendance—you will not be granted the rank of acolyte merely through slaying the beast alone."

"I understand, Archon, only... I do not believe I can be certain with a creature such as this," explained the young initiate. "The accounts I have heard are... conflicted to say the least. I myself have witnessed this creature from afar, but even having laid my own eyes upon it... I still cannot be certain what I hunt."

"Tell me then, Arlas, what is it you believe you are pursuing?" asked the archon as he tugged gently on his dark beard.

"It is a hybrid of sorts," began Arlas. "Only, the accounts differ as to which animals constitute its anatomy. My prevailing theory is that this creature is a manticore."

"A manticore!?" questioned Zadkiel, raising his eyebrows.

"Yes," confirmed Arlas. "It does not fit perfectly with all the evidence I've collected—but it is the closest match."

"A manticore is no trivial task," warned Zadkiel. "It is ill advised for any mage to pursue such a fiend alone; that goes double for an initiate. But you doubt your classification; tell me, why is this?"

"Its anatomy is inconsistent with what I know of manticores. It has the head and front limbs of a lion, of that I am more or less certain, but from what I have learnt and seen, it lacks wings—nor does it seem to possess the characteristic tail of a scorpion."

"And how *would* you describe the beast's tail?" questioned Zadkiel warily.

"Serpentine," responded the young mage.

The archon's eyes widened. "Anything else that you have noticed or heard that distinguishes it from a manticore?"

"Yes," nodded Arlas, "its tracks—paws without claw indentations for the forelimbs, but at the rear: cloven hooves. I believe its hindquarters are—"

"Hircine?"

"Yes," confirmed Arlas.

The archon swallowed. For the first time ever, the mage appeared anxious.

"You know what it is, don't you?"

"I do," nodded Zadkiel gravely. "The reason you could not identify the creature, my young student, is because I have never taught you to. It is what is referred to as a chimera."

"A chimera?" repeated Arlas.

"Yes," confirmed the Archon. "It is a beast of legend—one claimed only ever to come into existence during times of reckoning. I have never educated you on such a beast, because I did not believe you would ever encounter one."

"I see," mumbled Arlas, understanding now why the mystery had seemed unsolvable.

"Arlas, I cannot let you face this creature alone. It will kill you."

"The rules of the Rite specify that I cannot be aided," recited Arlas. "I must face this creature alone, or I will not graduate."

"True," nodded the Circle's archon, "but the Rite is designed to prove that you are capable of carrying out missions on your own accord, without the assistance of senior magi; it was not created to test the metal of young magi against monstrosities straight out of legend. Let me accompany you, Arlas. Your Rite of Ascendance can be completed another day against a creature that you can match by your lonesome."

"The statutes of the rite specifically forbid just that—an initiate must defeat the quarry assigned to them, whatever it may be," responded Arlas.

"The statutes were not decreed with circumstances such as these taken into account," returned Zadkiel. "I am at fault here," insisted the archon. "I assigned you this creature believing it merely a basilisk. I should have investigated further before issuing you the quarry. Because of this, I will use my power as head of the Circle to veto the assignment. The rest of the Circle need not know of this."

Arlas gazed north again, toward the mountainside, as crickets rattled through the undulating grass. "Thank you, Archon," he issued at last, "but I will complete the Rite of Ascendance today—as the scriptures of our order dictate."

"Arlas, do not be foolish. You do not need to prove yourself in this way... to me nor anyone else for that matter—especially not Azrael."

Arlas remained quiet as he brooded.

"I believe in you, Arlas. One day you will become a truly great mage. You have demonstrated your abilities time and time again throughout your training. Your time is near, but it is not today. Do not go after this creature."

"I only do what I must," returned Arlas ultimately.

"Do not be hasty, Arlas. You fail to understand what this creature's reappearance signifies."

"Then tell me," responded the young initiate.

"The emergence of a chimera portents disaster."

Arlas nodded silently.

"Your conviction is beyond admirable, Arlas, but... must I warn you about blindly following tenets? ... even those of our own order?"

"The rules of the Circle are what define us, Archon. If we are not beholden to the creed, then our oaths are meaningless."

The archon remained begrudgingly silent.

"This creature is too dangerous to not be stopped," warned Arlas. "If I am unsuccessful, send word to the rest of the order. It must be slain, or hundreds more will fall victim to it."

"Don't try this alone, Arlas," Zadkiel uttered gravely. "Please, let me help you."

"I believe in the Order," replied Arlas. "It is the first and only thing that has given me purpose. I cannot turn my back on its scriptures. The Circle's legacy is too important."

"I understand," sighed Zadkiel. "I will watch your progress from afar. I will not intervene… you have my word."

"Thank you, Father," returned Arlas.

With that, he stepped out from beneath the shade of the umbrella thorn and continued his trek towards the foot of the mountain.

Flies hummed around the mage's head as he marched out across the grassy plains. Distant herds of wildebeest grazed across the verdant hills whilst elephants paraded between leadwood trees. Arlas pressed on through the scorching heat, sipping sparingly on the last mouthfuls left in his waterskin. The sun rose high, reaching its zenith and drifting west. With noon at his back, the mage finally arrived at the foot of Mount Mlima. Raising his head and shielding his eyes from the sun's glare, he scanned the slopes above for any sign of his quarry. As of yet, the chimera remained hidden.

He began to climb. Continuing to survey the mountainside throughout his ascent, the mage caught sight of movement in the bush. Something was stirring, beneath the tangled mess of shrubs, prowling through the undergrowth, but given away by its movement all the same.

Arlas drew his ebony staff, feeling the grooves of its runic carvings beneath his fingertips. He stooped low, continuing to climb, creeping steadily closer to the movement up ahead. The minutes that followed drew out. The mage could feel his heart throbbing. His breath was short and sharp. He was downwind, with a little luck, beyond the monster's perception. His only hope of slaying the chimera was to take it by surprise. The question was, was Arlas the stalker, or was his prey stalking him?

The scrub rustled abruptly and vultures flocked into the skies. All fell still. Arlas hunkered down. Blood coursed fiercely through his veins. His senses were alive to the mountainside ahead. He could hear the cracking of dried twigs, the swishing of grass, laboured breathing. Almost crawling on hands and knees, the mage prowled further uphill, steadily approaching the site where he'd seen movement. Stooping beneath the brushwood, he crept closer inch by inch. Pushing aside a shrub, Arlas emerged at the exact spot he'd first sighted movement. A giraffe lay shredded in the grass, large chunks of flesh rent from its carcass, its innards strewn out beneath the sun, buzzing with flies, partially consumed by predator and scavenger alike. To Arlas's horror, the animal was not quite dead. It had been ravaged to within an inch of its life, but alive it was, if only barely. Its bloodied chest shuddered in stifled breath, and as the mage approached, its long eyelashes flitted open and the creature's large dark eye stared up at Arlas.

The mage peered down with pity. He knelt, gently resting his palm on the creature's elongated neck. Its pulse was near non-existent despite its once powerful heart. Arlas suspected it likely had only a few moments left. Even still, the mage could not bear to let the animal go on suffering. And so, mercifully, he sunk the blade of his staff through the giraffe's jugular, watching as the last few pints of scarlet blood seeped from the animal's neck. Its eye rolled silently shut, and all fell ghostly quiet.

Arlas could sense the danger before there was any sign of it. The tiny hairs on the back of his neck seemed to prick up, and an icy chill shuddered through his body under the heat of the afternoon sun. His fingers twitched tighter about his staff, as slowly, he rose to his feet. The crackling growl of a lion intermingled with serpentine hissing sounded behind him. It was impossibly close. As the mage apprehensively revolved, he realised the beast had snuck to within ten yards of him.

Its enormous head reared from out of the shrubbery, curving ram horns extending from out of its fiery mane. The golden fur of a lion transitioned to goat's wool near the creature's haunches, whilst further rearward, a scaled tail uncoiled, its tip barbed with venomous fangs. The chimera bared a maw of razor teeth. A forked tongue issued from the beast's gullet, wafting the air as it tasted Arlas's scent, two slitted eyes narrowing as they focussed on the mage.

Within striking distance, the chimera rose out of its prowling stance, standing nearly twelve feet tall as it padded a few final feet closer to Arlas, sizing up its prey. Muscle rippled beneath the fiend's hide with every step it took, until, ready to pounce, it rocked back on its haunches and locked eyes with the mage.

Reacting as fast as his arcane reflexes allowed, Arlas dove sideways, throwing himself to the ground, barely escaping beneath a set of hooked claws as the chimera sprung onto the body of the giraffe. Rolling to his feet, Arlas leapt back in disarray, the serpentine tail of the creature lashing for him, its poisonous fangs missing by mere inches. The chimera swivelled rapidly and swatted for Arlas. The mage stumbled clumsily aside.

Regaining his footing, Arlas dodged away

from the chimera's snapping maw and swung with his staff. A jet of lilac flame erupted from the end of the weapon, dousing the creature in fire. The monster reared up on its haunches and batted at the jet of flame with its feline paws as the searing heat enveloped it. The blast of fire subsided. Arlas leapt back in anticipation. Black smoke hung in the hot dry air as the brush smouldered. The chimera's paws thumped back onto the ground, and as the smoke cleared, Arlas's mouth fell agape in terror; not so much as singed, the mage's gout of flame had been utterly ineffective against the beast, succeeding only in angering it.

Arlas stumbled back in alarm, the chimera emitting a thunderous roar. Its forked tongue wagged, sensing the terror in the mage's sweat. The monster spread its jaws wide, the air around its mouth distorting as heat sparked with sudden intensity. Without further warning, a spout of fire gushed from the chimera's throat, spraying straight in Arlas's direction. Shielding his face with his arms, the mage threw himself back. His ankle snagging in the scrub, he toppled helplessly over.

Dazed and vulnerable, the mage felt searing heat blister the skin of his forearm. His sleeve was alight. He rolled over, extinguishing the flames, unintentionally dodging the next pounce from the chimera in the process. Once more, the creature's fanged tail struck at him, sinking into the soil barely an inch from the mage's thigh.

Arlas scrambled frantically to his feet, ducking as another set of giant claws scythed above his head. His boot snagged in the brush again, the undergrowth entangling his feet. He tumbled, head over heels, down the mountainside, in a sprawl of limbs. Flailing his arms and legs, he managed to slow himself, and somehow by accident, righted gracefully into a sprint. He was back on his feet and running for his life, but a swift glance over his shoulder revealed the hulking mass of the chimera was bounding rapidly after him. In a matter of seconds, the creature would close the distance and Arlas would be dead. Running wasn't an option.

Arlas pivoted left in a pirouette and let fly a short bout of flames from the end of his staff. The missile of smoke and purple fire merely deflected off the monster's mane. But, harming the beast had not been the mage's intention; all Arlas had meant to do was to dazzle the creature, and in that he had succeeded. The monster averted its eyes at just the wrong moment; just the right moment for Arlas: the instant it propelled itself from the ground into a second pounce.

Arlas dropped to his knees as the chimera bore down on him from above. He lunged with the tip of his blade, and as the chimera sailed overhead, Arlas drove the metal of his stave clean through the rear ankle of the beast. It was far from a mortal wound, but as the fearsome hybrid landed, its cloven hoof buckled. The chimera's momentum did the rest. Unable to control its impetus, the beast toppled over, careening sideways downhill.

Realising his last remaining chance was to end the affray in the next few seconds, Arlas leapt upright, charging after the fiend, casting forth a maelstrom of lightning, stone, and ice from his staff. The fusillade nearly rendered the mage unconscious from overexertion, but each spell hit its mark in rapid succession. The thunderbolt zapped into the chimera's eyes, instantly blinding the monstrosity as it howled in anguish. Swiftly following the lightning, a fist of stone hurtled downhill at blurring speed, crunching into the beast's ribcage and crumpling its chest, silencing the chimera's roar. The blast of frigid air was last to strike the monster, snap-freezing the chimera's serpentine tail, encasing it instantly in a crystallised layer of hoarfrost that rendered it rigid and immobile.

Charging the final few feet, Arlas leapt with every remaining ounce of strength he had left, lancing downwards with his blade. As he landed, the point of his staff speared through the creature's throat. Blood gushed from the wound, spilling over the monster's golden fur, dousing Arlas in the spray. The chimera's yellow eyes fell open, its narrow pupils swelling wide until its irises were fully eclipsed. Two hircine hind legs kicked in a final protest, whilst its hooked claws retracted slowly into the pads of its forefeet. The blood flow gushed thick and fast for a few short seconds, until its pulse grew feeble. Finally, the beast's head lulled back and the final wisp of breath exited its lungs. Arlas had done it. The chimera was dead, and he was not.

The mage collapsed on the mountainside, almost blacking out in exhaustion, the weight of what he had achieved not yet bearing down on him. He was sweating profusely, his gut quivering in uncontrolled breathing. His heart spasmed in his chest, on the verge of exploding altogether. But steadily, his body drew itself back to a resting state. His lungs and heart calmed and his skin cooled, but his mind was blank, unable to process the battle that had taken place. It had probably lasted less than a minute in total, but as his brain replayed each splintered second out over and over again, the whole affray seemed to have drawn on for hours.

"By all accounts you should be dead..." uttered Zadkiel from over Arlas's shoulder.

The initiate stayed silent, unable to so much as nod in response.

"I watched the battle in full. To have escaped so narrowly... so many times... and yet, somehow against all odds you prevailed."

Slowly, Arlas managed to rotate his heavy head to gaze upon the archon.

"For an initiate to achieve a feat such as this... it is unprecedented."

"I did…" laboured Arlas, "what I had to."

"An accomplishment such as this not only fulfils the Rite of Ascendance… it merits further promotion."

"What do you mean?" wheezed Arlas.

"Arlas Al'Asim, kneel before your archon."

Arlas fought his way up from the ground, struggling to his knees against exhaustion. The glare of the sun blinded him. He lowered his head.

Zadkiel raised his staff and lowered the flat of his blade upon Arlas's right and then left shoulder. "Arlas Al'Asim. From this day forth, you are no longer an initiate of the Order of Magi, nor shall you claim the rank of acolyte. Instead, rise, Paladin of the Circle."

"Paladin?" repeated Arlas, looking up in disbelief as Zadkiel gazed down on him with a smile.

"Yes," nodded the archon.

Slowly, Arlas clambered to his feet, the weight of exhaustion pressing heavily down upon him.

"I sense great things in you, Arlas. One day, you will be instrumental in bringing great change to the world. Of that, I am sure."

Rhys opened his eyes as rain bludgeoned the canvas above his head. The winds were howling and distant waves were raging up the beach. He was not in the south, nor on the mainland at all, but instead on a remote island of the north-eastern fringes of the continent. He was not Arlas, but Rhys. It had all seemed so real, because it was. Once more he was peering into the past, catching glimpse of things that had long ago happened. But what was the message this time? What piece of what puzzle was being unveiled to him from long into the past, conveyed to him through the medium of dream? Of one thing Rhys was certain: only time would tell.

THIRTEEN

"Here goes nothing," mumbled Rhys as he prepared to step out onto the swaying rope bridge, the lines ahead fading out into the foggy abyss.

"It's just like the other bridge," insisted Sol.

"The other bridge was attached to the world at both ends," replied Rhys. "This one is tied to a mountain floating in the sky."

"Whatever forces keeping it in the air are strong enough to hold an entire mountain aloft," assured Thia. "It's not likely to drop out of the sky the moment you set foot on it."

"How can you know for sure?" questioned Rhys uneasily.

"It probably weighs millions of tonnes. I don't think a few dozen pounds extra will upset it," replied Sol.

"If that's the case, why aren't you going first?"

"I did say *probably* won't make a difference."

"The small amount of extra weight could be all that is needed," began Nathaniel. "Send it over the tipping point... straw that broke the camel's back, and all that."

"I don't think you are helping the situation, Nathaniel," scolded Thia.

"I'm just saying," Nathaniel continued, "Rhys is right, we cannot know for certain."

"Rhys, I can go first if you'd prefer," offered Cade.

"No, it's alright," insisted the mage. "I don't suppose there would be a bridge across if the mountain couldn't take my weight. I'm just more comfortable on solid ground... anything that floats—ships... airborne mountains—they tend to unnerve me slightly."

"If you are going to cross, stop jabbering on and get on with it!" urged Ulfgar unsympathetically.

"You in a hurry, are you?" Rhys questioned the dwarf. "Some important meeting you need to get to?"

"No, I just hate all this standing around yammering, waiting for a dragon to fly out of the mist! The sooner we are back on the mainland, the happier I'll be."

"Alright," agreed Rhys, "I'll hurry up then."

The mage tightened his grip of the braided lines and tentatively lowered a foot onto the tightropes. The cords creaked slightly as they bore his burden, but once again barely so much as sagged underfoot. He shifted his full weight out beyond the precipice of the cliff, and as the mage edged further ahead, the others filed one by one onto the bridge behind him. Together they advanced into the swirling fog, the island behind them gradually fading away. Soon the lines began to ascend. Steadily they climbed, until finally, the shadow of the floating landmass loomed out of the haze, materialising like a titanic apparition.

The bridge anchored straight onto the mountain's underside, and to Rhys's amazement, a set of carved stone steps in an indenture in the rock appeared through the gloom before them. Rhys stepped off the ropes and placed his feet securely on the free-floating rock, which felt as solid as any other ground he had ever set foot upon. Moreover, due to the dense fog, were Rhys none the wiser, he would quite happily have accepted the mountain to be no different to any other he had climbed.

The other's each in turn dismounted the hanging bridge and took turns looking about the recess in the mountainside in which they were stood, the natural stone steps curving away around the eastern face of the horn.

"Seems stable," Ulfgar determined as he stomped about and proceeded to jump up and down on the spot.

"Stop that!" pleaded Nathaniel, only encouraging the dwarf to bound up and down more energetically.

"Come on, Ulfgar, stop messing around," insisted Alkis.

"Fine," grumbled the reluctant dwarf.

"Let's see where this heads," beckoned Rhys as he peered around the curvature of the bluff, trying his hardest not to gaze down from the ledge, the abyss plummeting hundreds of fathoms to nothing but mist and sea below.

Hugging the wall, the mage apprehensively began the ascent, following the natural corridor as the steps climbed around the eastern underside of the mountain. Soon, the craggy mountainside rebated back into a positive batter, and the overhang of rock receded overhead. The stone steps continued to carve out the side of the rugged bluff, and after the best part of an hour's climb, they reached the clifftops where they were granted a view of the grassy slopes blanketing the upper faces of the levitating landmass. The staircase continued up the tufted gradient, consisting now of granite slabs set in the soil at various intervals as the path snaked its way towards the summit above.

Rain continued to drizzle, but the fog lifted as they made their way further up the floating peak. Midday came and passed swiftly by, and the cloud canopy above thinned to a light veil. Sunrays spilled through the diluted murk, striking the twinkling rain showers, casting the brink of the world in an eery golden hue, a realm that since their arrival, had only ever been lit in shades of grey.

"Up there," indicated Sol through the swirling cloud cover.

"There are dozens of them," breathed Rhys, sighting an entire range of mountains hanging suspended across the heavens.

The scattered spine of levitating mountains was still visible only as a series of murky silhouettes, yet with the fog the thinnest it had been since the party had first sailed into the Wyrm's Triangle, Rhys could see farther than ever before. Peaks and ridges hung motionless against the drifting curtains of cloud, some hovering at similar altitudes to the slope they were on, others soaring far aloft. Vast massifs and ridges scudded through the haze, orbited by smaller hillocks and boulders gliding across the sky so imperceptibly slow, Rhys could not tell if their apparent motion was merely an illusion of the seething haze.

"How do we get higher?" asked Cade, surveying the heavens.

"There are bridges everywhere!" replied Sol, he and Rhys alone able to make out the faint network of rope bridges tying the scattered peaks together.

"This is..." began Thia.

"Unworldly," finished Rhys.

"No one back home would believe this," insisted Nathaniel.

"I'm not sure even I do," chuckled Sol nervously.

"There's the next bridge." Rhys gestured down the north face of the slope.

The far end of the lines anchored to a free-floating mound, after which the path split with a further three rope bridges trailing off into the mist.

"Something tells me it isn't merely a simple route to the top," remarked Sol, peering into the now thickening haze as he attempted to discern the way ahead before the gloom drew shut.

"Well, where next then?" asked Alkis as he stared blankly at the forked path laid before them.

"Up, I imagine," responded Rhys.

"Hang on," hesitated Sol, "what's that there?"

The mage indicated downwards into the swirling mist. Above, the clouds were drawing in, blotting out the faint sunbeams, rescinding the golden hue that had for a short time bathed their surroundings, but below, the haze was yielding, granting a rare glimpse of foaming waves. The murk continued to part, and suddenly the peaks of the archipelago were revealed. One islet in particular loomed steadily into view, not far beneath the underside of the horn on which they currently stood. Its sheer-sided cliffs swept around on the eastern shores to create a horseshoe alcove, out of which slanted a great spar. The angled post was unmistakable: it was a ship's mast.

"Its just a wreck," dismissed Ulfgar. "I'm not sure if you noticed on the way here, but there are hundreds littering the sea!"

"I wouldn't be so sure," Rhys disagreed.

"It's not the wreck that drew my attention," insisted Sol. "Look closer."

Immediately Rhys noticed what Sol had first seen. Too faint against the gloom for any of the others to make out, the mage sighted the thin yarn of smoke rising from the beach.

"There's someone down there," Rhys concluded aloud.

"Maybe," Sol played down. "It could merely be a fire from a lightning strike."

"A fire?" scoffed Ulfgar. "Here? Everything is piss-wrapped!"

"It is possible," insisted Sol.

Thunder suddenly drummed above their heads as if to emphasise the mage's point.

"Even still, it warrants investigation," insisted Rhys. "This is the first ship we've seen to make it this far into the Triangle other than the Marlin. It is not beyond the realm of possibility to think that someone else might have made landfall."

"That wreck could be hundreds of years old," argued the dwarf.

"Possibly," conceded Rhys, "or, it could only be a couple months old. In which case, there might be stranded castaways that need help."

"Rhys is right," agreed Sol. "It is worth taking a look."

"It could be several days out of our way," warned Thia. "It has taken nearly two to reach this far."

"We are stranded here for at least a week. What harm is another couple of days?" replied Alkis.

"If we head down a little further, we could gain a better vantage," suggested Rhys. "We might not even need to go down there."

"Very well," agreed Thia.

Rhys led them down the far slope towards the rope bridge, and just as uneasily as he had crossed the first two, he edged out from the brink. Making his way along the swaying lines, he soon planted boots on the hovering mossy hillock. Three more bridges branched away into the haze ahead; one climbed steeply upwards towards the next floating peak a few dozen fathoms above, whilst a second continued out into the mist, vanishing just as it junctioned further at a second levitating chunk of stone. The third path, the longest bridged they'd come upon so far, sank into the closing pall of fog, mooring the network of mountains to the first in a series of sea stacks rising from out of the breaking waves. A string of shorter bridges connected the rank of basalt towers with the clifftops of the island, the way thereafter ahead descending across solid ground towards the horseshoe bay.

"There is a pretty direct route down," concluded Rhys as he surveyed the way.

The party remained distinctly silent, and as Rhys looked round at them, he noticed that Sol's head was craned back as he peered into the murk.

"What is it?"

"Probably my own paranoia," replied the mage, "but for a moment I thought I saw something gliding between the mountains."

Rhys likewise peered skyward. Out of the corner of his vision he momentarily thought he saw a shape scudding through the murk, yet the second he fixed his gaze upon it, it faded into the mist.

"I think I saw it too," affirmed Rhys.

"It wasn't winged, was it?" asked Nathaniel.

Sol silently issued him a grave look.

"That dragon showing up is about the last thing we need," murmured the guardsman.

"We'll be fine," assured Rhys. "Come on. The sooner we get down to that beach, the sooner we can get back on track."

Making their way down the hanging lines, they descended towards the file of sea stacks below, smothering murk quickly enveloping them all the while, as the next swell of the eternal storm drew in.

"The weather never really lets up in this place, does it?" remarked Cade.

"We *are* in *the Stormy Isles*," reminded Nathaniel.

"Even still," replied the archer, "you'd have thought there would be breaks in the weather that lasted more than a few minutes at a time."

Delving further through the murk, Rhys reached the lowest point on the rope bridge and began the short ascent to its end, finally stepping off the lines onto the weathered top of a towering basalt sea stack. Brine foamed and crashed against the base of the stone spire below, the waves spraying high up the face, adding to the mist, tainting the air with a brackish note.

The top of the stack narrowed to a slanting ledge that offered too little room for more than one person at a time to stand on. As such, with the sea raging below, Rhys hastily mounted the next bridge in the chain, making for the clifftops ahead. The crashing swell continued to churn, spouting white geysers skyward each time the waves broke against the stacks. Seawater beaded off Rhys's cloak, the arcanely waterproofed fabric warding the mage against the saline downpour, but as Rhys dismounted the second bridge, a spout of brine gushed from directly below, the upward deluge washing straight under the mage's clothes, drenching him instantly.

Ulfgar and Sol broke into laughter at Rhys's misfortune, the mage slowly revolving to scowl their way. But an instant later, a subsequent saltwater geyser erupted across the bridge, soaking both the mage and the dwarf as severely as Rhys had been, silencing them both.

"I deserved that," conceded the dwarf as he wrung out his sodden beard and followed Sol in dismounting the lines.

One by one, the others darted across the final few yards of rope, each narrowly avoiding the near rhythmic jets of water erupting from a channelled inlet. A series of chuckles babbled throughout the group as they started to cross the next bridge in the chain, but over the tittering, Rhys's ears pricked at the sound of nearby voices.

"Quiet!" the mage suddenly hissed.

All at once, the others fell silent. Halting, Rhys leant closer, listening against the roaring waves and whistling gales. Concealed in the fog ahead, two voices, faint but distinct, murmured in conversation. As Rhys crept incrementally closer, their speech became clearer.

"What is it?" whispered Sol.

"People," breathed Rhys. "Just ahead."

"Are you sure?" mouthed Alkis quietly.

"Yes," nodded the mage, still unable to make out the exact words being said.

"What do you want to do?" questioned Sol.

"Be wary," advised Rhys, tentatively drawing his staff. "We don't know who they are, where they are from, or how long they've been here. There's no telling how they'll react to us—

especially if we catch them by surprise."

"You aren't expecting a fight, are you?" Sol nodded nervously to Rhys's weapon.

"I certainly hope not," assured the mage. "But anyone marooned here is likely desperate. If they suspect for a moment that we have a means of escape…"

"You are right," agreed Sol, his eyes widening to the realisation. "We cannot make any mention of the Marlin."

Rhys shook his head in accord. Pressing on, they crossed the next bridge to the final stack in the chain, close enough now that the others could hear the low chatter of talk.

"What do we do?" whispered Thia. "Should we announce ourselves?"

"Not yet," hesitated Rhys.

"Let's get closer first—see what they are saying," proposed Sol.

"Agreed," nodded Rhys, creeping out onto the final bridge as waves continued to bludgeon the basalt below.

The mage lowered his breathing and focussed his finely tuned hearing to the cliffs ahead. The bluffs were still concealed behind a dense pall of fog, the men atop likewise hidden, but with every step the mage drew closer, he could make out their discussion clearer and clearer.

"Has he always been this mad?" a man with a thick Westport accent asked.

"He's gotten worse over the years," returned a second voice with a Westvernessen accent that was harder to place.

"We're all crazy—this place does that to you... but he's a lunatic!"

"You've not been here half as long as he or I. If you'd survived what we have, you'd understand."

"But you're not anywhere near as mad as him! He's madder even then me!"

"He's gotten worse lately," conceded the second of the two. "He's grown more desperate."

"He thinks these islands are out to get us! He thinks we are in Hel itself!"

"And you think we aren't?"

"No," scoffed the first man. "This place is cursed; of that I am sure. But we are not in the underworld!"

"I would not be so sure, Brother."

"But to be in Helheim... you have to first die."

"Perhaps you did," proposed the second man. "Perhaps we both did. When your ship went down, all those years ago, maybe you drowned."

"No..." hesitated the first man. "If I were dead... I would know it!"

"Think about it, Kristoffer—Hel is in Niflheim: the Abode of Mist!"

"No," refused the first man again, the doubt weighing heavily in his voice. "No, I won't believe it!"

Rhys stepped closer and the edge of the bridge emerged from out of the fog. Up ahead, he could make out two shadows stood around the orange glow of a small fire crackling atop the cliff. Rhys stepped off the lines and hunched beside the anchoring pillars, unsure quite how to announce himself to the two men yet oblivious to their presence.

"I was a good man..." insisted the first of the two castaways. "If I died I'd have not gone to Hel—"

"Quiet!" one of the men hissed suddenly, cutting off his companion.

"What is it?"

"There's something moving in the fog... over there!"

Rhys's heart sank. He had been discovered.

"Quickly... pass me my bow," whispered the second man.

Rhys heard the groan of a bowstring as it was pulled taught.

"Don't shoot!" urged Rhys, standing upright.

"Don't listen, Brother!" insisted the man from Westport. "It is a demon. He is trying to trick you. Quickly, kill it!"

"I'm not a demon," replied Rhys, stepping forwards slowly to prevent startling the two men further.

"I've never heard a demon use the Common tongue," hesitated the second of the men.

"It is a trick!" replied the other. "Kill it! Before it is too late!"

"Don't!" warned Rhys stepping through the murk. "Please."

The mage drew closer, and from out of the mist loomed the two men. They were both scrawny and hirsute, their clothing ragged and weather-beaten, patched hundreds of times and heavily oiled against the elements. Their faces were gaunt, eyes sunken and cheeks hollow, each appearing on the verge of starvation.

"Human...!?" stammered the man holding a half-drawn makeshift bow.

"Yes," confirmed Sol, slightly perplexed by the remark as he two emerged from the mist with the others following close in file.

"Well..." came the voice of Ulfgar, "not all of us."

The two men startled back slightly at the appearance of seven strangers from out of the murk. The bowman raised his weapon and drew the string back further, aiming the arrowhead directly at Rhys.

"They are demons in disguise!" warned the other man, cowering behind the archer. "They are trying to trick us!"

"Who are you!?" demanded the bowman.

"My name is Rhys North," proffered the mage, edging closer, palms raised. "My friends and I were shipwrecked here about a week ago...

back on one of the islands south of here."

The two men eyed them suspiciously.

"You are well supplied for castaways," the archer issued, glancing at their packs and weapons."

"We managed to load a rowboat before our ship went down," bluffed Ulfgar.

A nervous silence lingered for several moments before the man let the bow slacken and unnotched the arrow. "I'm sorry," he issued with a grimace that vaguely resembled a smile. "You cannot be too careful in this place, as I'm sure you know by now."

"Are you sure about this?" interrogated the other castaway suspiciously.

"They are human," replied the bowman. "That is all I care about."

"What do you mean exactly?" questioned Sol.

"You mean… you've not seen them yet?" questioned the archer.

"Who?" asked Rhys.

The other man chuckled somewhat menacingly. "Oh, you'll find out soon enough."

"Forgive Kristoffer," apologised the archer. "He, like everyone here, startles easily."

"I'm sure you have good reason to," replied Alkis warily.

"My name is Bjorn," offered the archer. "It has been years since anyone new washed ashore —alive at least. You say you were shipwrecked about a week ago? What led you to sail to this godforsaken place?"

"We were an exploration vessel," insisted Ulfgar. "I funded this expedition here."

"To find what?" cackled Kristoffer.

"The legendary city of Annwn," explained the dwarf. "We were looking for some evidence of its existence here, but our ship struck a shoal several miles offshore."

"I bet you are regretting coming here now," smirked Bjorn uneasily.

"You are bloody well right I am!" agreed the dwarf.

"How long have you been here?" asked Thia, who until now had remained concealed at the rear of the group.

"You have a woman with you!?" remarked Bjorn suddenly as both his and Kristoffer's eyes widened.

"Yes," returned Rhys defensively.

"She's awful pretty," chuckled Kristoffer.

"That she is," agreed Bjorn.

"Hey!" warned Rhys as he stepped in front of the two castaways to block their view of Thia.

"Forgive us, my darling," apologised Bjorn. "We did not mean to make you feel uncomfortable. It has been... many, many years since either of us has even seen a woman!"

"It's okay," returned Thia coldly as she sidled in amongst the others.

"We've seen a few she-devils," smirked

Kristoffer.

"That we have," agreed Bjorn.

"What does he mean by that?" pressed Cade uneasily.

"There is plenty to tell, friends," replied Bjorn. "But first, Tobias will want to see you."

"Tobias?" questioned Sol.

"So many questions," smiled Kristoffer.

"And very few answers, it would seem," remarked Rhys.

"In time," promised Bjorn. "Come. We will introduce you to Tobias. He will give you the answers you seek."

"Very well," issued Rhys reluctantly. "Take us to Tobias."

Bjorn grinned and stomped out their small fire until nothing but a few embers were left. Then, without issuing another word, he marched out across the hillside with Kristoffer in close pursuit.

"I suppose we had better follow them," mumbled Sol uneasily, "but I don't in the slightest bit trust them."

"Just keep your wits about you," returned Rhys. "They don't pose much of a threat to us."

"Let us hope the situation doesn't change much then," growled Alkis as they all began to follow the two castaways.

"You never answered Thia," began Rhys as he caught up with the two men. "How long have you been here?"

"I've been here longer than almost any," replied Bjorn. "I was on the same ship as Tobias. We've been stranded here for near enough… twenty years?"

"Twenty years!?" repeated Nathaniel in disbelief.

"It certainly feels like its been longer though," returned the haggard man.

"And you, Kristoffer?" asked Sol.

"Nine years… maybe eight, maybe ten."

"It's hard to tell in this place," elaborated Bjorn. "Time doesn't quite work in the same way out here. Nothing does."

"We've noticed," replied Nathaniel under his breath.

"We're not far now," assured Kristoffer as they padded through the brown grass.

"We're camped just in the bay," explained Bjorn.

The two castaways led them over the hilltop, and as the mists momentarily thinned, they were granted a view of the sheltered horseshoe bay. The skeleton of a careened ship reclined on the grey beach, dozens of small figures at work on the hull. A bonfire was alight further up the sand with more men gathered around, whilst off the rocky bluffs, others appeared to be fishing, casting lines into the foaming waters.

"How many of you are there?" questioned Sol. "There looks to be at least a hundred men down there!"

"Give or take," confirmed Bjorn with a nod.

"But mostly take," chuckled Kristoffer.

"Why does he keep saying things like that?" grumbled a perturbed Ulfgar.

"Its this place," explained Bjorn.

"It rots your mind!" put in Kristoffer.

"Come on," beckoned Bjorn. "The storm will be back upon us soon. We had better head down to the beach."

FOURTEEN

Bjorn and Kristoffer marched down the steep hillside, descending into the cove with Rhys and the others cautiously following. Climbing down a run of hexagonal basalt pillars, the party soon found themselves plant boots on the ashen sands of the bay. The winds had picked up again and the rain grew steadily heavier; as Bjorn had promised, the storm was turning tempestuous once more. The two castaways continued from the foot of the hill, out across the beach, towards the careened ship under construction in the heart of the cove.

Dozens of men were fixing strakes to the futtocks of what appeared to be a longship. The portside hull was mostly complete, however, construction on the starboard side was lagging behind, the first run of boards having only been fitted just above the keel. The ship appeared to be built entirely from salvaged materials and the construction was crude at best, the clinker-built hull wonky, the ribs and keel askew. Heaps of scavenged driftwood, salvaged from flotsam washed ashore and plundered from the carcasses of nearby wrecks, were stacked further up the shore.

The castaway shipwrights hammered pegs and rivets into the strakes, most equipped with little more than pebbles. Other men meanwhile sifted through the great stacks of recovered material, sorting the usable timber from the rotten driftwood. Though the ship was erected with appalling craftsmanship, it was impressive nonetheless, given the materials and tools the men had to hand. These were no shipwrights; they were sailors. More than likely, few to none had any knowledge of carpentry or ship building. In spite of this, they were on track to complete something that appeared somewhat seaworthy; whether it was resilient enough to survive the perils of the Wyrm's Triangle was another matter altogether.

"How long has this taken you?" asked Sol as he stared in amazement at the longship.

"This one," replied Bjorn, "has taken about a year so far."

"This one?" repeated Alkis. "There have been others then, I take it?"

"Several," confirmed Kristoffer.

"Then, I am guessing none have been successful?" questioned Ulfgar.

"We have had varying degrees of success," responded Bjorn. "But no. None have ever made it beyond the borders of the Triangle."

"But the Endurance will make it!" asserted Kristoffer. "She's the greatest vessel we've constructed. She'll deliver us home! Tobias has declared such."

"Well, if he declared it, then it must be true," mocked Rhys under his breath.

They were approaching the fringes of the encampment and had now drawn the attention of almost every man in the bay. Some paid them little heed, offering only a fleeting glance of curiosity before continuing on with their tasks. Others were more inquisitive, chattering amongst themselves as they watched the newest batch of castaways approaching. The nearer they drew however, the more stares seemed to focus on them. It quickly became apparent to Rhys that the majority of attention was on Thia. The witch likewise was all too aware of the unwanted focus on her, strategically positioning herself right in the middle of her male companions, hood raised low over her brow to hide her silver locks. Thia bowed her head towards the ground, ignoring the lusting gazes that ogled her.

Rhys suddenly felt himself consumed with anger; he was defensive, on edge. The way the men across the beach had stopped in their tracks to leer lecherously at Thia made his skin crawl. The witch was surrounded by friends, several of whom were among the most skilled fighters in all of Cambria, yet despite this, Rhys was resisting the urge to shield Thia behind him, to draw his weapon and demand the castaways turn away.

Thia raised her gaze momentarily, catching eyes with Rhys to issue him an apprehensive smile. Rhys tried to offer one in return, but his unease perverted any reassurance the expression might otherwise have offered. As Thia's gaze returned to her feet, a sickening knot descended in Rhys's gut. Whereas moments before, the gathering of dishevelled sailors were merely watching from afar, whispering lewdly between themselves, now, the boldest men of the group had begun to advance, moving in, following the party as they made their way across the beach. The quiet whispers grew to sniggering and crude gestures, until soon, encroaching ever closer, the lecherous mob began to whistle and catcall in Thia's direction.

Before the mage had realised what was happening, his staff was in his hand. Steel sliding across leather rang out as Alkis unsheathed his bastard sword. In a matter of seconds, the party had instinctually closed rank around Thia, each of them brandishing their weapon as the witch meekly shrank behind the protection of her friends.

"Hey gorgeous!" a gruff voice called out from the enclosing rabble.

"We won't bite, darling!" sneered another.

"Come say hello, sweet pea."

"All of you, back away now!" warned Alkis fearsomely.

The encroaching ring of castaways continued to advance. Rhys's eyes flitted between their hands; several of the shipwrights were armed with hammers, whilst others began to menacingly unsheathe rusty daggers and shivs from under their belts.

"Why don't you come over here, poppet?" jeered a grimy oaf of a man as he twisted a rusted harpoon head in his grip. "We won't hurt your friends if you do."

"Not another step!" threatened Rhys through gritted teeth, striding forward to face down the man.

"Out of the way, boy!" snarled the villain. "You'll get your turn when I'm done with her!"

A hammer suddenly arced out of the air, thrown by one of the castaways, clanging as it bounced off Nathaniel's shield. A series of hollers and whoops roared from the mob, preceding a fusillade of similarly hurled projectiles. In the momentary disarray, the thug lunged at Rhys with his barbed shiv; but even with only half of his attention on the vagabond, the mage easily stepped clear of the thrust. He pivoted swiftly. The howl of his ethereal blade screamed across the beach, and in the blink of an eye, the mage had struck. In a flash of emerald, four fingers dropped from the villain's hand, each tumbling to the ground along with the rusted harpoon head, thick gouts of blood spurting from the villain's maimed palm.

The castaway screamed and clutched the

bloody stump where his hand had been cloven in half. The incoming barrage of stones and hammers immediately ceased, and suddenly, the men scattered. As the momentary chaos wore away, the group steadily regathered, forming back into a mob, this time hesitantly keeping their distance from Rhys.

"Back away!" roared the mage in fury, wildly brandishing his ethereal blade as he kept the point aimed ahead. "All of you!"

Everything had fallen silent, save for the whimpering of the injured castaway and the pattering of rain. The throng retreated tentatively at Rhys's behest, yet despite their wariness, they did not disperse.

"Get back!" shouted Sol as he too stepped out from their rank, his brow bleeding from where a stone had clouted him, his staff drawn and crackling with electricity.

Sol's advance encouraged the men to fall back a few steps further, but their stares flitted between Rhys and Sol to Thia. What was happening collectively in the castaway's minds was obvious; they were weighing up the risks at taking on the two magi in order to get to the girl. Rhys and his followers were outnumbered ten to one; it was a numerical advantage that was dangerous enough to negate the two magi, regardless of how poorly armed and malnourished the castaways appeared. They were at a standoff. Neither side dared strike the first move, fearing the impending slaughter that would ensue. But the castaways would not retreat, and Rhys and the others were surrounded, thereby lacking that same option.

The crowd in front of Rhys suddenly stirred, and through the mob emerged a burly man sprouting a thick fiery beard from his jaw. A set of ferocious eyes swivelled about the circle as he sighted Rhys and Sol, then Thia, before angrily, he glanced around at the surrounding horde of men. "If one of you lays so much as a finger on that girl, then I will have your guts for garters!" he scorned menacingly, conjuring a fear amongst the men that neither Rhys nor Sol had managed to arouse. "Get out of here!" he roared. "All of you! Get back to work!"

With that, the surrounding hundred or so men scattered, returning to work on the ship, or fleeing up the beach to watch from a distance. Only the thug that had lunged for Rhys and lost his fingers in the process remained, whimpering where he knelt, fumbling as he tried to pick up his severed digits from the bloody sand as he nursed his wound beneath his armpit.

"Get out of here, Gunnar," growled the castaways' leader. "You are lucky you didn't lose your whole arm!"

Gunnar wailed pathetically, abandoning one of his fingers as he clambered up out of the sand and staggered away.

"Thank you for not killing him outright,"

he uttered, toeing the rusted harpoon head protruding from the sand.

"Tobias, I assume?" returned Rhys.

Tobias nodded, croaking in gruff confirmation. "Why *didn't* you kill him?" he then asked.

"Things would have escalated had I done," replied Rhys.

"You are probably right," returned the ginger bearded castaway. "I'd've cut his head clean off. He deserved it." Tobias shrugged. "But spending a decade in this place without so much as seeing a woman… well, I am sure you can imagine what many of these men have gone through."

"I'm not sure Thia will empathise," returned Rhys, looking her way.

She was shaken, but still maintained her characteristic collectedness Rhys knew her for.

"I am sorry, my girl," apologised Tobias. "You reserve judgment—say the word and I shall see that Gunnar is executed."

Thia shook her head. "He was hardly alone—if you were to hold the others to the same account, half the men on this island would be put to death."

"I don't ask you to forgive," returned Tobias, "only to try to understand."

Thia scowled coldly back at him.

"The two of you," he directed to Rhys and Sol. "You are mages?"

"Correct," growled Sol, wiping the blood from the split in his forehead. "So, your men here had better think carefully before they try anything again!"

"They will leave you be," assured Tobias. "They fear me above all else on these islands. The Hounds included."

"The Hounds?" questioned Rhys.

"You have not seen them?" asked Tobias with disbelief. "Consider yourself fortunate then. They are the scourge of these isles."

"We encountered a dragon," replied Rhys. "Surely that's the most dangerous thing around here?"

"The leviathan is fearsome," agreed Tobias. "But it seldom ventures down to the lower islands—only to hunt beneath the waves. It is little danger, so long as you keep out of sight. The Hounds of Annwn are the true plight of those marooned here."

"The Hounds of Annwn?" repeated Rhys. "As in, Cŵn Annwn? The fairy tale?"

"Never heard of them," replied Alkis.

"A cavalcade of spirits that ride across the sky, preying on the souls of the living," explained Rhys.

"You mean the Wild Hunt?" returned Alkis.

"What?"

"They're called the Wild Hunt," explained the knight, "they are led by Woden."

"They're chief huntsman is Arawn… King of Annwn," retorted Rhys. "They are called the

Hounds of Annwn."

"You mean the Ghost Riders?" questioned Nathaniel.

"Ghost riders?" repeated Alkis.

"They are all the same myth," explained Sol. "They just go by different names in different realms. The same tale is told across Cambria, and depending on where you are from, a different figure leads the Hunt."

"They are no myth," insisted Tobias. "The Hounds are real. They prey upon the souls trapped here in purgatory and transport them to the underworld."

"You mean you have actually seen the Wild Hunt?" questioned Sol. "Here?"

"I have seen them many times. I have lost many friends to them over the years. I have even seen Arawn himself with my own eyes."

Lightning flashed.

"That was spooky," remarked Nathaniel.

"This can't be right," replied Rhys. "It can't be the actual Hounds of Annwn you have seen. They are just a folktale to scare children."

"I have seen them," insisted Tobias sternly. "As has every man here. They are real. And soon enough you will see them riding across the sky. When that time comes, you must hope they do not also see you!"

"That sounds rather ominous," uttered Cade.

"So, in Gwent the Wild Hunt is led by

Arawn, the king of Annwn?" questioned Alkis.

"Yes," replied Thia. "But in Gwent, Annwn is not located on the island of Thule. It is believed to be hidden somewhere in the White Mountains."

"It all seems rather muddled," replied Rhys.

"If the *'Wild Hunt'* is here," began Nathaniel, attempting to rationalise everything, "and we are referring to here as *'Thule,'* and Thule is supposedly home to the mythical city of Annwn, I figure it makes sense if we refer to the Hunt as the Hounds of Annwn."

"In Westverness, the Wild Hunt is led by Woden, King of the Titans," explained Alkis. "It is mentioned on the Tablets."

"But you don't believe in the Titans!" replied Rhys in confusion.

"No," conceded Alkis.

"I'm not so familiar with the tale," confessed Cade, "but I have heard the stories of Ghost Riders that ride the open plains of the sky, herding demonic cattle and ushering the spirits of the dead into the afterlife."

"So, in summary, everywhere across Cambria seems to have different versions of the same myth with merely a few of the details changed," concluded Rhys. "It sounds very similar to the major faiths if you ask me. I'm inclined to agree with what Ulfgar said earlier; everything seems plagiarised from everything else." To Rhys's surprise, no one protested his statement.

"What they are called isn't important," insisted Tobias. "Be they the Wild Hunt, Ghost Riders, or Cŵn Annwn, it doesn't matter. What matters is that each month I lose more men to those winged demons!"

"They are taking people?" questioned Rhys. "Alive?"

Tobias nodded. "They do not hesitate to slay us, but they take as many as they can alive."

"Where to?" questioned Sol.

"Into the sky," replied the leader of the castaways. "I cannot be certain where, but I suspect they are delivered to Annwn."

"Have you ever seen the city?" asked Rhys.

"I believe it resides somewhere in the heavens above us. But all who attempt to venture higher up the mountains do not return."

"Why do you think that is?" asked Thia.

"The higher you climb, the more the fogs thin. Whilst the mist is treacherous to sailors, it goes some way to conceal us from the Hounds. Further into the sky, there is little protection to be had."

"I see," mused Rhys.

"We were told you have been here nearly two decades," Sol directed to Tobias.

"How have you survived so long?" asked Alkis.

"By doing things most men could never conceive of," he uttered darkly. "I've had a few close calls over the years. Some with the Hounds, many with my own kin, but most with the sea."

"Kristoffer and Bjorn said that you've built several ships over the years?"

"It is the only way out of the Triangle," replied Tobias.

"The others have sunk though," return Rhys.

"The Endurance will not," replied Tobias definitively. "I am told your own ship went down a week ago."

"Yes," lied Rhys.

"A few miles off the shore of one of the southern isles?"

"We struck a shoal," put in Ulfgar.

"So Bjorn said," replied Tobias. "Tell me, is there anything left of your vessel? Any materials or supplies that might be salvaged?"

"Afraid not," fibbed Ulfgar. "It's at the bottom of the sea now. All we got off before she went down is the stuff we're carrying. Even our row boat was dashed against the rocks."

"That is unfortunate. We are in need of good timber for the Endurance," explained Tobias. "You were fortunate to escape with your lives. Of all who are shipwrecked in the Triangle, only a small few ever make it safely to the shores. Why is it you set sail for this place?"

"We came to investigate the legend of Annwn," responded Ulfgar. "I funded an expedition to land on these shores and investigate the legend of the city."

"And what did you hope to find?"

"You know, the usual," responded Ulfgar. "Gold, riches... the secret to immortality. Anything that can be sold back in Orthios."

"You are treasure hunters then?" questioned Tobias suspiciously.

"I prefer the term *'Fortune Seeker,'* but in essence, yes."

"And those who have journeyed with you?"

"We are here to investigate the myths surrounding the islands," explained Sol. "Ulfgar offered us passage in exchange for the protection that our order could offer his expedition."

"Everyone else is either muscle or hired help," added the dwarf.

"And what of her?" asked Tobias as he eyed Thia.

"I am his mythologist," explained Thia. "Without me there would have been no expedition."

"I imagine it is safe to say there is no expedition anyway now, given your current circumstances," replied Tobias.

"I wouldn't say that," replied Ulfgar. "I paid good money to get here."

"And since there is no way of leaving anytime soon, we might as well continue with the expedition," added Rhys.

"You want to head up the mountains?"

questioned Tobias sceptically. "After what I have just told you of the Hounds?"

"You forget that we have two magi with us," returned Alkis.

"Against the Hounds of Annwn... I fear it will make little difference."

"I fear you underestimate them," replied Cade.

"None of you seem particularly distressed at being marooned here," asserted Tobias.

"Well, if you are building that ship, I'd say we have a way off the island," replied Ulfgar.

"But I have not offered you passage," uttered Tobias sharply. "You are presumptuous to believe that I shall grant you salvation so easily."

"You'd refuse us passage home on your ship?" asked Nathaniel warily.

"I offer passage to those who prove themselves loyal and worthy," responded Tobias. "Only those who demonstrate their value can earn a place on the Endurance."

"And what does one have to do to prove their value to you?" questioned Rhys with his own scepticism.

"There are many ways," returned the leader of the castaways. "Those who are instrumental in the ship's construction are granted a place aboard, be they shipwright or scavenger."

"You want help constructing the Endurance?" surmised Rhys.

"I have plenty of hands," he explained.

"Unless yours have experience in either ship-building or carpentry, I have little use for them."

"Then what is it you want?" asked Alkis.

"There are many roles in our society," smirked Tobias.

"Society?" questioned Rhys suspiciously. "I trust you were elected leader then?"

"I earnt my place at the top here, the only way these men have come to understand."

"Violence then?" returned Rhys sardonically.

"I have only done what is necessary," uttered Tobias coldly.

"Somehow, I doubt that."

Tobias chuckled darkly. "You'd be amazed what can be achieved when you let go of the confines imposed by one's sense of morality. You have been here but a few fleeting moments. I have lived out half my life in this purgatory. In time, you will come to understand the terrors of these islands; they will transform you in the same way every other man has been changed before you. You will either mould and adapt, or you shall falter and die."

"Is that a threat?" questioned Sol, stepping forward.

"No," returned Tobias. "It is merely as statement of fact."

"I'm beginning to understand why these men follow you so obediently," replied Rhys. "It is not loyalty; it is fear."

"It's respect," returned the leader of the castaways. "Most of the men here had done far worse than I to survive. Take this advice: let go of your notions of ethics; they are relics created in the world you've left behind. They serve no purpose in this place."

"That doesn't sound evil at all," mocked Rhys.

Thunder tolled, and rain began to lash down in heavy squalls.

"There is room for each of you aboard the Endurance," assured Tobias. "But you must each prove your value." His eyes focussed on Thia suddenly and his gaze was filled with the same lecherous intent Rhys had seen in all the men that had cornered them several minutes ago. "For those who willingly accept the roles chosen for them in this place, there are benefits to be had... even here."

"No thanks," snapped Rhys as he moved to obstruct the man's view of Thia.

"Oh, I see," he sniggered. "You want her all for yourself."

Rhys scowled.

"Privileges are earnt here, boy," Tobias chided.

The mage felt his fingers constrict around the shaft of his staff.

"You think you can keep her from the rest of us here, but sooner or later they'll get the jump on you."

"I think we'd better leave, Rhys," urged Sol, planting a hand on Rhys's shoulder as the mage squared firmly up to Tobias.

"You lay a hand on her, or anyone else under my protection, and I will kill you," growled Rhys through gritted teeth.

"Come on, Rhys," implored Sol, pulling his friend away.

"You'll be back," insisted Tobias mockingly. "Soon you'll be starving. Soon the Hounds will be on your scent. Then you'll be begging for a way off this place. You'll sell that bitch to me for nothing more than a scrap of meat."

Lightning flashed as the sky continued to blacken.

FIFTEEN

"Are they still following us?" asked Thia, not daring to glance back over her shoulder.

"Yes," replied Rhys bluntly as they made their way across the beach, back towards the cliffs.

"How many are there?"

"There's a dozen of them," returned Sol.

"Weapons?" questioned Alkis.

"Four bows, two axes, and six harpoons," replied Rhys. "There are probably a few slings between them too, if I had to hazard a guess."

"What do you reckon they'll do?" asked Cade. "Wait to ambush us?"

"No," replied Sol. "If they were going to do that, they'd have waited till after dark."

"We need to get up the mountain—as high as possible, and quick," urged Rhys.

"Agreed," Sol concurred. "But they're going to attack before we even make it off the beach."

"What makes you so sure?" asked Nathaniel.

"Their weapons are drawn. They are gaining on us. And this is the safest place for a skirmish. If the fight doesn't go their way, they are close enough to successfully retreat, and they have near a hundred reinforcements close at hand."

"Point taken," nodded Nathaniel.

"It'll happen soon," determined Alkis.

"I reckon we've got less than a minute."

"My bow is still strung," assured Cade.

"And my crossbow is loaded," added Ulfgar.

"It'll be quick and messy," warned Sol.

"Sol and I will try and take out the archers before they can get a shot off. Cade and Ulfgar, you take out the first two who charge. Alkis, Nathaniel, get in front of Thia and don't let any of them near her. Thia, you watch for reinforcements, and make sure you are minding our backs; there's a good chance there is a second group of them who've slipped past us in the fog to try and head us off."

"Do you want to strike first, or should we wait for them to make the first move?" asked Alkis.

"We'll have to be first," explained the mage. "But we'll hold off until we are sure they are about to attack."

"They're speeding up," warned Thia.

"They're closing to within striking distance," explained Sol.

"Be ready," mumbled Rhys on bated

breath.

The mage halted. He swivelled on the spot. The others fell swiftly into rank behind him. Ahead, the band of castaways stopped dead in their tracks, realising they were now locked in a standoff, their chance of ambuscade passed. The storm glared and tolled across the black clouds as the two groups faced off in an impasse. Then, without hesitation, the four bowmen nocked arrows and drew back their bowstrings. Lightning crackled and thunder drummed once again, this time surging from the beach, not the sky, as the two magi's staves thrummed with energy, firing electricity and force across the sands with tremendous power.

The lightning bolt from Sol's stave connected with a pair of archers on the fringe of the sortie, arcs of white plasma sparking through their bodies, sending their half-drawn arrows blurring off across the beach as their muscles spasmed and contorted involuntarily in their death throes. Rhys's missile of kinetic energy surged across the ground, ploughing a great furrow through the sand as it careened violently into a third bowman on the opposite flank, launching the castaway down the beach as his body crumpled in the collision.

At that instant, chaos ensued. Like crazed berserkers, the assailants howled, continuing to roar at the top of their lungs as they charged, harpoons and axes brandished overhead as they stormed the final distance towards Rhys and the others. An arrow and quarrel took flight, streaking from behind Rhys to take down the final bowman and a harpooner at the head of the charge. In seconds, the gap had closed.

Rhys's ethereal blade chimed, unfurling from his staff in a whirl of emerald. The two ranks collided. Steel clashed against steel. Screams cut through the fog. A barbed harpoon head lanced for Rhys. A parry knocked the strike aside and the mage twirled his stave in a rapid moulinet, riposting past the harpooner's defences. The glowing emerald point of Rhys's weapon tore clean through his assailant's throat, carving out the rear of the castaway's neck, nearly decapitating the villain in a single blow. The beard of an axe clove through the murk. Rhys ducked, dropping and rolling. The butt of his stave swung wide, sweeping through the legs of the axeman, knocking him off his feet. In the blink of an eye, he was on top of the downed savage, sinking his blade into the helpless man's chest in a brutal coupe de grâce.

Renting his staff free, Rhys spun the weapon in a flourish, scanning the thick haze for a new target.

"Rhys!" Thia cried. "Behind us!"

A din of raging hollers swelled from the rear, a second ambushing party charging to join the fray, just as Rhys had suspected would happen. Skirting quickly around the fringes of the skirmish, Rhys dashed to Thia's defence, intercepting the head of the second charge, cutting down the raging berserker as he lunged through his flank.

A spearhead drove at Rhys, binding underneath the mage's fluke as their weapons locked and wound together in a contest of strength. The snarling spearman slammed his shoulder into Rhys, knocking the mage back in a stumble across the sand, their weapons disentangling. Rhys regained his footing, watching as the berserker reversed the grip of his weapon; raising the spear above his shoulder like a javelin, the castaway readied to hurl it the mage's way. As the spearman's shoulder drew back, a surge of lightning cascaded from out of the mist, flooring the berserker in the blink of an eye as Sol rushed to Rhys's aid.

Less than a second later, Rhys repaid the favour, the screaming silhouette of a raging axeman storming out of the mist to flank Sol. A fist of silver energy hurtled from Rhys's stave, churning through the fog and pummelling into the berserker, flattening the villain before he could bring his axe down at Sol. The mage's head flicked back to see the axeman struck down, swiftly returning Rhys a nod of gratitude, before together, both magi formed a defensive line against the incoming drive.

More villains materialised from out of the haze, weapons brandished overhead in their mad berserking assault. The veins of Rhys's staff flashed crimson and a tongue of flame licked across the sodden beach, vaporising the brine trapped in the sand in a puff of steam, and searing clean through an assailant's midriff. A sickening yelp snuffed out as the bisected torso and legs of the castaway slumped to the ground, but as the berserker was singed in half, the rest of the wave of assailants pressed up to push the advance, clashing suddenly into Rhys and Sol.

Driving the nearest adversary backwards, Rhys snared the hook of his blade around the man's ankle. Stooping under a wayward axe blow, Rhys yanked his staff, severing a foot from its adjoining shin. Changing direction in an explosive burst, Rhys switched targets, impaling the tip of his weapon into the axeman hounding his flank, returning then to finish off the footless barbarian howling from a patch of blood-soaked sand.

The beachside mêlée was a scene of anarchy, harrowing screams cutting through the swirling storm, weapons clashing in brutal exchanges partially concealed through densening murk. Rhys swivelled as another foe rushed his way, but as the challenger sprinted towards him, a shadow of wings plunged out of the mist to his rear. In a blur of darkness, Rhys watched a set of enormous black talons latch around the man's skull, snatching him from the beach. In the blink of an eye, the berserker had vanished, lifted into the sky, disappearing in the haze.

Rhys spun, sighting the next encroaching assailant, only to watch in horror as a second set of dark pinions swooped out of the fog, ensnaring the helpless castaway, taking back to the wind, carrying away its screaming prey into the storm above. Suddenly, wherever Rhys turned, great shadows were diving out of the sky, plucking unsuspecting castaways from the sand. Rhys tried to lock eyes on one of the winged beasts swooping out of the storm; he made out hooked beaks, splayed feathers, furred haunches, padded hind paws. The fiends moved so quickly that, despite his arcanely acute vision, Rhys struggled to catch a full glimpse of the blurring monstrosities through the mist. The bestial hybrids were raptorial, striking from the heavens with the precision of a hawk, yet bounding across the beach and taking back to the air, they pounced with leonine grace and prowess.

A terrified scream erupted from behind Rhys. The mage spun, watching as a castaway dove to the sand, narrowly avoiding a set of razor talons clamping shut overhead. The hulking hybrid touched down, rearing up on its hind paws, slashing at the air with its taloned forelimbs as the hapless castaway cowered and whimpered at its feet. Suddenly, a figure dismounted from the beast, dropping out of a saddle strapped to the fiend's back. Moving with unworldly speed, the rider pounced on the ill-fated castaway, lashing coils of rope around the man's hands and feet whilst he struggled. Rhys shook himself out of his stunned daze, readying to intervene, but with its victim restrained in mere seconds, the shadowy rider leapt swiftly back into the saddle and spurred its hybrid mount. A spread of black feathers unfurled, and the monstrous creature pounced back into the air; the line tethered to the fiend's saddle snapped taught, and with a harrowing yelp, the rope-bound castaway was hoisted skyward, in tow behind the ghost rider, vanishing in the glare of a lightning bolt.

"The Hunt!" a despairing castaway cried.

"Back to the caves!" screamed another, fleeing into the mist in panicky retreat before he too was set upon from above.

"The Hounds of Annwn," Rhys breathed in disbelief, watching the demonic riders diving from out of the storm to steal away the souls of the living.

The mage turned full circle as he steadily took in the turmoil unfolding all around. Rhys's companions were still stood back to back, locked in a skirmish with an assaulting force of castaways; the aerial ambush had struck so rapidly that half of the men on the ground were still oblivious to the Wild Hunt raiding party.

"Alkis!" Rhys alerted as shadowy wings descended suddenly on the knight.

A set of hooked claws closed around Alkis's shoulders. The force of the impact flung the knight's sword from his grip as he was plucked from the sand into the air. Reacting through pure instinct, Rhys felt his body uncoil like a spring. A blast of silver force erupted from his staff, hurtling airward, pummelling into the winged monster that had snatched up his friend. The hybrid monstrosity folded under impact, its wings crumpling, Alkis slipping from its clasp. The knight thumped into the ground, tumbling head over heels before painfully heaving himself up out of the sand. Above, the monster and its rider plunged out of the air, spinning through the murk in a writhing sprawl of feathers and claws, vanishing out of sight somewhere into the gloom.

Alkis faltered, clutching his side and dropping back to one knee in a winded daze.

"Get up!" implored Rhys as he snatched the man's bastard sword out of the sand, shoving it into his friend's grip. "We need to get out of here!"

"Thia!" Sol cried as another set of wings swooped down from out of the clouds. The mage fired a fork of lightning at the descending ghost rider, narrowly missing the hound of Annwn as it banked sharply, abandoning its dive for the witch.

"Rhys, look out!" warned Alkis as the mage helped him to his feet.

Rhys released Alkis, shoving his friend back to the ground. He spun. A spread of black pinions hurtled out of the murk. The mage slashed upwards with his staff. A mass of feathers smashed into him. Battered off his feet, Rhys felt two sets of razors slice through his shirt, tearing across his skin beneath. The world seemed to somersault around Rhys, and for an instant, he was weightless. Suddenly, the ground rushed up to meet him. The mage expected the sand to cushion his fall; instead, it felt no softer than if he had landed on solid rock. A jarring twinge fired down his spine as his shoulders collided with the beach. He rolled on impact, cartwheeling awkwardly until he finally came to rest, face down at the end of a furrow his body had tilled through the beach. The mage wheezed as he heaved himself up out of the sand. His head was spinning, his bones ached, his chest was on fire, but he was still alive, unlike the monstrous hybrid that had descended on him. Barely a dozen yards away, the dark feathered carcass lay broken, centred in a crater of sand. Rhys's strike had not spared him from the collision, but it had slain the beast nonetheless.

Coughing through a tightening chest, Rhys supported his weight on his staff and began to stagger closer, when to the mage's horror, a black figure sprung up from behind the monstrous creature. The rider had survived the crash landing. In a blur of speed, the ghostly cavalryman vaulted his dead mount, unsheathing an inwardly curved blade from a scabbard on its belt. Shrouded in black robes, clad in a hauberk of mirror armour, its head and face concealed beneath a tagelmust, the hound of Annwn cocked its head in challenge. The rider was both shorter and slighter than the mage, but moving with supernatural grace and speed, the ghost's shadowy demeanour was terrifying to behold.

A flick of the wrist sent the rider's blade dancing in a series of spiralling flourishes around its body, the hound brandishing its weapon with menacing dexterity. Then, with little warning, it charged across the beach, its feet leaving no impression in the sand as it glided spectrally Rhys's way. Suddenly, defying the laws of the natural world, the rider's material form disintegrated. Evaporating in an instant, the hound transformed into a blur of shadow, streaking through the air is it closed in on Rhys in the blink of an eye, before, just as quickly as the rider had dissolved, it rematerialized, lunging for Rhys with its blade outstretched.

Lightning reflexes from the mage spared him from death, a near impossible parry deflecting the strike at the very last second. Using his greater strength to his advantage, Rhys manage to turn the ghost's blade aside and drive the rider backward, but with in an instant, the fiend was on him again. They clashed blades a second time, the spectral cavalryman pirouetting away before Rhys could deliver any form of counterattack. Darting back for the mage, the ghost rider thrust past the mage's defences, clipping Rhys's hip with the curved edge of its knife.

Rhys winced, batting the weapon clear with the shaft of his stave before it could slice deeper. With all the strength he could muster, the mage drove his knee up into the rider's chest. Rhys's leg connected, but instead of being sent stumbling backwards, the spectral rider backflipped away in a mesmerising feat of acrobatics, planting its feet gracefully back on the sand before dashing for Rhys in another attack.

Rhys backpedalled, deflecting blow after blow, his parries wild and unruly as the hound wore away his defences. A mistimed block cost him, the tip of the rider's inwardly curled knife arcing over his horizontal staff to bite into his shoulder. The mage cried out, stumbling back as a redoublement grazed his thigh. A third successive strike sank the tip of the ghost's blade an inch into Rhys's bicep as he desperately retreated.

Swinging his staff in a series of wide arcs, the mage used the length of his weapon to his advantage, managing to momentarily repel the fiend's otherwise unrelenting assault. Using the brief respite to regather himself, Rhys readied for the ghost's next advance. Its blade whirled blurringly in another flourish, snaking tightly around its body as the spectral cavalryman prepared to deal the finishing blow, but in toying with Rhys, the rider had delayed too long and gave the mage the opening he needed for one last death-defying defence.

The ghost darted towards Rhys just as the mage struck the ground with his stave. A detonation of kinetic energy ripped outwards. A wave of sand erupted into the air, the explosion of energy surging out in every direction. Staggered by the blast, the rider stumbled away, toppling backwards into the sand. Rhys appended his attack with a successive salvo of kinetic missiles, but to his dismay, the rider flipped back to its feet as quickly as it had been grounded. Weaving left and right, the ghost darted aside as each fist of energy drilled into the beach, successfully dodging every attack Rhys sent its way. Then, with the fusillade at an end, it charged for Rhys.

Bounding across the sand, the ghost rider leapt high into the air, descending in another blurring arc of shadow as it vaporised once more at the zenith of its jump. It reformed with its blade outstretched, descending in a lunge for Rhys's neck. Unable to react fast enough, Rhys could only close his eyes.

Lightning flashed, and everything fell momentarily silent. Rhys's eyes crept slowly open. The ghost was dead; the body lay smouldering at his feet, slain by a thunderbolt from Sol.

"What is that thing!?" Sol's voice quavered.

"I don't know," swallowed Rhys. "But now is not the time to find out."

Together, they glanced about their surroundings. The beach was still in a state of turmoil. All the castaways had now turned to flee, but one by one they were being picked off by the winged creatures and their riders.

"Quickly!" urged Alkis. "Get to the base of the cliffs. We are vulnerable out in the open!"

"You heard the man!" shouted Sol, taking flight across the beach towards the bluffs.

Rhys took off after them, realising that the others were already some way ahead. The sand deformed beneath his boots as he powered on in spite of his injuries. Heavy rain began to lash down, drenching Rhys, splattering across his brow, streaming into his eyes, and blurring his vision.

The black clouds swirled overhead. Thunder drummed in a deafening crescendo. The cliffs enclosing the cove flashed suddenly into view. On he sped, the distant screams of castaways cutting through the storm.

Through the glare of lightning, Rhys spied another span of wings bearing down on him. Still on the run, he thrust his staff above his head. The emerald veins inside the weapon burned crimson and a gout of flames fanned out above Rhys. The hound of Annwn pulled out of its dive, swooping back into the sky to avoid immolation. Rhys continued to run, his wounds begging him to slow up, but he ignored the pain, spurred on by more dark shapes scudding across the electrically illuminated skies.

The Wild Hunt circled overhead, riders plunging down from the spectral cavalcade to harry Rhys and the others. Bolts of electricity crackled from Sol's stave up ahead, and a second geyser of fire from Rhys fended the harrying riders away. Together, the two magi kept the hounds at bay as they charged the final stretch towards the foot of the bluffs.

"Hurry, Rhys!" Sol urged, stood beneath the entrance to a cave sunken into the cliff face.

Rhys fought on, the cuts across his body burning in fiery pain.

"Get down!" Sol warned.

He dove to the ground as a set of sharp talons clamped shut above him. The creature swooped narrowly overhead. A fork of energy sparked from Sol's staff, connecting with the incoming ghost rider, zapping through the hybrid mount, slaying the beast mid-dive. The dead fiend's wings crumpled, sending the creature veering off into the cliffside. The rider was killed on impact, its body smacking against the face of the bluff as it unsuccessfully attempted to bail from the saddle.

"Come on!" urged Sol frantically as Rhys fought his way back to his feet and staggered the final few yards.

"Thanks!" Rhys wheezed, realising Sol had just saved his life for the second time in as many minutes.

"Don't mention it," returned the mage. "Now, quick, get inside!" Sol ushered Rhys into the cave.

The sound of thunder faded and echoed behind them. The storm raged on and the sky continued to dim as the last screams died on the wind. Darkness prevailed, and night gripped the world. And all fell ghostly still.

SIXTEEN

The fire crackled gently inside the cave, casting an orange glow over the black stone walls. Outside, the winds howled as white horses stampeded up the sands, illuminated by flashes of electricity across the skies.

"What were those things?" questioned Rhys as he removed his shirt and began tending his wounds with his wand.

"The beasts were gryphons," explained Sol. "A hybrid: head and wings of an eagle with the body of a lion."

"I think I've heard of them before," he nodded, beginning to close a gnarly gash across his chest dealt by one of the creatures' claws.

"They're supposed to have been extinct for nearly two thousand years," returned his fellow mage.

"Something tells me these islands have been isolated for a very long time," remarked Thia as she tended to Alkis's injuries.

"And what about the riders?" asked Rhys as he studied the cuts across his hip, thigh, shoulder, and bicep dealt by a hound's curved blade.

"I haven't the faintest idea..." returned Sol. "That is, other than—"

"The Wild Hunt?" finished Alkis.

"Yes," conceded Sol.

"The one I fought moved unlike anything I have ever seen," uttered Rhys. "It was so fast... and it faded like a ghost as it moved!"

"Maybe, because that's what it was?" supposed Nathaniel.

"You think I fought a ghost?" asked Rhys.

"A spirit of some kind," confirmed the guardsman. "The Cŵn Annwn: spectral riders. That is what they are described as."

"You think maybe they are undead? Creatures similar to wraiths?" Rhys directed to his fellow mage.

"It is possible," pondered Sol. "Undeath has never been well understood, even by history's most powerful necromancers. If the riders are spirits of the dead... well, I'm not the person to ask."

"I don't know," returned Rhys. "He seemed pretty alive during the fight... spirited, you might say—spritely even."

"There's an easy enough way to find out," proposed Sol.

"You mean...?"

"One we killed should be right outside the cave entrance."

"Okay," agreed Rhys rising to his feet, "let's bring it in and take a look."

"You sit back down!" ordered Thia. "And leave those wounds alone, you are making a right mess of them."

Rhys gazed down at the scabbed gash he had magically knitted closed across his chest. "I thought I was doing a decent enough job," he defended.

"Do you want them to scar or not?" asked the witch.

"I imagine they'll scar regardless," replied Rhys. "But I suppose I'd prefer you to tend to them."

"Then sit down and wait your turn," she insisted with a smile. "I'm nearly done with Alkis."

"You probably should have started with Rhys," remarked the knight. "My wounds aren't half as bad."

"Rhys's will take longer though," replied Thia. "Besides, he gets himself in this state so often, I doubt he even feels half the injuries he picks up nowadays, anyway."

"That's not strictly true," retorted Rhys.

"We'll fetch the body," offered Nathaniel.

"Wait... what!?" responded Cade, realising he had just been volunteered by the guardsman.

"Be careful," warned Rhys. "Remember that the Cŵn Annwn aren't the only threat here."

"I think the castaways are far more terrified of the Hunt than us," suggested Sol. "I shan't expect they'll emerge from the caves any time soon."

"Even still," replied Rhys, "keep a look out."

"We'll be fine," assured Nathaniel. "It is just outside the cave."

Nathaniel and Cade exited the cavern and Thia made her way over to Rhys.

"In my defence," began the mage as the witch routinely started healing the lacerations across his torso, "it's been about a month since you last had to patch me up like this."

"A month is hardly a long time," replied Thia with a smile.

"I know, but this time it is hardly my fault. You saw how fast those riders moved."

"I never said they weren't formidable," responded Thia. "I merely find it interesting that out of the two people injured in the party, one of them is yet again you."

"Well," returned Rhys, "I must be an obvious target. A glowing green staff tends to stand out on the battlefield."

Thia raised her eyebrows at him before turning her attention to the gash on Rhys's hip. Presently, Nathaniel strode back into the cave with a darkly clad corpse strewn over his shoulder.

"I thought Cade was supposed to be helping you with that?" commented Alkis.

"Don't look at me!" protested the huntsman. "He just went and picked it up all by himself."

"This guy weighs less than a child," explained Nathaniel, tossing the body onto the floor of the cave beside the fire.

"He doesn't look it," puzzled Sol.

"I know," returned the guardsman. "It's remarkable—like he has hollow bones or something."

"Well… let's take a look then," Sol proposed tentatively as he stooped over the body.

"Go on then," encouraged Alkis, equally wary.

"I've just… never examined a rider from the Wild Hunt before."

The mage knelt beside the body and carefully unwound the black shroud of the rider's tagelmust. As the layers of cloth were steadily removed, everyone within the cave slowly leant closer in anticipation, until only a single sheet of fabric obscured the rider's head.

"Here goes nothing," breathed Sol, tearing back the veil.

Everyone recoiled, expecting to see a ghostly skull strung with rotting flesh, yet as the light of the flames flickered over the creature's smooth bronze skin, they all leant closer, realising that the rider was not at all as they had expected.

"Oh…" remarked Sol as he observed the being's fine and attractive features.

"What is he?" questioned Nathaniel. "He

doesn't look human!"

"If I didn't know better," responded Sol, "I'd say this fellow was an elf. Look at the ears."

Sure enough, as Sol directed their attention, Rhys noticed the man's ears were not human at all; they were elongated and pointed.

Alkis next leant over the body and spread the creature's lips with his fingers. "He doesn't have the fangs of a demon," remarked the knight, revealing a normal set of white teeth.

Sol carefully drew back one of the being's eyelids, revealing a large dark iris that filled the orb of the eye almost to the very edges. "This creature is definitely not undead," insisted the mage.

"This was beside the body," put in Cade, presenting the creature's sword.

The blade was little more than a foot in length; it was single-edged, with an angled spine and an inwardly curving cutting edge. It thickened as it curved away from the haft and appeared to be weighted more like a hatchet than a blade, with the centre of gravity leaning towards the point. The damasked steel that formed the blade was ornately embossed to form a paisley-like motif. The haft was polished white wood with a grain so fine Rhys realised it could only be elder oak; it flared toward the butt with a gold metal band encircling the handle to form a grip. The knife possessed no guard of any kind, but more interestingly, the blade was notched at its narrowest point, just before where the tang inserted into the haft.

"I've never seen a weapon quite like it," remarked Alkis. "It's exquisitely made."

"That's definitely an elf," asserted Ulfgar.

"What?" replied Sol. "How do you know?"

"Because," explained the dwarf, "that there is an Elven kukri."

"A kukri?" questioned Sol. "Are you sure?"

"Every lord in Orthios has one in his house. Thing is, just about all of them are forgeries," explained Ulfgar. "I should know, I sold a few of them to nobles in my time. But one or two lords, Cromwell being among them, had the real artefact. Few men could ever spot a real kukri from the thousands of fakes being sold on the black market, but Cromwell was one, and I'm another. That there is a kukri, but it is no relic! And if that thing was carrying it, it can only mean one thing!"

"He's an Elven relic enthusiast?" jested Rhys.

"You are right, Ulfgar," uttered Sol, ignoring Rhys. "Everything seems to suggest that this creature is indeed an elf."

"I've never even heard of elves," stated Cade.

"Well," began Sol, "most consider them to be part of the Titan mythology. Those who don't worship the pantheon merely disregard them as a legend from Westverness. Only, the elves were once a people in Cambria. Supposedly, like dwarvenkind, they once were spread across the continent."

"Only, they did a much better job at dying out than dwarves did!" added Ulfgar.

"There's such little evidence they even existed," explained Sol. "They disappeared so long ago... we're talking over a thousand years before the dawn of the Cambrian Empire. They were even around millennia before dwarven society took shape!"

"You humans had barely figured out agriculture when these guys were at the height of their civilisation," chided Ulfgar. "You were still living in caves!"

"We seemed to have done alright for ourselves in the long run," responded Rhys.

"If I recall correctly, wasn't dwarven society built upon caves?" retorted Sol.

"Mines! Not caves!" growled Ulfgar.

"Same thing really," smiled Rhys. "They're both just glorified holes in the ground. You must feel right at home in here, Ulfgar."

Ulfgar scowled at Rhys but chose not to rise to the taunts.

"So, if elves died out thousands of years ago," continued Thia, returning the conversation to the matter at hand, "what is one of them doing in this cave with us?"

"Maybe he *is* undead," suggested Cade. "He was a Ghost Rider after all."

"No," dismissed Sol. "This elf was alive. Of that I am sure."

"Dragons, gryphons, and now elves," uttered Rhys. "These islands are lost to time. They are from another age altogether."

Sol nodded. "It is as if millennia have passed in the outside world and the Wyrm's Triangle has been completely untouched by the passage of time."

"Why are they taking the castaways?" questioned Thia.

"Who's to say," shrugged Sol.

"They are taking them somewhere up in the mountains," asserted Rhys. "At least that's what Tobias claimed."

"I suppose the way to find out would be to go looking then," proposed Sol.

"A good job we are already heading that way," smiled Rhys.

"First things first," interjected Alkis, "we need to get off this island and as far away from this beach as possible. It'll only be a matter of time before Tobias sends more of his men after us."

"You are right," agreed Rhys. "But I don't think it is safe to head out at night."

"We need to leave at first light," insisted Sol. "Before dawn—as early as possible."

"With a little luck, Tobias might assume we were taken by the Cŵn Annwn," added Thia.

"Let's hope you are right," replied Rhys.

They took turns guarding the cave entrance throughout the night, with two people on watch at any one time whilst the others rested. To their relief, all remained quiet as the storm raged outside; there was no sign of either the castaways or the Hounds of Annwn. When morning approached, the weather calmed, the downpour dwindling to a gentle spitting rain and the winds subsiding to occasional gusts. The fogs dissipated into wispy tendrils of mist that hung above the cove. An hour before sunrise, the first dim grey light of dawn appeared on the horizon.

Extinguishing the last embers of their fire, the party tentatively crept out beyond the mouth of the cave and surveyed the beach cast in half-light. A few corpses were scattered across the expanse of sand, most being those of slain castaways, either fallen during the affray with Rhys and his companions or killed during the raid from the sky. Amongst the dead however, were a couple of riders and their respective mounts. Glancing up and down the cove, Rhys made certain there was no sign of any castaways before moving closer to inspect the slain gryphon at the foot of the cliff.

Though Rhys had seen the creatures the previous evening, now, in the early light, he was granted his best up-close look of the monstrous hybrid. The creature was enormous, surpassing even the largest of stallions in height, its head almost exactly resembling a buzzard or eagle's; from its shoulders spanned an enormous set of black feathered wings, that if unfolded, Rhys imagined would stretch more than twenty feet across. Its forelimbs were giant raptor talons, whilst from the chest rearward, the creature's feathers transformed into a furry hide. The entire rear of the animal was that of an enormous cat, and though dead, Rhys could see the bulging muscles of its haunches, perfectly suited to launching such an immense creature into the air where it could take flight.

"Incredible," breathed Thia as she knelt beside the slain beast.

"I'm sure it would have appeared quite majestic, had it not been trying to kill us," quipped Rhys.

"Blame the rider, not the mount," replied the witch.

"Come on you two," urged Sol.

"He's right," murmured Rhys, scanning the bay once again. "It won't be long before the castaways emerge."

Along the base of the cliffs were dozens of openings that receded into the rock, forming a system of caves where Rhys suspected the castaways had taken refuge following the attack. None had yet emerged this morning, but with the Endurance careened in the bay, it was only a matter of time before Tobias and his followers would appear.

The party hastened towards the hillside that led up the cliffs. Retracing their steps from the previous day, they ventured back out onto the rope bridges, across the sea stacks, arriving soon after atop the small floating hillock from where three other routes forked. Electing to take the steep-rising bridge that climbed to the adjacent mountain, they once more began their ascent into the clouds.

The gales whipped the lines of the bridge back and forth. Steadily, the party climbed towards the rocky face of the mountain above. The ropes were anchored straight into the stone. A short flight of near vertical steps led them up over a ledge. The massive floating landmass from there ascended as a sweeping slope that rose to a pinnacle lost in the cloud cover. Reaching the summit, they found another bridge that ascended higher through the swirling mist. Thereafter, the next mountain revealed itself.

Dismounting the ropes onto a shingly hillside, Rhys surveyed the way ahead through the receding clouds. Before them, the terrain softened to one of tawny grasses; the massifs rolled into a series of adjoined peaks that rose steadily higher. On the more distant slopes, swards of green clung to the mountainsides with the occasional tree sprouting from the soil. The following ascent along the spine took the better part of the day, and as late afternoon arrived, just as they reached the final summit, golden sunlight began to glow through the white blanket of cloud that hung above.

"How much higher can this possibly go?" panted Cade.

"A long way I suspect," answered Sol. "If I had to guess, I'd say we've climbed to roughly half the height of Mount Arthest."

"Where?" questioned Ulfgar.

"It's a lone peak in southern Gwent," replied Sol. "Near the Virminter Range."

"Near Wythe," added Cade. "My village."

"Oh," replied Ulfgar.

"Arthest isn't even that tall compared to some of the peaks in the White Mountains," explained Rhys. "Some of the summits you could see north of Longford were snow-capped year-round."

"Even in the summer?" asked Cade.

"Yeah," nodded Rhys. "They're a lot further north than the Virminter Range."

"Not any further north than we are now, though," pointed out Sol.

"I suppose not," agreed Rhys.

"Look there," exclaimed Ulfgar. "That's our next mountain." The dwarf pointed ahead, beyond the peak before them, to a solitary conical alp floating in the mist.

Reaching the apex of the spine, they marched out onto the next swaying rope bridge. Suddenly, sunrays clove through the clouds, and for the first time since they had sailed into the

Wyrm's Sea, the burning orb of the sun presented itself in direct view.

"What's that bright thing up there in the sky?" joked Rhys.

"You mean the sun?" questioned Nathaniel.

"Oh," replied the mage. "I'd forgotten what it looked like."

"Very clever," uttered Sol sarcastically.

With the warming light spilling down on them, they each paused for a moment to bask in the rays. Out of the corner of Rhys's eye, a glimmer of light twinkled. He raised his line of sight to the peak before them and once more sighted a glint. Something was reflecting the sunlight from the tip of the peak, and as he focussed ahead, he realised there was a structure of some sort at the mountain's apex.

"What is that?" questioned Rhys, the glare from the sun preventing him from making it out clearly.

"Is that a building?" asked Sol.

"The tip of it..." mumbled Rhys, squinting to make out a glimmering pole rising out of a white domed structure. "Is that gold?"

"It looks like some kind of shrine..." remarked Sol.

"It's the first evidence of any structure we've seen in this place."

"Do you think it is Elven?" questioned Thia.

"Possibly," shrugged Sol.
"Let's find out," declared Rhys. "Onwards!"

SEVENTEEN

Rhys clambered up the rocky steps of the mountain slope. Cresting the brow, he sighted the golden tip of the shrine emerge above the grass. With each step he climbed, more of the ornate post revealed itself, and as he neared the summit, the mounded white rocks into which the golden pillar had been set rose into view. The gilded column was carved into a series of stacked orbs, each gradually diminishing in size until tapering into a spire, shimmering in reflected sunbeams at the pinnacle of the mountaintop.

Rhys and the others approached the drystone base of the shrine. Various wooden bowls filled with petals and burnt-out incense were arranged in offering before the structure. Surrounding the sanctuary, dozens of seemingly gravity-defying cairns balanced in the wind, many of the stone stacks appearing to teeter in impossible equilibrium, on the brink of collapse, yet never quite toppling, as if frozen in time.

"Remarkable," whispered Rhys.

"This is a holy place," Cade proclaimed. "I can feel it."

"You can *feel* it?"

"I can too," nodded Alkis.

"It is visited often," remarked Sol, observing the offerings at the base of the shrine.

"Whomever tends to this place might not appreciate our being here," warned Thia.

"Thia is right," agreed Rhys as he scanned the heavens.

Cloud was drifting in from above. The temperature quickly dropped as the sunrays piercing the canopy above were abruptly shrouded. The gloom condensed around them, and Rhys grew wary of their sudden loss of visibility.

"It's uncanny," uttered Sol. "The mist in this place has a mind of its own!"

"We can't stay here," insisted Rhys, glancing around for the next hanging bridge on the trail.

His eyes flitted about the gloom, and through the haze, he spied a swaying series of ropes extending out into the sailing cloud currently sweeping across the mountain top.

"There!" indicated the mage, looking around to ensure the others were ready to follow him, but as he peered back across his shoulder, a set of enormous feathered wings wafted the smoky air around him, a gryphon silently soaring up from below.

"Too late!" uttered Sol as the party huddled together and drew their weapons.

The gryphon planted its talons and paws

on the rocky slope, and from out of its saddle twirled an elf wreathed in the swirling mist.

"Behind us!" warned Rhys as two more beasts ghosted from out of the hazy sky, landing to their rear as their riders dismounted with unworldly elegance.

The elves darted through the fog. Rhys's ethereal blade unfurled in a verdant blur. Sol's staff charged with electricity. Yet before either mage reacted, an arrow loosed from Cade's bow. The missile whistled through the mist, aimed for the rider charging their way. The arrow flew true. It met its target. The elf halted. All fell still. Rhys's mind caught up with what his eyes had seen. He glanced the elf's way, expecting to see the shaft and fletchings of Cade's arrow protruding from his chest, but to Rhys and everyone else's disbelief, the realisation set in that the missile had never made it so far. The arrowhead had frozen mid-flight, its barbed tip still inches from the centre of the rider's breast, whilst around the shaft, the elf's grip was tightly enclosed. The rider had caught the arrow, plucking it clean from the air during its flight.

"Oh... shit," Rhys cursed under his breath.

The party watched in stunned disbelief as the arrow spun around in the elf's fingers. In the blink of an eye, the rider drew a recurve bow, notching and loosing the arrow, returning it to its sender. The arrowhead plunged into the soil at Cade's feet. The shaft twanged. Slowly, the elf reached for a quiver hanging at his waist and nocked his horn bow.

Rhys's head swivelled back to the other two riders. They were edging towards them with menacing deliberateness, kukris drawn. Prowling to within a dozen feet, they began encircling the tightly huddled party. The first rider, bow raised, arrow drawn, likewise stalked closer. The elves were adorned in disc armour like the Hounds of Annwn that had ambushed them the night before, yet unlike the winged cavalcade that had raided the beach, these creatures were garbed in bright ochre robes and tagelmusts. Their hauberks weren't black, but instead gilded and decoratively embossed; beads and jewellery hung about their persons, whilst woven beneath their headwear were ornate conical helms.

The archer padded closer still, his footing so light that his feet barely left any impression in the grass. His dark eyes scrutinised them beneath the cloth mask drawn over his face. A set of black eyebrows lowered in anger as he traced his aim between each of them.

"What do we do?" asked Alkis, his fingers twitching on the haft of his sword, but before Rhys could answer, the elven rider spoke loudly.

"Tapainle yasa pavitrara santhama trasa garen irsya garnu bhakocha!"

"Err..." Rhys hesitated in response. "Did anyone catch what he said?"

"Tyasapachi tapam eka yodha, ko yodha

akramaṇa!" the elf hissed in anger.

"I think he is annoyed at us," grumbled Sol.

"You don't happen to speak the Common tongue by chance?" asked Rhys.

"Yi aparadha haruko lagi saja mryyu ho!" the rider shouted, drawing taught his bow.

"He is definitely angry at us," uttered Alkis nervously.

"Why did you shoot him, Cade!?" reprimanded Thia.

"I thought that they were about to attack us!"

"Well, they probably will now," growled Ulfgar.

"Bahi," spoke a second of the elves, addressing the first in a more sympathetic tone. "Tinharu, madye eka ra kharaniko. Taravara cha." He pointed to Rhys's staff and the ethereal blade projecting from it.

"I think he likes your staff," whispered Nathaniel.

"This old thing?" smiled Rhys nervously, raising it slightly to grant the elves a better view.

"Uhale hamialai!" barked the third elf at Rhys's gesture. "Dhamki din uhuncha. Ma bhanna cahanchu ki hami harulai marcharum!"

"I don't think he does like it," mumbled Rhys

"Ra uniharu hamro mauntama khana khanchum!" the third rider continued.

"This doesn't seem to be going all that well," sighed Sol.

"What do we do?" Alkis asked again.

"Pray they don't attack us," returned the mage.

"Timi sahi ho, Bahi," hissed the first with discontent as he took closer aim with the arrow nocked in his bow. "Marnu parcha."

"Oh, fuck," growled Rhys in annoyance as he realised what was about to happen.

The elf let fly his arrow. It thudded into Nathaniel's shield; the guardsman having raised it in anticipation at just the right moment. At that same instant, the two elves wielding kukris disintegrated into streaks of orange that blazed towards the party with impossible speed. Rhys and Sol raised their staves as their unit broke apart in the chaos. Rhys caught the curving edge of a kukri on the shaft of his staff as the first of the elves materialised out of the air. The point of the blade halted barely an inch from Rhys's face as he parried away the lunge. The mage retaliated with a swing of his staff, but the elf ducked with preternatural reflexes before riposting with a slash for the mage's throat. Barely catching the edge of the kukri with his ethereal blade, Rhys successfully defended himself a second time.

The first elf snatched a handful of arrows from his quiver, nocking each one by one, loosing them rapidly in succession. The first thumped into Nathaniel's shield again, but the second glided past his defences, skewering the guardsman's shoulder. Nathaniel cried out; his shield dropped. The archer loaded another arrow, aiming the missile for the guardsman again, this time ready to deal a killing shot. The bowstring snapped taught and the arrow took flight, yet in a blur of ochre, the projectile span out of the air in two halves. The arrowhead and fletchings clattered to the ground at the guardsman's feet as a fourth elf materialised between Nathaniel and the archer.

The new arrival raised her voice in fury. Suddenly, the archer lowered his bow and the two kukri-wielding riders disengaged from the mêlée, sheathing their blades.

"Tapainle yasa pavitrara santhama ragata khanchum!?" the slender elf roared.

"Tiniharu trasa thie," responded the archer ashamedly.

"Tyo talavaralai baca uhuncha!" she scorned.

"I think they are arguing," whispered Rhys.

"Malai mapha gara," apologised the archer. He knelt before the female and offered his bow above his head to her. In response, the other two elves likewise knelt where they stood, bowing their heads in shame.

The female elf drew her kukri and held the edge of the blade against the bow as if she were readying to chop through it and execute the bowman in the same blow.

"Choda!" she hissed, sheathing her knife.

The archer's eyes widened in surprise. He bowed his head low and scurried away, remounting his gryphon. The other two elves followed the bowman's lead, skulking away to saddle themselves back on their monstrous mounts. The gryphons screeched and reared on their haunches before pouncing into the air, unfolding their wings, and taking to the wind. In seconds, they had faded into the mist, leaving Rhys and the others alone with the elf that had saved them.

Rhys's ethereal blade recoiled, sheathing itself in the air. The mage stepped forwards towards the she-elf. "Thank you," he offered sincerely.

"Tapai svagata hunuhuncha," she replied. "You are welcome here," she added in the Common tongue.

"You speak our language?" gasped Sol in disbelief.

"I do. I have learnt much from those of your kind who wash up on the shores of Sumeru," she returned. Without hesitation she began unwinding the veil concealing her face, removing her headdress and helm as she did so. Long, dark, flowing tresses uncurled about her bronze face and two piercing blue eyes beheld Rhys and the others.

"Who are you?" questioned Rhys.

"I am Maadurga."

"Rhys North," returned the mage, after which the others each introduced themselves in turn.

"Rhys North," she repeated, examining him closely. "You are human... and yet you wield the staff of Kalki?"

"Kalki?" questioned the mage, glancing down at his stave as it pulsed in rhythm with his heartbeat.

"The Protector," she clarified. "An incarnation of the Trimurti."

"The Trimurti?" recited Rhys, no more enlightened.

"The..." she hesitated, searching for the word in the Common tongue, "Trinity."

"Trinity?"

"Are the Trinity gods?" Sol asked, thinking he might better understand.

"Yes," nodded Maadurga. "The Trimurti are entities of Brahman. Brahma is the Creator. Kalki is the Protector. And Mahakala is the Destroyer."

"Slow down," urged Rhys, trying desperately to keep track of all the Elven words Maadurga was using. "You say my staff, is the weapon of one of your gods?"

"Yes," returned the elf. "Kalki."

"And Kalki is the Protector?"

"That is right, Rhys North."

"Well that is fortunate," smiled Rhys looking to the others.

"What do you mean?" asked Sol.

"Well, I'd much rather be the Protector god than the Destroyer," he explained.

"You might have a point," agreed Sol wryly. "People tend to fear deities of destruction."

"And you don't get invited to half as many parties," chaffed Rhys.

"The appearance of Kalki heralds the end of time," added Maadurga.

"The end of time?" repeated Sol in dread.

"In hindsight, I might have jumped to conclusions," backpedalled Rhys. "I'm not sure having the weapon of a god whose appearance signals the end of days is a good thing."

"Um... guys?" groaned Nathaniel.

"Its just a staff," Thia assured Maadurga.

"Well, its not *just* a staff..." protested Rhys quietly.

"Rhys and Sol are mages," she explained. "They are both protectors—of our people in our homeland."

"Jhakri," nodded Maadurga. "Controllers of Prana."

"Prana?" quizzed Thia.

Maadurga paused in a moment of deep thought. "Prana is the life energy that flows from Brahman through the world," she said finally. "It is life. It is Air. It is Fire. It is Earth. It is Water. It flows through all things in all places at all times."

"Magic?" nodded Sol.

"No," replied Maadurga. "Prana is more than magic. Magic is just an effect of Prana."

"The Aether?" murmured Thia in surprise.

"Yes," she added. "Yes, that's right. They are controllers of Prana."

"Thia, what is the Aether?" Rhys asked.

"It's an idea… a theory put forward by various members of the Occult," she explained. "One that attempts to understand and explain the existence of magic."

"It's an interesting theory," agreed Sol. "But there is no evidence to suggest it holds any merit."

"It is a better explanation than many others put forward," retorted Thia.

"Hello!?" moaned Nathaniel.

"What is the idea?" pressed Rhys.

"The theory suggests," began the witch, "that there is a metaphysical medium… a quintessence to the world, called the Aether, that connects everything to everything else. Energy and matter and consciousness… they are all connected. And magic supposedly is produced by ripples in the Aether; those capable of wielding magic can affect matter and energy through their consciousness."

"It's a nice idea," dismissed Sol, "but there is little to suggest that it's the case. Religion holds more definitive answers,"

"It's an elegant model of existence that

warrants consideration," argued Thia.

"It certainly is interesting," agreed Rhys. "I like that it is in principle secular."

"The idea is centuries old," replied Sol. "It never took off because every religion has its own explanation for magic. If like me, you worship the Titans, then you know that magic is an extension of their powers. This idea of an Aether subverts the fundamental beliefs of most of the major faiths throughout Cambria. There is good reason why very few people have ever taken it seriously."

"Its sounding more and more appealing to me."

"It might not correspond to *your* beliefs," derided Thia, "but Maadurga just used the word Prana to describe her Brahman: her gods."

"The Trimurti are entities of Brahman," confirmed the elf.

"And the Brahman is responsible for magic?" asked Thia.

"Brahman is the eternal truth," replied Maadurga. "It is the world and everything within it. From Brahman comes Prana, the force and energy that exists through Brahman on every level."

"It is different, but very similar to the idea of the Aether," insisted Thia, turning back to the others.

"This is all fascinating stuff," interjected Nathaniel agitatedly, "but I currently have an arrow sticking out of me!"

Rhys revolved to see that Nathaniel was not joking; an Elven arrow was sunk beneath the guardsman's collar bone and Nathaniel was stemming the bleed with his other hand.

"Oh...!" Rhys croaked guiltily as he realised they had been altogether ignoring the man's grunts of pain.

"Shit!" cursed Thia. "Sorry Nathaniel! I'll have you patched up quick."

"Hold still," instructed Alkis.

"No, wait!" protested Nathaniel, but before the guardsman could stop him, Alkis had rent the arrowhead from out of his shoulder.

Nathaniel roared and Alkis applied pressure to the wound. Thia drew her wand, and as Alkis held Nathaniel still, she carefully wove shut the weeping puncture to the guardsman's shoulder.

"Maadurga," began Rhys, addressing the elf once more as Thia tended to Nathaniel, "if I carry the weapon of Kalki, what does that make me to you?"

Maadurga studied the staff and looked upon Rhys. "If you carry the staff of Kalki, you are his incarnation. That you have taken the form of a human suggests that it is your people that will bring about the end of time—the end of the cycle. Only once the Destroyer has brought an end to the world, can the Golden Age begin."

"That doesn't sound good," sighed Rhys.

"I agree," nodded Thia.

"At least you aren't actually the one who ends the world," put in Ulfgar.

"I am definitely not a god," insisted Rhys. "You are mistaken, Maadurga. I am not Kalki."

"And yet, you arrive here carrying his jade staff," she responded with a smirk.

"But I don't even know the first thing about Kalki, or Brahman!" insisted Rhys.

"This form you have taken has not yet achieved enlightenment," replied the Elf.

"You aren't listening to me," urged Rhys. "I'm not a god. I'm just a mage. A magic user."

"Jhakri," nodded Maadurga.

"This isn't going well," grumbled Rhys.

"I think it is," replied Cade.

"How is she thinking I'm a god a good thing?" refused Rhys.

"She isn't attacking us, for a start," answered Alkis. "Unlike every other elf we've come across so far."

"There is that, I suppose," conceded Rhys. "Maadurga, why have the rest of your people attacked us on sight?"

"Jeet, Karun, and Samir did not recognise who you were," she explained. "This is a sacred place. They believed you trespassed here at this stupa—this shrine."

"As I suspected," nodded Rhys.

"Samir recognised your weapon, but the appearance of Kalki is feared by even his most loyal worshippers. When Kalki appears, it means that Mahakala, the Destroyer, will kill his father Brahma, the Creator, and lay waste to the world."

"But what about the rest of your people?" asked Rhys. "Why are they capturing the castaways? Where are they taking them?"

"The castaways?" questioned Maadurga.

"The humans on the islands below," explained Sol.

"My people do not take them," refused Maadurga. "You speak of the rakshasa; the black riders?"

"The Wild Hunt," nodded Sol.

"They are the corrupted worshipers of Mahakala," explained Maadurga. "They revere the Vritra. They believe it is the final incarnation of Mahakala."

"What's the Vritra?" questioned Thia.

"The dragon," breathed Rhys.

"Yes," confirmed Maadurga.

"Well, that's just perfect isn't it?" uttered Rhys. "The Hounds of Annwn worship the leviathan, believing it to be the embodiment of their god of destruction."

"The followers of Kalki are at war with the rakshasa," explained Maadurga. "We have been for longer than I have been alive."

"Where are they taking the castaways?" Rhys asked. "And Why?

"They are offerings to the Vritra."

"Are they sacrificed?" asked Thia.

Maadurga nodded.

"Great," groaned Sol. "More human sacrifice."

"What do they want?" pressed Thia. "What do they hope to achieve?"

"They wish to bring about the end of time. Only then can the cycle of rebirth end," explained the elf. "The rakshasa believe they are ushering in the dawn of the Golden Age."

"So, they are a dragon-worshipping apocalypse cult bearing an uncanny resemblance to Cŵn Annwn, kidnapping humans in the hope that their sacrifices will appease the Elven god of destruction to bring about the end of days," surmised Rhys. "Anything I left out?"

"They ride gryphons," put in Cade.

"How could I forget," sighed Rhys. "Maadurga, do you know of a set of standing stones anywhere on these mountains? A stone circle? One with magical properties?"

"The Chaitya," nodded Maadurga. "You seek the Chaitya. The sacred stones."

"That sounds about right," smiled Rhys. "Where are they?" he questioned. "How do we get to them?"

"The Chaitya is at the heart of Shambhala."

"There are a lot of words I am trying to get my head around," apologised Rhys. "What is Shambhala?"

"Shambhala is the Golden City," explained

Maadurga. "The sacred city of my people."

"And how would we go about finding Shambhala?" pressed Rhys.

"It sits at the top of Sumeru," she smiled. "But you cannot go there."

"Sumeru," Rhys repeated. "That is this place? These islands? Thule?"

"Yes," confirmed Maadurga. "Everywhere here is Sumeru. It was once one mountain with five peaks."

"But it was ripped from the world by the will of the gods?" asked Sol.

"Yes," replied Maadurga looking at Sol inquisitively.

"It is the same as Thule," explained Sol.

"Why can't we go to Shambhala?" pressed Rhys. "Is it forbidden?"

"No," replied Maadurga. "It is not forbidden. Not for you, Kalki."

"Then why can't we go there?"

"You cannot go there because of the Amara."

"The Amara?" questioned Sol.

"The Ascendant. The Undying."

"Please explain," urged Rhys.

"I cannot," returned Maadurga. "There is not time. The storm is returning."

"Wait," insisted Rhys. "You're not leaving, are you?"

"I must," apologised Maadurga. "It is not safe."

"But we have so many questions," pleaded Rhys.

"I have many answers for you Kalki," she returned. "You must find me again."

"Find you? Where? How?"

"You must travel to Suraksa. I will meet you there." Maadurga began walking towards a ledge that fell away to a steep mountain face.

"Suraksa?" questioned Rhys. "What is Suraksa? Where will I find it?"

"You must follow the trail markers," announced Maadurga. "They lead the way to the Temple of Kalki. Suraksa is along the way."

"Wait," urged Rhys. "You cannot just leave us here!"

"You must follow the way, Kalki," she smiled as she stepped right up to the very precipice and turned to face the mage. "If you follow the Sacred Trail, and arrive in the hidden valley, my people will help you. They will know you are Kalki by the staff you carry."

"Don't go," urged Rhys. "Can't you take us there yourself?"

"I am sorry, Kalki, but you must find your own way to Suraksa. Only then can I teach you what you must know."

Suddenly Maadurga turned, and before Rhys could call after her, she leapt from the precipice. Seconds later, the umber wings of a gryphon unfolded on the wind and Rhys watched as Maadurga glided away, saddled on the back of a striped beast.

"Wow," breathed Rhys as the others neared the clifftop beside him.

"Magnificent," exclaimed Cade.

"She was…" began Alkis.

"She was something alright," agreed Rhys.

"She was the most beautiful woman I have ever seen," replied Alkis.

EIGHTEEN

The darkling heavens shuddered with a drumroll of thunder and white fire seared through the skies as Rhys peered out from the precipice Maadurga had leapt from moments ago.

"What now?" asked Sol.

"We head to Suraksa," returned Rhys, "find Maadurga and get the answers we need."

"She was right about the storm," remarked Alkis as rain began to streak from above.

"She said to follow the trail markers," mumbled Rhys. "What do you think she meant?"

"My guess," began Cade, "those cairns." He gestured to the piles of balanced rock scattering the hill side.

Rhys surveyed the mountaintop; the various stacks led off down the slope towards the rope bridge he had sighted before the appearance of the elves. "I reckon you're right."

"The other huntsmen and I used similar markers in Southwood," explained Cade. "We'd use stone stacks and notches etched into trees to mark routes and indicate what game had recently been seen in the area."

"Then they lead to Suraksa?" questioned Sol.

"I should hope so," nodded Rhys.

"We don't even know what Suraksa is!" returned Sol.

"I imagine it is some kind of village," shrugged Rhys. "The elves have to live somewhere."

"I suppose that is true," conceded his fellow mage.

"Then let's not wait around for the Hounds of Annwn to turn up," implored Nathaniel, rubbing his freshly-healed shoulder.

"I'm not sure about this," grumbled Ulfgar.

"We have to keep moving if nothing else," insisted Rhys. "Come on," he beckoned, making his way down the hillside, following the markers towards the rope bridge swooping out from a clifftop into the pluming haze.

Crossing the suspended lines, they began a steep ascent up another series of steps carved from a rockface on the next mountain. The sheltered inlet staircase snaked its way back and forth as it climbed higher and higher, before eventually emerging out onto the upper slopes of the sky-bound bluff. When the rocky ceiling yielded above their heads, the party were quickly exposed to the full brunt of the raging tempest. Thick lashes of rain streamed sideways. Winds howled. The sky tolled with unceasing drumfire as thunderbolt after thunderbolt flashed. They fought their way uphill against the elements, staggering across the rugged grasses that matted the subalpine slopes. Coniferous trees swung back and forth in the unrelenting gales. Finally, they neared the peak, sighting the next cairn marking the trail above.

A sudden glare of electricity exploded as lightning struck the ground mere yards away from them.

"That was close!" cried Rhys as his heart thumped heavy with adrenaline.

"Too close!" shouted Thia.

A second bolt descended on their other flank, striking even nearer this time than the last.

"We need to get to cover, before we get hit!" hastened Sol.

Suddenly a third bolt blazed down out of the black sky, conducting into the copper prongs of the staff in Sol's hand. The arcane weapon fizzled and sparked as the energy from the thunderbolt slowly earthed through the blade into the mountainside.

"Whoa!" cried Nathaniel in alarm.

"Sol, are you okay?" asked Rhys.

The mage remained silent in stunned amazement.

"Sol!?"

"Yeah!" shouted the mage hesitantly. "I'm fine," he insisted. "That's never happened before."

As he finished speaking, another crackle of lightning struck his staff, conducting swiftly down the metal, discharging into the soil. Everyone jumped in alarm again, but once more, Sol seemed unharmed.

"You still alright?" questioned Alkis.

"Yes," nodded the mage. "Its just passing straight through my staff," he replied. "I can feel it conducting away."

"I'm not sure that makes me feel any safer," replied Ulfgar.

"I think it is safe," insisted Sol. "So long as it keeps hitting my staff and not any of us."

A third thunderbolt flashed and struck the weapon.

"Its bloody terrifying!" insisted Ulfgar.

"Let's find some cover and wait for the worst of it to pass," insisted Rhys.

"I think that's for the best," agreed Sol.

They hastened up the slope towards the next trail marker as the dark heavens continued to surge. Nearing the peak of the mountain, Rhys and the others approached the cairn. A sudden blast of lightning from above impacted the stone stack, obliterating the marker. In the seconds that followed the discharge, a fiery orb of plasma ejected from out of the soil and conducted into the air. The party stopped and watched in disbelief as a glowing orb of orange lightning took form before them, shocking and sparking as it levitated upwards. It flared and surged, discharging back into the ground with several forks of crimson electricity before finally the unworldly phenomenon burnt up in the air, dissipating only a few seconds after it had spawned.

"What was that!?" stammered Nathaniel.

"I..." began Rhys, lost for words.

"A sprite," answered Sol. "I've heard of it," he explained, "but never seen one for myself."

"We need to get out of this storm," urged Rhys. "Before it kills us."

"Where!?" protested Ulfgar. "We are completely out in the open."

"There has to be somewhere," insisted Thia.

"Come on," encouraged Rhys. "Let's at least get down from this summit."

They passed over the peak and made their way along the trail, out onto the next hanging bridge. The lines swung violently as the squalls continued to intensify. The distortions of gravity pulled the showers back into the sky and the rains began to once more batter them from below.

"Look ahead," boomed Sol. "There's a cave!"

Rhys squinted through the murk and made out a shadowy hollow in the rock face before them. The rope bridge itself was suspended through the gaping aperture in the cliff, extending into the dark depths of a cavern. Lightning flashed, conducting into Sol's staff once more. The frayed lines of the bridge thrashed in the churning updrafts.

"Hurry!" insisted Rhys, darting as fast as he could across the tightropes until the gargantuan opening in the mountainside loomed before him. As he passed under the threshold of the cave mouth, the streaming up-pour of rain yielded. Turning back, he saw a wall of rapidly climbing water resembling an inverted waterfall rising across the entrance of the cavern, through which, one by one his friends emerged, each as sopping wet as he was.

"I hate this place," grumbled Ulfgar grumpily, wiping away the excess water from his bald scalp and wringing out the braids of his beard.

"At least we are out of the weather," sighed Nathaniel.

Rhys spun back to face into the cavern. Several dozen fathoms below, a clear body of water had collected in the cave basin. Above, the ceiling domed away into a broad chimney through which rain was gushing, rippling into the water that had gathered over time in the giant cenote. Dim light from the fading day spilled into the naturally formed cistern and reflected off of the undulating waterbody to glint about the cavern. Ahead, the rope bridge was anchored to a large stone shelf extending from the cave wall, from which climbed a series of steps, traversing along the sides of the cavern, spiralling up into the shaft of the natural chimney overhead. The shelf itself was large enough for them to make camp, sheltered from the storm raging outside.

"Nightfall isn't far off," declared Rhys, glancing back out the cave mouth at the stormy twilight. "We should shelter here until daybreak."

"Good idea," agreed Sol.

They set up camp there and then as the final glow of daylight surrendered to night, constructing a meagre fire from the last pieces of kindling they had carried up from the beaches below. Darkness consumed the cave as they ate their meal. Rolling out their bedding on the shelf, they quickly slipped into slumber.

Arlas raised the green trimmed hood of his paladin robes and waded into the frigid waters of the lake. His bare feet sunk into the mud of the lakebed, and with each step he took further out into the glassy waterbody, ripples flowed ahead of him and quivered in his wake. As the water rose beyond his waist, the mage revolved and planted his staff vertically in the mud, before finally taking his position amongst those already gathered in the partially formed circle of men. The mirrored starlit sky undulated, finally settling into perfect stillness once more as Arlas waited for the other magi to appear. Over the next few minutes, the remaining dozen members of the Order emerged from the treeline and likewise waded out into the lake, each in turn driving their weapons into the silty lakebed before taking their places in the water.

Finally, the last of the sixty odd magi appeared and made his way out into the lake; Zadkiel, adorned in black and purple archon robes, planted the final staff in place to complete the circle. As he took up his position in the water, tangents of flame flickered up off the lake's surface and crept around the gathering magi to encircle them, separating them from both the shore and their respective weapons.

"Brothers!" Zadkiel's voice boomed with arcane influence. "I have summoned your presence for the Conclave of Magi. We are gathered to discuss matters of both the Order and all else. Speak freely within the circle, for here the voice of any can be heard! What say you?"

Arlas glanced about the gathering of men, awaiting to see who would be the first to speak.

"Zadkiel," rasped the voice of Azrael from beneath the hood of a figure draped in scarlet hemmed robes. "Why is it you have summoned every mage in Cambria to converse in this tiny woodland in the foothills of the White Mountains? The continent is rife with conflict, and you choose now to draw every arcane warrior in existence away from their personal missions? Please explain this irrational behaviour."

"By now, Brother, I am sure you have heard the rumours brewing of a secret faction that has arisen within the Occult," replied Zadkiel sharply. "The Dark Sisterhood has grown in merely a few years from a few radicalised individuals to numbers that far surpass the size of our order. Though it cannot be verified, several sources have indicated to me that they may well constitute an entire third of the Occult."

"We've all heard of the Dark Sisterhood, Zadkiel," interjected Darren Sayer. "But to say they are so deeply embedded within the Occult is absurd. They are a fringe faction, little more than a small coven. To say otherwise without providing any evidence... it mocks the principles on which our order is founded."

"I have a plethora of evidence to back up my assertions, Sayer," responded the archon with zeal. "I have dedicated the past months to studying the Dark Sisterhood—Arlas Al'Asim meanwhile, the very member of our order who first drew my attention to this threat, has spent over a year investigating them."

"What merit do the findings of Arlas hold?" mocked Azrael. "He may wear the robes of a paladin, but everyone here knows that he is barely worthy of the rank of acolyte."

"Do not be so quick to judge the worth of others, Azrael," scorned Zadkiel. "Arlas has proven his capabilities countless times, and he deservingly earnt the rank of paladin years ago when he single-handily slew the chimera."

"Once again, I would like to bring that claim into question," rebuked Darren. "You have admitted yourself that you were present during the encounter. Your account of a mere initiate slaying a creature of such legendary prowess— it is very hard to swallow. We are supposed to believe that you watched Arlas defeat the beast alone? Whilst *you* merely observed the encounter from afar? I believe that you aided Arlas— or perhaps more likely, you engaged the monster entirely on his behalf."

"And what purpose would the archon have for constructing such an elaborate deception?" demanded the paladin, Michael Hemsworth. "Why would Zadkiel go to such lengths to promote Arlas to his current rank?"

"Do not pretend to be naïve, Hemsworth," scorned Azrael. "We all have heard of the relationship between the archon and Al'Asim's whore mother. The rumours of the boy's parentage are undoubtedly true."

"You are audacious to speak so bluntly," snarled Zadkiel. "Watch your tongue, Magistrate, and remember your place here in this Order. My relation to Arlas is of no significance. His ascendance was conducted in complete adherence to the traditions of this Order, and Arlas was awarded his rank because of the merits of his achievements. If any others here, aside from the two who have already made their opinions well known, believe that Arlas Al'Asim is undeserving of the title of paladin, then please speak now."

To Arlas's relief, silence prevailed across the lake as the three scores of hooded figures looked to one another without uttering a word.

"Very well," growled Zadkiel. "Then if we are done squabbling amongst ourselves and exchanging insults, let us return to the matter of debate."

"I wish to hear the young paladin's testimony," spoke out the voice of Magistrate Arabis. "Tell us Arlas, what is it you have come to discover of the Dark Sisterhood?"

"As the archon says, it is difficult to determine the extent to which they have infiltrated the Occult," explained Arlas. "But I have reason to believe that the leader of this necromantic organisation is a priestess of the Occult."

"You believe this corruption has risen to the highest ranks of their order?" questioned Arabis in surprise.

"No, Magistrate," replied Arlas. "I believe it has *descended* from the highest ranks."

"Please explain," insisted Arlas's friend Ross Baines.

"Start where it all began," insisted the archon.

"I first stumbled upon the Dark Sisterhood when arriving in a small village in the southern foothills of the Virminter Mountains, in Mediussex. I had heard rumours along the road, far away, in a different shire altogether, of a man whose wife had returned from beyond the grave; such rumours are more often than not hearsay, as you all know. They are seldom little more than exaggerated accounts of people recovering miraculously from the brink of death, their body successfully fending off some fever or malady that had killed many others before them. But as I heard more and more of this tale the closer I drew to the town, I came to realise that there was likely something to the story after all.

"The tale had spread nearly a hundred leagues in little more than a month; the reason it had travelled so far so fervently was due to the efflux of villagers from the town. The townsfolk were fleeing their homes, and as I investigated further, it seemed to me as if they had fled for their lives.

"Ten miles south of the village of Bryntywyll, I finally met one of the villagers in person. They spoke of a widower whose wife had died in childbirth, his daughter likewise perishing during the traumatic birthing. They spoke of the day his wife and child reappeared, risen from the dead, nearly a week after their passing. The man, no longer a widower, heralded it as a miracle, yet the townsfolk were understandably wary. The woman with whom I spoke claimed the man's wife did not return from death the same person she had been in life. At first, the risen woman supposedly resumed her day-to-day affairs, living with her husband and new-born child, but as the days went by, more and more of the townsfolk began to question the man on his wife's reappearance. During this time, a sickness began to grip Bryntywyll and the villagers started perishing one by one.

"The husband gave no answers that satisfied the village's apprehensions; after little more than a few days, he no longer allowed his wife to set foot outside his house. The town's apprehension turned to fear and anger, all the while, more of their family members and friends continued to fall victim to the perilous sickness spreading about the town. They confronted him, insisting his wife's reappearance was unnatural; they urged him to return them to their graves. Blows were exchanged, and afterwards, he locked himself away with his wife and child. The townsfolk would stand outside his home with torches; they threatened to burn down his house with him inside—warned him to leave, yet still he remained locked away.

"The villagers continued to perish, and soon those few that remained decided their only chance of survival was to flee their homes."

"So far Arlas, you have provided no firsthand account to verify any of this," interrupted Azrael. "You have given us nothing to go on nor even linked this whimsical tale to the matter of discussion!"

"Perhaps if you were to demonstrate a

modicum of patience and would allow Arlas to finish his account, you might be surprised, Azrael" scorned Arabis. "Please, Al'Asim, continue."

"Thank you, Magistrate," Arlas bowed his head. "I journeyed myself to Bryntywyll to find it all but deserted. There was a deathly presence that hung within the air and it became all too apparent that the place was wreathed in a dark curse. Not only had every villager perished, but the entire settlement's livestock were rotting in the paddocks, and the crops in the surrounding fields blighted. I located the man's home—to my amazement, he answered the door to me.

"I revealed my nature to him, and he immediately confided in me. He granted me entry, and I saw first-hand his risen wife and child. Their flesh had begun to putrefy, their forms had withered, yet they were not like any undead I have ever encountered. His wife was not merely an animated corpse; she was not a puppet of necromancy; she held in her some corrupted fragment of soul."

"What do you mean exactly?" pressed Arabis.

"The woman could speak. The baby whimpered in its crib. They were risen, but they held some remnant of what they had been in life."

"Impossible!" asserted Darren Sayer.

"Impossible because you do not believe such magic exists?" questioned Zadkiel. "Or impossible because you do not believe Arlas's testimony?"

"But Archon," began Michael, "such magic has not existed since..."

"Since the War of the Arcane," confirmed Zadkiel.

"Knowledge of such magic was wiped out along with its practitioners nearly a thousand years ago!" asserted Azrael.

"And yet we hear of it now," replied Ross.

"Please, finish your account, Arlas," urged the archon.

"I questioned the man on the true nature of his wife and child's miraculous return from the dead. He broke down, haunted by regret. One evening, a few days after his wife and child's funeral, he had journeyed to the village graveyard beyond the borders of the town. It was after dark, later than many would dare visit such a place; he explained that he merely intended to place fresh flowers on the graves. Yet upon his arrival, he described meeting a trio of women cloaked in black. They offered him a dark bargain—one that in his grief he could not refuse. They promised to return his wife and child to him; in exchange, for every additional day they lived, another soul would be committed to the grave.

"They performed a short ritual, taking his blood and a lock of his wife's hair as offerings. They promised his wife and child would rise in the days to come, but in order for such to happen, they needed to first be exhumed. The man spent the night digging. When he was finished, he claimed the coven of witches instructed him to carry their bodies into the forest, where he would find a stone altar. The man did as instructed, despite having never heard of such an altar so close to the village, yet he discovered one nonetheless, precisely where the witches had described. He left their bodies upon the stone and returned home.

"The following day, the first victim fell to a chilling sickness. The day after, another perished from the same mysterious disease. On the third, the man's wife appeared on his doorstep, cradling his new-born child in her arms. He explained that when she had first appeared, she looked as she had done in life, young and beautiful, yet her mind was distant. She seldom uttered a word and she moved slowly and clumsily. The baby rarely cried and never suckled from his wife's breast, yet his family had returned, and these issues seemed insignificant. Day by day, more of the villagers perished, and after the townsfolk threatened to come for his wife and child, to lift the curse from their town, he boarded himself in with them.

"When all but a final few villagers had perished from the sickness, and the last had fled their homes, his wife and child began to slowly decompose."

"There were no longer nearby souls to

feed the curse," concluded Arabis.

"I believe so," confirmed Arlas. "Already feeling the draw of the curse upon my own body, I explained the nature of the black magic to the man. He consented to me ending his wife and child mercifully. I do not believe they had a true comprehension of what had happened. I fear only a small portion of her consciousness had been restored, yet I choose to believe she welcomed the mercy I offered.

"I left the man for a few hours whilst I went to investigate both the graveyard and the forest. The graves had been disturbed and there was indeed an altar constructed within the woods from a slab of sarsen lain across the stump of a great oak. But I found little evidence of the coven of witches he had described. In the time I was gone, the man hanged himself—I returned to find him dangling from the rafters of his house. And so, with no leads to investigate further, I decided to head north to contact Zadkiel.

"Along the journey, I asked after the coven of witches, and to my surprise, a trio of women had been described travelling west along the same route I followed. For several weeks, I pursued this illusive triad, but before long, the trail ran cold. After journeying between several towns however, I discovered an initiate of the Occult lodging in an inn along the highway.

"At first I suspected the woman might be

one of the three witches I pursued. But after conversing with her at length, I began to doubt such. I revealed myself as a member of our order—she willingly cooperated, answering every question I pressed her with. She spoke of rumours of a grimoire obtained by a sister of the Occult; this dark tome supposedly held magic lost to time. She claimed to know little, but spoke of the formation of a sect within the Occult—one for which there was little evidence that it truly existed. But, she *had* overheard whisperings of a coven—one calling themselves the Dark Sisterhood.

"A little over a month later, Zadkiel and I met in the Capital Realm, and I spoke of all I had discovered."

"I met Arlas upon his behest," clarified the archon, "and heard him out. I myself was sceptical of what the young paladin told me," he confessed, "but believing in Arlas, I arranged a meeting for the two of us with a contact I have in the Occult. She too had heard whisperings of the Dark Sisterhood, and believed them to be real. She knew little more than the witch with whom Arlas had conversed sometime earlier, however, she divulged that this supposed grimoire had origins north of the White Mountains."

"You believe the Dark Sisterhood has obtained a lost tome from the Carparthian tribes?" asked Paladin Artemis Flamel.

"The evidence suggests such," confirmed Arlas. "On direct instructions from the archon,

I continued my investigations. I travelled to Orthios, and Iarbhaile, and many places in-between. I have unearthed the remnants of dark rituals and uncovered further rumours of dead rising from their graves. These stories of necromancy share much in common with the tale of the man and his wife and child. The dead are rising across the realms, but they are not the animated corpses we have come to expect. Each of the risen is rumoured to resemble that which they were in life, even if they are merely a shadow of such."

"Arlas and I have uncovered much, all of which we will discuss this evening," explained the archon. "But know this now: he and I have come to believe that a priestess of the Occult is at the head of the Dark Sisterhood. We believe that there is a high-ranking witch within their order who is directly descended from the bloodline of Morgain Caddick, the very witch who served as High Priestess to the Occult nearly a millennium ago; the very same Morgain Caddick who led the order to war with the Circle of Magi."

"Then, this grimoire…?" began Flamel.

"You think it is the lost grimoire of Morgain?" asked Arabis.

"I do," confirmed Arlas.

"As do I," concurred Zadkiel. "Magic such as this has not been practised on the continent since prior to the reformation of the Occult. It was its previous resurgence that first sparked the War of the Arcane. The fact that it has reappeared has widespread implications that could shake the foundations of Cambria.

"Brothers, this evening is far from over. There is much that you must hear of before dawn. But I shall make it clear here and now that, from this point forth, we are at war with the Dark Sisterhood. I believe the Occult is not a lost cause. For the better part of a thousand years, they have been a force for good, and they have aided our own order in its endeavours countless times. The High Priestess and those loyal to her are still our allies, and will be instrumental in uprooting the corruption within their order. However, after tonight, every one of you here must pursue this mission to cleanse Cambria of the darkness that has arisen beneath our very noses."

NINETEEN

Rhys sat upright on his bedroll. He rubbed his face in his palms, shaking his mind back into the present. He sat with his head in his hands, the others still sleeping, and pondered for a time the images that were steadily being revealed to him through the medium of dream. Like that which he had been shown before, he knew some revelation would eventually be conveyed, but as of yet, the dreams seamed irrelevant and obtuse. Why was he seeing these events that had transpired so long in the past?

Lowering his hands, Rhys gazed around the cavern to realise it was bathed in an unworldly green glow. The light was spilling down through the chimney of the cenote and flooding the cave in undulating pulses of verdant light that glinted off the water and twinkled across the stone. Rhys stood up and studied the ethereal luminosity as it slowly tinged yellow over time.

The mage peered up towards the oculus in the cavern ceiling, yet his position atop the shelf offered no view of the sky above. He made his way over to Thia and placed a hand gently on her shoulder. She stirred, gazing up into Rhys's eyes before she noticed the strange light bathing the cave.

"Rhys?" she murmured, rising from her bedroll to stare around in awe. "What is this?"

"I have no idea," remarked Rhys. "Would you like to find out?"

She smiled at him gently, her eyes locking with his. "Yes."

"Come on," the mage whispered, pulling on his boots and waiting for the witch to do the same.

They crept towards the edge of the shelf, stepping out onto the stairs rising towards the chimney. The carved spiral staircase hugged the walls to the cavern, traversing up through the hollow in the roof. Rhys and Thia steadily climbed, emerging through the rising shaft to the mountainside above. Helping the witch up the final step, Rhys lifted her onto the summit, and together they craned back their heads and peered up into the shimmering sky.

Waves of violet and red burnt across the atmosphere as an aurora shone through the parted clouds. The heavenly display effervesced and wove in shining curtains that slowly bled from purple to crimson, then amber to gold, finally transitioning from emerald to azure. Stars twinkled through the ethereal fires, whilst in the distance, white lightning flickered silently across the mountain ranges suspended in the sky.

"Its..."

"Beautiful," finished Rhys as he found himself lost in Thia's gaze.

Their fingers interwove as they moved side by side. They stood in silence lost to time. The colours continued to blend and the clouds boiled past overhead, and for a moment that seemed to stretch on forever, Rhys and Thia stood motionless, hand in hand.

"Should we wake the others?" questioned Thia.

"Not yet," breathed Rhys, praying that the moment could stretch just a little farther.

"What is it?" questioned Thia.

"My guess," suggested Rhys, "the Northern Lights. But when I saw them before they were not half as incredible as they appear now."

"I've never seen anything so beautiful in my entire life."

"I have," breathed Rhys nervously, turning to face Thia.

Thia revolved slowly, raising her sapphire gaze to meet Rhys's swirling emerald stare. The mage felt his heart clench tightly in his chest. His lungs seized, and he seemed incapable of drawing breath. For a brief instance, he felt as if he was observing this moment from outside his own body. He felt himself toppling forwards, only he wasn't toppling, he was leaning, and Thia was doing the same. They drew close. He could feel her gentle breath against his neck.

Rhys watched as Thia's eyes fell heavily shut. She leant nearer still and her lips quivered. Rhys felt his hand glide steadily across her back until his fingers curled around the smooth skin of her neck. He closed his own eyes. His heart convulsed in his chest. Their lips pressed together, and in a moment that drew on for eternity, they kissed beneath the glowing heavens, beyond the edge of the world, as storms raged in the distance, the aurora glinting in a thousand colours overhead, a million stars sparkling above.

"Thia..." Rhys whispered as they parted.

She shushed him, placing a finger upon his lips, before running her hands through his hair and kissing him once more. Together they stood cradling each other, neither uttering a word as they peered up at the marvels around them. Time became abstract and meaningless as they held each other in their arms. Finally, they turned to gaze into one another's eyes once more.

"I don't suppose the others would forgive us if we didn't wake them," Thia sighed.

"No," Rhys beamed at her. "I think you might be right."

"We best go get them then," she smiled.

"No," refused Rhys. "You stay here. I'll go."

Her grin widened and Rhys moved away from her, making his way back towards the stairwell.

"Rhys?" Thia called back after him.

The mage paused on the top step as her

platinum tresses fluttered in the breeze.

"What took you so long?"

"I..." the mage hesitated. "I was just waiting for the right moment, I suppose."

Her smile broadened even further. "I think you chose well."

Rhys felt his pulse stutter momentarily. Finally managing to break away from her gaze, he turned and made his way back down into the cenote to waken the others.

TWENTY

"Incredible," remarked Sol as the mage stepped out of the shaft and up onto the mountainside.

"What is it?" questioned Nathaniel in amazement.

"The Northern Lights?" asked Alkis.

"No," replied Sol. "I... don't think so."

"Then what is it?" quizzed Rhys.

"I'm not sure," responded his fellow mage. "But I've never heard of the Aurora Norteius being visible so far south... not at anything like this intensity at least."

"Then what else could it be?" questioned Rhys.

"It's impossible to say."

"Perhaps it has something to do with the storm," suggested Thia.

"And the force keeping the mountains suspended in the sky," added Rhys.

"Possibly," agreed Sol. "Its as good an explanation as any without us knowing more."

"It's magnificent," croaked Ulfgar.

"Ulfgar... are you... crying!?" questioned Cade.

"No!" snapped the dwarf, rubbing his face. "I've just got sleep in my eyes!"

"Look," gesticulated Alkis, pointing to the amber light surging above the horizon to the east. "Dawn."

"It won't be visible soon," remarked Sol. "There's likely only a few minutes left before it fades into daylight."

"Then let's use that time wisely," suggested Cade, peering up at the undulating ribbons of light.

As the sun rose up above a floor of cloud tops, the white ocean of fog boiled amber in the dawn. The aurora steadily faded in the brightening sunbeams just as the last stars winked out of sight. Cool winds surged around them, and the clouds brewed steadily about the hundreds of floating peaks.

"Come on," encouraged Rhys, "let's set off."

They headed back into the cave and packed up camp, before climbing back out of the cenote, setting out once more along the marked trail. Another hanging bridge extended out from the northern face of the summit, strung through a bottomless pass between two floating hillocks. The ropes extended through a veil of mist, emerging to a curving ridge that climbed steadily, via slopes blanketed in ferns, to a pyramidal horn. Small copses of alder and silver fir dotted the mountainside, whilst further up the slopes, emerald swards of grass reigned supreme. Reaching the base of the horn, the party followed another set of steps scaling the rocky faces of the rise. Along the way, they came upon several small shrines consisting of altars laden with offering bowls of petals and sprigs, and prayer beads coiled in heaps upon the stone.

Reaching the western face, the party continued out across the next bridge, passing beneath the underside of an aerial spine, dismounting the lines in the bottom of a ravine carved through the saddle of two escarpments. The path snaked higher into the sky, the twisting gorge climbing steadily. More offerings were set at various intervals along the trail, and lines of vibrant prayer flags were strung across the top of the canyon.

The trench eventually opened to a domed hill, atop of which was set another golden-tipped stupa, though this second shrine was different from the last, its spire rising as a narrowing helix, its base square rather than circular. More bunting adorned with prayer inscriptions was pegged in slanting lines that stretched from the tip of the stupa's post to the ground.

"Religion seems integral to their society," commented Sol as they took a moment to pause and observe the religious monument. "Their shrines aren't dissimilar than those constructed in reverence to the Titans."

"In what way?" questioned Nathaniel.

"The golden posts," began Sol. "If I had to

guess, I would say it represents some sort of Tree of Life."

"Tree of Life?" questioned Rhys.

"Yes," nodded Sol. "I might just be imposing my own religious symbols on to these," he conceded. "But the World Tree is at the heart of the Titan faith. It connects all realms of existence to one another. A post rising from a stone structure... it's seen often in places of worship of the Titan Pantheon."

"I find it curious then, that your religion originates in Westverness, the realm positioned closest to the Stormy Isles," alluded Rhys.

"What do you mean?"

"Well," responded Rhys, "there just seem to be many similarities in Titan mythology to this place."

"Perhaps it is merely because the Tablets portray the world as it is and was, accurately," suggested Sol.

"Maybe," nodded Rhys. "Or, perhaps the reality of this place is what inspired much of the mythology inscribed on the Tablets."

"You think the elves, and the nature of this place influenced the formation of the Titan beliefs?" questioned Thia.

"I do," the mage confirmed. "And I think we are just scratching the surface of it."

"But the Tablets are millennia old!" protested Sol.

"And so does this place seem to be," remarked Rhys.

"Come on," urged Cade, looking to the east where black anvil shaped clouds were brewing out of the lower blankets of mist. "The storm is circling back this way."

They ventured out from the ledge on a winding system of short bridges that spanned the gaps between a convoluted scattering of hillocks and mounds, before ahead of them, a sierra of closely grouped peaks emerged from the pluming mists. The tight massif floated high in the skies above them, several of the summits rising taller than the rest. Together, the collection of mountains formed the largest mass of land they had seen so far, the various ridges ascending to a singular apex standing sharply above all else in the surrounding heavens.

"That looks a likely place for a village," suggested Rhys.

"It would certainly be a lot more sheltered than just about anywhere else in these mountains," agreed Thia.

"We'll need to hurry," warned Alkis, "the sun is already going down."

"We might just make it over there by dark," concluded Sol.

They marched out onto the next bridge, still following the cairns that marked the way. Navigating the random assortment of airborne boulders and hills via the ever-diverging network of hanging bridges, proved more time consuming than any of them had feared. The winds rose sharply as the fringes of the thunderstorm pressed down on them, whipping the ropes back and forth. As darkness descended, the fiery shades of the aurora melted through the skies, but minutes after the phenomenon's reappearance, the heavenly glow was blotted out by swirling black clouds.

Raindrops hammered suddenly downwards and flashes of lightning flared in the tumbling fog. Clinging to the handrail lines, the party fought their way out onto the final bridge on the trail, the cords tethered to the foot of the nearest mountain in the skyborne range ahead. Reaching the halfway point along the furlong of ropes, Rhys glanced into the black skies the moment a bolt of electricity seared through the cloud cover. Dark feathers flocked through the storm in droves. The Cŵn Annwn were on the hunt, stampeding across the currents of the tempest as they rode down from high out of the heavens.

"The Wild Hunt!" gasped Sol.

"Quick," urged Rhys. "We need to get over to those mountains before it's too late!"

"They're heading back down to the cove," asserted Ulfgar as he watched the cavalcade plummet down through the raging storm in helical formation.

"Then let us hope they don't catch sight of us!" warned Rhys as he hurried along the tightropes.

They rushed the final hundred yards of the lines, venturing out onto a set of steps etched from the outer cliff face of the nearest mountain in the tightly spun chain.

"We're still exposed," cautioned Sol. "We need to find our way into the heart of the range."

"Then hurry up!" urged Ulfgar shoving the mage in front of him.

The seven of them clambered rapidly up the uneven steps, ascending the broad wall of bare stone that jaggedly edged around the periphery of the ridge. Reaching a turn in the bluff, the steps ended, the trail extending forwards with a short bridge that led over to the next sheer face on the adjacent mountain. A cairn stacked near the pillars of the bridge indicated the way ahead.

"That's not good," grumbled Sol, realising that the path continued to skirt the outer faces of the mountains.

"There'll be a way in," insisted Rhys, stepping out onto the hanging bridge anchored between the two faces. "We just have to find it."

Reaching the middle of the ropes, Rhys peered down the corridor formed between the two closely associated alps, gaining a brief view into the heart of the mountain chain. Smaller floating hills and gentle forested slopes briefly flashed into view as lightning surged across the sky, but as the short-lived glare of electricity waned, the mountain pass was wreathed once more in shadow.

Rhys dismounted the lines onto the next ridge of steps, venturing out now along the face of the second landmass in the airborne ridge.

"Rhys!" cried Thia, pointing skywards.

The mage glanced upwards as another flash exploded in the clouds. A winged rider cloaked in black scudded rapidly overhead.

"They've seen us!" cursed Sol.

"Come on!" shouted Rhys, leaping up the narrowing ledge of steps. Reaching a landing in the staircase, he skidded suddenly. The stairs had swerved sharply back in the opposite direction, and Rhys only noticed the looming precipice at the last second. The mage's boots slipped across the wet stone. His shins clattered into a cairn perched on the lip of the ledge. Rhys scraped to a halt as the stacked stones toppled over, tumbling from the precipice, vanishing into the darkness below. Regaining his balance, saving himself from following the cairn over the brink, Rhys swivelled and accelerated up the next flight of steps.

Thunder clapped, and from out of the blaze of lightning appeared a gryphon rider. The monstrous beast flared its wings as its talons and padded hindfeet touched down on the narrow steps above Rhys. From out of the saddle, leapt its master, who lunged high into the air. In a dazzling display of acrobatics, the elven cavalryman unsheathed his kukri in mid-air and connected with the wall of stone. Running a palm across the cliff face, the elf planted his feet along the wall, and in a gravity defying stunt, sprinted at a downward trajectory towards Rhys across the vertical surface.

A flash of emerald glared on the dark staircase as Rhys's ethereal blade unfurled in anticipation. The elf descended upon him, kukri scything out of the air. Rhys lurched suddenly forwards, dipping beneath the arcing pounce of the Wild Hunt rider. Slicing upwards with his staff reversed, he snagged the elf's ankle with the hook of his blade. A glancing cut brushed across the rider's calf, disrupting the elf's otherwise elegant descent. The black robed warrior tumbled from the face of the cliff headfirst, but with supernatural grace, righted himself in the air, rolling swiftly as he struck the flight of steps, bounding back to his feet. The rider stopped inches before toppling over the precipice and span, ready to charge back up the stairs for Rhys. Having anticipated the elf's recovery, Rhys thrust his staff rearward with little more than a glance over his shoulder. A missile of force careened down the stairs, smashing into the elven warrior balanced precariously on the ledge, launching him from the brink. The creature's screams faded below as Rhys charged onward, surging ahead up the steps.

The riderless gryphon reared up on the path ahead, letting out a deafening shriek. Its tail thrashed and its wings beat, lifting the enormous hybrid back into the air above Rhys's head. Its talons sliced downward for the mage. Rhys ducked, narrowly evading the monster's grasp, and lanced upwards. His ethereal weapon punctured the gryphon's breast. Its wings crumpled. With an anguished screech, the beast dropped out of the sky, slamming into the thin ledge of steps before toppling to the flight below, thereafter, plummeting off the cliffside all together.

"Nice!" remarked Sol as he came to Rhys's aid several seconds too late.

"Watch it!" cried Ulfgar from the flight of steps below where he had very narrowly avoided being crushed by the gryphon as it had fallen from above.

"We've got more incoming!" warned Alkis, his finger pointing out into the raging storm.

Sure enough, more and more riders were peeling off from the body of the main hunt, banking on the turbulent draughts as they dove the party's way.

"Move!" cried Rhys, spurting further up the sloping steps.

He came once more to a turn in the way, the stairs doubling back again along the face of the bluffs. Rhys charged onwards, but soon staggered to an abrupt stop as the first Hound of Annwn swooped past. The gryphon rolled in a spiral of feathers, and as the lightning flared,

Rhys saw the rider clutching a nocked bow. As the mounted archer revolved beneath his corkscrewing gryphon, his bowstring twanged, and the arrow hurtled the mage's way.

To Rhys's relief, the arrow clattered off the rock a foot away from him. The elf had missed, yet as the rider's mount continued to roll, the archer's hands moved rapidly, pulling arrow from quiver, loading, drawing, and loosing the bow in swift and fluid singular motions, unleashing a quickfire salvo at Rhys. The hail of arrows shattered and bounced across the steps as Rhys frantically sprung up the stairway, the fusillade ceasing only as the winged cavalryman banked out of range. But the aerial assault had only just begun, as the moment the first mounted archer glided away, the next in the flying hoard swooped down towards the party. Rhys stooped as he continued to climb amidst the rain of arrows and water, firing covering blasts of force to repel the incoming rakshasa strafing run.

An arrowhead slashed across the back of Rhys's thigh; the mage stumbled, falling to his knees across the stairs. From out of the thunderstorm, a spread of black wings descended. Rhys lunged upwards to defend himself as a set of talons bore down on him. A quarrel loosed from Ulfgar's crossbow struck the creature in the eye, seconds before it snatched hold of Rhys. Swerving out of control, the leonine raptor crashed into the cliff wall above the mage, its hulking carcass tumbling from the ledge. In the split seconds before plummeting into the abyss, a smoky blur of energy ejected from the beast's saddle, the rider magically vaulting from the falling gryphon, rematerializing on the lip of the precipice.

A kukri clove for Rhys's head, but before the defenceless mage's skull was split open by the blade, an arrow slung from Cade's bow pierced the elf through the neck. The rider slumped atop of Rhys, his curved knife clattering to the steps as the mage threw the elf's surprisingly light corpse off him, sending the body falling into the tempest below.

Rhys bounded back to his feet and looked down at the party closing in on his rear. "Everyone alright?" he called out to them as he sighted the next incoming band of the Hunt break away to bear down on them.

"Yeah," replied Sol. "None of them are going for us!"

"Why are they only attacking Rhys?" cried Thia.

"Its his staff!" shouted Cade. "They think he is Kalki!"

"You've got to be fucking kidding me!" cursed Rhys.

More arrows rained down through the storm, but the hail was offset by the surging winds. The projectiles whirled all around Rhys, splintering as they collided with the rockface. Miraculously, Rhys was left unharmed, but only seconds elapsed before the next flight of Annwn' hunt circled back on him. Rhys continued to ascend, the rest of his friends following up the steps in close pursuit. A bolt of lightning crackled down from the heavens, striking Sol's staff. Rhys peered back to watch as Sol inspected the fizzling weapon. Ensuring not to let the copper stave earth, the mage thrust outwards from the ledge. A blinding surge of energy thundered deafeningly back into the storm. An immense bolt of plasma forked and crackled, bifurcating over and over within the splintered fragments of a single second. The enormous outpouring of electricity singed into the oncoming brigade of rakshasa. Suddenly, a half dozen electrocuted gryphons and their riders dropped from the sky, slain instantly by the colossal discharge of energy from Sol's weapon.

"What in the world!" cried Rhys in disbelief.

Breathing heavily, Sol peered down at the lightning conductor in his hands before gazing back up into the surging storm.

"Can you do that again?"

"I don't think so," panted Sol, "Not unless my staff is struck by the storm again."

"Well, let's hope it is!" prayed Cade.

"More of the Wild Hunt are heading our way!" shouted Alkis as the main body of the descending hunt turned towards the mountains.

"We won't make it!" despaired Nathaniel. "There are too many. We can barely fight them as it is."

"Then we had better move fast!" rallied Rhys, urging them up the cliffs as the Hounds of Annwn bore down on them from out of the raging heavens.

TWENTY-ONE

Rhys scampered up a steep ladder of ledges on hands and knees. Thunder roared, winds howled, gryphons screeched, and arrows whistled throughout their chaotic charge up the cliffside. A streak of shadow accelerated across the shelf. An elf reformed into existence in the blink of an eye. Rhys clashed against the curved edge of the rider's Kukri with his ethereal blade. Sol's staff thrust past him, impaling the unsuspecting creature through the gut. The elf crumpled. Rhys and the others leapt over him, sprinting up the narrow straight towards the next turning in the winding staircase.

An arrow sliced across the back of Rhys's hand. Blood ran between his fingers. A second missile ricocheted off the stone wall to his flank, the bouncing shot stabbing shallowly into Rhys's calf. The mage winced whilst on the run as the arrowhead dug in; a few steps later, weighted down by the splintered shaft, the barbed tip shook free, dropping out of the surface wound. Unhindered by the rapidly dulling pain of his weeping leg, he spurted on.

The Hounds of Annwn were flocking in droves around Rhys and the others, the cavalcade swelling as more and more of the rakshasa descended from out of the tempest to join the swarm. Suddenly, in front of Rhys, a gryphon planted itself on the rockface, its talons and retractable feline claws grappling the cliffside, anchoring the enormous beast to the vertical surface. The rider raised his bow. A bowstring twanged, but from the rear, not ahead. An arrow from Cade screamed past Rhys's ear, stopping mid-flight as the elf effortlessly snatched the projectile clean from the air. A finger twirl spun the arrow back around, and with rapid dexterity, the black rider threaded the notch, drew, and took aim.

A second bowstring snapped between tolls of thunder, once more to the rear. A quarrel took flight, accelerated across the wind by Ulfgar's crossbow, the bodkin head puncturing clean through the hound's mail. The rider slipped sideways out of the saddle. His fingers slackened; the string of his composite bow loosed from his dead grip. Cade's arrow took flight for a second time, returning the way it had come. Rhys ducked. The fletchings brushed through his hair as the arrow sailed a fraction of an inch overhead, dipping in its arc towards his companions on the staircase below. More through luck than anticipation, the wayward arrow glanced off the face of Nathaniel's half-raised shield, deflecting back skyward, vanishing into the dark.

Rhys fired a blast of force at the rockface on which the rider's monstrous mount was still perched. The slug of energy crunched into the stone, ejecting an eruption of shingle and dust. The beast was sent sprawling as the rock beneath its talons disintegrated. Thrown from the precipice, the hybrid disappeared in a fading tumult of shrieks.

On they sped, every second more of the Wild Hunt diving towards them.

"We're near the top!" cried Rhys as lightning flashes illuminated the crest of the clifftop one final flight of steps above their heads.

"Hurry!" yelled Sol, rallying them forward.

A bout of fire cast from Rhys's stave licked outwards from the stairway. The plume of flames domed above, repelling the incoming charge of rakshasa plunging down from the sky. Swooping to avoid the burning bulwark, the hunt veered out of their dive, circling back into the heavens to line up for another strafing run. Sol fired a line of thunder after them, the bolt only narrowly curling wide as the riders banked out of range.

Rhys dashed up the final few steps. Reaching the top of the stairway, he leapt over the lip of the cliff, summitting atop a flat plateau. Ahead, a rope bridge extended across a chasm towards a second shelf, the gulf walled either side by inwardly sloped cliff faces forming a natural choke point to the valley beyond. Across the chasm stood an ornamental stone gateway, a pair of decoratively carved pillars topped by an equally ornate lintel. Beneath the entrance, a dozen elven figures shrouded in shadow formed a firing line, their bows drawn and aimed Rhys's way, their arrowheads sparkling in the lightning flashes.

"Rhys, look out!" cried Sol, tackling his friend to the ground.

From out of the sky behind them, dove a mounted rider of the Wild Hunt. The beast touched down, having only narrowly missed the two magi with its razor claws. It thrashed rapidly back around, granting its rider a shot at the prostrate magi. The elf took aim. An ochre blur blazed from out of the darkness. A second elf leapt cleanly onto the gryphon's saddle. Maadurga drew a pair of kukris from behind her waist, and in one swift motion, decapitated the bewildered rider in a scissor of blades. Another gryphon landed on the plateau alongside her, yet before the rider could even nock an arrow, Maadurga had flung one of her kukris, impaling the rider through the chest.

A blaze of black lurched from out of the

storm, another Hound of Annwn materialising, bow aligned for Maadurga. Maadurga moved with unworldly speed, bounding from aback the first gryphon to the saddle of the second. Renting her blade from the breast of the rider's corpse, she flipped backwards, pouncing down towards the rakshasa bowman below. Still in the air, she skewered the archer through the nape of his neck. Rolling her weight over the hound's shoulders, she finally landed, curling her shortsword through the remaining flesh of the rider's neck, cutting his throat in a shower of blood.

Rhys and Sol clambered back to their feet after watching the display from the ground in astonishment, when suddenly, all hell broke loose. Gryphons and elves touched down all around, some the black riders of Cŵn Annwn, others the orange robed warriors of Suraksa. Arrows took flight from every direction. Feathers and wings clashed through the glare of lightning. Steel clanged as scores of kukris collided in a maelstrom of blades. Streaks of shadow and flashes of amber blurred all around, the two forces engaging in a deathly skirmish outside the gates of Suraksa.

"Kalki!" Maadurga cried, darting over to Rhys and Sol.

"Rhys," the mage corrected her, glancing around frantically, fearing at any moment they would be flanked.

"We must get you past the gate," shouted

the elf over the din of battle. "The rakshasa will not set foot into the Sacred Valley."

"We need to make it across... to there!?" fretted Sol, gazing through the whirlwind of blades, over the rope bridge, where a rank of Suraksa archers stood defending the gateway to the valley beyond.

"Easier said than done," warned Rhys.

"My people will hold the rakshasa at bay!" the elf assured.

"We'll move together," declared Alkis, the knight and the others arriving from the rear.

"Once you make it through the gates, the rakshasa will flee," promised Maadurga.

"Why are they after us?" questioned Rhys.

"They see you bear the weapons of Kalki!" explained Maadurga. "You are an enemy of their god Mahakala."

"Well that's just perfect!" groaned Ulfgar.

"We must move fast!" urged Maadurga.

Rhys nodded. "Let's go."

Their elven escort dashed into the foray, stooping and spinning between foes in a frenzy of knives as she carved a path through the sally towards the rope bridge. Rhys charged after her, but was instantly met with resistance, an elf materialising in front of him. They clashed weapons, exchanging a quick bout of blows before Alkis stormed into the elf's flank, carving the rakshasa open with his bastard sword. The knight spun suddenly, a second hound rushing out of the fray for the swordsman. They locked blades, steel sliding over steel as the elf delivered a rapid moulinet, flinging Alkis's sword wide, opening the knight's defences. The rakshasa drew back for a death blow, but before he could deliver his strike, his legs were torn out from under him by the hook of Rhys's blade. Grounded, the black rider was suddenly impaled, Sol darting into the fray to deal the finishing blow.

The party pushed forward, the bridge inching closer step by step, as one after another, the Hounds of Annwn leapt out of the saddles of their diving mounts, landing in the heart of the skirmish to harry Rhys and the others. Another rider darted for Rhys, sliding beneath a cleave from Alkis, dodging one of Cade's arrows, and dancing clear of a sweep from Sol's staff, to lunge kukri-first for his target. Rhys raised his stave in defence as the face of Nathaniel's shield smashed sideways into the elf. The hound staggered off balance, desperately attempting to recover its footing, only to be cut down in a slash of emerald. Sweeping his ethereal blade through, Rhys parried another incoming assault. The mage felt his blade lock out, the notch in the rakshasa's kukri biting into the edge of his ethereal weapon. The elven fiend manipulated Rhys's staff out wide, disentangling their bound blades the moment the mage's guard had been broken. Rhys flinched defencelessly, preparing to be struck, when the steel arms of Ulfgar's crossbow rang out, a quarrel bulleting through the elf's neck. The rim of Nathaniel's shield crunched through the skull of a rakshasa engaged with Sol, whilst Cade riddled the elf besting Alkis with a rapid salvo of arrows. Spinning on the spot, Rhys fired a blast of force rearward, narrowly saving Ulfgar as a gryphon swooped down from the rear, whilst Sol paid Cade the same favour, a fork of lightning unsaddling a rakshasa diving out of the sky.

On they advanced, working together, pulling into tighter formation, Maadurga carving a way ahead, the defending Suraksa warriors holding off the greater hoard of the Cŵn Annwn on their flanks. The chaos intensified. Rhys swung his blade left and right, deflecting incoming blows, rending limbs, cutting down the rakshasa in his path. Time after time he was saved at the very last moment by one of his companions; each instance he returned the favour mere seconds later. Inch by inch, they crawled closer to the bridge, towards the gulf, to the gates of Suraksa.

A hound blurred out of the shadows, pouncing with his kukri drawn, arcing down for Rhys. The mage span, staff raised horizontally overhead. Steel and crystal collided. Rhys stumbled, tripping over a corpse under his feet. He caught himself from falling, but the elf was upon him. A blinding flash glared to the rear.

The rakshasa halted, shielding his eyes against the dazzling flare summoned from Thia's wand. Without delay, Rhys struck, cutting down the stunned elf in his momentary hesitation.

The bridge was close at hand. A coordinated succession of thrusts alternating from Rhys and Sol's staffs overwhelmed the defences of a rakshasa in their way. A simultaneous lance from both magi ran the rider through, spearing him off his feet, impaling him against the ground, opening the way ahead.

"Hurry!" urged Maadurga, darting out onto the lines of the bridge, gesturing the others to follow.

"You first!" insisted Sol as he shoved Rhys out onto the tightropes.

Rushing across the lines, Rhys ducked on instruction from behind, a set of talons clamping shut above his head. The swooping beast plummeted past the bridge, riddled with a volley of arrows loosed from the ranks defending the gateway to Suraksa. Re-righting himself, Rhys charged onwards, sprinting halfway across before daring a peek back over his shoulder.

Another gryphon plunged towards the bridge. Rhys and Sol aimed upwards. Lightning and kinetic energy took to the sky, striking the airborne monster, crippling its wings as it raced down towards them. No longer kept on course by its crumpled wings, the gryphon nosedived over their heads, colliding with the ropes. The tumbling beast bounced off the taught lines and the entire bridge sprung upwards. Rhys felt his stomach lurch. Suddenly he was weightless, flung from the cords into the air. His hands instinctively snagged hold of the handlines, but as the bridge rebounded back downward, it flipped, tangling over itself.

A tumult of screams sounded behind, the entirety of Rhys's party now dangling from the cords of the upturned rope bridge.

"Shit!" cried Alkis as their legs flailed beneath them.

"What do we do now?" shouted Thia.

"Hold on!" insisted Rhys as he began to swing his legs back and forth.

"Rhys!?" blurted Ulfgar anxiously from behind. "What are you going to do!?"

"Trust me!" the mage called back.

With only a single hand preventing him from plummeting into the dark chasm below, the mage gripped the line and slashed upwards with his staff. The hook of his blade cut through one of the handlines, and with the rope severed, the bridge uncoiled. The party cried out as the cords lurched, untwisting sharply before coming to a rest. Hanging on its side, the partially cut bridge now dangled vertically.

"Now what!?" demanded Ulfgar angrily.

"Climb sideways!" instructed Rhys as he heaved himself up to grasp the other still intact handline.

Slotting his feet between the tightropes that had once formed the floor of the bridge, the mage began to shimmy sideways. As he reached the far side of the chasm, Maadurga's hands clasped hold of his sleeve and helped him up over the ledge. Rhys knelt beside the elf and began aiding the others up over the precipice. Within moments, they were all clear.

"Quickly," insisted their elven companion, "through the gates!"

Together, the group darted for the ornate stone archway. The line of archers saw them coming and stepped clear of the gate, allowing them to run through. Maadurga halted and turned back to study the onslaught raging across the bridge.

"Pirta linuhos!" she cried.

One by one, the warriors of Suraksa disengaged from the fray, leaping out across the chasm, each in turn landing atop the tightropes. In an unworldly feat of acrobatics, the retreating elven warriors ran across the lines, arms spread eagle for balance as they dashed across the tightropes in file, dismounting the remnants of the bridge each in turn when safely across the gulf.

"Bloody hell," mumbled Ulfgar in disbelief.

Several of the rakshasa attempted to pursue, but the Suraksa warriors that had already made the crossing rapidly reformed a firing line, loosing an onslaught of arrows, slaying every

Hound of Annwn that dared attempt the crossing, and deterring any other from trying. As the final Suraksa archer skipped off the ropes, the Wild Hunt amassed on the precipice across the way. The volley of arrows ceased, and both sides were locked in a standoff. Several suspenseful moments endured, punctuated by tolls of thunder and lightning flashes, before one by one, the black riders leapt back into their saddles and took to the air, climbing steadily into the howling winds astride their demonic mounts. The sky continued to blaze white with electric fire, as steadily, the dark cavalcade vanished into the eternal tempest.

TWENTY-TWO

Rhys stirred as thin beams of sunlight streamed through the shutters across his face. He yawned, sitting up from his bed of goat hides, allowing the cashmere blanket to slip from his shoulders. He shivered in the chilly air and gazed about at the others; they all still lay throughout the room asleep. Rhys rose and dressed quietly. Checking he had not disturbed any of his exhausted companions, he picked up his staff, crept over to the intricately carved doors, and slowly pushed them open. The glare of the sun dazzled him as he stepped out into the cool morning. He shielded his eyes from the rays, carefully closing the door behind him, and turned to gaze in wonder.

The vibrant mountainsides rustled with verdant alders, cedars, and pines, whilst crimson maple canopies danced in the alpine breeze. Lower down in the valley, meadows and fields were terraced into flooded rice paddies, fed by flowing rills that wove from the rocky peaks high above, draining thereafter into small lakes pocketed between adjoining slopes. Further below, Rhys caught glimpse of white clouds drifting beneath the bottomless basin of the valley, occasional breaks in the cloud floor granting lofty views of the Wyrm's Sea far beneath.

Rhys made out the colourful timber rooves of the village of Suraksa some way down the track; he could hear the bustling of elves carried his way by the mountain breeze. Rhys leisurely set off down the path, descending a set of wooden steps to enter the small settlement. Chickens clucked and goats bleated nearby as he passed between two stone houses. Lines of prayer flags were strung between the rooftops, the bunting fluttering in the soft air currents. Above, the sky was almost entirely clear of clouds, and to Rhys's amazement, he could make out the faint emerald ribbons of the aurora even in full daylight.

Rounding a corner, Rhys stumbled upon an elven woman dressed in an ornately embroidered pink sari, a red shawl woven with various teardrop motifs draped across her shoulders. She was perched on a stool milking a yak into an earthen ewer. At seeing Rhys, she stood immediately, bowing her head with her hands pressed together.

"Prasansa," she smiled, approaching Rhys, taking his hand in hers.

"Hello..." hesitated Rhys as he looked down on her.

She beheld him with her large dark irises, studying his face as Rhys in turn studied her. She appeared older than Maadurga, in a way almost elderly, yet Rhys could not figure out why; her complexion was wholly youthful, her physique spritely. Yet somehow, the way she held herself and a certain look in her eyes conveyed a sense of wisdom and inner peace which Rhys only associated with age.

"Pransa Kalki," she beamed, pressing her forehead to the back of Rhys's hand.

"Err... I think you have the wrong man." Rhys smiled, realising she hadn't understood a word he had said.

Gently, she released Rhys, taking several steps back, but instead of returning to her business, she remained stood, silently watching the mage, almost in anticipation.

"Um... do you know where I can find Maadurga?"

"Hi'umda," she responded politely.

"Maadurga?" Rhys repeated.

"Hi'umda," she nodded once more.

"Okay," Rhys grinned awkwardly. "Don't worry, I'll just take a look around for her."

Rhys slowly walked around the corner, glancing back over his shoulder every now and then to see the woman was still watching him. Once she was out of sight, he followed a fence railing a steep grassy bank to the adjacent street.

"Pransa Kalki," a male elf with long dark braided hair uttered upon sighting Rhys. He rose from his doorstep where he had been tanning a goatskin and approached the mage, taking his hand in much the way the woman had done. "Tapai svagata hunuhuncha," he added.

"Once again," Rhys smiled, "I'm not Kalki."

From the waist down, the elf was dressed in a dhoti, his bronze and slender chest on show. Much like the woman, Rhys found it difficult to estimate his age; everything except his appearance indicated that the elf was elderly. His voice, the way he held himself, the sense of weariness soothed by inner calm that pervaded his demeanour, all of it hinted at maturity concealed by a veil of youthful vigour. The villager bowed his head respectfully, retreating much as the woman before him had done, continuing to observe Rhys as the mage carried on down the way. Several other elves called out to him from their doorsteps, some merely watched him from afar, whilst others rushed up to him to take his hands in theirs.

Climbing a set of steps to a street on a higher terrace, Rhys could hear the sound of string and wind instruments intermingled with chiming bells and percussion. Children giggled from behind a wall, ducking down out of sight the moment Rhys turned to look their way. One child, braver than the others, no taller than

Rhys's hip, crept out and wandered over to the mage.

"Hi there," Rhys smiled friendlily as the wide-eyed girl shuffled from side to side, clutching the fabric of her sari as she beamed up at him. "How can I help?"

"Pransa Kalki," she giggled.

"Why am I not surprised?" Rhys chuckled back.

Suddenly, the young elf's large eyes focussed on Rhys's staff as it rhythmically pulsed green with the beating of his heart. A state of wonderment took her over and she cautiously reached out, pressing her fingertips to the crystal surface of the shaft. Immediately she withdrew, cackling in hysterics before scampering off out of sight.

Rhys quickly realised a crowd of elves had gathered about him.

"Pransa Kalki," several chanted.

"Tapai svagata hunuhuncha," uttered a number of others, all smiling broadly at the mage.

"Hello," offered Rhys uncomfortably as he tried his hardest to upkeep his own smile. "I'm looking for Maadurga?"

He received only blank grins in response.

"Anyone know where I can find Maadurga?"

"Maadurga, hi'umda," returned an adolescent girl in response.

"Maadurga," nodded Rhys in attempt to overcome the language barrier.

"Hi'umda," responded the girl once again.

"Come on, help me out here," replied Rhys, his smile fading.

"You are looking for Maadurga, Kalki?" came the voice of a young male.

"Yes," Rhys sighed with relief upon hearing the Common tongue, quickly scanning the surrounding faces for the source of his own language.

"She is making peace," replied a handsome elf in a white sherwani with an umber turban. "Up the hill," he added.

"How can I find her?"

"Follow the prayer flags," instructed the elf, tracing his finger across the slopes rising above the village.

Glancing where indicated, Rhys spotted a trail marked by posts strung with runs of the colourful flags.

"They will lead you to the stupa."

"Thank you," smiled Rhys, bowing his head respectfully.

"Pransa Kalki," he replied in response.

"Err..." Rhys hesitated, "thanks."

The crowd parted before the mage as he made his way down the main street. Various stalls were being set up for the day to come; shop shutters and awnings drew steadily open, revealing a broad assortment of wares. Reels of silk and cashmere dyed in every conceivable colour hung from racks, the cloth floating in the cool winds swelling about the sheltered valley. One male elf was stacking earthenware outside his shop, another was splitting wood with his kukri. A third stoked a fire beneath a wide pan of simmering yellow stew; the spicy aromas wafting from the food stirred a hunger pang in Rhys's gut. The mage caught sight of a fletcher making arrows, whilst in another nearby street he could hear the chiming of a smith's forge. The sound of music grew louder until Rhys passed a group of elves sat playing various unfamiliar instruments in the morning sun. All through the street, people stopped to watch Rhys, greeting him with smiles and taking his hand in theirs.

Eventually, he made it to the foot of the slope from which the path exited the village. The lines of prayer flags fluttered gently overhead as the mage began to climb. He paused along the way, glancing back down at the village beneath. At this distance, the bustle of the town had now faded, the multicoloured roofs glinting beneath the sun's golden rays. A serene tranquillity bathed the secluded dale; the entire valley seemed so far removed from the tempestuous climate of the Stormy Isles that it was difficult to believe he was still in the same part of the world.

Cresting the brow, Rhys sighted a golden spire rise out of the land, the village's stupa unveiling itself from behind the verge. Rhys approached the white cairn forming the base of the shrine. He soon sighted Maadurga, her legs crossed as she sat in silent meditation before the stupa. He hesitated, not wanting to draw any closer for fear of disturbing the elf from prayer. After a moment of silence, she spoke out.

"Good morning, Kalki."

"Please," urged the mage, "call me Rhys."

"Very well—Rhys," returned the elf as she rose from her meditation and turned to face him.

In a word, Maadurga was stunningly beautiful. Sapphire eyes gleamed Rhys's way in the sunlight. Dark hair curled in silky braids across her shoulders, framing the caramel skin of her flawless complexion. Since their last meeting, she'd doffed her ochre mirror armour, garbed now in a gold-frilled scarlet sari. A navy shawl draped across her shoulders, the elf hugging it tightly across her slender frame as the cooling winds soughed around the hilltop shrine.

"How are your injuries?" she inquired, sauntering over to him.

"All closed up," Rhys assured her as he rubbed a faint pink scar across the back of his hand.

"Good," she beamed, taking it in hers to inspect it.

"I've had a lot worse," Rhys assured, "trust me."

Maadurga nodded and looked up at his

face. "Your friend is a great healer," she concluded.

"She really is," agreed Rhys, aware that Maadurga was still holding his hand in hers.

"Come," beckoned the elf, finally releasing Rhys. "Let us talk."

She led him over to a grass verge that granted them the best view of the valley and village below.

"This place is incredible," remarked Rhys. "I'm not sure I've ever seen anywhere quite so beautiful."

"Is your home not beautiful, Rhys?"

Rhys chuckled and lowered his gaze as he twiddled his fingers. "It *was*," he smiled wistfully as he gazed back out across the valley. "But that was before it was destroyed. I have no idea how it looks now."

"That is very sad," remarked the elf. "Sumeru was destroyed long ago. The five peaks were torn apart in a disaster many aeons past. The mountain will never be the same. But there are still places for beauty to be found."

"Like here," nodded Rhys.

"Yes," agreed Maadurga. "This is the Sacred Valley. It is one of the last havens of Sumeru. It is the home of my people: the followers of Kalki."

"What happened?" questioned Rhys. "What was it that tore Sumeru apart."

"The rakshasa," she explained. "They

sought to bring an end to the cycle of rebirth."

"What did they do?"

"They used a magic weapon of old—one that fell from the heavens, to wound Brahaman and Prana."

"Prana?" questioned Rhys. "They wounded the Aether?"

"Yes," nodded Maadurga. "Or so say the stories my people tell. The scar can still be seen to this day," she pointed skyward. "The Akasa: The Rift."

Rhys gazed up and realised Maadurga was pointing to the faint aurora glowing in the daytime sky. "The aurora? That is a wound to the Aether?"

"Yes," confirmed the elf. "The Rift is what powers the storm and lifts the mountains from the sea."

"And you say that it was done by a weapon?" pressed Rhys.

Maadurga nodded. "The Cintamani Stone."

"How did a weapon cause this?" questioned Rhys.

"I do not know," confessed Maadurga. "We are told the Cintamani Stone was a gift from the sky. It fell to the world and was an artefact of great power. It was given for safe keeping to the worshipers of Brahma, the Creator. But the bringers of doom, the worshippers of Mahakala that came to become the rakshasa, stole it and used it to destroy Sumeru."

"But why would they want to destroy this place?" questioned the mage.

"Only when the destroyer has brought an end to all things can the cycle of rebirth finish, and can our people achieve enlightenment."

"I'm not sure I understand," replied Rhys. "What is the cycle of rebirth? And what is enlightenment?"

"Of course," smiled Maadurga. "You do not know our ways."

"Then explain to me."

"Samsara is the cycle," she began. "Our world is in the Forth Age: the Dark Age. In the First Age, after Brahma created the world, it was a time of perfection; our people were pure of heart. We were honest, kind, and untainted. Our people did not spoil the world. There was plenty for all. There was no war. There was no sickness, or age, and elvenkind was immortal. There was no need for worship, for the Trimurti walked upon the world, but they were just different faces of Brahman. All was good."

"Sounds perfect," responded Rhys. "I'm guessing it did not last."

"The first age ended when the Trimurti divided. When the three faces of the Trimurti broke apart, the sky quaked and the Cintamani Stone fell from the stars. It struck the sea, and a great flood covered the world, leaving only a small continent in the great ocean. In other places, the rivers receded, leaving barren wastes of desert.

"The world was no longer plentiful, and so our people were forced to farm the land and mine the mountains for the treasures they held; in doing so, they began to taint the beauty of the world. There was still enough for all, but greed had come to the world, and elvenkind began to fight for resources. The first wars were waged amongst the elves as their purity was diminished. We came to know death and disease, yet still our kind lived many thousands of years. Kings were needed to rule, and laws were needed to keep chaos at bay. It is in this time that the holy city of Shambala was built atop Sumeru for worship of the Trimurti, who now in their division spent less time upon the world. In their absence, the elves were often left to themselves, and in time they discovered knowledge that allowed them to manipulate Prana."

"And how did this age end?" asked Rhys.

"The Second Age ended when the Trimurti left the world and did not return," answered Maadurga. "Death became more common—elves lived only a few thousand years at a time. Our faith became vital in a world the gods did not visit, and the worshipers of Trimurti became divided across the peaks of Sumeru. They fought wars often between themselves. But throughout this age, our knowledge of Brahman and of Prana increased. We learnt of the Cintamani Stone and of its power; but it was soon considered too dangerous and was given to the followers of Brahma to protect. But the radical worshippers of Mahakala, the rakshasa, attacked Raraprambanan, the temple of Brahman, slaughtered his worshipers, and stole the Cintamani Stone for themselves. They took it to the Chaitya at the heart of Shambala and destroyed it. The destruction of the Cintamani Stone tore open a wound in Brahman and sundered Sumeru; the mountain's five peaks were scattered to the sky and an eternal storm raged across the seas. It is this apocalyptic event that ushered my people into the Fourth Age."

"Hence it being referred to as the dark age," surmised Rhys.

"Correct," nodded Maadurga. "The city of Shambala now sits atop the highest peak of Sumeru, high above the rest of the world where none can reach it, for it is protected by the Amara. The Amara will not allow any who has not achieved Nirvana, Enlightenment, from entering the city. With Sumeru torn apart, and entrance to the Golden City forbidden to the rest of my people, an age of darkness fell. We have lost the knowledge and wisdom of our ancestors. Food and wealth is scarce. We fight to defend our home against the rakshasa. We have begun to know age, and elves only live a few centuries at most."

"Wait!? A few centuries?" questioned

Rhys.

"Yes," replied Maadurga.

"How old are you?"

"I am young," she replied. "I am only recently one hundred and twenty-two."

"One hundred and twenty-two!?" Rhys repeated in disbelief. "You don't look it."

"I have been told by many that I appear mature for my age," she smiled, having clearly misinterpreted Rhys's surprise.

"Well," began Rhys, "let's just say you have a good few years on me."

"How old are you, Rhys?"

"Only twenty-four," responded the mage.

Maadurga studied his face for a long moment. "Your vessel ages fast," she declared. "Humans live such short but intense lives."

"You are telling me," returned Rhys.

"Curious, Kalki, that you should choose this body."

"What are the Amara?" asked Rhys. "Why do they prevent anyone from entering Shambala?"

"The Amara are the Ascendant, the Undying. They are those who have reached Nirvana and escaped the cycle of rebirth. They attack any outsiders who approach the fringes of Shambala."

"Undying?" questioned Rhys. "Like immortal? And what do you mean by the cycle of rebirth?"

"Samsara is the cycle of eternity. Our people believe that the Atman, the soul, is immortal, and that the body is merely a vessel."

"Most human religions believe the same," replied Rhys.

"We believe that when the body dies, the soul is reborn once more in a different vessel after each death. Whilst in the First Age the bodies of our people were immortal, the passing of the ages has seen the mortal lifespan of our physical bodies reduce drastically over time."

"A few hundred years doesn't seem so bad," replied Rhys.

"No, it is not," agreed Maadurga. "But our people, much like yours, fear death. The ultimate goal of any individual of our people is to follow Dharma, their duty and role within the world. Those who follow Dharma can achieve enlightenment and escape the cycle of reincarnation, liberating themselves from Samsara. Those that achieve Nirvana are known as the Amara. They are no longer beholden to the laws of mortality, for their vessels do not age."

"Okay," nodded Rhys, beginning to get a hold of all the Elven words Maadurga was using to explain the concepts. "What I still don't understand is, why would the rakshasa want to destroy Shambala? Why do they want me dead?"

"The prophecy."

"Sounds ominous," remarked Rhys.

"It is told that, after the Dark Age will

rise the Golden Age. The world will return to the state in which it was first created. All of elvenkind will achieve Nirvana and be liberated from Samsara."

"I follow," nodded Rhys.

"However, in order for the Golden Age to begin, the world must first be destroyed."

"And this is where the Destroyer, Mahakala, comes in, I'm guessing?"

"You are right. Mahakala is destined to destroy the world. Kalki the Protector is destined to reappear and stand in his way, but ultimately, he will fall in battle against Mahakala. Kalki, although the protector of the world and of our people, is also the harbinger of the end of time. That is why the rakshasa want you dead. You are the enemy of their god. They have seen your staff, and they know you to be what stands in the way of Nirvana."

"That doesn't make much sense," puzzled Rhys. "The end of time seems like a good thing in this story. And if Kalki is destined to be slain by Mahakala, then why do the rakshasa wish to kill me themselves? Why not allow their god to do it?"

"The prophecy has many interpretations," replied Maadurga, "and there are different versions of the foretelling. The Golden Age is believed by the followers of Mahakala to be the final age. However, the followers of Brahma and Kalki believe it to be the cycle restarting."

"You think the Golden Age is the same thing as the First Age?"

"Yes," confirmed Maadurga. "However, there are doubts as to whether the cycle will restart. Why would Kalki wish to stand in Mahakala's way? If he is the Protector, then why would he not want our people to achieve enlightenment?"

"Maybe Kalki isn't all that good," replied Rhys. "Or maybe he just doesn't think your people are ready."

"Or, maybe the end of time is just that," suggested Maadurga.

"You think there is not another age after this one?"

"We cannot know," replied Maadurga. "If Mahakala succeeds in destroying the world, and there is no Golden Age, then all will come to an end."

"I think I understand," nodded Rhys.

"We as the followers of Kalki do not deny the Golden Age, but we do not claim that it will come with the end of time. We do not know, and so, like Kalki himself, we fight to preserve and to protect the world in which we live. We know that enlightenment is possible without the end of this age. The Amara are proof of this. There is virtue and peace to be found, even in this dark time."

"But what of Mahakala defeating Kalki? If Kalki is destined to die in battle against

Mahakala, then what is the point in it all if it is predetermined?"

"In many accounts of the prophecy, Kalki fails and Mahakala brings the end of time. However, in others, in the versions that are told by our people, he is slain by Mahakala, but succeeds in stopping the Destroyer from ending Samsara. The Rakshasa fear these versions of the prophecy, as we fear the versions where Kalki is defeated. What is not clear, is whether Kalki is killed by Mahakala's own hand."

"Just that he is defeated in battle by him," replied Rhys.

"Yes," nodded Maadurga. "That is why the rakshasa come for you. They fear you possess the power to prevent Mahakala from ending the Dark Age, and they believe it might be the followers of the Destroyer rather than Mahakala himself that will slay Kalki."

"I understand now."

"It is a story that has endured for thousands of years, and one that speaks of the fate of our people. The rakshasa used the Cintamani Stone to destroy Sumeru. They believed they were already living in the Dark Age. They sought to destroy the world, believing they acted on Mahakala's behalf. The rakshasa at that time were a radical sect of the worshippers of Mahakala. The rest of the Destroyer's worshippers did not believe that they were living in the Fourth Age. Now however, it is clear that darkness is upon the world. We live in a desperate time and have done so for thousands of years. They seek the end of this age now more than ever. With the appearance of the Vritra, the dragon, the rakshasa came to revere it as the final incarnation of Mahakala."

"Why?" pressed the mage.

"It is said that Mahakala has taken many forms over time, but that his last incarnation would be his most terrible. Just as the weapon of Kalki is a jade staff, the weapon of Mahakala is a trident of fire."

"Ah..." uttered Rhys. "That makes a lot of sense."

"They revere the Vritra. They sacrifice your people who land upon the shores of Sumeru in offering to the beast. Perhaps it is because of this, that you have taken this human form, Kalki."

"Maadurga, I'm not who you think I am. I'm just a man. I'm not an incarnation of your god," Rhys insisted. "I am not Kalki."

"You do not believe it," replied Maadurga. "But I do. With each reincarnation, the souls of our people lose the memories of our previous lives. However, through meditation, one can occasionally catch glimpses of the past. It might be possible for you to see your previous lives."

"Glimpses of the past?" Rhys questioned. "Like dreams?"

"Dreams?" questioned Maadurga.

"You know..." began Rhys, trying to explain through the language barrier. "When you sleep, the images you see."

"Sleep?" questioned Maadurga.

Rhys shot her a curious look.

"Ah yes," she smiled. "When you humans lie down to rest."

"You can't seriously mean that—"

"Elves do not sleep."

"Uh huh," Rhys's eyes narrowed sceptically.

"It is true," Maadurga insisted.

"Sounds awfully tiring."

"We do rest," confirmed Maadurga. "But we merely need a few hours of meditation each day."

"Hmm," Rhys mumbled, at a loss of what else to say.

"Why do you ask of these dreams?" Maadurga questioned.

"You say that I might be able to see images of the past if I meditate?"

"Yes," nodded Maadurga. "Those of our people who spend their lives in worship, the Sadhu, can achieve a deep spiritual connexion to Brahman. This connexion can show whispers of that which once was."

"You don't say," chuckled Rhys.

"You have already heard these whispers?"

"Yes," nodded Rhys. "In dreams."

Maadurga smiled. "Because you are Kalki."

"I still don't know about that," resisted

Rhys.

"Then there is more for you to see."

"How can I see it?" questioned the mage. "The dreams don't come to me every night. They are random! Sometimes I go months without seeing anything. And when I do, it is only a short glimpse of a bigger story."

"I cannot teach you," Maadurga expressed regretfully. "My connexion to Brahman is as Kshatriya; I am of the warrior caste. You must speak to a Brahmin, a teacher of the holy caste."

"You mean like a priest or a monk?"

"Yes," nodded Maadurga. "We must take you to a sadhu."

"I'm not sure," hesitated Rhys. "I'm not one for religion."

"Sadhu study the ways of Brahman. They understand Prana in ways the rest of my kin do not."

"Alright," Rhys agreed. "Are there any down in the village?"

"No," smiled Maadurga.

"Of course there aren't," groaned the mage. "That would just be too easy."

"The Sadhu live in the Temple of Kalki."

"And where is that?"

"It is atop the highest peak of the Sacred Valley of Suraksa, Suraksameru, one of the five peaks of Sumeru"

"Oh, okay," grinned Rhys, scanning the valley to determine which was the highest peak.

"Its not too far then?"

"No," agreed Maadurga.

"Would you be able to fly me there on your gryphon by chance?" Rhys beamed at her.

She shook her head.

"Why's that?"

"It is forbidden to enter the temple from the skies. Any who reach the Temple of Kalki must follow the sacred trail and climb the mountain."

"Even Kalki himself?" Rhys smiled wryly.

"Even Kalki himself," Maadurga smiled back.

"I see."

"It is Kalki that first made the climb."

"I take it that it is some form of pilgrimage?"

"Yes," nodded Maadurga. "You understand."

"Do I have to go alone?"

"No," assured the elf. "Others may accompany you on your journey."

"Well, at least there is that," replied Rhys. "Will you come?"

"I will," agreed the elf amiably.

"Thank you," beamed the mage.

"The Sadhu will help you if you make this journey. It will prove to them that you are Kalki. They will help you to see Brahman as they do."

TWENTY-THREE

Rhys and Maadurga entered the village together from down the hillside to see the elven inhabitants gathering in the square. As the mage and elf drew nearer to the crowd, many of the villagers turned and greeted them both, parting slightly to reveal Rhys's friends centred in the group.

"Rhys!" Thia called out upon seeing him.

There were cries of greeting from the elves in their own tongue, all referring to him as Kalki as they lowered their heads; then, to Rhys and his friends' amazement, one by one, the elves began to kneel in the street, bowing in reverence to the man they believed an incarnation of their god. Silence quickly descended as Rhys and the others stared around at the veneration directed his way.

"What are they doing?" Rhys whispered to Maadurga.

"They are praying," she replied.

"To me?"

"Yes."

Rhys glanced to his friends; they each shot him confused looks. He turned his attention to the congregation gathered at his feet. "Tell them to stand," insisted the mage.

Maadurga nodded. "Khada," she uttered.

After a few moments, the villagers all slowly rose to their feet.

"Explain to them that I am not Kalki."

"They will not believe it," replied Maadurga.

"Why?"

"They have long awaited your arrival, Kalki. Times have grown desperate. The rakshasa close upon the borders of the Sacred Valley, and yesterday they dared attack the gates, something they have never done before. They did so in pursuit of you. You have arrived at the darkest hour—when you are needed most, just as it was foretold you would. You may not believe it, Rhys, but the rakshasa do. My people have been taught the stories of Kalki since before humans first walked this world. You carry the weapon of Kalki, and you are Jhakri, a sorcerer. To them, and to me, you are Kalki."

"Okay," paused Rhys. "Well tell them that I don't want to be worshipped. I want them to treat me the same as they would my companions."

"As you wish," nodded Maadurga. "Kalki

puja garna cahamdanan. Usala jasto yavahara garunhola."

"Kalki vinamra cha!" cried several of the elves.

"What does that mean?" questioned Rhys.

"They say that you are humble."

Rhys peered around himself once more at the dozens of smiling faces silently observing him. "Are they just going to keep watching me like this?"

"Sathihara, tapa inko kamama parkanuhos," spoke Maadurga, addressing the throng.

The gathering of elves chatted amongst themselves, several bowing their heads respectfully Rhys's way before the crowd steadily dispersed and the elves once more went about their business.

"What did you say to them?" questioned the mage.

"I merely said you wished for them to return to their preparations for the festival."

"Festival?"

"Karkasankranti," replied Maadurga. "The long day."

"The long day?" repeated Rhys. "You mean Midsummer? The solstice?"

"Yes," smiled Maadurga. "It is tomorrow."

"Already!?" questioned Rhys in disbelief, his mind wandering rapidly to visions of home.

"What was that about?" questioned Sol as he and the others emerged through the dispersing elves.

"They just think I am the reincarnation of their god," replied Rhys nonchalantly. "No big deal."

"Right," replied Sol warily. "Glad to see it's not gone to your head."

"Where have you been?" asked Thia eyeing Maadurga at his side. "We've been looking for you."

"I couldn't sleep," replied Rhys. "I didn't want to wake the rest of you."

"What time is it even?" questioned Nathaniel. "I'm not sure I've ever slept so late into the day before!"

"I reckon its late morning," replied Cade glancing at the sun's position in the sky as it approached its zenith. "Probably not long past eleven o'clock."

"Maadurga?" Alkis addressed her gently. "Are we safe here? From the Wild Hunt?" he added, looking up at the open skies.

The elf nodded. "The rakshasa will not enter the Sacred Valley. It is the abode of Kalki, not Mahakala; the Trimurti swore in the Second Age not to trespass in each other's domains. They cannot enter unless welcomed through the gates; to do so from the sky violates Dharma."

"Right," remarked the knight, clearly having not understood much of what the elf had said.

"Dharma is their religious duty," explained Rhys from what he had been told by Maadurga. "Entering the valley would be a sin," he surmised.

"Oh—okay," nodded Alkis. "So, we are safe then?"

"Yes," smiled Maadurga.

"It seems you two have been talking," remarked Thia.

"Is that where you have been?" questioned Sol.

"I figured if I can't stop the elves from seeing me as a religious figure, then I had better brush up on the basics," replied Rhys.

"What did you learn?" questioned his fellow mage. "Anything that can help?"

"I reckon I got the short story," replied Rhys, looking to Maadurga. "But I think I understand."

"Well, tell us then," insisted Thia impatiently.

"To make a short version of a long story even shorter," began the mage. "Kalki is one of the three Elven gods. He is the protector, destined to stand in the way of Mahakala, the destroyer. His appearance heralds the end of the world, that may or may not usher in a golden age, after he either is or isn't defeated by Mahakala. The elves think I'm Kalki because my staff resembles his jade weapon. Because of this, the Cŵn Annwn want me dead so that they can end the world, so the Golden Age can begin.

"What about the conduit?" questioned Sol.

"It's in Shambhala, the ancient holy city of the elves. I reckon its on the highest peak of what seemed once to be a single mountain range. The problem is, the city is said to be inaccessible, and is protected by supposedly immortal elven guardians from anyone who would try and enter it."

"Well that's problematic," sighed Thia.

"It would seem that the Stormy Isles were once a single mountain range. Maadurga said that Sumeru was ripped apart when the Cintamani Stone, an ancient arcane weapon that fell from the sky, was detonated in the conduit in the heart of Shambhala. The destruction of the Cintamani Stone ripped a hole in the Aether, hence the aurora visible overhead, the result of which tore the mountain apart and lifted it into the sky."

"That seems unlikely," doubted Sol as he peered up at the faint whispers of purple weaving between the clouds.

"It lines up with your stories of Thule, doesn't it?" questioned Ulfgar.

"Vaguely, yes," conceded Sol. "But the Aether is only a theory, and not even a widely accepted one at that. Ripping a hole in it doesn't exactly sound feasible. And a magical weapon that fell from the sky capable of rending mountains from the world? It just seems a little far-fetched."

"Wait a moment," protested Ulfgar. "Didn't Woden's spear supposedly come from the sky?"

"It was a lightning bolt," replied Sol. "Of course it came from the sky."

"But the Tablets say that Woden's spear, the weapon belonging to the king of the Titans, came from the sky, don't they?" pressed the dwarf.

"Technically yes," agreed Sol.

"Don't the tablets also say that the Titans destroyed the island of Thule with a storm?" questioned Rhys.

"Yes, they do," nodded Sol.

"A lightning spear from the sky, and a storm that rips an island from the sea; a magical weapon that falls from the heavens, used to tear a mountain apart, which in turn causes an ever-raging storm," recited Rhys. "Stop me if anyone disagrees, but I'm noticing a lot of similarities here."

"Me too," nodded Ulfgar.

Sol scowled silently at Rhys and the dwarf.

"And if Woden is the head of the Wild Hunt..." continued Rhys. "Did I forget to mention that it was the rakshasa that used the Cintamani Stone to destroy Sumeru?"

"That is a remarkable coincidence," agreed Thia.

"That's just it," insisted Rhys. "I don't

think it is a coincidence at all."

"It is," resisted Sol, though Rhys could tell from the doubt in his friend's eyes that he did not wholly believe it.

"Rhys!" intervened Alkis, noticing that Sol had become visibly upset.

"What is the plan then?" asked Thia, changing the subject. "There must be some way to reach Shambhala."

"There are no bridges," explained Maadurga, "and the city is guarded by the Amara."

"Would it be possible to fly there?" questioned Rhys.

"It is not impossible," responded the elf. "But the storm is at its worst there. The closer to the Akasa, the fiercer the Sakti becomes."

"Sakti?" asked Rhys.

"The force of the world," explained Maadurga. "It moves things towards ground."

"Gravity?" questioned Thia.

"Yes," replied Maadurga. "Here, the Sakti moves mostly downwards. But higher up in the storm, closer to the Akasa, the Sakti moves in twisting paths. But the flow of the Sakti is often invisible without rain. It makes it difficult to read and very hard to fly. Only riders that know the hidden ways can follow the paths of Sakti safely and make it to the upper peaks of Sumeru."

"But there are those who know the way?" questioned Thia.

"Not any of the followers of Kalki," returned Maadurga.

"Then who does?" questioned Alkis.

"The rakshasa," returned the elf. "The Vritra's lair is on Kalapa, the second highest peak of Sumeru. It is not far from Shambhala. It is there the rakshasa take their prisoners to be sacrificed to Mahakala."

"If its not far, then you think we could make it across from Kalapa to Shambhala?" questioned Rhys.

"It would be very, very dangerous," returned Maadurga.

"But do you think it would be possible?" pressed the mage.

"Maybe," returned Maadurga.

"Wait," interjected Sol. "I'm having a bit of trouble keeping up here. Are you suggesting that we follow the Wild Hunt into the heart of the storm, to the lair of a leviathan in order to fly across to an ancient city protected by immortal guardians, so that we can reach the conduit?"

"I have to agree with Sol on this one," sighed Alkis. "It does sound pretty crazy."

"I'm not suggesting anything of the sort," assured Rhys.

The others exhaled in relief.

"At least, not right now," added the mage.

"You mean you are considering it then?" asked Thia.

"If it is the only option, then I am not ruling it out," replied Rhys. "But if we were to entertain such an insane idea, then I wouldn't do so without some sort of plan."

"You would need many warriors to make it past the Amara," insisted Maadurga.

"I figured as much."

"My people," began the elf, "they would fight for you."

"Why would they?" questioned Thia.

"To help Kalki reach the holy city."

"No," refused Rhys. "I'm not having your people serve as martyrs for my cause."

"If you ask, they will," assured Maadurga.

"Rhys," murmured Nathaniel, gesturing for a private word with the mage

Rhys shuffled away from Maadurga and leant in towards the guardsman.

"Maybe you should think about her offer," suggested the guardsman.

"You can't be serious!?"

"If these elves would fight for you..." he began. "All I am saying is, we came all this way to find the stone circle. If this is the way to reach it —I reckon you should think very carefully about refusing this kind of help."

"And just use these people to achieve our own goals?" disapproved Rhys.

"People have fought and died for you before," insisted Nathaniel. "Think about it; the Kings' Crypt, the Battle for Orthios? How is this any different?"

"Because those fighting weren't doing so

for me! They were fighting for our cause. They were fighting for their home. They were fighting to stop Indus!"

"And these people would be fighting for their beliefs!"

"I'd be exploiting them through charlatanry!" refused Rhys. "I'm not what they think I am. I cannot ask them to fight for me."

"It could be the only way," insisted Nathaniel.

"We'll find another way."

"What will it be then, Kalki?" questioned Maadurga as Rhys and Nathaniel turned back to the others. "Do you wish us to fight for you."

"No," Rhys refused. "We'll find another way to Shambhala."

"As you command," replied the elf. "Then you wish to make the pilgrimage to the Temple of Kalki? To learn the ways of Brahman and hear the teachings of the Sadhu?"

"I think so," nodded the mage.

"The teachings of the Sadhu?" questioned Thia.

"There is a temple, just up the mountain from the valley," explained Rhys. "Apparently the Sadhu, the monks there, know a lot about the Aether."

"If the Rift is as Maadurga says, a tear in the Aether, then it would certainly help to learn more about it," replied the witch.

"Hang on," interjected Sol, "where has this

come from? The Temple of Kalki? Why are you heading there?"

"There are things I need to understand," Rhys returned, vaguely alluding to his dreams. "Maadurga says the Sadhu can teach me about the Aether, and I think she might be right."

"But you don't believe in any of the gods. Why would you want to visit a holy temple?" questioned the mage. "You aren't converting to the Trimurti?"

"No," assured Rhys. "All I know is, magic behaves differently in this part of the world than any other place we have visited. If there is a chance that we can learn more, then it would better prepare us if we are to venture higher up the mountains. If there is any truth to the Elven myths about the Rift and the Cintamani Stone, then I think it is worth investigating. The more we know, the better we understand, the better we can plan for reaching the conduit."

"Alright," conceded Sol. "How do we get to this temple?"

"You have to make the journey on foot," explained Rhys. "Maadurga is going to show me the way. It is located atop the highest peak of the Suraksa valley."

"You are going alone?" questioned Thia.

"This is something I have to do," insisted Rhys. "I don't expect any of you to come with me."

"Would the rest of us be welcome?" asked

Sol.

"All followers of Kalki are welcome," insisted Maadurga.

"But we don't believe in the Trimurti," replied the mage.

"And yet, still you follow Kalki," she smiled, looking then to Rhys.

"She has a point," murmured Cade.

"But Rhys isn't Kalki," replied Sol.

"They think he is though," chuckled Nathaniel.

"Do you even want any of us to come with you?" questioned Thia.

"Of course I do," asserted Rhys. "But I'm not sure there is much point in us all going. It could be a waste of time. There is no guarantee there will actually be any answers."

"I want to come," insisted Thia. "If there is anything to be learnt of the Aether, then I should probably be there. I know a bit more about it then you do. Besides," she added with a wink, "we can't let you have all the fun!"

"Thank you," beamed Rhys.

"I suppose I should probably come too," agreed Sol. "I don't buy into the concept of the Aether, but if there is something to be learnt about the magic in this place, then I would like to hear of it."

"And the rest of you?" questioned Rhys.

"Say the word and I'm with you," replied Cade. "But the arcane is beyond my area of expertise. I'm not sure what help I'd offer."

"The lad is right," agreed Ulfgar. "This journey is for the three of you. The rest of us have no business coming."

"I agree," concurred Alkis. "Rhys, if you want me to come I will, but I don't think there will be any merit in it. If this valley is safeguarded from invaders, then my sword is of little use to you."

"We might be better off saving our strength and resting here in the valley," added Nathaniel. "If we do decide to make an attempt at Shambala, we will need to be at our best."

"Okay," agreed Rhys. "So it is Thia, Sol, and I."

"When do you want to leave?" questioned Thia. "Today?"

"We cannot leave today," returned Maadurga. "We must wait until after the festival."

"Festival?" questioned Sol.

"Karkasankranti," replied Maadurga. "It is against Dharma to begin such a pilgrimage during the holy time."

"Its their Midsummer celebration," explained Rhys.

"Of course!" exclaimed Sol. "The solstice is tomorrow, isn't it? I had almost completely forgotten!"

"Very well," agreed Rhys. "I've never been one to miss a party. We'll leave once the festival is over."

"There is something else," put in Sol.

"What is it?" questioned Rhys.

"Arne, Vidar, and Eirik. Now that we know about the Wild Hunt, about how they take the castaways to be sacrificed to the leviathan... we must see if they are okay. We have to warn them!"

"*We* could head back down to the beach," suggested Alkis.

"You have friends?" questioned Maadurga. "Outside of Suraksa?"

"Yes," explained Sol. "They are repairing our ship. They don't know about the rakshasa."

"My kshatriya can find them," assured Maadurga. "They can be brought here where it is safe."

"I'm not sure they'd want that," replied Sol. "I doubt they'd abandon the Marlin... the ship that is. I need to head down, I need to explain to them about the Hunt... about the castaways."

"Sol, the beach is at least three days away!" warned Alkis. "That's almost a week there and back."

"I can send kshatriya to watch over them," offered Maadurga. "I can tell your friends of the rakshasa, and my warriors can watch the beach and ensure no harm comes to your friends."

"That would be amazing," sighed Sol with relief.

"I will prepare to ride out after noon," returned the elf.

TWENTY-FOUR

Rhys wandered along the path as it skirted the hillside above the flooded rice paddies; dozens of elves were stooped, wading through the water-logged fields, harvesting the verdant crop with kukris in the baking sun. The path doubled back as it ascended the subalpine slope. Rhys followed the crisscrossing runs of prayer flags until the hilltop prevailed beyond the brow. The mage could hear Maadurga before he saw her, speaking softly in the melodic Elven Tongue. When Rhys first caught sight of her, garbed in her mirror armour, he paused suddenly in his tracks. She was tending to her mount: an enormous gryphon with a burnt orange coat and plumage; black striations banded across the beast's back and flanks, whilst the feathers of its breast and the pelage of its underbelly transitioned to a snowy white. The giant hybrid nuzzled its raptor head against Maadurga's hand as she ran her slender fingers over the creature's monstrous hooked beak and rustled its feathers, all the while, she whispered sweetly to the gryphon.

Overcoming his trepidation, Rhys stepped closer. Upon noticing the mage, the gryphon reared its head and screeched, raising its hackles and flaring its wings in a warning display. Maadurga peered back over her shoulder to see the mage approaching. Palming her mount's beak, she promptly calmed the beast. The gryphon bowed its head, soothed by his master, and with the creature at ease, Maadurga revolved steadily to face the mage.

"How can I help you, Kalki?" she greeted him, surprised to see Rhys atop the hill.

"It's okay. I'm not after you—just needed to get away," explained Rhys. "I didn't realise you were here."

She smiled affably. "Why is it you wish to get away?"

"It was just a bit much," began Rhys. "The village... everyone staring at me..." he continued, evading the truth.

"You wished to be alone," surmised Maadurga.

"Yes."

"Why?" she pressed bluntly.

Rhys couldn't help but chuckle at her forwardness. "I don't think the others realise," he started, now giving the elf the true reason he had set off to wander aimlessly alone through the valley of Suraksa. "Remember how I told you that my home was destroyed?"

"Like Sumeru," she nodded.

"Well," continued the mage diffidently, "it was a year ago tomorrow."

Maadurga blinked slowly in understanding. "The memories return to you now."

Rhys smiled weakly, offering a single nod.

"What happened?"

The mage emitted a low sigh, the kind that proceeds the telling of a story delivered countless times before, the coupled pain dulled with each retelling. "It was a curse," explained Rhys. "Dark magic—conjured by my enemy."

Maadurga nodded slowly in response, clearly realising that Rhys would rather not speak of it. "Come closer," she gestured, turning back to rustle her gryphon's plumage.

"Are you sure?" queried Rhys, warily taking a few tentative steps towards Maadurga and her monstrous mount.

"His name is Dawon," reassured the elf. "He will not hurt you."

"He *looks* pretty dangerous."

"Come!" she insisted.

Apprehensively, Rhys approached. Maadurga reached out and took Rhys's hand in hers. Delicately, she cupped the back of Rhys's hand in her palm and manoeuvred the mage's fingers to within inches of the gryphon. Dawon cocked his head without warning and clicked his beak. Rhys withdrew anxiously.

"Santan," breathed Maadurga, calming her mount. "Do not worry," insisted the elf, once more moving Rhys's finger's closer.

Seconds later, Rhys felt the beast's plumage beneath his fingertips. Carefully, he caressed the creature's soft pinnae. Dawon tilted his head and stared at Rhys with his two enormous eagle eyes, and to the mage's wonder, the creature began to softly nuzzle his beak against the mage's arm.

"Wow," exclaimed the mage with a half chuckle.

"He likes you," remarked Maadurga as Rhys stepped back to admire the fiercely majestic animal from a safer distance.

"How do you even train a creature like that?"

"We rear them from eggs," elucidated Maadurga. "They are our Vahana—our mounts. They are important to our culture. Dawon is my companion as much as he is my servant—I am the same to him. There is a bond between rider and Vahana. Some will not let any but their masters mount them."

"That's okay," replied Rhys. "I have no intention of flying any time soon."

"Dawon has taken to you," insisted Maadurga. "If you earnt his trust, he might in time let you ride him."

"No, I'd rather keep my feet on the

ground," assured Rhys sheepishly. "I have enough trouble staying on the back of a horse —I had a bad experience not that long ago," he added, his memory quickly flitting to when he was dragged several furlongs by the stirrup during their flight from Orthios.

"As you wish, Kalki," smiled Maadurga. "Will you help me ready Dawon? I am preparing to ride to your ship."

"Yes, of course," beamed Rhys, noticing now the pile of tacking lain upon the ground.

"Rest your hand on Dawon's neck," instructed Maadurga.

Hesitantly, Rhys approached the gryphon once more and rested his palm on the creature's feather's, drawing the hybrid's predatory gaze. Deftly, whilst both Rhys and Dawon's attention was on one another, Maadurga dropped a leather hood over the gryphon's head, lacing it tightly around the back of his neck, effectively blindfolding the beast. Rhys leapt back as Dawon softly clicked his beak, expecting the enormous mount to rear up in protest; instead, the response was in complete juxtaposition to what Rhys had predicted. The moment the beast's gaze was covered, Dawon relaxed; his jittering head movements ceased, his wings slackened, and his entire demeanour became eerily sedate. Sitting back on his haunches, Dawon's hooded head faced forwards, his frame falling entirely still as if he'd settled down to roost.

"They are calmed when they cannot see," Maadurga explained. "Here," she added, handing Rhys a saddlecloth for the mage to drape over the gryphon's back.

Together they tacked Dawon, securing a leather saddle with unusually short stirrups and a flat backed cantle atop the saddle cloth. Maadurga effortlessly slotted a bit into the gryphon's beak, and loosening the hood, positioned the bridle. Then, removing the hood altogether, Maadurga fastened the headgear swiftly around Dawon and leapt up into the saddle, taking the reins.

"I will find your friends and give them your message," assured Maadurga. "Some of my kshatriya will join me in flight. They will remain behind, to keep watch and ensure no harm comes to them."

"When will you be back?" questioned the mage.

"Before nightfall," promised the elf as she flashed a smile at Rhys.

"I'll see you then."

"You might want to step back," warned Maadurga, gesturing for Rhys to give Dawon a wide berth.

Rhys retreated several steps and watched as Dawon's enormous wingspan unfolded on the gentle mountain breeze. The gryphon flared its pinions, and with several powerful strokes, it pounced into the air and took to the sky. In mere seconds, Maadurga was soaring high above, making her way towards the peaks on the far side of the dale. As she neared the top of the ridge, several more gryphon riders took to the sky, assembling into a vee formation behind Maadurga and Dawon. Rhys smiled to himself as he watched them fade from view. Once they had vanished into the clouds, he turned and made his way back down the path towards Suraksa.

Arriving back in the village, Rhys was once more greeted by the smiles and stares of the elven inhabitants. Preparations were underway for the upcoming solstice festival; a bonfire was being constructed in the square, windchimes were being hung from the eves of every building in the village, and women and children were braiding hundreds of jasmine garlands. More instrumentalists had joined the band playing in the street and the smells of sweets and spices melted through the air.

Rhys sighted the others sitting gathered on a grass verge overlooking the village and made his way over to them.

"Hey," smiled Thia as Rhys planted himself on the sward beside her.

"This is all a bit surreal, isn't it?" determined Cade as he greeted the mage.

"Yeah," nodded Rhys. "I'm not quite sure what to make of it."

"I did not know what to expect when we first set sail for the Stormy Isles," confessed Sol.

"This... I couldn't even conceive of it."

"Where have you been?" questioned Thia.

"I just went for a walk," replied Rhys. "Came upon our friend Maadurga."

"Oh yes?"

"I stroked her gryphon," added the mage.

"Is that some kind of euphemism?" questioned Ulfgar.

"What!? No!" objected Rhys.

"Just checking," chortled the dwarf.

"Let's not get too friendly with the locals," warned Sol.

"What are you talking about?" questioned Rhys.

"All I'm saying, Rhys, is that it seems like Maadurga likes you an awful lot," explained Sol. "These elves are the only people we have come across on these islands that haven't immediately attacked us. We cannot risk complicating things."

"Maadurga likes me because she thinks I am an incarnation of her god," assured Rhys agitatedly. "There is nothing else to it!"

"And that puts you in a very dangerous position," warned Sol.

"You don't think I know that?" scoffed Rhys.

"I know you do," conceded Sol. "Just... be careful."

"I will—I *am* being careful," insisted Rhys.

"I trust you," reassured Sol, pausing for

a moment before he continued. "You have what Indus wants: reverence. The way these elves perceive you... that's what he wants for himself back on the continent."

"I don't know," Rhys shook his head. "I think there is more to it."

"What do you mean?" questioned Sol.

"He wants to be worshipped, that much is clear, but I can't help but think it goes deeper than his own ego."

"It grants power," replied Sol.

"Its more than that," insisted Rhys. "Lords and kings have power, but only the sort of power that comes from loyalty or fear. Whereas gods... their power is greater, it comes from veneration. There is a level of devotion that can only come from believing someone or something to be divine; that level of devotion does not *inspire* loyalty, it necessitates it! It doesn't just conjure fear but ensures it. Lords, kings, and even emperors can be overturned and overthrown; they can be betrayed by those closest to them and conquered by enemies that come from afar. But a god's rule..."

"It's eternal," finished Thia.

"You are right," agreed Sol. "It would make his rule unquestionable."

"The level of following which religion inspires... it is blind and infallible. It can make people commit atrocities without thinking. It can dictate and replace an individual's own moral values without question or scrutiny. Faith can bend people into servitude in ways mortal rulers cannot. Kings and emperors themselves are considered to be beholden to their gods' divine will. If Indus is successful in convincing the populace that he is a god, then he guarantees his reign."

"It is self-policing," added Thia. "The gods themselves do not exact punishment on those who commit crimes against their religions—sinners; punishment is dealt upon those who do not conform by the followers themselves."

"It is not crucial for everyone to believe, so long as enough do," continued Rhys. "Religious leaders—those who supposedly hold the strongest of faiths, they are more often than not those left to judge and convict; they ensure that the laws of religion are followed to the letter. If such a system were established in a kingdom or empire, as Indus intends, then he has established one that maintains itself with little influence on his behalf."

"I hadn't given it so much thought," confessed Sol.

"I understand the dangers of belief," summarised Rhys, "more than you know Sol. I fear what these elves think of me in much the same way I fear what the people of Cambria believe of Indus. Faith is a very dangerous thing."

TWENTY-FIVE

Rhys sipped hot chhaang through a straw out of a wooden mug as he watched the bonfire rage; elven bards chanted in their hypnotic tongue, plucking the strings of sitars, strumming sarangi, fluting shehnai, banging tablas, and jingling kanjira. All around the fire, dancers wove with supernatural elegance and grace, wending to and fro with chimes and bells jangling from their wrists and ankles. The Rift burned emerald in the night sky, weaving in gleaming ribbons under a galaxy of stars. Down beneath the heavenly display, cool winds swilled about the valley, carrying the bonfire's embers upward into tumbling currents; the sparks hung suspended aloft in the airflow for a time, before finally descending like glowing snowfall as they faded and cooled throughout Suraksa.

"Quite nice, this stuff," remarked a cheery Sol as the mage took another swig of the warm fermented rice drink.

"Remarkably similar to ale," agreed Rhys as they watched the elves celebrating. "As far as midsummer festivals go, this isn't half bad."

"Its certainly beats eating rotten fish," chirped Sol. "Do you think they are alright?" the mage added more sombrely. "Arne, Vidar, and Eirik?"

"I'm sure they are fine," smiled Rhys reassuringly. "Maadurga went herself, and she took half a dozen kshatriya with her."

"I know," replied Sol, "but she's not come back yet. Arne, Eirik, Vidar... they are family to me."

"I understand," affirmed Rhys. "Trust me, they will be fine. They are probably celebrating themselves right now!"

"Probably insisting Maadurga try their surströmming!" jested Sol.

"That sounds like them," agreed Rhys. The mage's eyes unfocussed from the crowd, as through the movement of the dancers, he sighted Maadurga making her way towards them. "Look," gestured the mage, pointing out the elf as she drew nearer. "Here she comes now."

"Maadurga!" Sol accosted her enthusiastically as he and Rhys rose to greet her.

Maadurga was dressed for the celebration, adorned in a colourful gold embroidered lehenga choli. Her dark hair was up, revealing the delicate golden jewellery linked in fine chains about her slender bronze neck. Across her fingers and forearms, intricate patterns of henna decorated her smooth skin. Her large blue eyes twinkled in the firelight as she gazed on the two magi, her lips curving into a warm smile as she offered them a subtle curtsy. She was breath-taking, such that Sol fumbled at his next words before eventually managing to compose a sentence.

"You... what... Ahem." He cleared his throat and started over. "How are they?"

"They are good," beamed Maadurga. "A little wary at first. But when your names were said, they were put at ease."

"Thank goodness," relaxed Sol, audibly sighing with relief.

"They were friendly," responded Maadurga. "They were very insistent that we try their fish."

"They didn't!?" questioned Rhys with disbelief.

"I'm so sorry!" apologised Sol with embarrassment.

"It was... interesting," smiled Maadurga.

Rhys laughed heartily.

"You can say that you hated it," replied Sol. "Neither of us will be offended."

"I very much hated it," returned the elf smiling broadly.

"Thank you," beamed Rhys, "for checking on them. You didn't have to do that."

"They are friends of Kalki," she returned. "You are most welcome."

"It means a lot to me," added Sol.

Maadurga nodded. "Come," she gesticulated, offering a hand to Rhys, "let us dance."

"I don't know about that," hesitated the mage. "I wouldn't want to embarrass you."

"What do you mean?"

"I am not really one for dancing."

"You can't dance?" questioned Sol in disbelief. "That's impossible. I've watched your footwork when we spar. Its amazing! No way you can't dance."

"You'd be surprised," remarked Rhys.

"Trust me, *I am*," insisted Sol.

"Everyone can dance," returned Maadurga. "It is like breathing. We all must do it when our body demands. It comes naturally to all."

"Well, I can certainly dance," assured Rhys. "Just not very well."

"You must," urged Maadurga, holding her hand out.

"I can't," apologised Rhys. "But I tell you who would love to…"

"You're not roping *me* into embarrassing myself in front of everyone," insisted Sol.

"The thought hadn't even crossed my mind," lied Rhys.

"Sure it hadn't," returned Sol with a knowing grin.

"Alkis," Rhys suggested, nodding in the direction of their friend. The knight, sat not far away, was tapping his feet and swaying his head as he watched the fluid elven figures encircle the flames. "I'm sure he would love to dance with you, Maadurga."

Maadurga beamed warmly at Rhys. "I will ask him," she returned, bowing her head gracefully as she excused herself from their company.

"A woman that beautiful..." Sol began. "Some would say you are a madman for turning her away, Rhys."

"Wasn't it *you* that recommended me, only a few hours ago, not to get too friendly with the locals?" returned Rhys as the two of them watched Maadurga make her way over towards Alkis, the knight oblivious to her coming.

"I never actually expected you to heed my advice," smirked Sol. "You never normally do!"

Maadurga greeted Alkis and the two exchanged a few words before the elf extended a slender hand to him. The knight grinned dumbfoundedly, nodding his head with enthusiasm before rising to his feet and taking Maadurga's hand.

"All I know is," continued Sol, "you've really done Alkis a favour there."

"What are friends for?" returned Rhys as they watched Alkis follow Maadurga out towards the fire.

Together, the elf and the knight began to dance, Maadurga elegantly weaving her arms and swaying her hips as she lightly pranced around the bonfire. To both Sol and Rhys's amazement, Alkis likewise began to rock rhythmically with composure. With little warning, the knight broke into an Iarbhaile step, the jig performed with fluid military precision. Despite the dance's striking juxtaposition to the Elven lavani his partner was performing, the two somehow complemented one another, Alkis and Maadurga coming together, moving synchronously in a bizarre yet captivating exchange.

"Well, I'll be..." chortled Sol. "The bastard can really dance."

"You doubted he could?" questioned Rhys. "He was a knight of the Iarbhaile Courts!"

"I suppose it should have been obvious, really," concluded Sol. "His footwork is maybe even better than yours."

"Let's not get ahead of ourselves here."

"He's showing the rest of us up."

"Its not exactly difficult to do," mocked Rhys, indicating to Ulfgar who was stood not much further away.

The dwarf was swaying out of time with the music with an inebriated grin stricken across his bearded face. He clutched not one, but two large mugs of chhaang.

"Someone isn't going to make it until dawn," remarked Sol.

"I wouldn't be so sure of that either," argued Rhys. "This is *Ulfgar* you're talking about."

"Point taken," agreed Sol. "He can drink

more than the both of us combined."

The two mages chuckled, continuing to chat light-heartedly with one another as the evening drew on. They drank, ate spicy food, and watched the village dance to the music around the warmth of the fire. After a time, Rhys was left on his own, as Sol, now under the influence of half a dozen mugs of chhaang, joined the merrymaking around the bonfire. The mage remained seated on the bank, watching the shadowy figures of elves and men undulate around the flames as instruments hummed, twanged, and chimed late into the night. The aurora overhead continued to blaze, and Rhys's mind was transported to six months earlier, to the winter solstice, the night he first became a mage. Then, his memories delved further back still; exactly a year earlier, Rhys had been merely a few hours away from awakening to find the world dead. The Grey had come during the night, sapping all life from Longford. He remembered waking in an icy chill, stepping out into a sullen world consumed by curse. He remembered their vacant glassy eyes, the dead gazing hauntingly back at him. He remembered the smothering gloom. Then, he remembered the soft glow, that against all impossibility, pierced through the deathly haze and summoned him forth into the light.

"Is this seat taken?" came the genteel voice of Thia, stirring Rhys from his wallowing.

Rhys gazed up, offering a forced smile and

meeting the witch's eyes. It was the first Rhys had seen of her this evening; she was dressed in a teal and silver sari that hugged her slender figure, the colours mirroring her sapphire eyes and platinum tresses. She smirked at Rhys flirtatiously and suddenly the mage's painful reverie faded to distant memory, his own smile losing any sense of falsehood.

"Do you like it?" she questioned, twirling from side to side as she caressed the silken fabric between her delicate fingers.

Rhys nodded speechlessly. "You look..."

"Nice?" suggested Thia knowingly.

"I think that might be underselling it," returned the mage with a wry smirk. "Where did you get it?"

Rhys had only ever known Thia to wear her threadbare travelling gear. Apparelled now in fine silks, the grime of their long arduous quest washed away, her face subtly painted with makeup, her hair neatly combed and plaited, it was if he was seeing her for the first time anew.

"Maadurga lent it to me," explained Thia. "But you still haven't answered my question."

As Rhys looked Thia up and down he realised he was gawking. Snapping out of his ogle, he respectfully returned his gaze to eye level. "Your question...?"

"Is this seat taken?" repeated Thia, gesturing to the unoccupied sward of grass beside Rhys.

"I'm afraid I'm saving it for someone special," teased Rhys.

"Oh?" she raised an eyebrow. "And who is this mysterious someone?"

"Why don't you take a seat, and maybe you'll find out?"

Thia giggled and planted herself on the bank close to Rhys. "You know—you can be quite the smooth-talker when you want to be."

"It's all a facade, I promise," assured Rhys. "I just say whatever first comes into my head, and as if by some incredible streak of luck, it often works out in my favour."

"No, it's not," insisted the witch as she subtly shuffled even closer to Rhys so that their shoulders touched. "You say what you mean... not what you think other people want to hear. No one else does that."

Rhys turned and beamed warmly at her, and amongst the blades of grass, their fingertips found each other.

"It's Longford," asserted Thia. "Isn't it?"

Rhys nodded solemnly, his gaze drifting vacantly back towards the celebration at the foot of the slope.

"We all know," assured the witch. "None of us have forgotten that it was a year ago. We agreed between us not to mention it, lest you be reminded. Foolish really—since we first entered this valley, your mind has dwelt on little else—even with all that is happening around us."

"What do you want me to say?" pressed

Rhys, unable to divert his eyes from the festival.

"Nothing," returned the witch. "Or everything. Or something." She wrapped herself gently around Rhys's arm, hugging him tight, resting her head on his shoulder as she too gazed ahead at the dancers. "If you want to talk, I'll listen," she assured. "But equally, if you don't, I'm still here."

Rhys tilted his head so that it came to rest against Thia's. "Thank you."

They sat in silence for a time.

Eventually rising, they wandered hand in hand beyond the borders of the village. The silver moonlight intermingled with the ephemeral shades of violet, amber, and jade weaving through the Rift, illuminating the valley in a transient light that could never settle on a single shade. The mage and the witch exchanged few words as they sauntered amongst the flooded paddies. They ambled over fast flowing rills, listening to the susurrus of water that filled the silence; they strolled through copses of red maple and listened to the sough of leaves fluttering in the valley breeze. Nature spoke in the quietude for them. Neither Rhys nor Thia felt the need to speak as they meandered through the still and tranquil dale; each other's company and the splendid wonders of the world around them said all that needed to be said.

After a time, they arrived atop a shelf perched high in the foothills, overlooking the village some hundred fathoms below. The bonfire had reduced to smouldering cinders, yet still the elvenfolk danced and frolicked about Suraksa. Their instruments echoed softly on the wind and their joyous chanting and singing faintly followed. To the east, the sky was bathed in half-light as the fiery red of dawn ignited behind the mountain peaks. The first light of midsummer glowed steadily warmer as twilight intensified. The instruments fell quiet and a single voice bellowed an Elven hymn that carried up the mountainside towards Thia and Rhys.

The Elven ballad sang of the coming of summer; it heralded the daybreak of the year's longest light. It praised the ripening of fruits, the warmth of the night, the changing of the wind, and the beauty of the land. It told of sweet rain, and golden sunshine. It celebrated luscious grass, the fall of blossom petals, the humming of bees, the scent of pollen, and the chirrup of birdsong. The meaning of the words were lost to Rhys in the harmonious Elven Tongue, yet the very melodies of the composition were enough to conjure all of these sights, sounds, and smells as he and Thia listened from the mountainside.

Suddenly, the top of the sun's orb surfaced from behind the ridge, and warm amber light spilled down from the peaks, flooding the valley. As dawn broke, the solo became a chorus as the entire village below joined the ballad. The sun floated wholly above the mountains and the shadow of the night slowly faded away. Rhys turned to face Thia and she him. He felt his hand move without instruction. He brushed his fingers gently across her cheek. She stepped closer. Their bodies pressed against one another as Rhys tucked a single strand of Thia's silver hair behind her ear. The mage stooped as the witch tilted her head back. Their lips met as the warm sunbeams of Midsummer struck them.

TWENTY-SIX

Rhys and Thia re-entered Suraksa to find the celebrations still in full swing. The fire was little more than a heap of white ash, yet still the elves danced about it, now bathed in the morning sun. Rhys looked around, sighting each of his friends in turn. Several were dozing on the grass, whilst the others sat tiredly watching the elves weaving exuberantly about the extinguished firepit, perplexed by their complete lack of fatigue.

"I guess they really don't need to sleep," remarked Rhys, now finally believing what Maadurga had told him the morning before.

"Hey!" called Sol, rising to his feet as he sighted the two of them. He stumbled over in an exhausted daze. "Where have the two of *you* been?"

"We went for a walk," returned Thia as her and Rhys exchanged a subtle knowing look.

Sol studied them for a moment and his eyes narrowed. "Did something happen between you two?"

"No," replied Rhys ever-so-slightly too quick.

"What do you mean?" asked Thia, chuckling nervously.

Sol laughed to himself. "You just look guilty," he remarked giddily, revealing that he was still slightly drunk.

Rhys smiled, changing the subject. "I'm surprised you are still up?"

"I *was* going to get some sleep," explained the mage, "but Maadurga said I'd miss the contest."

"Contest?" repeated Thia.

Sol shrugged. "Apparently it is worth staying awake for. But seeing how these elves don't need to sleep—I don't think Maadurga is qualified to make that assessment."

"Where is she now?" questioned Rhys, scanning the crowd for any sign of the elf.

Sol shrugged once more. "I haven't seen her in a while."

"What's going on up there?" asked Cade as he approached the three of them.

Rhys gazed up the slope of the hill to see a number of elves moving about in the morning sun, erecting several wooden frames across the brow. They moved quickly, setting them at equal distances apart, facing out into the valley. Presently, a series of archery targets were hung from the frames.

"It looks as if the contest is one of archery," surmised Rhys, seeing that the huntsman's interest had been piqued.

"You are right," agreed Cade, realising the rest of the village were now amassing in audience at the foot of the hill.

Rhys's ears pricked at the distant screech of a raptor. He revolved just in time to see a dozen mounted gryphons dive from the sky. Swooping over the village mere fathoms above their heads, the flight of riders glided in single file, breaking formation as they climbed back upwards, each beast banking on the wind, peeling off in a different direction and soaring higher still to circle back above the hillside. The elven audience that had amassed broke into applause, cheering and chanting excitedly in Elvish as the mounted kshatriya looped and twirled acrobatically in the morning light.

"Come on!" urged the hunter enthusiastically, gesturing Rhys and the others to follow as he made his way to join the elves gathered at the bottom of the slopes.

"Get up!" asserted Sol, delivering a gentle kick to Ulfgar as he snored obliviously on the grass.

The dwarf sat bolt upright, spilling the mug of chhaang that had been balanced on his chest all over his face and beard. He wiped his eyes and peered about groggily, his grumpy stare finally settling on the mage who had roused him from inebriated slumber.

"What did you bloody do that for!?" he grumbled.

"You are going to miss the contest," chided Sol.

"I don't care about a bloody contest! I was sleeping."

"Well, you are up now," smiled Rhys. "So, you might as well watch."

Ulfgar gazed hazily around and finally caught sight of the throng of elves awaiting the archery competition to begin, then, shielding his eyes from the sun, he looked up into the sky to see the swirling formation of gryphons.

He sighed laboriously. "Fine!" Rising to his feet, muttering under his breath, he followed the rest of them to join the spectators.

The circling gryphons cumulated and effortlessly aligned into a vee formation, plunging back down towards the ground in another flyby. Dawon was at the tip of the vee, distinguished from the others by his distinctive black and umber stripes; on his back was saddled Maadurga, once more adorned in her mirror armour, bow in hand. The formation sped rapidly overhead and scattered again to the wind as they rose back into the sky. As the other gryphons took to circling high above once more, Dawon plunged groundward, flaring his wings to catch hold of the mountain gusts as he swooped passed the series of targets erected across the hillside.

Almost faster than Rhys's eyes could make out, the elf released her grip of the reins and drew a handful of arrows from the quiver hanging at her side. Nocking the first missile whilst clutching the others between her fingers on the same hand, she rapidly drew back the bowstring. The exaggerated curves of her bow's limbs flexed rearward, and an instant later, the bowstring twanged, slinging the arrow into rapid flight. A flick of her fingers guided the next arrow onto the string, and in the same motion, she drew taught the bow and loosed it. Her fluidity continued as she notched the third arrow, loosed, notched the fourth, let fly. Each arrow had been nocked and fired, one after the other, before the first had even struck its target.

A quartet of thuds rhythmically sounded as Dawon shot back into the air. Four targets were swaying back and forth. Rhys examined each in turn with disbelief. All four were perfect bullseyes. The entire feat had happened almost too fast to be seen, and as if to make it seem wholly impossible, the unworldly display of dexterity and skill had been carried out from aback a flying gryphon at speed. Rhys merely stared agape as the next rider plunged from the air and matched Maadurga's display, followed swiftly by a second, then a third rider, each loosing a handful of arrows in the blink of an eye, every shot striking a target dead centre.

The crowd gasped and cheered as one by one the remaining mounted archers dove from the sky and rapidly unfurled successions of arrows that clattered into the wildly swinging targets. Rhys and the others meanwhile were awestruck with silence.

"What..." breathed Cade in disbelief, his own archery skills now rendered unimpressive by all accounts.

The final gryphon rider climbed back into the sky, leaving the targets each riddled with a dozen arrows. The spectators on the ground applauded. Dawon emerged from the circling formation above, gliding rapidly back down towards the hilltop. Rhys watched as Maadurga slumped in her saddle; she lowered herself until she hung upside down from Dawon, one leg hooked over the saddle horn, the other wedged firmly in the stirrup. She drew two more arrows from her quiver, nocking both at once. The missiles took flight towards the first of the swinging targets, but this time, the bullseye wasn't Maadurga's aim; instead, the circular target dropped from the frame as the two ropes suspending it were severed. It plummeted towards the slope, landing on its side, bouncing as it rolled, finally coming to a halt just before the audience at the foot of the hill. The target fell flat, the tight grouping of fletched shafts pointing skyward so that all could see the dozen perfect bullseyes.

"I don't believe it," uttered Cade.

"Nor I!" groaned Ulfgar as he rubbed his tired eyes in bewilderment.

The next mounted archer dove from above, climbing out of the stirrups to balance standing upright on the back of his gryphon. He too loosed a duo of arrows, both slashing the tethers that hung the next swaying target in place. The circle of wood tumbled down the slope, coming to rest aside the other, its grouping of arrows as tight as the first. The next archer performed the same feat riding backwards, the next lying supine in the saddle. Rhys and the others found themselves staring at four target boards at the base of the hill, each bullseye riddled, the outer rings of the target utterly unscathed.

Four mounted archers now descended to circle low above the hilltop, Dawon and Maadurga among them. One of the riders drew an arrow and pulled back the bowstring, taking aim at Maadurga. Rhys felt a pang of sudden trepidation as the elf loosed his bow. The arrow shot straight at Maadurga, but somehow she snatched it clean out of the air. In the same movement, she notched the once-fired arrow and drew back her own bow, taking aim for the next rider in the circling formation. She released her bowstring and the arrow set sail, grabbed in mid-flight by the next archer in the chain. He sent it on its way to the final rider, before the last bowman drilled the arrow into another hanging target.

The circle of riders peeled off and four more mounted archers took their place. The incredible aerial performance continued for several minutes. Rhys and the others watched arrows shot out of the sky by other arrows, and bows shot from behind the elves' backs. At one point, a rider leapt from the saddle, plucked an arrow from its flight, and sent it on its way again, all before landing back astride his gryphon. Flying targets were tossed into the sky and riddled from multiple directions, caught thereafter by the riders before they struck the ground. Arrows were split in half, cut from the sky by kukris, and even loosed skyward to land back in the quivers of the same archers who had fired them. All these impossible exploits and more were performed without effort and without error. The audience gasped, cried, oohed, aahed, and applauded, yet overall, the elves' reaction to the unbelievable skill displayed seemed understated and muted. Genuine shock meanwhile, came from Rhys and his friends, who throughout the entire contest, uttered only a few words, exchanging a mere handful of looks between themselves; for the most part, they merely gazed silently with their jaws agape, staring as hard as their eyes could manage to watch the rapid movement of elven fingers on bowstrings, trying to spot some form of trickery or subterfuge that could explain away the impossible unfolding in the air overhead.

Finally, with every bullseye stuck with arrows and the mounted archers' quivers empty, the gryphons dispersed, flying back to the roosts where their mounts dwelt. Rhys turned and looked to Sol and the others, waiting for someone else to speak first.

"Worth staying awake for?" Rhys finally directed to the mage beside him.

Sol nodded. "Yeah," he chuckled almost deliriously. "But I could really use some sleep now."

"I think we all could," agreed Rhys, looking around at the rest of them.

"Where's Cade?" questioned Thia as they suddenly realised the hunter was nowhere to be seen.

"He left as soon as the contest ended," replied Nathaniel.

"Why?" questioned Rhys.

Ulfgar shrugged. "Maybe he felt shown up."

"Don't be ridiculous," dismissed Sol.

"Its not ridiculous," protested Ulfgar. "We all thought the lad was hot shit with a bow! Now we know he's a novice when compared to the likes of these elves."

"He's still a remarkable archer on the mainland," insisted Sol.

"But not here he ain't," chided Ulfgar.

"Cade's ego is not such a fragile thing," refused Rhys. "I very much doubt he cares what the rest of us think—you most of all, Ulfgar."

"I'm just saying..." returned the Dwarf, "he was in a hurry to make his escape."

"What about you?" put in Alkis. "You now look like a novice with a crossbow when compared to the elves."

"Nice try," chortled Ulfgar. "I never claimed that firing a crossbow required any great skill; especially when they are dwarven-built. I put more pride in my other skills."

"You mean your aptitude for subterfuge, espionage, and deceit?" asked Rhys wryly.

"You know me better than I thought you did, lad," laughed Ulfgar, patting the mage firmly on the back.

"I'm not sure he was complementing you…" uttered a bewildered Alkis.

"Yes he was," insisted Ulfgar assuredly.

Rhys smiled. "To each his own."

The party continued to chat wearily amongst themselves over the next few minutes before Maadurga appeared over the brow of the hill and walked back into Suraksa; she hadn't yet doffed her disc armour, but her bow was unstrung and carried at her side bundled with Dawon's saddle and tacking. She smiled at sighting Rhys and the others and made her way over to them.

"What did you think?" she beamed.

"You were incredible!" insisted Thia enthusiastically.

Maadurga smiled warmly. "Archery is important to our people. We each receive our first bow when we are just children."

"I'm guessing a hundred odd years of practise goes a long way," supposed Rhys.

"Yes," nodded the elf. "Like all of my people's kshatriya, I practise every day."

"How old are you?" asked Thia in wonder.

"One hundred and twenty-two."

"No wonder you are so skilled!" returned Alkis.

"You look amazing for your age," smiled Thia.

"How old are you, Ulfgar?" questioned Nathaniel.

"I dunno," shrugged the dwarf.

"What do you mean you don't know?" questioned Alkis.

"I've lost count."

"Well, take a guess then," suggested Nathaniel.

"Eighty-five? Give or take of few years," he offered, shrugging again.

"So, if you are eighty-five, and Cade is only twenty-five, I'd say you have more to answer for about your marksmanship than he," smiled Alkis.

"I like my crossbow," explained Ulfgar, "but I'm not married to it."

"I should hope not," jested Rhys. "You're not exactly faithful! As far as I can tell, you have at least two other crossbows that I've seen."

"It's more of a hobby for me," declared Ulfgar. "Besides, any fool with half a mind to work it and a decent eye can get good with a crossbow. If I gave any of you mine and taught you up, in half an hour you'd be shooting straight. That's why I like it; it requires little commitment, unlike archery which takes years of shooting at practise targets before you even stand half a chance of hitting something!"

"So, what you are saying is, you have no specific skill to speak of?" chided Sol.

"I'm still a bloody good shot!" protested Ulfgar.

"But it's easy," teased the mage. "Crossbows pretty much aim themselves. All you have to do is look at what you want to kill and squeeze the tickler."

"I know what you are doing," replied Ulfgar, "and it won't work!"

"I haven't the faintest idea what you are talking about."

Rhys continued to half listen to his fellow mage wind Ulfgar up as he gazed about. To his surprise, he sighted Cade emerge from out of the village; across his back was his quiver, brimming with arrows. In his hand was his recurve bow, readily strung. The huntsman was marching with determination straight towards them, the look on his face purposeful. Rhys shot his friend an inquisitive look, but Cade did not notice; his attention was squarely on Maadurga.

"Cade?" Rhys questioned as he walked straight past him.

The hunter halted suddenly before the elven kshatriya and knelt, offering up his bow to the elf. "Teach me."

Maadurga smiled and gestured for the hunter to stand. "I cannot," she returned apologetically.

"Why not?" questioned Cade pleadingly. "I am able to learn. I have a good eye and I can hit a bullseye at a hundred yards."

"I cannot because I do not have the time," apologised Maadurga. "Tomorrow I head to the Temple of Kalki with Rhys, Sol, and Thia. But if you wish to learn, then I can have one of my kshatriya teach you."

"Yes," nodded Cade insistently. "Please!"

Maadurga held out her palm facing upwards, and after a moment of hesitation Cade placed his bow in the elf's hand. She looked over the recurve composite bow methodically, turning it in her hands; she then raised it and drew back the bowstring, aiming as if she had an arrow notched. Slowly, she released the tension.

"This will not do," explained the elf, returning Cade's bow to him.

"But..." began Cade, appearing almost offended. "This is a fine bow!" he insisted. "It's composite, like yours. It has a draw weight of seventy odd pounds... that's enough to go through mail! Its as much as some longbows—and its only two thirds' the size! It was my great grandfather's; it uses the Cambrian warbow design; very few of these even exist on the continent. I'm told it is worth a fortune!"

The hunter offered the bow back to Maadurga, who, seeing Cade's insistency, took it again. This time Maadurga flexed the bow and unstrung it. The horn limbs straightened from the recessed grip and the tips pointed away from the elf. She looked the bow over once more and shook her head solemnly.

"I am sorry," she apologised. "This will not suffice."

"Why?" questioned Cade. "I've used it all my life and it has never failed me."

Maadurga set her saddle and tacking down on the ground and produced her unstrung reflex bow. Unlike Cade's weapon, not a single portion of the limbs were straight; instead, the entire length of the shortbow was curled into an exaggerated curve, so distorted from the shape of the hunter's unstrung Cambrian bow that its limb tips were less than an inch from meeting. She extended her arm and offered the reflex bow to Cade, who stared at the weapon in amazement before taking it in his hands and examining it intently.

"How do you even string this?" questioned the huntsman as he flexed the composite limbs.

"With great difficulty," assured Maadurga. "Watch," she then added, taking the bow back from Cade. Producing her bowstring, the elf looped an end over one of the notches, then, rifling through her tacking, she produced a leather strop and seated herself on the ground. Passing one bow tip through the leather strop, Maadurga wrapped the broad sling around her back and midriff before passing the loop knotted in the other end of the strop over the second limb of her bow. Pressing the soles of her feet against the grip, she used her legs to draw back and tension the bow, flexing it out of its exaggerated horseshoe shape and into the more familiar curvature of her reflex bow. Passing the second end of the bowstring over the other notch, she then released the force of her legs on the bow and stood up, discarding the strop as she did so, her bow now strung.

"Here," offered Maadurga, handing the bow back to Cade.

Cade drew the string, adopting his accustomed archery stance, yet as he tensioned the bow, he grimaced, his face reddening with strain. Unable to pull the bow to full draw, the huntsman carefully released the tension and rolled his shoulder uncomfortably.

"What is the draw weight on this?" asked the huntsman.

Maadurga smiled. "I do not know."

"It must be near enough a hundred pounds!" exclaimed Cade as he half drew the reflex bow once more. "If not more! How is it so strong? Its little more than half the length of my bow."

"It must be short," explained Maadurga.

"If it were not, it could not be fired from the saddle."

"I can fire my bow from astride a horse," insisted Cade.

"But a horse does not have wings beating at your side when you ride it," returned the elf. "From Dawon's saddle there would not be space enough to aim a bow as long as yours."

"I don't ever plan on shooting from the back of a gryphon, if I'm honest with you," replied the hunter. "I've done very little archery from horseback as it is."

"Even still," assured Maadurga, "a shorter bow is better. It is quicker to aim; it takes less time to think between every shot. If you are in a forest, you can move swiftly between the brush, and shoot on the run."

"Okay," nodded Cade, convinced by Maadurga's arguments. "What else do I need to know?"

Maadurga circled the huntsman, examining him closely. "Your quiver."

"What about my quiver?"

"Why do you wear it on your back?"

"It's out the way," insisted Cade. "And I can easily draw from it."

"It is in the wrong place," declared Maadurga, smiling mockingly. "You will be very slow to nock an arrow."

"I can fast draw," insisted Cade.

"Yes?" questioned Maadurga. "Show me,"

she added, picking up Cade's own bow.

"Now?" questioned the hunter.

Maadurga nodded.

Cade adopted his shooting posture, and pausing for a moment to ensure the elf was watching, he swiftly moved his hand behind his head and pulled a single arrow, nocking it onto the string and drawing the bow in a fluid motion. Yet, in the brief moment that the hunter had performed the motion, Maadurga had drawn an arrow of her own and had notched, drawn, and aimed the arrowhead straight at Cade, all before the hunter had managed to place his fingers on the bowstring. Cade's eyes focussed warily on the arrowhead pointed at his heart from only a few feet away.

"See," returned Maadurga as she slackened her bowstring and lowered her aim, "slow!"

"Alright," conceded Cade, "my quiver should be on my hip."

Maadurga smiled enthusiastically as she took pleasure in dismantling all of Cade's prior notions of archery.

"What else?"

"Aim for that target," insisted the elf, pointing up the slope of the hill to one of the hanging targets riddled with bullseyes.

Cade raised the bow and tensioned the string. He looked down the shaft of the arrow and took aim. Once more Maadurga circled him, scrutinising his positioning and posture.

"Loose," commanded the elf.

Cade exhaled forcefully as he released the weight of the drawstring and let the arrow fly. It flexed left and right as it sailed to the top of the hill and thumped into the lower rim of the target, causing it to sway back and forth. The huntsman rolled his shoulder once again and turned apprehensively for judgment from Maadurga.

The elf pondered Cade for a short moment in silence before announcing, "There is much to improve. But, you are not beyond teaching."

"Thank you," replied Cade, accepting the backhanded compliment.

"I will see that Ehani begins your lessons tomorrow."

Cade smiled broadly. "What about my bow?" he asked after a moment.

"You will not train with this," insisted Maadurga as she handed back the Cambrian recurve to Cade and took her own elven reflex in return. "Ehani will bring you a child's bow for your training."

"A child's bow?" questioned the hunter, slightly humiliated.

"Yes," nodded Maadurga. "When you have the strength to draw a full-powered Elven bow, then you will begin training with one."

Cade looked down at his slim, yet well-defined arms, then gazed upon the slight frame of Maadurga. "But I must surely be as strong as you, if not more so!"

"You are strong here, yes," agreed the elf as she clutched Cade's bicep. "But not here," she added, tapping the small of his back with her bow. "Or here," she insisted, touching then his abdomen with the other end of her bow. "Once you have the right stance, the strength will come. Until then, you shall shoot a child's bow."

"Very well," begrudged Cade.

"What is the secret to catching arrows from out of the air?" questioned Alkis. "That is something I would like to learn!"

"There is no secret to it," returned Maadurga. "You just need a quick eye and an even quicker hand."

"So, you are saying I cannot learn to do it?" asked the knight disappointedly.

"If you have both of those things, then you can practise. If not, then no, you will never learn."

"Even still," replied Alkis politely, "whilst you are away, I would consider it a great honour if myself and Nathaniel were allowed to train with some of your kshatriya."

Maadurga nodded compliantly. "It might better prepare you if you are to face the rakshasa; you should know how to fight those trained in the way of the kukri."

"My thoughts exactly," agreed Alkis.

"I will arrange for Cetan and Shankha to train with you whilst I am away."

"My thanks," smiled Alkis warmly.

"I will tell you now that they will not go easy on you," warned the elf. "They are both fierce fighters."

"I'd be disappointed if they did."

"Good," smiled Maadurga.

"What are you going to be doing whilst everyone else is training?" questioned Sol, turning to Ulfgar.

"I'm sure I'll think of something," chuckled the dwarf as he picked up a wooden mug laying on the ground and drank the last dregs of chhaang that had been left in the bottom.

"Don't cause any trouble," warned Rhys sternly.

"Maybe I'll teach these elves a thing or two about drinking," suggested Ulfgar.

"No," refused Rhys somewhat confoundedly. "That is literally the opposite of what I just told you."

"Come on," grinned the dwarf. "I've got to have some fun while you're gone!"

Rhys sighed heavily. "We've got a good thing going here. Don't mess it up for us!"

"Yes sir!" saluted Ulfgar mockingly, but before Rhys could scold him any further, his attention was drawn skyward.

The mage shielded his eyes against the glare of the sun to see the vast wings of a gryphon beating down on them. The beast landed on its paws and talons, and from out of the saddle sprung a kshatriya. The elf drew back the veil covering his face and spoke urgently in Elvish to Maadurga, his eyes flitting to Rhys and the others, then back to his commander.

"Maadurga! Manisaharu Kalaki ko jahak ma hamala garchana!"

Maadurga turned to look at Rhys and Sol, her expression creasing suddenly into one of concern.

"What is it?" questioned Rhys.

"Your friends…" she began, "they are in danger."

TWENTY-SEVEN

"In danger!?" repeated Sol. "From the Wild Hunt?"

"No," Maadurga shook her head. "From your kind."

"The castaways!" hissed Rhys. "They have found the Marlin!"

"Oh shit!" cursed Sol. "They'll kill them to get onboard. Especially if they've finished the repairs."

"Some of them have been marooned for decades. I hate to think what they'd do to commandeer the Marlin," warned Thia.

"Maadurga, Tayamha kehi samaya cha!" urged the Kshatriya.

"He says there is little time," translated Maadurga before responding to the elven messenger. "Hamie ahil uni haruka, samana garana. Savari garchana." She stuck her fingers to her lips and let out a piercing whistle that carried across the mountainside.

"We need to help them," Rhys insisted to Maadurga as she gathered up her saddle and tacking.

"There is not time to head down on foot," warned Maadurga. "Vihaan and I will ride down. We will meet the others and scatter the humans before they reach your ship, Kalki."

"There could be as many as a hundred of them," warned Rhys. "A hundred versus half a dozen makes for terrible odds; even if those half a dozen are elves."

Maadurga nodded solemnly. "There is not time to ready the village's kshatriya."

"Then take us with you!" insisted Sol.

Maadurga looked sombrely at Sol, understanding his desire to defend his friends.

A screech suddenly echoed through the dale. The wingspan of Dawon scudded across the sun as the gryphon dove from the air, responding to his master's summons. An instant later, he thumped onto the ground beside Maadurga. The elf turned away from Rhys and the others and draped the hood from her riding gear over Dawon, securing it in place.

"Two magi will certainly help to balance things better," insisted Rhys as he rushed to aid Maadurga in securing the tacking.

"It is not so simple," warned Maadurga. "You must ride with us."

"I know," Rhys swallowed, looking apprehensively at the two gryphons.

"Dawon may allow you to ride with me, Kalki," explained the elf. "But…" she looked at Sol hesitantly, then to Vihaan's black and white mottled gryphon as it groomed its feathers with its hooked beak.

"What is it?" questioned Sol, realising that he was going to be left behind.

"I understand," nodded Rhys. "But can't we at least try?"

Maadurga cocked her head anxiously. "If it goes badly, he could be injured... or killed."

Rhys sighed closing his eyes in frustration. "It is your call, Sol."

"What do I have to do?"

"Tapa inle timra jhakri linu parcha," Maadurga spoke to Vihaan.

Vihaan looked at Maadurga sceptically before turning briefly to his gryphon and then eyeing Sol. "Kee tapa gambhira hunuhuncha!?"

"Ho!" insisted Maadurga.

Vihaan conceded, stepping away from his mount hesitantly as he stared at Sol.

"You must touch his mount on the neck," instructed Maadurga. "Move slow. Speak gently. Do not look Igala directly in the eyes."

"Okay," nodded Sol nervously.

"I'll get your staves," whispered Thia in Rhys's ear as the mage watched his friend revolve to face Vihaan's mount.

Rhys nodded as the witch darted off into the village, keeping his attention squared on Sol. The mage stepped apprehensively towards Igala. As if by some premonition of what Sol was going to attempt, the gryphon suddenly reared its head and locked its gaze intimidatingly on the mage. Sol lowered his stare to avoid eye contact, slowly but surely approaching closer to the hulking beast. Igala let out a low screech and flapped his wings, churning dust up into the air; even his rider, Vihaan, stepped back warily.

"Taya hamiko lagi samaya chaina!" growled Vihaan impatiently.

"Santan," returned Maadurga, seemingly silencing Vihaan's protests and calming Igala in one word.

Sol continued to step closer. Igala growled, clicking its beak as it intensified its gaze on the approaching mage. "This thing is going to kill me," hissed Sol.

"Do not back away," urged Maadurga. "If you do, Igala will think you are weak and afraid. He will not let you mount him if he thinks this."

"But what if he attacks?" questioned Sol, still nervously edging closer.

"Then you must run," replied Maadurga, "before he kills you."

"Not very reassuring," muttered Sol.

Igala suddenly reared upwards, brandishing his razor talons and flaring his enormous dark wings. Sol hesitated, no doubt fighting every instinct within himself to retreat. Igala refolded his wings and planted his talons back on the ground. Sol drew to within a couple feet. Clenching his body tightly and lowering his gaze to the floor in dread, the mage then outreached with a hand. To his amazement, and everyone else's, Igala seemed to relax. Sol cautiously lay his palm on the beast's neck. Taking a deep breath of relief, the mage opened his eyes and softly ruffled Igala's feathers.

"Come," uttered Vihaan in broken Common as he leapt gracefully into the saddle of Igala and offered down a hand to the mage. "Up. We go."

Sol nodded, accepting the elf's hand, heaving himself up across the gryphon's back. Vihaan shuffled as far forward as he could in the saddle and Sol slumped tightly in behind him, perching on the low cantle.

"We must go now," insisted Maadurga as she too leapt astride Dawon and reached down to pull Rhys up behind her.

Rhys mimicked Sol and slid onto the cantle of the saddle behind Maadurga.

"Rhys!" called Thia appearing at Dawon's side, offering up his staff.

Rhys took his weapon and shot a weak smile back at the witch. Wrapping his free arm tightly around Maadurga's waist, but unable to wedge his feet into the stirrups, he merely clutched at Dawon's sides with his thighs until his hips began to burn under tension. Suddenly, Rhys was frantically nervous. His mind was filled with flashbacks to their highspeed pursuit on horseback across the Capital Riviera only a month earlier. Back then he had never ridden a horse before. This was only the second time he had ever ridden anything, and though now he was not in control of his mount, it would be soaring through the skies rather than galloping along a bridleway.

"I am definitely going to die," the mage breathed under his breath.

"Just hold on," insisted Maadurga. "Dawon will not let you fall."

"Just, try not to do any loops or anything," pleaded Rhys.

"No loops," promised the elf. "My people would be most displeased if I let Kalki fall from my saddle."

"I think I might be even more displeased," returned Rhys.

"Are you ready?" questioned Maadurga as she took the reins and led Dawon away from the others to give the gryphon room to take off.

"No," replied Rhys honestly.

"Good luck," offered Thia, taking several steps back.

Rhys issued her another anxious smile before Dawon suddenly spread his pinions; with several large thrums of his wings, he sent torrents of wind surging beneath them. Dust swirled as Igala likewise beat his enormous wingspan. Rhys felt his stomach lurch, as suddenly he and Maadurga were airborne.

Rhys swore under his breath as he clutched Maadurga tightly. His weight shifted as Dawon pitched backwards and he felt on the verge of slipping completely out of the saddle. On either side, the orange and black striped wings of Dawon flapped furiously as the beast climbed upwards. Rhys peered back over his shoulder to see the ground spiralling rapidly away. In a matter of seconds, Thia and the others had shrunk smaller than ants, the village of Suraksa receding with them. Wind ripped passed the mage's ears and wafted violently at his unkempt hair. His gut continued to turn over in his belly and his head spun. The foothills of the vale were tumbling away below and the rugged mountainsides sinking. The air grew crisp and cold and the peaks of the valley ahead drew level with their altitude. Up they continued to climb, the fringes of Suraksa's valley haven receding below. The golden sunbeams cut slantingly through the sky as storm clouds boiled from the ever-raging tempest encompassing the Stormy Isles. The faint lilac of the Rift was blotted out by an anvil-shaped tower of cumulonimbus, and the familiar crackle of thunder gurgled through the clouds as white fire arced above.

The moment they passed beyond the limits of the Sacred Valley, Dawon pitched sharply downwards, plunging into the mists below. Rain streamed through the fog, immediately drenching Rhys; in the turbulent air currents buffeting him from all sides, the mage could not tell if the deluge was falling from above or rising from below. Igala drew alongside Dawon, and through the howling gusts and streaking water, Rhys made out Sol clutching desperately to Vihaan.

The gloom surrounding them intensified,

yet the darkness was rent open every few seconds by the white glare of lightning. Dawon began to bank and swerve through the smoky mists as the shadows of hovering boulders and floating hillocks blurred by in the haze. Rhys made out the thin trails of rope bridges, and through thinning patches in the floor of the clouds below, he sighted the foam of breaking waves across the sea's surface.

Suddenly, the cloud canopy tore open as Dawon swooped out beneath the smothering gloom. Jagged cliffs of black basalt and crescent coves of grey beaches linked together to form the rugged island chain, raging foam crashing along the shores, the eternal tempest boiling the cauldron of the Wyrm's Sea. Up ahead, Rhys spotted the slanted mast of the Marlin rising out of a sheltered bay, the ship's distinctive sun-bleached hull gleaming in the pallid light.

"Look!" cried Maadurga, pointing to the staircase of hexagonal basalt pillars leading down from the cliffs to the beach.

Rhys traced her line of sight; clambering down the distant steps of dark stone were scores of the castaways. The mage turned his vision now out across the sands to the careened ship. On the beach, four gryphons were steadily being tacked by their elven riders as the Anderssens' kshatriya protectors readied for the fight to come. Meanwhile, on the slanting decks of the Marlin, Rhys could make out the three seamen reeling in the ropes cast down over the bulwarks to the sand, and readying hammers and harpoons.

"Where do you want me to set you down?"

"On the beach," returned Rhys. "Sol and I will pick them off from afar; see if we can force them to retreat before they make it to the Marlin."

"These men are desperate," warned Maadurga. "Many have been stranded on the shores of Sumeru for years. I fear they will not flee—not whilst your ship is there for the taking."

"I reckon you are probably right," agreed Rhys. "But we have to try."

"Vihaan, the others, and I will keep to the air," explained the elf as Dawon began to glide towards the sands. "We will pick them off with arrows until our quivers are empty."

The gryphon touched down joltingly on the beach, kicking up sand as he slowed from a sprint to a halt. Rhys, grateful to be back on the ground, and solid ground at that, hastily dismounted.

"Good luck," the mage called back, meeting eyes with Maadurga.

"And to you, Kalki," she returned, before spurring her feet in the stirrups.

Dawon spurted forwards, spanning his wings and taking to the sky once again. The other four kshatriya took off from the beach ahead of their leader, their gryphons assembling in aerial formation as they climbed, racing towards the horde of amassing castaways charging across the beach towards the Marlin.

"Rhys! Sol!" cried Arne from over the bulwark of the Marlin as the captain and his sons sighted the two magi come to their aid.

"For once I am glad to see you, Sol," chided Eirik.

"I can't say the same for you," mocked Sol, calling back to them as he dismounted Igala and waved Vihaan off as the elven gryphon rider soared back into the air.

"Thank Woden you are here," declared Arne sternly.

"Don't worry," called up Rhys. "We'll see you through."

"Just stay up there," shouted Sol. "And don't do anything stupid—I'm looking at you, Vidar!"

Vidar opened his mouth to shout something back but closed it again against his better judgement.

The screams of the charging wall of berserkers carried over the wind as the castaways drew closer. The kshatriya were circling above them now, loosing down a rain of arrows, but many of the castaways were brandishing shields above their heads, their bulwarks cobbled together from driftwood; some loosed arrows skyward from makeshift bows, forcing Maadurga and the other elves to veer evasively this way and that. The castaway numbers were thinning, but the elven riders were not enough to stem the tide. In mere moments, the attacking force would close the distance and arrive at the hull of the Marlin.

"You ready?" questioned Rhys as he and Sol stood shoulder to shoulder, waiting for their foes to draw within range.

"Readier than when we last faced these bastards!"

"Let's hope the Hounds of Annwn don't make an appearance this time," returned Rhys.

"Don't jinx it," warned Sol. "There's still time."

The two magi looked ahead as a curtain of gloom drawn inward by the onshore winds swept over the waves and up onto the sand. The vee of gryphons broke apart in the chaos, swooping and diving above the charging mass of castaways as their elven riders picked them off one by one. A sudden shriek pierced through a toll of thunder as a harpoon hurled from the horde speared into the breast of a low swooping mount. The gryphon tumbled from the air, plummeting to the beach with its rider still caught in the saddle. The creature ploughed into the sand, churning up a cloud of grit into which both gryphon and rider were momentarily lost; as the dust settled, Rhys saw the elven rider pinned beneath the body of her dead mount. Seconds later, the castaways were on top of her. Her screams were drowned out by the roars of the charging mob as she vanished beneath a stampede of feet. The mist swept inwards, shrouding the Marlin in gloom. In the moments that followed, the oncoming charge of berserkers storming across the beach likewise faded from view beyond the pall of vapour.

"Damn it!" cursed Sol. "They are still out of range."

"Just a few more seconds," insisted Rhys.

Their quiver's depleted of arrows, the kshatriya peeled away just as they were enveloped by the pluming fog, banking on the winds as they turned back towards Rhys and Sol. Before the two magi caught their final view of the sally of exiles, Rhys reckoned their numbers still greater than fifty.

"This doesn't look good!" warned Sol as the charge of men faded completely from sight ahead.

"We don't have to defeat them all," calculated Rhys, "just enough to force a retreat."

Lightning crackled, a fork of electricity striking the sand mere yards from their location. Another bolt struck, closer than the first.

"They must be within range!" urged Sol impatiently.

"Hold! Just a bit longer," implored Rhys, knowing Sol's personal stake in the fight was getting the better of him. If they unleashed their arsenal of magical attacks too early, they'd find themselves exhausted before the enemy had even closed in on the Marlin; the mêlée was where the real fighting would begin

"Rhys!" panicked Sol. "I can hear them getting close!" he insisted, the roars of charging men building to a crescendo above the storm.

"Now!" commanded Rhys, flourishing his staff and letting fly the first missile of the cannonade.

An elemental maelstrom exploded from the firing line of magi. Bolt after bolt of electricity snaked into the swirling mist, punctuated by an unrelenting bombardment of kinetic shells. Screams and howls cut through the deafening detonations; Rhys and Sol were firing blind, their foes obscured by the screen of murk ahead, yet the agonised cries informed them that at least some of their shots were hitting their mark. Ejections of sand blasted in geysers from the beach, the dust raining down as the incoming mob stormed ever closer. Suddenly, the first silhouettes of the charging barbarians condensed out of the wall of fog, the frontline erupting from the veil moments later. Rhys and Sol ceased fire, the vanguard of berserkers closing the last few yards in seconds.

Rhys's ethereal weapon swirled out of the velvet mist, its green blade casting an unworldly jade glow through the murk. The first challenger closed in, darting across the sand for the mage. Almost effortlessly, Rhys ducked, stepping calmly aside as a woodcutter's axe swung wildly overhead. Reversing his staff, he snagged the man's thigh; the hook of his blade tore into the castaway's flesh, the assailant's own momentum opening the wound deeper. The berserker toppled, collapsing to the sand, clutching his limb in a din of agonised screams, still alive, but dispatched.

Pulling his stave back around, Rhys fired. The blast of force sent the next incoming barbarian flying, launched back the way he had come. A third rushed in, snarling as he thrust at Rhys with a rusted harpoon. Rhys dodged the lancing strike, parrying the next attack, before hewing the harpoon's head from its shaft. A knee to the chest sent the harpooner reeling, giving Rhys the breathing room he needed to counter a swinging cleaver from another foe. Dismembering the arm wielding the butcher's knife, Rhys skewered the assailant through the gut. Renting free the tip of his blade, he pivoted, twirling his staff in a wide arc, impaling the harpooner through the temple with his fluke.

Carrying his momentum in a rapid pirouette, Rhys's body uncurled like a spring. He leapt, thrusting whilst airborne, the entire impetus of his body driven through the length of his stave. A sickening crunch clove through the din of battle as Rhys skewered clean into the forehead of a villain charging his way. Killed instantly, the exile's feet flailed out beneath him, his skull lurching back as it was driven into the sand. Rhys landed, rolled, and turned to the roar of a raging berserker storming his flank.

Still on his knees, Rhys raised his stave horizontally. A jolt of vibration shuddered along the length of his weapon, the beard of an axe hooking down over the shaft, the cleaving edge having halted mere inches from the top of Rhys's pate. The mage twisted. The weapons locked. A two-handed jerk rent the axe from its wielder's grip. Rhys twirled, planting a heel in the barbarian's breastbone. The disarmed axeman staggered back, swallowed an instant later by a gout of fire as Rhys's stave flashed crimson. Another villain rushing to the axeman's aid met the same fate, the screams of both men waning as they were immolated in the inferno.

As the pair of smouldering corpses collapsed, Rhys turned his head just quick enough to realise he had been flanked. He stooped, staggering off his feet, half tripping as a scythe slashed narrowly above his head. Through providence, the missed hew swung into another castaway's side, the hooked blade embedding deep into the unlucky victim's hip. The impaled barbarian screamed as his ally attempted to rent the corroded weapon free from the bone. From the ground, Rhys slashed upward. He parted the scythe from its owner, hand and forearm still attached. Scrambling back upright, he finished off the dismembered berserker, swivelling then to cut down the barbarian trying to prise free the scythe lodged in his hip.

A shank stabbed out of nowhere, scratching across Rhys's shoulder as the mage flung himself clear at the last instant. He danced away, twirling his stave to retaliate when an oar shattered across his back. Rhys felt a rib crack as the oar snapped clean in half, the force of the blow buckling him to his knees. He tried to gasp for air, but his lungs had seized shut, the wind knocked entirely from his chest. A suffocated wheeze sucked through his mouth as Rhys's head lulled back on his shoulders. An axe clove down for him. Rhys flailed his staff, clumsily deflecting the incoming strike, but the recoil from the blow was enough to floor him completely. Thrashing his body on the sand, Rhys managed to cast off a bolt of force. The missile exploded from the tip of his staff, and through sheer luck, smashed into the face of the axeman assailing him. The villain's neck snapped backwards and he fell dead in front of the mage.

Summoning the strength to fight his way back to his feet, Rhys pulled himself out of the sand and craned his head to catch sight of the oarsman that had struck him down.

"He fights for the demons now!" cackled Kristoffer, wielding the snapped oar shaft.

The castaway speared the jagged end at Rhys. Flopping back to the sand, Rhys rolled away and Kristoffer's thrust missed narrowly, instead impaling the body of the axeman Rhys had slain seconds earlier.

"Tricky, tricky!" shrilled Kristoffer as he pulled the bloody broken oar from the cadaver. "But you never fooled me! Never!" he shouted in a deranged manner, lunging for Rhys again.

Rhys scrambled to retaliate, only to realise he had lost his staff in the scuffle. Kristoffer cackled, dancing after Rhys as the mage frantically scurried across the beach towards his weapon. The madman snarled, lancing for the mage with all his might when suddenly, an amber streak of energy blurred out of the mist, rematerializing to intercept the strike.

"Shedevil!" Kristoffer hissed, baring his teeth as Maadurga deprived him of his kill.

With a flourish of her kukri, Maadurga clove through the castaway's wrist and thrust, driving her blade into the madman's gut. Kristoffer barely made a sound as his dismembered hand dropped to the sand, the broken oar still gripped tightly in his dead callused fingers. Instead, the lunatic seized hold of the elf with his remaining hand, pulling the kukri deeper into his abdomen before gnashing and snarling like a rabid dog. He struck Maadurga with his bloody stump and snapped his teeth, trying to bite at the elf's throat.

For a brief moment, Maadurga lost her preternatural grace and composure as she scrapped with the crazed amputee. A roar thundered as another berserker charged for them both. Bjorn stormed out of the fog, axe raised above his head as he rushed to Kristoffer's aid. Rhys watched helplessly from the ground, scrambling to reach his staff. Maadurga glimpsed Bjorn charging her way from over her shoulder, bloodlust in his demented gaze, but entangled in Kristoffer's grapple, she was defenceless against the charging barbarian.

Stomping on Kristoffer's foot, Maadurga managed to shrug momentarily free. She twisted to face the berserker rushing her, and drew back her kukri, ready to cut him down, but as Bjorn closed in, Kristoffer threw himself at her once more, his fingers clasping around the edge of Maadurga's blade. Blood oozed from Kristoffer's hand as the elf tried to free her grappled kukri, but Kristoffer merely gripped tighter, the edge slicing through his fingers to the bone.

Rhys locked hands around his staff as Bjorn's axe descended for Maadurga. With no time to react, he channelled all his energy through his weapon into the ground. A low thrum shook the air and a shockwave imploded around the core of the stave. Gravity suddenly gave way. Rhys's stomach lurched into a summersault and the beach tumbled away beneath him. In that instant, he was weightless. Grains of sand floated into the air, and as the mage tumbled in the gravity wake, he saw that Bjorn, Maadurga, and Kristoffer had likewise lifted from the ground.

Bjorn's momentum sent him tumbling in an upwards fall, toppling head over heels. He flailed his arms wildly as he glided passed Maadurga, beyond the influence of Rhys's magic. Gravity seized him once again, and without warning, he thumped prone into the sand. Maadurga acrobatically righted herself in the air whilst Kristoffer snarled and screamed upside down, his fingers still locked around the edge of the elf's kukri. Blood was still pumping from his cloven forearm, now collating into incarnadine globules suspended in the mist. Maadurga ripped her blade free, severing the four fingers' from Kristoffer's remaining hand.

Rhys flipped himself upright as the fleeting well of antigravity began to fade. The laws of reality swiftly took hold again and Rhys and Maadurga planted boots back on the ground. Kristoffer, who had tumbled highest into the air, dropped headfirst to the beach, his neck breaking during the impact, finally silencing his deranged howls. Bjorn staggered up from the ground, swaying around disorientatedly, his daze lasting long enough for his throat to be slit unopposed by Maadurga.

"Are you alright, Kalki?" asked the elf in the momentary lull of fighting.

"Yeah," wheezed Rhys, grimacing against the throbbing pain beneath his shoulder blade. "Are you?"

She nodded. "Fulan, Naahbi, and Tivi, are dead."

"I am sorry," lamented Rhys, readying himself as more shadows charged from out of the gloom.

"So am I," mourned Maadurga, likewise preparing to do battle once more.

The veins of Rhys's stave shimmered blue as he thrust at the first approaching foe. A cone of ice chilled the mist and the castaway snap-froze, rapidly encased in sheet ice, his statuesque body toppling rigidly over. Maadurga dashed into the fray, cutting down two more men before vanishing into the boiling murk. Rhys followed, quickly dispatching anyone in his way.

A hulking shadow loomed out of the fog, and Rhys span to see Tobias appear before him. His fiery beard bristled with fury as he beheld Rhys, shouldering a large twohanded battle axe.

"So, you turned against your own kind, mage?"

"No," refused Rhys, "just you."

"And sided with the Hounds?"

"They aren't the Cŵn Annwn. They are elves—and not the ones kidnapping your men, at that!"

"You fight for Arawn now," scoffed Tobias. "You are an enemy to your own kin!"

"What you and your men have become in this place is hardly human anymore," returned Rhys.

"You don't know!" spat Tobias. "You can't possibly understand what this place is! We are in Hel! Niflheim: The Abode of Mist!"

"No, we aren't!" refused Rhys. "This is Sumeru. This is Thule. It is still part of the same world where sits the rest of Cambria. A part of it lost to time, but still of the same world!"

"Lies!" roared Tobias, brandishing his axe. "This place is the underworld! It tortures your soul! It whispers into your mind. It makes you do things—made *me* do things... things no man should do!"

"Nothing has made you do anything," returned Rhys. "Your crimes—they are all your own doing; they are all your own choices. It doesn't matter how desperate you were; you only have your self to blame for whatever atrocities you have committed!"

"Don't you understand boy!?" he snarled wide-eyed. "All of us are drowned. We all perished when our ships sailed here!"

"Then why do you want our ship!?" demanded Rhys.

"To escape from here!"

"You've tried and failed many times before. What makes you think its even possible to escape here on a ship?"

"If there is a way here, there must be a way back. Now stand aside, before I kill you and your friends to get what I want."

Rhys peered over his shoulder to see that

several of the castaways had made it to the keel of the Marlin. Now, they were attempting to climb the hull by wedging harpoon heads and knives between the strakes. Waves were crashing up the beach and water was foaming around Rhys's ankles. Lightning continued to toll, louder now as darkness pressed in. The nearby clamour of fighting somewhere off in the mist meant Sol and Maadurga at least were still alive.

"Order your men to retreat," uttered Rhys as he turned back to face the insane gaze of the castaway's leader, "and I'll offer them passage aboard the Marlin when we set sail back to the mainland. You have my word."

"Only my word counts for anything in this place," snarled Tobias. "Now surrender, and I will leave you alive to watch me sail away from these shores aboard that ship!"

"Fuck you," uttered Rhys coldly. A rapid flourish of his staff launched a bolt of force energy. The kinetic fist cascaded into Tobias, staving in his chest, driving him into the sand.

Rhys stood over the madman in his final seconds, watching the fear and hate fade in his eyes as he realised: only now was he truly dying.

TWENTY-EIGHT

"Kalki!" cried Maadurga urgently, drawing the mage's attention back to the surrounding skirmish.

Rhys swivelled to see the elf. Maadurga pointed with her Kukri towards the Marlin; the castaways climbing her hull had leapt back down to the beach the moment Sol had charged in to engage them; but the mage was outnumbered more than a dozen to one and was rapidly being overwhelmed. He danced back and forth, slashing and parrying in a flurry of exchanges with his surrounding foes, mere seconds from being overcome as the castaways pressed his flanks.

Cutting down the villain in her path, Maadurga dashed across the sand, wading into the breaking swell to aid Sol. Rhys took aim for the gang of exiles surrounding the mage, but with his friend skipping back and forth at the heart of the scrimmage, there was little chance he could get off a clean shot. Unwilling to risk Sol being caught in the crossfire, Rhys cursed, lowering his staff, and took off after Maadurga, sprinting the sixty yard stretch of beach towards the Marlin.

Ankle deep foam splashed beneath Rhys's boots as he drew level with Maadurga, quickly overtaking the elf, but up ahead, too far away for Rhys to intervene, Sol's time had run out.

"Sol!" Rhys screamed, watching as the assailing mob of castaways choked around him.

Without warning, the sky flashed white and lightning struck from out of the storm. A blinding glare of light exploded, the jagged tines of a thunderbolt cleaving down from the heavens, connecting with the copper stave in Sol's hands. A shockwave of energy ripped outwards from the explosion. Sand and spray erupted up into the air. A solid wall of air slammed into Rhys and Maadurga, throwing both the mage and elf clean off their feet.

The world spun in dizzying disarray. The gurgle of thunder proceeding the lightning bolt peeled through the dark skies as up became down and down up. Frigid brine embraced Rhys, his broken rib exploding in sickening pain as he slammed hard into the sand. He gasped in agony and cold saltwater gushed into his throat, burning through his nose and stinging his eyes. A second wave broke over Rhys's head as he heaved his throbbing body out of the foam, wiping the brackish water from his eyes.

His vision blurred by the seawater, Rhys

coughed and sputtered, frantically thrashing his head back and forth as he searched for Sol. White sparks glared out of focus up ahead, the very air surrounding Rhys prickling with static electricity. Rhys staggered drunkenly to his feet, his lungs screaming, his ribs aflame. He whipped a palm down his brow, clearing his eyes once more, his vision finally clarifying enough for the scene ahead to draw into focus.

Bands of discharging plasma were crackling across Sol's staff and body, the energy of the thunderbolt radiating out from the mage. His eyes burned white, sparks fizzling across his skin, the air alive with electric current.

Sol stood calmly gazing down at his hands, studying the supernatural effects of the unworldly phenomenon gripping him. Thrown backwards by the same shockwave that had grounded Rhys and Maadurga, the gang of castaways were only now staggering back to their feet. As they each shook themselves out of their daze, one by one, their attention fell on the mage in front of them.

Unnerved by the electrical energy spilling out from Sol's body, all at once, the band of savages slowly raised their spears, harpoons, and axes, backing anxiously away from the fizzling mage. Rhys watched Sol close his fingers into a fist, the grip of his staff tightening in his other hand. The mage clenched his teeth, slowly raising his head as he turned his attention on the anxiously retreating band of castaways in front of him.

Sol strode menacingly forwards, forks of lightning crackling across the surface of the lapping waves as he marched towards his foes. Conducting across the frothy brine, the discharging plasma snaked through the water, electrocuting the nearest of the exiles as they stood ankle deep in the sea. Their bodies convulsed as fingers of lightning zapped up their legs, channelling across their chests, penetrating their hearts. They spasmed and thrashed, before each in turn collapsed dead into the swell.

Cries of terror sounded from further up the beach as Sol marched out of the sea towards his remaining foes. Some turned and fled in fright, whilst the braver of the band steeled their resolve, emitting battle cries as they raised their weapons and charged.

Sol suddenly lurched into motion, sparks trailing behind him as he blurred with lightning speed. Thunderbolts forked through the air as the mage launched a salvo of strikes, immolating the first of the mob to rush him. In an instant he had closed in on the rest, his fizzling staff slashing in wild furious swings as the mage cut all his remaining adversaries to pieces in a matter of seconds. Hurling himself several yards in the blink of an eye, Sol impaled his smouldering blade clean through the heart of the last man in his sights. Tearing his stave back out of the castaway's chest, he let the corpse slump dead at his feet.

As the final villain fell slain, a mere handful of straggling deserters fleeing up the beach in the distance, the last dregs of electricity drained through Sol's body, earthing into the sand.

Sol collapsed to his knees; his whole body quivered, his chest rising and falling in heavy pants as the white glow in his eyes petered out.

"Sol!" Rhys wheezed, clutching his side as he stumbled out of the bubbling wash to his friend's side.

"I'm fine," the mage assured, emitting a long exhale. "Just... drained," he explained.

"I should think so," Rhys returned, both with concern and admiration.

All around, cadavers bobbed in the lapping swill. Blood stained the beach, whilst great tracts of sand snaking away from Sol had solidified into black glass.

"That was..." Rhys croaked. "That was something else entirely!"

"My staff..." breathed Sol. "It conducted the lightning... channelled it. For a few moments... it were as if I had the charge of the lightning bolt stored in me!"

"Like a storm cloud?" asked Rhys, trying to understand.

"No..." the mage shook his head as he struggled momentarily to articulate the sensation. "More like... a bow—pulled to full draw. I couldn't hold the energy long. It was seeping out of me. Each time I cast a bolt, or struck an enemy, it was like releasing the tension in a bow. It wasn't my own strength, it was borrowed… something that needed to be paid back."

"Amazing," breathed Rhys, helping pull Sol up as the mage attempted to climb back to his feet.

"But now…" Sol grimaced as he pushed Rhys away to stand by himself. "Now I feel drained. Like I had to pay it back with interest. Does that make any sense to you?"

"Yes," nodded Rhys. "And no," he added with a wry grin.

"I think it is the rift," explained Sol. "This storm holds more power than any back on the mainland."

Rhys nodded.

"Is it over down there?" called Vidar from over the bulwark.

"Its over," Rhys shouted back in confirmation.

"Sol!" cried Eirik. "Is that Woden's spear?"

Sol chuckled. "No. It's just my staff."

"It looked like Woden's spear to me," agreed Arne as the captain too peered down from the deck.

"Was it a gift, or did you take it from him?" asked Eirik jovially.

"He defeated Woden in single combat and claimed it as his prize!" joked Rhys. "Sol is now the head of the Wild Hunt."

"Shut up, you," smiled Sol.

Ropes were suddenly lowered over the Marlin's gunwales and the three sailors abseiled down, splashing into the swell.

Arne embraced Sol, then moved to do the same for Rhys, but as the hulking sea captain enwrapped the mage in his arms, Rhys felt a blinding spasm of pain shoot across his back. The mage groaned loudly, the nerves beneath his shoulder blade firing in agony. Arne immediately released Rhys in alarm, steadying the mage as he faltered.

"Are you alright!?" the sea captain gasped.

Rhys nodded nauseously, swallowing hard as he waited for the pain to abate.

"Rhys!?" Sol questioned concernedly.

"I'm sorry..." apologised Arne, not understanding exactly what he'd done to cause the mage such agony.

"I think I've broken something," wheezed Rhys, every breath he took sending ripples of blunt throbbing pain across his chest and back.

"Hold still," soothed Sol, moving to his friend and untucking Rhys's shirt, lifting the clothing to inspect the blow across Rhys's back.

"Ouch!" exclaimed Vidar as the injury was unveiled.

"Is it bad?" questioned Rhys, taking shallow breaths to dull the pain.

"It's already black with bruising," explained Sol.

"Certainly feels that way," quipped Rhys, grimacing the moment he started to chuckle.

"I can have a go at it," offered Sol. "But it might be a bit beyond me. You'd be better off having Thia take a look."

Rhys nodded, lowering his clothes back over the wound. "Its alright," insisted the mage jovially, "it only hurts when I breathe."

Sol shook his head, fighting back a smile in his annoyance.

"Thank you for saving our lives," beamed Arne sombrely as he gently laid a hand on Rhys's other shoulder. "Both of you."

"You should really be thanking Maadurga," insisted Rhys, looking to the elf and her two surviving kshatriya stood watching a dozen yards away.

Arne nodded solemnly and both he and his sons walked over to the elves to express their deep gratitude for what they had done.

"What a senseless waste of life," grieved Rhys as he peered around at the graveyard the beach had become.

"There was nothing to be done," insisted Sol. "It was them, or us."

"I just wish they could have seen reason," begrudged the mage. "We could have taken them back with us. We could have helped them…"

"They had descended into savagery," insisted Sol. "We saw their true colours when we first encountered them days ago. They tried to murder us! Thia... they would have—"

"I know," interrupted Rhys, cutting his friend off before he could finish the sentence.

"They were brutal and unconscionable."

"They were desperate," argued Rhys.

"They were lunatics," countered Sol, "driven mad by this place and the things they had done to survive here. Had we taken them back to the shores of Cambria... they couldn't have lived normal lives. At best, they'd have turned to banditry. At worst—well, I'd rather not think about it!"

"You think they were beyond redemption?"

"I'm not sure it's a matter of redemption," replied Sol. "I think it is a matter of condemnation. Their souls and minds were marked—scarred by this place. Those are wounds that can never be healed. At least now we will not blame ourselves for unleashing a group of deranged cutthroats back into society."

"No," refused Rhys. "It can't be that definitive. There has to be redemption. People *can* change—otherwise there is no agency in this world—no freewill!"

"Of course there is freewill," agreed Sol. "But only within the confines of our nature."

Rhys gazed down at the sea foam babbling around his feet; it was died pink with the blood of the slain. Dozens of bodies were being washed up the beach whilst others were being drawn out into the deeper water of the bay. The dark mist was evaporating, but the ceiling of cloud hung low, dispensing a fine drizzle throughout the cove.

"This is gruesome," shuddered Arne sombrely as he approached Sol and Rhys.

Rhys nodded weakly.

"You can't stay here any longer," declared Sol. "Come with us. The elves can offer you refuge in their sacred valley; you'll be safe there!"

Arne shook his head. "Repairs aren't yet done," he replied. "And... I can't abandon her."

"Surely after all this you can see its too dangerous to stay," argued Sol.

"You killed enough of them so that they won't attack again," replied the seaman. "In that sense, we are safe. But if we abandon the Marlin, those that remain will come for her again," assured Arne.

"You are right," agreed Rhys. "But the castaways are far from the only danger here. There is still the Cŵn Annwn; and let us not forget the leviathan."

"Exactly!" emphasized Sol. "You can't stay here alone. I won't let you!"

"They not alone," announced Vihaan, sheathing his Kukri as he approached. "I stay. I protect."

"You don't have to do that," insisted Rhys, peering through the thinning mist to see Maadurga laying out the bodies of her three fallen kshatriya on the sand some way away.

"No. I must," insisted the elf, using the few words he knew in the Common Tongue. "I do for Kalki."

Rhys's insides knotted with inner turmoil at those words. They were words of blind faith; faith stemming not from Rhys's character, nor his mission, but from a misconception of his identity.

"If the Marlin is taken, then we have no way home," insisted Arne.

Sol and Arne continued to dispute the matter, but Rhys wished to hear no more of it. He walked out of the splashing foam and onto the damp sand of the shoreline. He wandered through the littering of bodies and finally came to stand behind Maadurga as she positioned her three slain warriors side by side with their hands crossed on their breasts. She took the kukris and scabbards from their belts and stowed them in a saddlebag hung from Dawon as the gryphon lay out on the sand beside his master.

"I'm sorry," offered Rhys regretfully, not knowing what else he could say.

"They have returned to Samsara," returned Maadurga, rising to meet Rhys's eyes. She appeared troubled, but not overly grief-stricken. "But for them to be reborn, we must perform Antyesti."

"Antyesti?" repeated the mage.

"The last sacrifice," explained the elf. "Their bodies must be cleaned and burnt."

"A cremation," nodded Rhys. "Do you want to do it now?"

"No," Maadurga shook her head. "Antyesti will be performed here—it is by the sea. But, it will be a day from now. And their families should be the ones to do it."

"I understand," confirmed Rhys. "And what of their blades?" he asked, indicating to Dawon's saddlebag.

"I will present them to their families when I deliver the news."

A period of silence lasted between the two of them as they looked at the three elves lain peacefully on the grey sand. The tide continued to roll in, and raindrops splattered down through the tolling thunder.

"Vihaan will remain here and watch over your friends," announced Maadurga.

"He doesn't have to," returned Rhys.

"But he wishes to nonetheless. I did not ask him to; he asked me."

"At least the castaways are of little danger now," conceded the mage.

"I will ask for other volunteers from my kshatriya to help Vihaan in his watch once we return to Suraksa."

"Thank you," murmured Rhys, looking back to see Sol shaking his lowered head at Arne, Vidar, and Eirik. From his defeated look, Rhys suspected he had been unsuccessful in convincing the three sailors to accompany him back to the Sacred Valley.

"Come," beckoned Maadurga. "We should return. Your other friends will wish to know what has become of us."

TWENTY-NINE

Cold air washed through Rhys's hair as he clung silently to Maadurga aback Dawon. The storm buffeted the gryphon's great wings as the majestic beast soared ever higher into the tempest. The flight back to the Sacred Valley was as gentle as both Dawon and his master could manage, but even still, with each lurch caused by the turbulence, Rhys clenched his teeth, fighting to remain conscious, every spasm of pain pushing him closer to blacking out. Touching down on the slopes of the vale's foothills, Rhys was saved from tumbling out of the saddle by Maadurga, the elf grappling him tightly, easing the mage down to the ground when they finally came to a stop.

The two of them made their way silently down the path back into the village of Suraksa. The elf bid the mage farewell as she departed to seek out the families of Fulan, Naahbi, and Tivi. She offered Rhys a warm smile and they went their separate ways on the fringes of the elven settlement.

Midday was approaching and the Midsummer celebrations appeared to have come to a close. The sunlit streets of Suraksa were peaceful and mostly empty. A few elves sat on their doorsteps or on benches in the various small garden plots scattered about the hillside. Many nodded placidly the mage's way as Rhys passed them by, but few so much as uttered a word of greeting. The rest of the villagers, Rhys suspected, must have been meditating in their homes following the night's nonstop festivities.

Finally, the mage made it back to the intricately carved doors of the small house where he and his companions had been put up by Maadurga. Knowing his friends were almost certainly asleep inside, he gently pressed his palm against the door and slipped in through the gap, trying not to let any of the bright noontime sun spill into the darkened room. Closing the door quietly behind him, Rhys gazed around the shaded interior to see his friends were indeed resting on the array of hides and blankets scattered about the living quarters. All were asleep, except Thia.

The witch sat up slowly when Rhys entered. The slatted beams of sunlight streaking through the shutters fell over her in a near ethereal manner; Rhys smiled as he admired how, even after being awake for more than a full day, she still was as beautiful as ever. She greeted Rhys with a whisper, but narrowed her gaze suspiciously as she noticed him cradling his side.

"What have you done now?"

"Someone broke an oar across my back," confessed the mage. "Or was it: I broke my back across someone's oar? I can't quite recall—things tend to get a bit hazy in the heat of battle."

Thia rolled her eyes. "Well, come on then," she huffed, rising to her feet. "Let's have a look at it." The witch aided Rhys in removing his cowl and shirt. For a brief moment, her slender fingers hovered above his chest before she encircled him to inspect the injury on his back. Gently probing the tender skin, Thia offered her reassurance. "It's just a fractured rib; nothing too serious."

"It feels serious!" grimaced Rhys as Thia's fingers explored the bruising.

"Here," she gestured to the mage's bed, "lie down."

She eased Rhys to the ground and the mage sprawled prone across his bedroll. The witch straddled his lower back and produced her wand, holding it over the darkened skin below his shoulder blade. Within a matter of seconds, Rhys felt a jarring crunch as his rib fused itself. His own hand slapped over his mouth so as not to awaken everyone else in the room as he stifled a cry. The throbbing steadily subsided and Thia turned her attention then to the bruising itself; after a few more moments of the witch weaving her magic, there was little more than a lingering dull ache. Thia shuffled off the mage to sit on her own bedroll. Rhys panted heavily as a bead of sweat trickled down his brow.

"Better?"

"Better," Rhys nodded, reaching for his undershirt and draping it back over his torso, before slumping once again onto the goat hide.

Thia reclined beside him, meeting Rhys's gaze as he groggily opened his eyes. She smiled gently. "Do you want to tell me what happened?"

Rhys nodded, rolling over onto his side before beginning his account of what had transpired in their battle for the Marlin. Throughout it all, Thia lay listening attentively in silence.

"Sol is right," assured the witch when all was said and done. "They were loyal enough to Tobias to die for him, and from what he told of himself, he seemed an irredeemable character. Any who would follow a man like that to their grave has lost a part of themselves. You only feel remorse because you pitied their situation—but a man's circumstances don't justify his actions."

"There is wisdom in that," conceded Rhys as he reclined on the goat hide next to Thia, his eyelids now lulling heavily.

They exchanged a few more tired sentences between them, before almost simultaneously, they both succumbed to lassitude and slipped deeply into sleep.

It was evening when Rhys next opened his

eyes. Most of his friends were still resting, but the soft murmurs of Alkis and Nathaniel whispering in the corner carried through the stillness. Sol was asleep beneath a blanket on the far side of the room; Rhys didn't know how long the mage had been there, but he had not awoken anyone when he had snuck in after returning from the beach. From the amber tint of the light spilling through the slats in the shutters, Rhys estimated that it was dusk outside. Still drowsy, he rolled over and quickly drifted back into slumber, awakening once again to cool moonlight gleaming through the open shutters.

Most of the party were chitchatting quietly amongst themselves now, though Sol was still laying silently in the same position he had been earlier. Rubbing his eyes, Rhys sat upright and stretched before rising and making his way over to the ewer of water resting on the table in the corner. Pouring himself a mug and sipping it slowly, Rhys joined his friends' conversation. Not long later, Sol roused, likewise entering the discussion.

Venturing out in search of food a short while later, they were very quickly sighted by an elven man and woman stood waiting at the threshold of their house. Speaking exclusively in Elvish, the partners warmly greeted Rhys and the others, hurriedly shepherding them inside their home. Stepping through the door, the party were greeted by another elven couple sat around a table laden with bowls of rice, dals, spiced pickles, and tarkari, with stacks of flatbreads heaped in the middle. Directed in both Elvish and by an accompanying array of enthusiastic hand gestures, they were all instructed to take seats on the floor cushions surrounding the low dining table. Moments later, they were each handed a mug brimming with hot chhaang.

Their hosts seated themselves around the same table, and without pause, the four elves began helping themselves to the array of colourful dishes, indicating that the others should do the same. Seemingly not a word of the Common Tongue was understood by the hosts; regardless, conversation moved back and forth between the elves and Rhys and his companions all the same. It was clear that their hosts had been expecting them; there was more than enough food, even with eleven squeezed around the table. What wasn't clear however, was whether their hosts had taken it upon themselves to feed their guests entirely out of their own initiative, or were doing so by request from Maadurga, or perhaps some village elder. Nonetheless, the food was delicious, the chhaang flowed freely, and the conversation, though largely incomprehensible, was warm and friendly.

Once they had eaten and drunk their fill, the group offered their gratitude and said their goodbyes to the elves, before venturing out into the night. Together they strolled the valley around the outskirts of the village, admiring the moon and the changing colours of the Rift above. Returning in the small hours to their accommodation, they chatted for a time longer, before sleeping thereafter until sunrise.

The following day, the village seemed to have recovered in full from the solstice celebrations; the streets were once again rife with bustling activity as the elves went about their daily routines. Rhys was greeted frequently as he made his way about Suraksa, many bowing their heads his way, smiling, pausing from their business to stop and stare at the mage, often for prolonged durations. The mage wandered somewhat aimlessly, admiring the wares of the various merchant stalls set up around the village, but the majority of his time spent strolling, he was searching for Maadurga.

As far as Rhys could tell, the elves had no specific currency, instead bartering in exchanged goods. Some came to the stalls with baskets of eggs and ewers of milk to purchase spices and rice, others brought sacks of firewood and bamboo barrels of fermenting chhang to trade for plucked chickens or goat meat; one man offered a live pig to a bowyer in exchange for one of the reflex bows hung on the rack erected on his porch. Some exchanged no visible items, merely bartering in words before walking away with their goods, presumably having offered some service or debt in exchange.

Haggling was rife, and on the verge of aggressive in some cases, yet it always remained civil; when a deal was finally reached, the two elves involved in the trade always exchanged friendly goodbyes. Eventually, Rhys found himself outside the forge of Suraksa's blacksmith. Three elves altogether worked the smithy; one clutched a glowing length of steel above an anvil with a set of enormous tongues, another swinging the sledgehammer, dealing heavy blows to the heated metal, denting it slowly but surely into the curving shape of a kukri. In the rear of the workshop, the third smith was engraving a near finished blade with an intricate teardrop pattern.

On display out front, were racks of the finished item, each kukri more impressive than the last. The collection of Elven blades were each individually decorated with their own unique finish, some gilded, others etched, some inlayed and encrusted, all forged from fine damasked steel, and each likely worth a fortune back on the mainland.

The smiths slowed their efforts as the mage studied their work, curious as to what Kalki would make of their craftsmanship, yet before Rhys could appraise the incredible weapons too closely, the distant cry of a gryphon sounded high in the sky above; Rhys caught sight of Dawon gliding down into the Sacred Valley, Maadurga in the saddle. Without delay, Rhys departed the forge and swiftly made his way out of the village, up the path towards Dawon's roost.

Halfway up the hillside, Rhys was met by Maadurga coming the other way. She greeted him with a warm smile, her saddle and tacking bundled under her arm as her dark hair wafted in the late morning breeze.

"Hello Kalki," she beamed, pausing for a moment before the two fell into step with one another back down the path to Suraksa. "How is your injury?"

"Better, thank you," replied Rhys, rolling his shoulder in a display of wellbeing. "How did it go?" questioned the mage. "Antyesti?"

"They have returned to Samsara. Their souls are at peace; their bodies have returned to the five elements, but their Atman is immortal."

"But the funeral… the ritual: the last sacrifice—it went well?"

"Fulan, Naahbi, and Tivi's families wept," replied Maadurga. "They still mourn. But our people know life begins anew. In time, their Atman will find new vessels. They will be reincarnated and will live on."

"It's a nice sentiment," offered Rhys, wishing he could have faith in such a thing.

"You do not believe in the immortal soul, do you Kalki?" questioned Maadurga knowingly. "Yet you see things from your past lives?"

"My dreams aren't from my past lives," Rhys assured. "I have a connexion to them, yes.

But they aren't the different vessels my immortal soul has inhabited. One person's past I have seen is someone I have met; he was alive at the same time as me. I trust I am right in assuming your beliefs say one soul cannot exist in two bodies at a time?"

Maadurga remained quiet for a long moment before conceding, "This is true. But the sadhu in the Temple understand Samsara and Brahman in ways I do not. They might know how it is you see the past of other souls."

"I hope so," pondered Rhys, still unable to make sense of the dreams he had been subjected to since setting sail for the Wyrm's Triangle.

"I need a short time to prepare for the pilgrimage to the Temple of Kalki, but I will be ready to leave Suraksa by noon."

"I wasn't sure if we would still be beginning the journey today," confessed Rhys. "With what happened yesterday, and with Antyesti..."

"It is the day after Karkasankranti, the first day of Dakshinayana," responded Maadurga. "Today is the day to begin the journey. Many others have already set out."

"Very well. I'll find Sol and Thia. We'll be ready at noon," he assured her.

"There are things you will need for the journey," explained Maadurga. "I will bring them to you."

"Thank you," smiled Rhys as they arrived back at the village outskirts.

They parted ways once again. Rhys returned to his lodgings to find all of his companions were there, eating a breakfast of steamed rice with egg and vegetables.

"Are the two of you ready for the climb up Suraksameru?" asked Rhys as he seated himself between Sol and Thia. The mage plated up a larger helping than normal, figuring that, if he was due for an alpine ascent in the afternoon, he could do with all the sustenance he could stomach.

"We are still going?" questioned Sol somewhat in surprise as he polished off the last of his breakfast.

Rhys nodded, unable to respond otherwise through a mouth stuffed with rice.

"I've already packed," replied Thia, nodding to her bag stowed neatly in the corner of the room.

"When are we leaving?" pressed Sol, rising to his feet.

"At noon."

Sol approached the window to see the sun nearing its zenith. "So... any time about now then!?" realised the mage, rushing to shove all of his possessions back into his bag.

Rhys eyed his mostly packed knapsack as he scoffed the last few mouthfuls of food when a knock came at the door.

"Shit," cursed Sol as he tried forcing the last of his clothes into the poorly organised pack.

Thia rose calmly to her feet to answer the call. Stood there in the midday sun was a kshatriya carrying a bow in each hand.

"Cade?" questioned the elf as she looked around the room.

"You must be Ehani?" the huntsman spoke up, rising from his cushion to politely greet his teacher.

"Yes," she replied bluntly, lingering silently in the threshold thereafter.

"You are my teacher?" questioned Cade. "Archery?"

"Dhanurveda," replied the elf, nodding as she did so.

"Do you speak any of the Common tongue?" questioned the hunter.

"Yes," replied the kshatriya.

"Other than the word '*yes*,'?"

"Yes."

Cade sighed. "Such as?"

Ehani raised her hand clutching the smaller of the two reflex bows and offered it to Cade. The huntsman apprehensively took hold of it. Ehani released her grip before uttering another single word, "Come." With that, she turned her back on Cade and marched off down the path.

Cade glanced back into the room, realising Rhys, Sol, and Thia would not be there when he returned. "I guess I'll see the three of you when you get back. How long do you think you'll be?"

Thia and Sol both shrugged, deferring to

Rhys for a response.

"However long it takes to learn all of the secrets of the Aether," replied Rhys with a wry smile.

"That sounds like code for: *I haven't the foggiest idea!*" mocked the hunter.

"Sounds about right," confirmed Rhys.

Cade peered out the door to realise that Ehani had no intention of waiting for him. "I had better go."

"Good luck," issued Thia, hugging him.

"I'm sure I've got a lot to learn," sighed Cade as he moved to Sol, shaking the mage's hand.

"You'll be fine," assured Rhys as the two of them embraced. "Watch Ulfgar for me whilst we are gone," he added with a not-so-subtle whisper

"Hey!" protested the dwarf through a mouthful of rice.

"I'll see you soon," he declared, vanishing out the door.

With Cade gone, Rhys began shovelling the last of his own possessions into his pack, ensuring they were tightly rolled to avoid the pains of reorganising the knapsack Sol was going through. Thia waited patiently as the two magi finished gathering their possessions when another shadow appeared in the doorway. Rhys revolved, expecting to see Maadurga, yet in the threshold were stood two more kshatriya.

"Cetan and Shankha, I presume?" asked

Alkis, rising from his seat, reaching for his bastard sword sheathed in its scabbard.

"I am Cetan," confirmed the taller of the two with a thick Elvish accent.

"Shankha," nodded the other gesturing to himself.

"You come to train with us?" asked Cetan, looking to Alkis.

"We do," nodded Nathaniel as the guardsman likewise rose, gathering up his heater shield and axe.

"Come!" instructed Cetan, motioning for the two men to follow.

"Just a moment," delayed Alkis, gesturing for the elves to wait. "We'll see you when you get back—whenever that might be," conceded the knight, shaking Sol and Rhys's hands firmly before embracing Thia.

"I hope you find what you are looking for," offered Nathaniel, smiling as he too said his goodbyes.

"I'm not sure I know what that is," returned Rhys, meeting the guardsman's eyes as they shook hands tightly.

"In which case, I hope you find *out* what you are looking for."

"As do I," nodded the mage waving the two men off as they followed the kshatriya out of the door. "As do I," he repeated again, this time under his breath.

Within seconds of Alkis and Nathaniel's

departure, Maadurga appeared in the threshold; the elf wore boots and fur leggings, her torso draped in a plain ochre shawl: far more conservative clothing than the silken saris and cholis he normally saw her in outside her mirror armour. Across her back was a small pack and bundled under her arms were three sheepskin coats.

"You are ready?" she asked, looking at Sol as the mage finally succeeded in pulling taught the drawstring at the top of his traveller's pack and buckled it shut.

"Yes," replied Rhys as he too closed his knapsack.

"I have brought you these," declared the elf, offering them each a jacket.

"A little warm for these, isn't it?" questioned Thia.

"In the Valley, yes," agreed Maadurga. "But atop Suraksameru, at the Temple, it will be cold."

"How long will it take to get there?" questioned Sol.

"We will reach the start of the trail by nightfall," explained Maadurga. "We begin the climb early the next morning and arrive before dark."

"And how difficult *is* the climb?"

"There is a trail," explained the elf. "Young children make the journey. When a child decides they wish to seek enlightenment and become a sadhu, they journey to the Temple, where they remain until they die."

"If young children can make the journey, it shouldn't be too difficult," surmised Sol.

"Young *elven* children," reminded Rhys. "I'm sure there is a world of difference there."

"You make a good point," conceded Sol.

"You are strong and fit," assured Maadurga looking to the three of them. "You will be fine."

"Well," chirped up Ulfgar, "have fun on your little mountaineering expedition."

"We'll miss you too," returned Rhys mockingly.

"See you around, lad," the dwarf nodded as he began stuffing his pipe with tobacco.

"Behave," warned Sol.

"Never."

Sol shook his head silently as the four of them left the house.

Together, they made their way through Suraksa. Many of the elven villagers bowed their heads respectfully as they passed; Rhys heard Kalki murmured repeatedly amongst the susurrations of Elvish whispers as every resident of Suraksa seemed to congregate throughout the streets to see them off.

"I trust they all know where we are going?" questioned Rhys.

"It is an important day," confirmed Maadurga. "Kalki is returning back to the place where he first saw fit to build his temple. They believe you will achieve Nirvana. When you return from the Temple, you will have all the knowledge and memories from your past lives; it is then you will be able to stand with your followers against the rakshasa; against Mahakala."

"No pressure then," jested Rhys as they left the villagers amassed in the streets behind, setting out on the path into the foothills.

With the village quickly receding, Rhys peered down the slopes and caught sight of Alkis and Nathaniel sparring with Cetan and Shankha in a small paddock below. The two men, though seasoned and admired fighters back in their respective realms, were outmatched by their elven opponents. The mage watched a quick exchange between the four warriors. Within seconds, the two kshatriya had broken the guards of their human counter parts, quick dodges and deft counters being enough to overwhelm both Alkis and Nathaniel's usually stalwart defences. They each reset, the next bout breaking into sudden action, only for it to be over just as quick as the last. Time after time, the two soldiers readopted their stances, just to be bested mere seconds later when the sparring resumed. Even from this distance, Rhys could make out the disdain and frustration of his friends' body language, their frequent and rapid successive defeats proving somewhat humbling.

Meanwhile, on a hilltop not far from the other two, Rhys spied Cade and Ehani. They were stood facing a hanging target. Cade was aiming his child's reflex bow at the target ahead, the string drawn but no arrow nocked. After a short moment, Ehani encircled him, tapping his ankle, his forearm, the small of his back, and his neck each in turn with her own bow. Cade loosened the tension in the weapon, rolling his shoulder and lowering his head in annoyance as he received a lecture, most likely in Elvish, from his new archery instructor. Rhys smiled to himself, continuing to watch his friends from over his shoulder until they drew out of sight for the last time.

They trekked through acres of rice paddies, out beyond the limits of the village's farmland, and continued further still, further than Rhys had yet explored throughout the valley of Suraksa. Passing several hilltop chortens, their golden spires rising from white shrines strung with lines of prayer flags, they journeyed on through maple and cedar groves, steadily climbing the slopes of the dale throughout the day. Halting briefly by a gushing rill to replenish their water supply, the group continued on late in the afternoon, skirting the northern fringes of the valley.

The rift glowed a faint emerald in the blue skies overhead and the sun was periodically blotted out by drifting clouds, but as evening drew in, a fiery sunset igniting the western peaks, storm clouds brewed from over the ridge above. Shortly after dusk, a sudden squall rushed down the slopes out of the black heavens. Within the hour, the heavy shower blew over and the murky cloud cover evaporated into starlight bathed in the violet shades of the rift. The peak of Suraksameru loomed forever in a pall of white mist. Portions of the summit periodically emerged from behind the veil of cloud, yet the Temple itself, supposedly sat atop the summit, remained illusively hidden at all times.

As night fell, they made camp on the border of an alder copse nestled in the foothills of Suraksameru itself. Ahead, a mile or so further up the path, Rhys made out a set of wooden posts rising from two large cairns set either side of the trail; across their tops sat a wooden lintel wrapped colourfully in prayer flags.

"That marks the start of the sacred trail," explained Maadurga as she stood beside the mage and looked ahead up the slopes of Suraksameru.

Rhys followed the path with his gaze, tracing the twisting track and trail markers as they seemingly encircled the mountain dextrally, ascending various steep faces towards the lofty zenith: one of the five great peaks of Sumeru.

THIRTY

Rhys inhaled deeply as he perched on the mountain precipice. Winds buffeted his face, rustling his hair as it whistled through the upper atmosphere. He stood gazing out from the vertical ledge, down at the sierra ringing the Sacred Valley. Verdant paddies carved out from the mountainsides in great flooded steps, whilst further up the subalpine slopes, the red canopies of hundreds of maple copses swayed in the breeze. Gazing down through the gaps in the basin, where the feet of the mountains nestled together but failed to touch, the mage glimpsed distant scudding clouds breaking occasionally to offer brief glimpses of the dark waters of the Wyrm's Triangle.

Roughly halfway up the slopes of Suraksameru, they'd now climbed above the height of any of the Sacred Valley's other surrounding peaks. Gazing out across the floating jagged spine, Rhys watched clouds seething beyond the natural walls protecting the vale; outside the haven of the valley, the storm clouds plumed into dark anvils, flashing silently with sheet lightning. In the distance, nestling in a crook between the foothills, on the far side of the floating dale, Rhys could descry the village of Suraksa itself.

Done surveying the sweeping vista for the time being, the mage turned away from the expansive view to the sound of laboured puffing. He grasped Thia's hand firmly and helped her up the final step onto the shelf. As the witch caught her breath, Rhys guided Thia over to a nearby cairn, easing her to the ground. Thia sat and rested, the others waiting patiently for her to stop panting.

"I don't know why I'm struggling so badly," she apologised.

"It's the air," explained Rhys, flaring his nostrils as he sucked down a wispy lungful. "It is getting thinner the higher we climb.

"He's right," agreed Sol. "I can feel it. There's less substance to it."

"I'm finding it harder to breathe myself," assured Rhys.

"Look," exclaimed Sol, gesturing to the slopes below. "We are above the treeline."

Rhys and Thia both peered out from the ledge, quickly noticing that the last canopies of the subalpine region were now well below them. Glancing then uphill, Rhys spied only a few final trees clinging to life on the barren slopes above, the dwarfed specimens so deformed and twisted that they barely resembled trees at all.

"Your body will grow accustomed to the air," assured Maadurga, kneeling beside the witch as she finally succeeded in steadying her breathing. The elf produced a waterskin hung around her waist and offered it to Thia. "Here, it will help."

Uncorking the waterskin, Thia took a few tentative sips in between laboured breaths before returning it to Maadurga.

"You ready?" Rhys asked sympathetically.

Thia nodded, clambering back to her feet, pausing for a moment to admire the views. There on, they followed the ledge around the curving cliff face, proceeding up the next run of narrow steps carved out the mountainside, tightly hugging the near vertical walls of stone as they followed the trail of cairns and prayer flags.

Rounding a turn in the path, they sighted an elven pilgrim up ahead lying prone on the floor.

"Is he alright!?" questioned Rhys, moving to offer the prostrate elf assistance, yet before he could get close, the pilgrim rose steadily to his feet. Once upright, the elf continued several steps down the path, only to then bow, lowering himself back down to the ground into another prostration, where he remained for several seconds before repeating the process all over again.

"What's he doing?" questioned Thia, as together they watched the elven pilgrim repeat the ritualistic movement over and over.

"He performs the Kora," explained Maadurga. "He left Suraksa two weeks ago. He has journeyed the whole way like this."

"He is making the entire pilgrimage whilst prostrating the whole way?" questioned Sol in disbelief.

Maadurga nodded. "It is an act of devotion to Kalki. This mountain is sacred. Some believe the Kora is the only true way to make the journey to the Temple."

"Wow," breathed Rhys in admiration for the level of devotion, steadily approaching the elf circumambulating the mountain from behind.

The moment the elf saw Rhys, he faltered, his eyes almost instantly falling to the crystal staff strapped across the mage's back, the veins of jade pulsating gently within. His gaze widened and suddenly the elf fell reverently into another prostration, this time his hands directed straight towards Rhys.

"Pransa Kalki!" he wept from the floor.

"Its okay," Rhys assured the pilgrim. "You can stand up."

But the elf remained prone, his face pressed to the trail. "Pransa Kalki."

"Maadurga?"

"Pransa Kalki!"

"He will not rise," she assured Rhys. "Not so long as you are here."

Rhys sighed heavily. "Come on then. Let's move. He's already spending enough time on the ground as it is."

"Pransa Kalki," uttered the pilgrim one final time.

They overtook the elf and continued along the trail, passing beneath various wooden torana erected over the way. Prayer flags were strung intermittently across the mountain steps, flapping in the strong winds, whilst at regular intervals, cairn trail markers balanced impossibly on the lip of the path, forever threatening to topple over the precipice, but never doing so.

The four of them climbed higher, steadily encircling the mountain, passing various elven pilgrims along the way, each stopping in their tracks to bow reverently Rhys's way when he passed. Some were performing the Kora, making their circumambulation in an unending series of prostrations, whilst others were merely walking the trail, taking the time to pray at the various wayside shrines erected along the path. Some were little more than slabs of stone laden with prayer beads and smouldering incense, whilst others were ornately sculpted wooden altars set inside arches carved out of the rock; these more established worship sites were often laid with offerings of alpine flowers, and on occasion, small gems and pieces of jewellery could be seen amongst the prayer beads. At each shrine they passed, Maadurga herself stopped to kneel, closing her eyes in a moment of silent devotion before rising to lead on.

Wending northward, the trail guided them around the northern face of Suraksameru, the view of the valley vanishing behind the mountain. A wall of cloud sank across the path and the winds swelled into ripping currents, the party exposed to the elements now that they had left the shelter of the Sacred Valley. Thunder began tolling loudly and sporadic squalls lashed from out of the tempest. They marched on through the rain and gales, along the ever-narrowing path and up the steepening staircases. Occasionally now, they witnessed cairns toppling in the winds; each time, Maadurga paused a few moments to rapidly rebuild the collapsed trail marker. At first Rhys and the others had offered the elf help in restacking the stones, yet after watching the kshatriya deftly pile the first set into a tall stack in a matter of mere seconds, they decided silently between themselves that they would only hinder her efforts.

As thicker and thicker cloud drew in, Rhys began to truly appreciate Maadurga's efforts at restoring the cairns, for in the continually congealing fog, the silhouettes of the trail markers stood out against the dense gloom, forever signing the way ahead. Though for the most part, when following the carved steps and narrow shelves lipping around the circumference of Suraksameru, the trail was easy enough to follow, at oft times it became somewhat ambiguous, traversing over shingly slopes and through great mossy carpets matting the alpine tundra.

The day wore on and the weather only worsened as they looped around the north face. The lashing rain frequently solidified to stinging hail that clattered off the cliff faces, and Rhys, Sol, and Thia quickly came to appreciate the sheepskin coats Maadurga had gifted them. The higher they rose, the more the air thinned. They took frequent breaks to catch their breath, even Maadurga by this time finding the ascent taxing. During one such pause, whilst their elven guide bowed in reverence before a wayside shrine, Rhys discerned something moving across the path up ahead. He moved closer to inspect, only for the shadow to dart off into the murk.

"What was that!?" gasped Rhys, creeping closer to where he'd spotted it.

"I don't know," replied Sol. "I barely saw it."

The wind lulled in a moment of eerie silence as Rhys inched closer still. He finally reached the place where he'd seen it; there was nothing there. He glanced around, searching for some sign of whatever had been stood watching him, when suddenly, out of the mist, a shadow pounced down from the ledge above. Rhys instinctually drew his staff as his heart leapt in his chest. The shape bounded over the scree at speed. Two enormous curving horns scythed through the mist, its hooves rattling as they clattered across the stone.

Rhys let out a sigh of relief as he watched the mountain goat scamper away down the slope; a moment later, both Thia and Sol broke into laughter.

"Alright," Rhys conceded, appreciating that from their point of view, watching himself being startled by nothing more than a mountain goat would have been quite entertaining.

"The look on your face!" chortled Sol.

"It can't be that funny," returned Rhys, supressing his own laughter as Thia and Sol both cackled in hysterics.

"It was," insisted Thia.

"It could have been anything!"

"But it wasn't," mocked Thia.

"What else has horns like that and would be this far up a mountain?" questioned Sol mockingly.

"I don't know," shrugged Rhys. "Let's not forget that this place is home to both gryphons and a dragon! Who knows what else is here!?"

"You make a good point," conceded Sol, wiping away a tear from his eye.

"You are right to be cautious," warned Maadurga, rising from her knees before the shrine. "There are many dangers throughout Sumeru that reside higher up the mountain—some that *do* have horns like a goat."

"Really?" inquired Sol. "What are they?"

"I have not seen one myself," explained the elf, "but my people tell stories of the men of the snow: the yeti."

"Yeti?" repeated Rhys.

"Part bear, part ape, with white fur, and the horns of a mountain goat; they stand on two legs and walk around like men or elves. It is said that high up the slopes of Sumeru, you can hear their howls during the night."

"Are they dangerous?" asked Thia.

"They hunt goats and yak, but they have been known to take elves."

"Take?" questioned Sol. "Where to?"

"Back to their lairs," replied the elf. "To their caves hidden deep within the mountains."

"But you've never seen one?" questioned Rhys.

"No," replied Maadurga.

"Do you know anyone who has?"

"My people do not head much higher up Sumeru than the Sacred Valley. Above here is the realm of the rakshasa, Mahakaleshwar, the temple of Mahakala. We do not venture into their territory. Above that is the peak of Kalapa, where the Vritra has made its lair; higher still is Shambala, guarded fiercely by the Amara."

"It is just a legend then?" asked Rhys.

"One that comes from a time before the Cintamani Stone brought ruin to Sumeru."

"Then I suppose there is every chance that they are real," returned Rhys. "There was a time not all too long ago when I did not even believe that magic was real—yet here I am now, little more than a year later, stood atop a mountain floating in the sky, beside an elf, a witch, and a mage, with dragons and gryphons flying about."

"And yet you still aren't open to the possibility that deities might be responsible for it all?" questioned Sol.

"Nope," replied Rhys bluntly, entertained by the fact that his response irked Sol.

"Come," Maadurga led on, "we must reach the Temple by nightfall."

Rhys and Sol nodded, falling into rank. The path further narrowed as it ascended higher into the smoking clouds. The temperature continued to drop, but as they circled back around the southern face of the mountain, the winds died down and the hail and rains surrendered to a light drizzle persisting through the heavy mist. Suddenly ahead, Maadurga stopped dead in her tracks. Her abrupt halt set Rhys and Sol on edge, both men instinctively pausing, their hands primed to draw the weapons across their backs. Seconds later, they were put at ease when the elf turned back to look at them with a smile across her face. She gestured for them to approach, and as they cautiously obeyed, Maadurga pointed up ahead. As the pall of gloom drew open, Rhys descried what the kshatriya had spotted.

A small creature sat atop a rock a few dozen feet ahead; its body was covered with silver fur, a long tail coiled around the stone on which it perched. A pink face bore two large humanoid eyes that beheld the four of them, behind which Rhys sensed an intelligence absent in most animals. In his hand the creature gripped a piece of fruit, perhaps obtained from a pilgrim that had passed by not long ago. Still staring intently their way, the animal sank its fanged teeth into the fruit, taking a bite.

"What is it?" questioned Rhys.

"Bandara," replied Maadurga, shrugging her shoulders as she realised the common name for the creature was outside her vocabulary.

"It's a monkey!" announced Sol with a grin across his face. "I've never seen one before."

"There are many in the temple," explained Maadurga. "They bring good fortune."

"He looks so… human," puzzled Thia.

"Here," gesticulated Maadurga, rifling through her knapsack to produce a kumquat. The elf handed the small yellow fruit to Thia and motioned for the witch to offer it to the monkey.

Tentatively, Thia took the fruit and slowly approached the silver-furred creature. The animal's eyes widened, his attention fixing squarely on the kumquat Thia was holding as he sat munching the remnants of the fruit in his own hand. The witch neared, offering up the kumquat. The monkey continued to chew and outreached with his small fingers. Snatching the food dexterously from Thia's palm, the creature stood up on its haunches, his tail snaking in the air, swiftly bounding off the rock on which he was sat. Discarding the rind in his other hand, the monkey stuffed the kumquat into his mouth and scampered up the rocky slope, disappearing into the mist. Thia giggled with delight as she watched the animal retreat with his prize, before turning back to face Rhys with an infectious smile from cheek to cheek.

"He was gorgeous!" she chirped to Maadurga.

"He was," agreed the elf.

Thia wrinkled her nose as she smiled at Rhys and the mage beamed back at her, yet the two of them averted their gaze from one another as they realised Sol had registered the exchange.

"Come on," beckoned Rhys. "It cannot be much further now."

"We are close," confirmed Maadurga.

Setting off again, they continued for the next hour across the southern face of Suraksameru as the invisible summit drew steadily within their reach. They passed further pilgrims along the way as they looped once more around the mountain, out towards the western slopes, away from the sheltered inner face of the horn, where the winds picked back up and the rain refroze to hail. Out on the exposed north face, howling gales roared across the mountainside in deafening blasts in which the four of them struggled to stand upright. To make matters worse, the tight walkways continued to narrow; at points, they were forced to shimmy along ledges little more than a foot across, the precipice falling hundreds of fathoms away to the slopes below. A single wrong step or an unexpected gust could send a pilgrim tumbling off the sheer drop to their death. Fortunately, these sections of narrow shelf often had handholds cut into the cliff faces with the occasional rope serving as a handrail.

Circumambulating the mountain for a second time, they found themselves back on the southern face, and almost immediately, the roaring winds and thundering hale died. Rhys peered up through the billowing haze and sighted the summit high above: a single horn with sharp angular sides cutting like a knife into the swirling murk. The zenith of Suraksameru held no plateau or mesa, its slopes were near vertiginous with no flattening or even an ease in their incline. No temple could possibly sit atop such a harsh and dramatic peak. The mage stopped in his tracks, fearing there had been some mistake, or that he had been duped for some reason into climbing the mountain on false promises; yet, as he continued to peer upwards through the effervescing fog, the secrets of the Temple of Kalki revealed themselves.

In some impossible feat of architecture, the Temple hung from the vertical face of the mountainside. Tiers of halls and pavilions snaked back and forth across the rockface, clinging to the sheer wall in a gravity defying marvel, sheltered by the inward curve of the peak's concaved southern face.

"I don't believe it," exclaimed Rhys, craning his neck to survey the suspended system of buildings and wooden walkways.

Thia and Sol paused ahead of him, turning back as Rhys uttered the words, yet before they could look up to see the Temple in its illusory magnificence, the gloom drew back over the summit like a closing curtain.

"What is it?" questioned Sol.

Rhys chuckled. "You'll have to wait and see."

Ascending another set of steps that bore more semblance to a ladder than a stairwell, the party completed the final leg of the pilgrimage. Atop the rise before them, for the first time in the entire trail, the path reversed in direction, cutting back along the southern face of the horn before yielding to what lay beyond. Ahead, a large decorative gold and crimson torana stood marking the gateway to the Temple. Past the archway, extending outwards from the precipice, stretched a wooden walkway suspended above nothing more than swirling mist. The catwalk was fastened to the cliff face by a series of wooden crossbeams driven deep into the stone; boards were fastened between them, forming the path. There were no railings along the ledge, nor a single handhold in the stone. Although the wooden walkway was rigid, not prone to swaying in the breeze like the rope bridges interconnecting the islands below, the prospect of balancing along the structure ahead seemed infinitely more terrifying.

"Who's first?" joked Rhys nervously as he realised they had all come to a halt beside the final trail marker.

"Kalki must be the first to pass through the gates," explained Maadurga, looking sombrely to Rhys.

"Why am I not surprised?" groaned the mage with disdain as he stood watching a curtain of mist pour across the gateway like some kind of spectral waterfall.

Psyching himself up, Rhys slowly edged forwards. He passed beneath the ornate torana and planted a foot on the wooden walkway. The planks creaked, and for a brief moment the mage was plagued with visions of the ancient road giving out and tumbling to his death. He began to shift his weight, but as the wood groaned louder, he withdrew his foot. The temple was ancient, the planks and supports were likely centuries, if not millennia old. Furthermore, though they frequently bore the weight of pilgrims across to the Temple, the key distinction was that they were elven pilgrims, not human. Rhys, though far from heavyset, was broad-shouldered, currently carrying the most muscle he had done in his life. He recalled how light the body of the rakshasa rider had been back down in the cave several days earlier; Nathaniel had described the hound as weighing little more than a child.

Rhys couldn't begin to explain how, but elves had a supernatural lightness about them; blades of grass scarcely bent beneath their boots; they seldom left so much as a footprint in sand. There was no assurance whatsoever that the walkway ahead would take his weight; it perhaps even seemed unlikely. But it was the only path ahead, the only way to the Temple, and the only way for Rhys to learn the cause of his dreams. He summoned a courage from deep within. It was the same courage that had led him up the hillside to the Northern Circle, the same courage that had led him into the Grey at Llanmyd, and the same courage that had led him down into the catacombs of Orthios. It was a courage driven by determination. It was a courage driven by faith; faith derived not from religion, nor from belief in some higher power, but from himself, and the world around him.

Inhaling deeply, clearing his mind of premonitions of tumbling to his death, Rhys stepped out, shifting his entire weight in one swift motion onto the walkway. The boards flexed and groaned under his mass, yet the sturdy weightbearing crossbeams sunken into the stone stood fast beneath the mage, just as they had done so over thousands of years against the elements.

Hesitantly, the mage began to walk,

watching the bowing of the planks underfoot until he was more than a dozen yards out beyond the gateway. He peered back, realising that neither Maadurga, nor Sol, nor Thia were following him. He understood that for whatever reason, entering the Temple was something he was supposed to do alone.

Taking another deep breath to slow his racing heart, Rhys marched purposefully on. The mist continued to seethe gently about in the air, and in a moment of quietude, Rhys heard the jangling of windchimes from up ahead. He advanced step by step along the walkway, watching as the veil of mist steadily unravelled before him. The wooden path came to an abrupt halt as it reached a protrusion in the rockface. As Rhys neared, he spied an aperture in the stone. The trail continued into the mountainside, the path leading through a stairwell tunnelled out of the rock. Stooping into the carved passage, Rhys began to climb, cautiously ascending the dark confines of the rising tunnel before the stairway opened to a grey light once more. Stepping out onto another shelf, Rhys stopped suddenly in his tracks.

Atop the plateau, towering twenty feet high a piece, were two stone statues. Both effigies depicted a four-armed elf. The arms of the statue to the right flailed outwards, the various hands each aggressively angling a different weapon, all four carved from solid jade. The two lower limbs clutched a spear and a mace slanted groundward, the upper limbs clasping an axe and a kukri crossed overhead. The figure's pose was combative, poised ready to do battle, each of its four weapons primed to strike. The second statue of the two however stood in meditative juxtaposition. Still armed with the same axe, kukri, spear, and mace as the statue on the right, the leftward effigy held each of the four jade weapons aligned down the central axis of its body, the pose altogether unthreatening and somewhat peaceful by comparison to its counterpart.

With the four weapons stacked vertically, the shaft and handles of each aligned, the axe, the kukri, the spear, and the mace appeared to take on a different form, their individual silhouettes combining to become a new distinctive profile. From where Rhys was stood, the effigy of Kalki erected before him appeared to be holding a staff, and not just any staff.

Rhys felt his flesh turn cold as the frightening realisation hit him. The spear aligned central to the statue represented a shaft, with the mace head resting on the ground overlapping to form the stave's butt. At the top of the four transposed weapons, the spearhead, the leading edge of the axe, the axe's rearward spike, and the curving blade of the kukri all combined, stacking atop one another to take the form of an ethereal blade, edge, point, fluke, hook, and all. The effigy before Rhys was unmistakably that of Kalki; but he was holding Rhys's staff!

THIRTY-ONE

It was more than just coincidence. The resemblance was uncanny. Everything down to the emerald shimmer of the jade matched the likeness of Rhys's stave. Until this point, Rhys had dismissed every assertion that he was the re-embodiment of Kalki as mere superstition. Faced with the evidence mounting in front of him now, it was becoming increasingly difficult by the second to argue otherwise.

After a long moment of internal debate, Rhys manage to overcome the stupor seeing the two effigies of Kalki had brought on. Pushing several burning questions to the back of his mind, he resumed his journey through the Temple. Stepping between the two statues, he passed beneath a torana, before venturing out thereafter onto another timber walkway.

Out of the fog loomed the steeply pitched roof and flaring eaves of the first pavilion fixed to the vertical face of the mountainside. A light gust wafted the mist ahead and a sudden overwhelming tintinnabulation drowned all other sounds. Rhys edged closer to see, hanging from the eaves were hundreds of windchimes, some made from little more than lengths of metal, or hollow bamboo, others were crafted from delicate ornate brass bells and assortments of seashells dangling in clusters. Each gentle stir of the air currents caused the instruments to clink and jangle in a random yet melodic cacophony of tinkling percussion. Each lull in the mountain breeze meanwhile, returned the roofed walkway back to near preternatural tranquillity.

The thinning murk revealed a series of brass cylinders affixed to vertical axes mounted on the rock face walling the covered walkway. Rhys paused and inspected the half dozen wheels to realise they were each embossed with the same set of Elvish Sanskrit characters. Rhys reached out with his fingertips and gently rotated the first in the series, watching as the fluid script revolved before him, the Elven characters reading in a cyclical mantra that repeated with each turn of the prayer wheel. The mage watched the wheel slow to a stop, before spinning it again, followed by the other remaining wheels in the series as he ran his fingers along each in turn, continuing then along his way.

Handrails and balustrades now guarded the ledges of the walkway as the mage progress from pavilion to pavilion. Monkeys perched atop the banisters, watching Rhys as he passed the various shrines erected beneath the sheltered terraces. Several smaller statues of the four-armed Kalki stood at intervals down the path;

some were small jade figurines perched atop altars carved out of tiny grottos in the rockface. Others were wooden, leafed in gold. Each shrine was laden with bronze bowls filled with blossom petals and scented oils, flickering candles and smouldering incense, heaps of prayer beads and strips of cloth inked with Elven Sanskrit. Rhys passed each shrine slowly, studying the assortment of offerings laid before the idols as he traversed the temple's first level.

Throughout the entire lower tier, there was not a single elf to be seen, and to his rear neither Maadurga nor Sol or Thia had yet appeared. The only other creatures he had yet seen were the half dozen monkeys sat inquisitively watching him pass them by. Coming to the end of the first level, Rhys ascended a set of steps carved out of the rock that doubled back along the cliff face, rising above the flared eaves of the pavilions to the tier above.

Arriving atop another ledge, Rhys passed beneath the next torana, venturing out across a wooden bridge lit with flaming torches extending towards the first of the great halls. The mist ahead stirred, a crouching silhouette looming through the vapour. Rhys approached to find an Elven monk garbed in saffron robes, head shaven, pressed to the ground in prayer, his arms extended in prostration towards Rhys.

The mage stood over the elf, gesturing for the sadhu to rise, yet the monk remained flattened across the stone, muttering in Elvish as he revered the mage. Looking up, Rhys sighted another sadhu further along the bridge, who just like the first, was sprawled prone in devotion, his arms aimed in Rhys's direction.

"Please—stand," Rhys urged the two of them loudly, but they would not move. Were he not certain they were praying directly to him, the mage would have thought they were ignoring him.

Concluding that there was nothing he could do to stop the monks' prayers, he continued over the arching bridge. On the far side, Rhys discovered a dozen more sadhu laying on the ground, their hands and fingers once more aimed towards the mage's coming, their bodies almost entirely motionless. The whispering of their lips, the tightening of fingers around the lengths of prayer beads wound about their palms, and the subtle flattening of their noses as they pressed their faces harder against the ground when Rhys passed, were the only signs the sadhu were even alive.

The level of devotion the brahmin caste paid Rhys was troublesome. None of the sadhu bowing before him had ever met the mage before; even now they wouldn't lay eyes upon him. Yet despite this, they threw themselves at his feet, heralding him as the incarnation of their god. They likely knew of his coming by way of the pilgrims that had arrived at the Temple ahead of Rhys, but clearly the claims of Kalki's imminent return to his temple had gone unquestioned without any level of scepticism, accepted as fact, no proof required. To these monks, Rhys's coming was the fulfilment of prophecy; there was no room for doubt in religious beliefs so firmly held.

Dismounting the bridge, Rhys found himself before the open doors to the first great hall. He stepped through the threshold into an atrium lit with hundreds of candles and oil lamps. A giant ornate gong hung suspended from a frame in the centre of the hall, whilst rows of prayer wheels lined the walls of the vestibule. Wind drifted through the openings around the rafters, allowing the aromatic smoke from the burning incense to be drawn out of the hall. Gathered about the floor of the building were dozens more sadhu, each adopting the same reverent prostration as those Rhys had already passed. Now, enclosed within the hall, their quiet chanting reverberated in chorus to a steady incantation of prayer that echoed throughout the atrium.

Eager not to linger, the mage hastily strode through the building, exiting via the far doorway, out onto another bridge towards the next tabernacle. The second hall of worship was partially excavated from the mountain face, receding into the stone as an expansive grotto with bas-reliefs carved out of the walls. More sadhu filled the chamber, each adorned in the golden robes of the brahmin caste, some with shaven scalps, others with their dark hair drawn back into tight braided buns, all praying prostrate on the ground, facing the mage as he made his way through the building and out to the other side.

Exiting the second hall, Rhys arrived at the foot of another set of steps cut out of the cliffside. Heavy mist draped over the way, shrouding the mage's view of the top. Gazing back through the doors to his rear, Rhys turned to see all of the monks still laying in prayer, none having so much as moved an inch since he had passed them. With a heavy sigh, he continued his ascent, beginning the climb to the third tier.

Reaching the top, the mage set foot onto a plateau extending from the southern face of Suraksameru. Barely a hundred feet above, the mountain summit speared through the turbulent clouds. The gloom momentarily parted, unveiling to Rhys the final portion of the Temple of Kalki. A towering pagoda was carved intricately from the stone of the peak, hugging the rockface from which it was cut; rising seven stories, its golden finial climbed just beyond the zenith of the summit, standing as the highest point in the Sacred Valley. Rhys beheld the impressive tower for only a few moments before a bolt of lightning thundered out of the clouds, the blinding fork striking the finial atop the pagoda. Stepping back in momentary surprise, Rhys watched as the electricity was conducted harmlessly away.

As the storm quelled once again, the mage's line of sight fell across the plateau before him. Rhys was not alone. Prostrate across the terrace were more sadhu, this time numbering more than a hundred. Each had been lying in wait, starting their prayers before the mage had even climbed to the base of the pagoda. Yet amongst the congregation of reverent monks, a single sadhu sat cross-legged in meditation atop a dais in the centre of the terrace, his sinewy body layered white with ash, a red pottu dotted between his eyebrows. Of all the elves Rhys had seen since arriving in the Sacred Valley, this single sadhu bore the weight of age more than any other; beneath the layer of ash painted to his skin, the sadhu's face was creased with wrinkles. His frame, though far from frail, was beginning to appear haggard, centuries of life finally having caught up with him. The brahmin sat with his eyes shut, his body relaxed and his face emotionless as the mage observed him from afar. Aside from the tintinnabulation of windchimes from the terraces below, all was eerily still and silent atop the peak of Suraksameru.

Anxiously, Rhys stepped forwards and approached the meditating sadhu. The moment Rhys drew within a dozen feet of the monk, his eyes shot widely open and met instantly with Rhys's. This was enough to halt Rhys suddenly in his tracks. The mage opened his mouth to speak, yet he was at a loss for words. The sadhu beheld him for a long moment as the mage returned his gaze. Feeling a sense of unease, Rhys lowered his eyes and glanced around at the surrounding monks lying silently prostrate. Turning back to the sadhu atop the dais, Rhys realised the monk's attention had moved to his staff.

"Tapai svagata hunuhuncha, Kalki," spoke the monk. "Merolam samayadeki tapa inko agamanko cha pratiksa."

Rhys hesitated. "I don't understand."

"Welcome, Kalki," returned the brahmin in the Common Tongue. "I have awaited your arrival my entire life."

Rhys sighed a breath of relief at hearing the elf speak his own language. He began to relax as a dozen potential responses sifted through his mind. Momentarily, he felt the urge to play along and assume the role of Kalki; if they believed him to be the incarnation of their god, his time at the Temple could be a lot easier, the knowledge he sought shared freely with him. Snapping out of his brief disillusion, Rhys despaired at the idea. He was not a god. He was not chosen. He was not the incarnation of one of the Trimurti, nor did he want to be. He was a mage. He was a man, and nothing more. He was not part of some prophecy to be caught up in a sequence of predestined events. He had been brought to this place through his own choices; through his own freewill. There was no great destiny that had brought him to the Temple of Kalki, only his own drive towards his goal of restoring the Nexus and stopping Indus. He could lie. He could feign divinity to achieve what he wanted. But if he chose to do such things, then he was no better than the man he was trying to stop.

"I am not Kalki," replied the mage assuredly.

The sadhu's eyes narrowed momentarily with intrigue. "And yet, you carry his staff?" quipped the sage.

"The Kalki I saw depicted in your idols does not carry a staff," returned Rhys. "I saw him wielding four weapons, none of which were a staff."

"But together—" replied the monk bringing his palms against one another and entwining his fingers, "they form his staff. The spear, the mace, the axe, the kukri—each are but individual facets of the staff. Apart they differ, but together, they are one of the same."

"Even still, that does not make me Kalki."

"He who carries the staff is the reincarnation of Kalki," insisted the sadhu. "Rhys North is the name you were born to, the name your people gave to you, but it is not your first name. Dharma has brought you here. You seek wisdom. You seek Nirvana."

"You seem to know a lot about me," remarked Rhys upon hearing his name.

"Your coming has been foretold for thousands of years," returned the sage.

"And yet, I know nothing about you," replied Rhys. "Before our ship landed upon the shores of Sumeru, I knew nothing of this place or of your kind. If I were the reincarnation of your god, surely some of this would have been known to me, the very least of it Sumeru's existence."

"I am Guru Shakyamuni, High Brahmin, leader of the Sadhu of the Temple of Suraksameru, servant of Kalki," replied the monk with a wry smile. "Now you know of me. As for Sumeru, you may not have known it to exist across the Samudra Vritra, but you came to this place all the same. Why? Because you did know of it; not with your waking mind, but with Anussati —remembrance. Through Anussati you learnt of your dharma. Dharma is what brought you here to Sumeru. Dharma is what brought you to Suraksameru. Dharma is what brought you to me."

"I brought myself here," insisted Rhys. "I came to these islands for the conduit: the stone circle that lies in the heart of Shambhala. What brought me here, to this temple and to you, was a need for answers, something entirely different. I came to ask for your help to make sense of the dreams I've been having."

"You seek the Chaitya?" questioned Shakyamuni.

Rhys nodded.

"Do you know what the Chaitya are?"

Rhys nodded, though in truth he had only

suspicions. "They are sites of power throughout Cambria, all connecting to the central Nexus."

"The Chaitya *are* Anussati. They hold the memories and the knowledge of what has been. They are understanding. They are the key to the deeds of the past. They show the lives of those who have come before. They show us what we cannot remember from our past incarnations. It is this purpose that the first elves, the vessels our Atman first inhabited, built them for. They are relics from the First Age, from a time when our kin were enlightened, constructed as gifts for our people now, here in the Dark Age, trapped in Samsara, so that we might know of your coming, so that we might know of the end, and so that we might know of the Golden Age that will follow. Now the Chaitya in the heart of Shambhala is guarded by the Amara, those of our people who have achieved Nirvana and have once more become undying. The Amara have escaped Samsara because they have learnt the secrets of Dharma from the Chaitya.

"You say Rhys North, that you are not Kalki. You say that you were brought to Sumeru and to Suraksameru for two different reasons. But they are one of the same. You come here to the Temple of Kalki for Anussati; you wish to understand the visions that come to you through Prana. And you came to Sumeru seeking the Chaitya. Both are the same ultimate goal. You may not yet see the forces that guide you Kalki, yet you cannot deny they are what move you along your path."

Rhys remained silent. For once he had no argument with which to respond. He knew Shakyamuni was right about the conduits. At the Nexus, he had come to understand the circle was an archive of knowledge and memories. It was for this understanding that he fought. It was for this knowledge that he had sailed to the Stormy Isles and travelled deep into the catacombs of Orthios beforehand. For whatever reason, he believed the understanding the Nexus could grant him was knowledge he needed to stop Indus. This simple notion had been instilled into him the day he had discovered the Nexus. Now it was the driving force for his main motivation. It was a powerful incentive, one that led him constantly into the fray.

Rhys remembered back to when he had first discovered the conduit in the King's crypt; Morgwen Caddick and her Black Coven had just sacrificed an ash warrior in a blood ritual to enthral several willing zealots before the rest of the Church of Ashes. Rhys had felt something come over him in that moment. The conduit had drawn him towards it, and had Sol not laid a hand on his shoulder to stop him, he feared he might have simply walked straight into the Kings' Crypt to reach it in spite of the threat that laid below. The conduits held some power over him, this much he could not deny, but was it merely his own mind driving him to restore the Nexus, or could something else be in control? The elves believed strongly in Dharma. Its concept seemed difficult for Rhys to truly comprehend; there seemed no direct translation in the Common Tongue. The closest Rhys knew was the word 'duty,' yet he suspected that this was an incomplete interpretation. It seemed to him that Dharma also meant fate. Fate was an idea that Rhys detested. It meant predetermination. Predetermination meant freewill was nothing more than an illusion. If freewill was merely an illusion, then every decision Rhys made or ever would make had no real consequence. Whatever it was that brought Rhys to where he was stood in this very moment, he refused to believe it to be an act of fate.

"If what you say is true," began the mage, "then teach me how to see for myself. Teach me what you know of the Aether and show me how to control my dreams so that I can draw my own conclusions."

Guru Shakyamuni smiled and nodded. "To do so is my life's purpose. Showing you the way is my dharma."

"I just need answers," replied the mage. "If I can see for myself, then I might understand."

"And so you will," returned the guru. "Tell me, Kshatriya Maadurga," Shakyamuni spoke past him, "what of the other two who made the pilgrimage with Kalki and yourself?"

Rhys revolved to see Maadurga, Sol, and

Thia had now appeared atop the steps to the plateau. The elf knelt on one knee respectfully, whilst Thia and Sol peered around at the congregation of monks prostrate in worship of Rhys.

"They wish to learn of Prana so that they might better understand Brahman," replied Maadurga, bowing her head as she did so.

Shakyamuni scrutinised both Thia and Sol for a silent moment, his gaze drawn to the copper stave Sol had strapped across his back for a length of time, before finally he asked, "are these two pilgrims Jhakri?"

"Suelamana Thamasa eka Kshatriya Jhakri ho," explained Maadurga in Elvish whilst looking at Sol. "Ustai Kalki."

"Unako barema kē?" returned Shakyamuni.

"Thiya Smitha eka Brahmin Jhakir ho," replied Maadurga.

Shakyamuni nodded, studying them both before he addressed them in Common. "To understand Brahman, first you must understand Dharma. Solomon Thomas, you are a warrior of Prana, Kshatriya Jhakri. Thia Smith, you are a scholar of Prana, Brahmin Jhakri. Together you represent body and mind, but Nirvana cannot be achieved without mastery of both, and mastery of one cannot be achieved without mastery of the other. Together you will study Gatka and Yoga and fulfil your dharma. This will grant you understanding of Brahman."

"What are Gatka and Yoga?" questioned Sol.

"Gatka is the way of the warrior," explained Maadurga. "It is a collection of fighting disciplines in which kshatriya are trained."

"And yoga is the way of the Brahmin," added Shakyamuni. "It is control over the body and mind, so that one's Atman can be understood. It is the path to Nirvana; liberation from Samsara so that enlightenment can be achieved."

"And studying both Gatka and Yoga helps to understand the Aether?" questioned Rhys.

"There is much knowledge of Prana in the teachings of Gatka and Yoga," nodded Shakyamuni.

"I am willing to learn," declared Thia stepping forwards, bowing her head respectfully to the guru.

Sol looked somewhat more apprehensive than Thia. He stood in hesitation. Rhys could see the mage pondering the offer before him, but he knew that Sol did not believe in the concept of the Aether himself. The religious sanctity of Suraksameru seemed to speak to him, however. Rhys could tell that Sol held a deep appreciation for the sacred aura of the Temple, admiring the role that faith played in the lives of the elves; though their religions were worlds apart, there seemed some parity between the Trimurti and the Titan pantheon.

"I too am willing," the mage announced after a time, likewise taking a step forwards and bowing his head as Thia had done.

Shakyamuni nodded with approval. "During your stay here atop Suraksameru, the Sadhu will instruct you in the teachings of yoga, whilst those kshatriya who have followed the sacred trail to the Temple in the time after Karkasankranti will instruct you in gatka."

Sol and Thia nodded respectfully, as did Maadurga, who then gestured for the other two to follow her back down the steps towards the lower levels of the temple. Yet, before the elf could take her leave, the guru called after her.

"Maadurga?"

"Ho, Guru Shakyamuni?"

"You are Rajanya Kshatriya, First Warrior of our people. My role in the days to come is to instruct Kalki in Brahman; I will serve as his teacher in yoga and Anussati. But like those he has travelled with, Kalki must also study Gatka. Your Gatka is the greatest of all of Kalki's followers. It is you who must instruct him."

Maadurga seemed somewhat taken back. Suddenly she knelt, placing a fist against her chest and lowering her head solemnly. "Masam manitachu." The elf then rose and strode over to Rhys, drawing a kukri from one of the scabbards strapped across the small of her back. Halting before the mage, she knelt once more and offered the blade flat across her palms to Rhys. "Kalki, please accept my teachings in the way of Gatka."

Rhys peered down at Maadurga, wishing desperately that she would stand to look him in the eye. But he knew that it would not happen, not so long as they stood within the inner sanctum of the Temple of Kalki; not before the Temple's Guru, and not so long as an audience of over a hundred Brahmin lay around them with their faces pressed to the stone.

Sighing internally, Rhys offered his response, picking his words carefully. "You would do me a great honour by serving as my mentor."

With a dextrous flourish, Maadurga sheathed her kukri and rose to her feet. She bowed her head with a smile on her face and turned then to look upon Shakyamuni, awaiting what the guru would say next.

"The day is at an end," declared the sadhu. "Kalki's vessel is not of our kin; no doubt he grows weary. He and his followers must rest. Solomon Thomas and Thia Smith will be given a place to rest in the halls below. Kalki, you are to be given quarters within the pagoda."

Rhys peered back at Sol and Thia. Both stood silently listening. The mage would have much preferred to stay with his friends, but he knew that asking for such would be improper. Instead, Rhys simply nodded in agreement.

"At first light, your teachings will begin. Until then, rest. Food will be brought to you, along with water so that you may bathe."

"My thanks," Rhys bowed his head.

"Your pilgrimage up Suraksameru was but the first step in a long journey, Kalki. Few ever achieve Nirvana. I have spent my entire life seeking it, yet still I am imprisoned to Samsara. But you are one of the Trimurti, and you have achieved Nirvana once before. It may take many years, but in time you will come to understand Brahman. And when the day comes, you will stand against Mahakala and lead us into the Golden Age."

THIRTY-TWO

"Breathe in," whispered Shakyamuni. "Breathe out."

Rhys inhaled and exhaled through his nose in rhythm with the guru's words.

"Breathe in. Breathe out."

The mage's eyes remained shut as he sat cross legged on the cold stone. His hands rested upturned on his knees; staff lain across his lap. Rhys's whole body relaxed of all its tension, his mind still, his senses dulled to the stimuli around him. He felt the waft of a cold mountain breeze as the air currents flowed over the peak of Suraksameru. He heard the compressions of his heart pumping deep within his chest. Tiny droplets of rain pattered intermittently on his skin. The warming flames of the nearby brazier crackled softly. Yet his mind remained dark. No visions had come to him. He had felt no unworldly sensations, no sights or sounds from a time or place far from the present. Hours upon hours of tranquil meditation in the week he had spent in the Temple of Kalki, and still he felt no closer to understanding the dreams that came to him in the night. Not only could he not summon the visions at will, but he had not even dreamt since the night before his arrival in the Sacred Valley.

"Breathe in. Breathe out," Shakyamuni's voice echoed.

Rhys tried harder to clear his mind. Wandering thoughts had seeped into his meditation. He reflected on Thia and Sol, wondering how their own training in yoga was progressing. He thought of the others back in the village of Suraksa, of Arne and his sons, lower down on the beach. His mind wandered back to the mainland: Orthios, now occupied by Indus and his forces, and the other magi, wherever they might be. His mind was roving wide and far, now uncontrollably so. The more he tried to reign in his thoughts, the faster his mindscape began to race from place to place. It had begun to affect his body. His posture had slouched. The muscles in his neck knotted and threatened to cramp. His eyes twitched and pressed tightly shut. His breathing became shallow and irregular. Annoyance quickly grew into frustration; unable to sit still a second longer, Rhys opened his eyes and abruptly stood upright.

"Patience, Kalki," schooled Guru Shakyamuni.

"My name isn't Kalki," returned Rhys sharply as he gazed out from the precipice.

He was stood atop a small outcrop protruding from the northern face of Suraksameru. Ahead, anvils of black cloud raged with distant thunderclaps and lightning flares, whilst above, the emerald glow of the Rift shimmered through the haze. Heavier raindrops began to splatter down against the perch, darkening the paving stones in blotches. He peered back along the dark pass leading through the mountain, back to the inner sanctum on the southern face of the peak, hoping that Shakyamuni might dismiss him so that he could resume his training with Maadurga.

"Kalki may not be the name you were given at birth, but, whether you believe you are the reincarnation of one of the Trimurti or not, Kalki is the name my people have given to you."

Rhys looked coldly back at Shakyamuni.

"Please," the guru gestured to the slab Rhys had been sat on for near an hour. "Sit. Padmasana."

"I'm done meditating," replied the mage frustratedly. "I've spent days doing it and achieved nothing. When are you going to teach me about the Aether?"

Shakyamuni looked back at Rhys as calm as ever. "No meditation," he nodded. "Sit. Listen. Breathe."

Rhys reluctantly sat back on the cool stone and crossed his legs, readopting the padmasana pose. He closed his eyes, slowed his breathing, and listened.

"Dhyana means contemplation," began the guru softly. "Through dhyana, samadhi is reached—focus, stillness of the mind, wholeness of the body, connexion with your higher self: enlightenment. Samadhi is the path to many things and is the main goal of Raja Yoga. Through samadhi comes remembrance: Anussati. Anussati will allow you to see the visions of what has been. It will help you remember your past lives in other vessels. Through samadhi comes Nirvana, escape from Samsara, the cycle. Samadhi holds the answers you seek, answers I cannot give; answers you must discover for yourself."

"But what role does the Aether play in all of this?" asked Rhys.

"Prana is the force of life, the force of mind, the force of energy. It flows through all things, living and unliving, at all times. It comes from the sun, the air, and the ground. It is the breath in your lungs, the beat in your heart, the thought in your mind. It is woven through Brahman and is inseparable from it. Through Prana, and only Prana, can Brahman be perceived."

"Prana is magic?" replied Rhys, settling once more into a relaxed state.

"Magic is the word your people use to describe the effects of Prana that can be seen in the world. The fire summoned by a Kshatriya Jhakri is not Prana, but the use of it to control the element. The healing of a wound by a Brahmin Jhakri is not Prana, but the product of its manipulation."

"Then, Prana is the Aether."

"Yes," confirmed Shakyamuni. "This word better describes Prana. Prana flows through this world and everything within it, yet it is channelled more strongly through certain places and vessels. Sumeru is one such place where Prana is focussed, the chaitya being the point of greatest intensity. It is for this reason that the first elves built Shambhala atop Sumeru's peak and erected the chaitya stones at its heart. Your people have a name for these channels of Prana that flow through the world; they call them ley lines. It is along these ley lines, at the point where they intersect, that the chaitya are built. The stones focus Prana and allow for it to be absorbed or manipulated with wide ranging effects. Sometimes, these effects can be terrible."

At these words, memories of the Grey were conjured into Rhys's thoughts. He stepped out of his house and into the murky colour-drained streets of Longford. He wandered through the icy fog and saw the eyes of countless deceased gazing back hauntingly at him.

"Akasa, the colours you see in the sky above you: The Rift—this is a tear in Prana."

"How did it happen?" questioned the mage as the recollections of his desolated home fleeted.

"With the division of the Trimurti, the Cintamani Stone fell to the world from out of the heavens and brought an end to the first age. The world was flooded, and the first golden age drew to a close. By the time of the Third Age, our people had come to understand the concept of Prana, and with it came knowledge of the Cintamani Stone. Like the Chaitya, it could focus Prana. It is said that a jhakri armed with the Cintamani Stone would be unstoppable. It was a powerful tool that could be used for immense good, but one that was ultimately used as a devastating weapon. The Cintamani Stone was given to the safe keeping of the followers of Brahma, the Creator, but the most radical followers of Mahakala, who have now come to be the rakshasa, attacked the temple of Brahma, Raraprambanan, butchering every last one of his followers to steal the stone. Seeking to bring an end to the world to begin the cycle of ages anew, heralding in the Golden Age once more, the rakshasa fought their way to the heart of Shambhala, using the power of the Cintamani Stone to reach the Chaitya. Placing the Cintamani Stone upon the altar of the Chaitya, and using the power of blood, they destroyed the Stone, fracturing it into thousands of pieces that were scattered across Sumeru. This act distorted Prana so violently that it caused a rupture in its fabric and wounded Brahman. The Akasa ripped Sumeru from the sea and created a storm that has lasted since the dawn of the Dark Age—over five millennia"

"Five millennia?" remarked Rhys with disbelief. "How can you possibly know about something that happened five thousand years ago?"

Shakyamuni uttered a single word in response, "Anussati."

"Remembrance?" repeated Rhys, opening his eyes to look now on the Guru. "You have seen it for yourself?"

"I have," nodded Shakyamuni. "So far back in history, the memories are like whispers in another tongue. They are difficult to interpret and so rarely hold decipherable meaning; but a lifetime of dedication to yoga and Nirvana has allowed me to make sense of all that I have seen. There is much that is uncertain from the Third Age and those that came before, but of the Cintamani Stone, the Akasa, and the destruction of Sumeru—of these things there is little doubt."

"How can you be so certain?"

"Every action that you, or I, or anyone who has ever lived in this world takes, causes ripples in Brahman. Like ripples across a pond, they fade with time, but even the most distant events in history are still recorded as faint whispers in Brahman. The actions we take shape the world around us; actions tending towards good and order, those in keeping with dharma, bring balance to Brahman, whilst actions that are chaotic and evil, actions considered adharma, bring darkness and unbalance. The ripples of Brahman are echoed in Prana and can be read and seen by the enlightened mind. Those who achieve Nirvana can see the whole of history, understanding all that has ever transpired, and all that which will come to pass. But those who have not been liberated from Samsara can also read the echoes of Brahman, in samadhi."

"You are saying that if I can achieve samadhi, stillness of mind, then I will be able to see anything in history?" asked Rhys

"Samadhi grants sight of Prana, but not understanding. Nirvana is true understanding. With Nirvana, you will indeed be able to read the history of the world as if it were recorded in scripture before your eyes. Without understanding, samadhi will grant you sight, but not the knowledge of where to look. Your unconscious mind will guide you, but the visions you see might not be of your choosing."

"Like knowing the right chapter of a book, but not which page to read?" mused Rhys aloud as he attempted to make sense of Shakyamuni's teachings.

"As an analogy, this works," agreed Shakyamuni. "The visions you have seen in the past have granted you understanding for questions you sought answers for. These visions have come to you during sleep, because it is at this time that your waking mind is still. Your first vision came to you when you were betrayed. You wished more than anything to understand why. Though your waking mind did not know the answers, your unconscious mind knew where to look. You watched the events unfold that led to the deaths of your friends, and saw first-hand how the traitor Indus executed the leader of Kshatriya Jhakri.

"Next came the answer to your heritage. Having never met your mother, you always desired to learn more of her. When you came face to face with your relative, Morgwen Caddick, your unconscious mind sensed through the echoes recorded in Prana, that the two of you were connected by blood. Through your dreams, your higher mind guided you towards the single moment in time that assured your existence: the meeting of your parents. But, this event laid further back in time. The betrayal of your order transpired mere days before your visions of it, and thus it was easy to find. The meeting of your parents was decades in the past. Because of this, the whispers in Brahman were fainter—your mind found it harder to discover the exact moment in time in which it occurred. You witnessed the chain of events play out over several nights, throughout which time, your higher mind was navigating to the moment your mother and father first met."

"And what of the dreams I am having now?" pressed Rhys. "Why am I seeing the life of Arlas play out?"

"In order to find out, you must let your higher mind guide you through the sequence of events. Only when you have seen the answers your mind seeks will you understand."

"That sounds like just another riddle," grumbled Rhys.

"Perhaps so," agreed Shakyamuni. "Once a riddle is understood, the answer seems obvious."

Rhys chuckled at how easily Shakyamuni had turned his remark into a proverb. "I'll give you that one."

"To understand, you must see. Samadhi is the path to many things, Kalki."

"So you said."

"Dhyana. Focus. Breathe."

Rhys relaxed again and concentrated on little more than the air flowing in and out of his lungs.

"The air you breathe is one of five elements that make up the world: Earth, Water, Fire, Wind. What is the fifth?"

"Lightning?" answered Rhys assuredly.

"No," refused Shakyamuni. "Lightning is the amalgamation of Fire and Air."

"Ice then," responded Rhys.

"No," insisted Shakyamuni. "Ice is the amalgamation of Earth and Water."

"Magma?" suggested the mage after a moment of contemplation.

"That is Earth and Fire combined."

"Clouds?"

"Water and Air."

Rhys sighed audibly. "There's definitely a

fifth?"

"The five elements relate to our senses," explained Shakyamuni.

Rhys felt a smooth pebble press into his palm, placed there by the guru.

"Earth can be seen. It can be heard. It can be felt. It can be tasted. And it can be smelt. It can be perceived by every sense our body possesses. The next element is Water."

As Shakyamuni said this, Rhys felt a droplet of rain splatter on his forehead and trickle down the bridge of his nose.

"Water too can be seen, and heard, and felt, and tasted, yet it is odourless and completely imperceptible by smell. Next comes fire."

Shakyamuni took the mage's free hand from his lap and positioned it nearer the flaming brazier.

"It's warmth can be felt, its light seen, and it can too be heard, but fire cannot be tasted, nor can it be smelt," explained the Guru. "Then comes Air."

Rhys felt a swell in the chilling air currents as a gust swept across the mountainside.

"The wind can be felt and heard. But it is itself invisible; only its effects can be seen."

Rhys nodded.

"The final element can only be seen. But even then, not by all."

"Prana," whispered Rhys. "Prana is the fifth element?"

"Correct," replied Shakyamuni. "Our vessels comprise of the five elements. Our bodies are made of Earth: our skin, muscle, and bones are solid. Through our veins flows water in the form of blood. In our hearts burn fire, giving warmth to our vessels, and the Wind flows through our lungs as breath. Tell me, Kalki, how does Prana form the vessel for our Atman?"

"Our Atman are Prana," replied Rhys.

"An interesting thought," replied Shakyamuni, "But our Atman are instead a part of Brahman."

"Prana flows through the entire body," offered Rhys, giving his second answer.

"Yes. Prana is channelled through all the four other elements, through our vessels as it is the entire world. It flows through our bodies in channels, similar to the ley lines that stretch across the world. In the body, these channels are known as nadis. The greatest of nadis, is the mind."

"Prana is consciousness?"

"Yes," confirmed Shakyamuni. "Just as Prana stems from Brahman, the mind stems from the Atman. Consciousness is the channelling of Prana by the Atman. Prana forms the mind of the vessel, connecting it to the Atman, the Soul. To most, the Prana flowing through their vessel and through the world is unperceivable; but to a few, to the Jhakri, it can be controlled. Through dhyana, focus, the elements around you, can be manipulated by control over the Prana that flows through you."

"What of the differences in magic users?" questioned Rhys. "Why can Magi affect the elements directly, whilst witches can only form secondary effects?"

"Prana flows differently through different vessels," explained the guru. "The distinction is obvious when our peoples are compared. Through elves, Prana flows in different ways to humans. It grants us better sight, longer life, faster control over our bodies, yet we lack the strength, the resilience, and the versatility of humans."

"Versatility?" questioned Rhys.

"Perhaps versatility is not the correct word," pondered Shakyamuni. "Elves have these gifts because of the flow of Prana through our vessels. It grants also jhalaka."

"Jhalaka?" questioned Rhys.

"Jhalaka, means to blink," replied Shakyamuni.

"I still don't follow," puzzled Rhys.

"To have made it to the Sacred Valley, you will likely have seen it," insisted Shakyamuni. "It is called jhalaka, because it is to move within the blink of an eye."

"Yes!" realised Rhys, suddenly understanding what Shakyamuni was referring to. "I have seen several elves do it. They disappear in one place and then appear in another, only they don't vanish altogether... they dematerialise—transform into a blur of energy and reform in another place."

"That you see so much means that you already observe Prana in parts. Most do not see what you do. To most, an elf that performs jhalaka vanishes completely before reappearing."

"What is happening?" questioned Rhys. "How do elves blink?"

"Just as the elements can combine, they are mutable. They can transform from one to another. Wood becomes Fire when burnt, then Wind in the form of smoke. Water can become Earth or Wind as ice or steam; equally, ice can become Water, as can clouds when rain falls. When you conjure Fire, or Wind, you are manipulating Prana and converting it directly into other elements. When elves jhalaka, they perform the same feat yet in reverse. The elements of their body are momentarily converted from Earth, Water, Fire, and Wind, into Prana. When their vessels take form in Prana, they are able to flow from one place to another in a very short time. The Prana is then transformed back into the other four elements, and the elf has seemingly moved without time passing. To most, the blur of energy that you can see is invisible. You are able to witness the Prana form of the elf as they move from one place to another."

"Is blinking something all elves can do?"

"Through training in Gatka, yes," confirmed Shakyamuni.

"Is it something I could learn?" questioned the mage.

"I do not know," replied the guru. "It might be possible. Jhalaka is the greatest manipulation of Prana that an elf can achieve. Beyond this, the way Prana affects our kind is passive. It flows through our eyes, and bodies, granting sharp sight and agility, and it staves off the effects of age. Yet, beyond these gifts, our control of Prana is limited. Whereas with your kind, there is a greater variety in the way Prana can be controlled. The Jhakri have not existed amongst the elves since the start of the Dark Age, yet amongst humans exist both Brahmin Jhakri and Kshatriya Jhakri."

"You are saying elves have no witches or warlocks, or magi of any kind?"

"We do not," confirmed Shakyamuni. "It is said that in past ages the Jhakri existed amongst my people, but even then, not in the same way they exist amongst humans. The only true Jhakri of the elves are the incarnations of the Trimurti."

"That is what you mean by *'versatility?'*" questioned Rhys.

"Yes," nodded Shakyamuni. "You as Kshatriya Jhakri can transform Prana directly into the other four elements and their amalgamations. And as Brahmin Jhakri, you can perform more subtle manipulations of Prana, repairing flesh, altering perceptions of the senses, and more. Though not all of your kind are capable of performing these manipulations of Prana, a select few can. The same cannot be said of my people."

"What about blood magic?" questioned Rhys. "Why does blood hold the power it does?"

"The flow of blood is the most direct route that Prana can travel through the body. Converting Prana into the other elements requires expenditure from the body's reserves. As a Kshatriya Jhakri, you can only conjure so much fire before your reserve of Prana is exhausted; after it is depleted, you must wait for it to be replenished from the surrounding world, rechannelled back into your body through your mind. If you do not wait for balanced to be restored by the flow of Prana, your mind's reserves are drained—you can lose consciousness, or in extreme cases, death is possible. The same can be observed with the jhalaka. An elf can only move so far before the Prana channelled into their body is exhausted. Once their reserve is expended, they must wait for the flow of Prana from their surroundings to rejuvenate the supply within their body. For this reason, the jhalaka can only be performed so often.

"Blood allows for greater reserves of Prana to be expended, because it exceeds the normal limits of Prana that flow through the body. Even when a Jhakri or an elf's usable reserves are spent, Prana is still abundant in the body; it still flows through all the other elements that make up the Atman's vessel. Prana is responsible for breath, warmth, consciousness, strength, wellness, and far more. If all Prana were used, then not only would a Jhakri die, but their vessel would cease to exist. This Prana, though constantly flowing, is not the same as the pool from which a Jhakri draws when summoning the elements. However, if the skin is broken, and the flow of Prana through the blood tapped, more energy is available, at the cost of wellbeing, strength, consciousness, and often life. Expending the power of blood will leave a vessel weak for days or even weeks, if not killing it outright. What's more, the blood of others can be tapped for its Prana, not limiting a Jhakri solely to the reserves contained within their own vessel."

"That makes sense," nodded Rhys, considering all that Shakyamuni had said.

"Now, I have explained to you what Prana is, and how it works, do you wish to learn how to read it: Anussati?"

"Yes," nodded Rhys, pressing his eyes even tighter shut.

"Then dhyana," insisted the Guru. "Breathe in. Breathe out."

THIRTY-THREE

Rhys wiggled his toes in the sand, his feet planted defensively in the training pit. He twirled his bamboo staff, the steel-capped ends of the sparring weapon spinning in the periphery of his vision as he watched Maadurga prowl the circumference of the pit. The elf whirled her wrists, flourishing her two curved ebony otta sticks as she strafed around the mage. He studied her every move, waiting for the moment she would strike. The elf continued to pace the circumference of the ring as she tested his defences. She stopped. Rhys's finger's twitched. Maadurga exploded forwards onto her right foot, but in an instant, she had reversed direction, pivoting on her toes. Rhys raised his staff in anticipation, falling for Maadurga's feint. She began pacing again, studying how Rhys had reacted.

The mage exhaled, returning his focus to breathing control. He continued to stare down Maadurga, watching for any slight twitch of muscle that would give her away before she struck. Rhys took several steps back, feeling for the edge of the training pit with his heels. He rotated his hips and began to tread the ring's perimeter himself, his shoulders constantly kept facing the elf. A single bead of sweat trickled down the ridge of his spine.

Rhys rolled his shoulders. He watched. He studied Maadurga intently. Then she moved. Faster than Rhys could react, Maadurga blinked. Her body vaporised in an instant, transcending into an ethereal form. As a blur of energy moving rapidly through the Aether, she hurtled for Rhys. The mage could both feel and see her coming. He moved, unleashing the elastic tension in his thighs, darting sideways as fast as his body could respond. In motion he uncoiled his back, swinging his bamboo stave for the spot where he predicted Maadurga would rematerialize. Yet before Rhys had moved more than a foot, his opponent took form once again. An ebony otta whacked against the inside of his knee, buckling it instantly. He toppled backwards, his staff flailing wildly off target, and thumped into the sand.

He felt a second ebony stick press gently against his throat the instant after his head struck the ground. As his vision refocussed, he saw Maadurga's blue eyes staring down into his own.

"Surti, Kalki," schooled Maadurga as she helped him back to his feet. "Awareness," she repeated now in the Common Tongue. "Dhyana."

"I *am* focussing," insisted Rhys. "I saw you coming; you just cheated!"

"I did not *cheat!*"

"You just blinked!" replied Rhys. "How am

I supposed to react that fast?"

"You must be ready," returned the elf. "You must develop surti. With surti, you will see my actions before I take them."

"If I could blink, then I'd have been able to get out of the way; otherwise I cannot possibly move that fast!"

"You *must* move that fast," insisted Maadurga. "Or you will be defeated."

"Shakyamuni said it might be possible for me to learn how to blink," returned Rhys.

"You wish me to teach you jhalaka?" questioned Maadurga, taking a step back in surprise.

"Can you?" pressed Rhys.

Maadurga withdrew into a moment of intense rumination. "It might be possible," she concluded.

"Then teach me," urged the mage.

"No," refused the elf. "You are not ready."

"When will I be?"

"When your gatka improves."

"I thought I was doing well," replied Rhys.

"You are," agreed Maadurga. "You have learnt more in a week than most kshatriya learn in years of schooling. But you are not yet ready."

"What do I need to improve on?"

"Your footwork," replied the elf without hesitation. "Your stances," she added. "Your yudhan..."

"I've always been told my footwork is excellent!" retorted the mage defensively.

Maadurga smirked. "For a child, yes. For a human, yes."

"But not for an elf?"

Maadurga shook her head.

"I'll pretend not to be insulted by that,"

jested Rhys.

"You fight lazy," explained Maadurga.

"What do you mean?"

"The way you have been taught to fight works for those you have trained to fight against. You move only as much is necessary, relying on your strength and prana to win. For fighting humans, this style works—humans are slow. But elves are quick and agile. Elves do not fight lazy. You will not be able to defeat a great kshatriya by fighting lazy."

"I have beaten *you* a few times since we started training," retorted Rhys.

"Have you?" questioned Maadurga, her eyes widened as she smirked.

Rhys sighed heavily. "I'm guessing you let me win?"

"The way you have been trained to fight as Kshatriya Jhakri is similar to gatka in many ways," explained Maadurga. "You have learnt forms similar to the yudhan; but you favour some over others, in ways that make you fight lazy. There are four yudhan, one for each of the four arms of Kalki. Kalki uses all of his four weapons together, each forming a different part of his staff. The yak is Kalki's mace. It is strong and powerful; it can break defences and flatten foes, knocking them to the ground where they can be trampled; but it can be slow and predictable. The monkey is Kalki's axe; it is a smarter way of fighting. The monkey grapples its opponent; instead of using brute force, it waits for the enemy to strike first, using its challenger's own strength as a weapon. By fighting with the monkey yudhan, you can turn a foe's blade to your advantage, blocking and countering his attacks to grant opportunity. But the monkey yudhan puts you at great risk of being struck."

Rhys nodded silently, having already heard Maadurga explain and demonstrate the four yudhan to him at length over the course of the week. "You are saying I need to use the four yudhan in equal measure," assumed the mage, hoping to skip to the end of the lecture.

"No," replied Maadurga. "The opposite."

"Oh?" grumbled Rhys, the smile fading from his face as he awaited Maadurga to recap the other two fighting forms.

The elf knelt and began drawing in the sand with one of her ebony sparring sticks. Carefully, she traced the shape of Kalki's staff, talking as she did so. "The mace is the lowest point on Kalki's staff; the yak is the basic yudhan, using mostly aggression and strength to overcome enemies. The axe sits above the mace, and the monkey is the second yudhan taught to kshatriya. It builds upon what is taught in the yak yudhan, but it is the second lowest of the four."

"So there is a hierarchy to the different forms?"

"Yes," nodded Maadurga, smiling as Rhys came to the realisation that to her seemed so apparent.

"Above the axe sits the kukri."

"The leopard," put in Rhys.

Maadurga nodded. "The leopard awaits the perfect moment to attack. It strikes quick, from the shadows. The leopard's prey does not see its doom coming until the moment it is struck. The leopard seeks to take down its foe with a single blow; to do this, it must be patient, and it must draw close. A long time may pass before an opportunity presents itself, but when it does, it is not missed.

"Finally, the top of Kalki's staff is the spear."

"The eagle," nodded Rhys.

"The eagle watches from afar and sees all. Like the leopard, it seeks to strike fast, and kills its foe swiftly, but until the moment it deals the finishing blow, it remains far beyond the reach of its enemies. Once it has struck its prey, it retreats back into the skies, where once more it watches, waiting for the next opportunity."

"And the eagle is the greatest of the yudhan?" questioned Rhys.

"To counter and block is better than to attack with blind aggression. To dodge and avoid is always better than to counter and block. And to remain beyond you opponent's reach is better than to dodge and avoid; no matter how powerful a warrior, it means nothing if they cannot reach their opponent."

"If the eagle is the superior yudhan, then what is the purpose of the other three?"

"Each yudhan serves a purpose. There will always come a time when your enemy draws close, when you cannot remain beyond his reach; there will come a time when your enemy strikes true and you cannot dodge. And there may come a time where pure offense is the best option. The four yudhan must be used together. The superior yudhan are not separate from those below, but build on their foundations. A kshatriya must first learn the yak yudhan before the monkey, and the monkey before the leopard, and the leopard before the eagle. Each must be mastered in turn before the next can be taught.

"With you, I have taught the four yudhan together, because you have already been trained to fight. I do not wish to unteach you what you have learnt in the past, only to adapt what you already know to gatka. I had seen you fight before our training began, both on the beach when defending your friends, and when you arrived at the gates of the Sacred Valley. You use each of the four gatka, but you do not often change between them, and you favour the monkey and yak too much."

"I keep at range when I can," insisted Rhys. "But I can't cast spells with this!" He held up the bamboo training weapon. "So, what is the point of me staying at a distance during our training?"

"The eagle includes fighting with a bow, or in your case Prana, yes," agreed Maadurga, "but the eagle is also to fight using a spear, or kukri, or axe, or mace. The eagle yudhan is about remaining just beyond your opponent's reach, darting in close when you wish to strike, only to retreat to a safe distance once you have struck. You do not do this, in training, or in battle. Once an enemy draws close, you strike and never retreat."

"But if I retreat, my enemy follows," insisted Rhys. "If all I did was seek to put myself beyond an enemy's reach, then I'd be forever running backwards."

"To retreat does not mean to move backwards," insisted Maadurga.

"No, it does," corrected Rhys. "That is the literal meaning of the word."

"Oh," puzzled Maadurga. "Then, what is the word that means: *'to pull away, but to keep moving forward,'* in the Common tongue?"

Rhys paused for a moment. "You know, I'm not sure there is one."

Maadurga let out a frustrated sigh. "Pravaha."

"Pravaha?" questioned Rhys.

"Constant motion. Always flowing towards and away. Waves on a beach."

"Okay," nodded Rhys. "Pravaha."

"To fight with the eagle yudhan is to never stop moving. Both hands and feet, body and weapon. It is to move faster than your opponent can strike, and to always watch and be ready."

"I think I understand," returned Rhys.

"Then let us begin again," insisted Maadurga, taking several steps back and readopting a combative pose. "Dhyana: focus. Surti: watch. Pravaha: move."

※ ※ ※

"How is it going for you?" Rhys asked Thia now that the two of them were alone. The mage leant against the bridge balustrade as they gazed out into the mists swirling in the night air.

"It doesn't seem right that they are instructing Sol and I in gatka together," she explained. "I'm happy to learn how to fight—especially from the kshatriya, but Sol was trained to fight nearly a decade ago. He's an acolyte of the Circle of Magi—probably one of the best warriors in all of Cambria, whereas I barely even know the pointy end of a blade from the hilt! Yet, we are being taught together, as if we were on the same level!"

"Surely they can't expect you to be anywhere near as experienced as Sol?"

Thia giggled. "They didn't expect me to have *any* martial training—and rightly so."

"Then I don't quite see what the problem is?"

"They made the same assumption of Sol."

"Oh," chuckled Rhys in realisation. "I can't imagine he was happy about that."

"He wasn't," confirmed Thia. "They started us both with jat ka."

"Jat ka?" questioned Rhys.

"I can't imagine Maadurga would have wasted your time with it," explained Thia. "It comes before the yudhan. Its basic footwork: positioning, stances—there's a little hand-to-hand training—escaping grapples—that sort of thing; but there is no weapon training in it whatsoever."

"All things Sol would no doubt find infuriatingly trivial."

"Precisely," smiled Thia.

"But he is going along with it?"

"Even I've moved past jat ka now," nodded Thia. "But they are gauging Sol on a step-by-step basis. Instead of taking him on his word that he knows how to block, parry, and counter, they insist on giving him the lesson before letting him demonstrate his capability."

"But they aren't holding him back at your level?"

"No. We are training together, but the kshatriya have let Sol move quite far ahead of me now."

"I suppose that makes it better," conceded Rhys.

"It's all a means to an end though," shrugged Thia. "Ultimately I think Sol enjoys learning gatka more than the teachings of the Brahmin. Whereas, for me, its very much the other way around. The training is a distraction from what I am really here for. What about you?"

"I'm not really sure," replied the mage. "I'm enjoying training with Maadurga, though I must say, she's knocked my confidence a bit."

"Its about time someone did," chided the witch.

"Very funny," mused Rhys sarcastically. "She sees fit to demonstrate time and time again how easily she can get past my defences. And she's so fast that I can barely keep up with her. If she wanted to, she could dance around the training pit and I wouldn't be able to get within ten feet of her!"

"Maybe you'll learn a thing or two then," suggested Thia teasingly.

"I'm definitely improving," agreed Rhys. "If nothing else, I'm fighting a lot smarter."

"But what about your time with Guru Shakyamuni?"

"It is interesting," contemplated Rhys. "Frustrating and vague at times, but interesting. I'm trying to filter out all of the religious connotations to focus on the key concepts. Obviously, I am not Kalki, and I don't think the Trimurti exist. And I can't say for a moment that I buy into their ideas of reincarnation, or the immortal soul. Nor am I convinced by their legends of the four epochs; though, Shakyamuni has an interesting story about how Sumeru was destroyed that involves the conduit in Shambhala. But as far as the Aether goes, the Elven theories about

Prana and the other four elements... it all seems to line up with everything I know about magic."

"I've asked a great deal of questions, and only received answers to a few," confessed Thia. "But from what they have told me, I agree; it all seems very compelling. The nomenclature is all foreign, though you'd expect that from a completely different language; but, Prana— it lines up so closely with the Occult's theories of the Aether. Considering how the ideas were conceived completely independently from one another, they are profoundly similar. They are so identical, that if I didn't know better, I'd assume one was plagiarised straight from the other."

"Other than what you've told me about it, I don't really know much," confessed Rhys. "But everything Shakyamuni has explained about Prana seems to fit elegantly; not only with the laws of magic, but with the conduits, my dreams, and how it effects everything and everyone in the world around us."

"If Elven civilisation is truly as ancient as we are told, then they have had a lot of time to refine their theories of magic," concluded Thia. "The reason the theory of the Aether is not a popular one, even among the Occult, is that it is secular. The vast majority of people throughout Cambria are religious. The Aether conflicts with most people's world views and is mutually exclusive from all the major religions. Here however, the Elven religion: Brahman and the Trimurti—it all appears to have been constructed around the theory, rather than the theory being constructed to uphold the religion."

Rhys nodded in agreement. "Prana can almost be completely separated from any belief in the Trimurti or Brahman whilst remaining wholly intact. Their faith and their understanding of the world go hand in hand, but they are not mutually *inclusive*."

"Exactly!" exclaimed Thia somewhat excitedly.

The two shared a moment of silence as they beamed at one another, gazing longingly into each other's eyes. They moved closer, electricity flowing between their separated bodies, but as Rhys prepared to steal a kiss, his ears pricked up to the sound of gentle footsteps appearing from behind. The mage peered over his shoulder to see a bald monk slowly ambling over the bridge. He halted at sighting Rhys and a broad smile stretched across his face.

"Pransa Kalki," praised the elf softly as he pressed his palms together in front of his chest.

Rhys smiled politely and nodded back to the sadhu, hoping he might continue on his way and give the two of them some privacy, but the brahmin loitered, continuing to smile widely as he beheld Rhys with awe.

"It's getting late," declared Thia, raising an eyebrow.

"It is," agreed Rhys dimly.

Thia smiled and embraced Rhys, pecking him on the cheek before they released one another.

"I've missed you," announced the mage, dwelling on the fact that they'd barely spent little more than a few minutes together since they had first arrived at the temple.

"I know," she quipped with a wicked grin before turning and wandering off across the bridge.

"Same time tomorrow then?"

"Same time tomorrow," repeated the witch without turning back to face Rhys.

THIRTY-FOUR

From the shadows of the trees, Arlas sat watching the cave entrance bathed in the wan light of the moon. A gentle wind rustled the foliage as he waited patiently, his eyes never averting from the subterranean passage sunken into the outcrop.

"Where is Azrael?" questioned Artemis Flamel. "He should be here by now!"

"Something isn't quite right," agreed Arabis Ibrahim.

"Patience, my friends," hushed Zadkiel. "He will be here soon enough."

"He's already more than an hour late," protested Flamel. "What if he has been discovered!?"

"Have faith," insisted the archon. "We have been cautious. Neither Eryn Caddick, nor any of her dark sisterhood, save those we have taken captive, know we are here. We have the element of surprise."

"Regardless, I am not sure it was wise to involve him in this plan," replied Flamel.

"You do not trust Azrael?" questioned Zadkiel.

"Not entirely, no," whispered the mage in response. "Do *you*?"

"It's no secret that I do not like him," replied the archon wryly, "but I do trust him."

"Azrael is a magistrate like you and I," put in Arabis. "It is right for him to be here."

"You hate him more than I," insisted Flamel.

"I have never said such a thing," replied Arabis ever calmly. "Nor ever would I."

"You don't need to," returned Flamel. "But I can tell," he insisted. "You are not an easy man to read, Arabis, but I have known you for over two decades. I can tell when you despise someone, even if you don't show it."

"Azrael is not an easy man to like," agreed Arabis. "But he is a talented and resourceful mage, and a true asset to the Circle. For the sake of the Order, it is important we all are civil, regardless of our personal opinions of one another."

"I knew it!" smirked Flamel. "He shouldn't be coming with us, and you think it too, even though you won't admit it."

Arabis turned away to survey the mouth of the cave, offering Flamel only silence in return.

"What do you think, Arlas?"

"I am not a magistrate," replied Arlas. "It is not for me to decide."

"If tonight goes to plan, you could well be," insisted Flamel, looking to Zadkiel as he did so.

The archon returned Flamel's gaze with an unreadable expression, yet when the magistrate looked away, Zadkiel met eyes with Arlas, offering a brief knowing smile.

"Besides," continued Flamel, "this is your plan. Without you we wouldn't have this opportunity, and we wouldn't be here now. You should have a say on who we involve."

Arlas sighed internally, knowing Flamel would not leave him be until he offered the man some response. "Azrael has made no effort to keep his opinions of me a secret," began the paladin. "I think therefore, my opinion of his character should be clear to you," offered Arlas diplomatically. "However, I agree with both Arabis and Zadkiel. He is a magister of the Order, and rightfully so. We would be foolish not to involve him tonight; there is too much at stake."

Flamel was silent for a long moment after Arlas stopped speaking, before finally he gave his response. "You continue to surprise me time and time again, Arlas. One day, I hope you will make a very wise archon."

Arlas did not reply, but smiled quietly to himself in the darkness of their lookout.

A quarter of an hour passed as they continued to keep watch from the cover of the trees, until the four magi were alerted by a rustling to their rear. From out of the brush emerged Azrael.

"Where have you been!?" demanded Flamel in a whisper.

"Apologies," returned Azrael. "I was on my way here when I came across a patrol of mercenaries along the road."

"The Shadow Sons?" questioned Arlas.

"I believe so," nodded Azrael. "There were nearly a dozen of them—they were moving this way."

"Then our suspicions are correct," concluded Zadkiel. "They are undoubtedly in league with the Dark Sisterhood."

"What happened?" questioned Arabis.

"I dealt with them," returned Azrael coldly.

The other mages exchanged a series of looks between them.

"Very well," returned Zadkiel. "You did what you had to."

"Hopefully, when tonight is done, it will all be over," prayed Flamel.

"And just as well," nodded Arabis. "I fear the devastation Cambria would see if the Dark Sisterhood's plague of blood magic were allowed to spread any further than it has done."

"Agreed," returned Azrael. "Arlas," he began, turning now to the lowest ranking mage there.

Arlas looked to the man; his dimly lit face wore an expression of sincerity.

"I owe you an apology. You were right about the Occult and the Dark Sisterhood from the very beginning. You have been instrumental in uncovering their secrets, and without you, we would not be here now. Please forgive the way I have treated you in the past. You truly are the mage Zadkiel has claimed you were since the start. I see that now. You deserve everything you have fought to achieve. What happens tonight—it is all because you brought us here."

Arlas studied his rival with disbelief. Never would he have expected such an apology. He was taken back. Perhaps he too had misjudged Azrael. "There is nothing to forgive," insisted the paladin. "You have only shown scepticism: something that is necessary within the Order; lest we devote our time and resources to every wives' tale and unfounded superstition that reaches our ears."

"Even still," replied Azrael, "know that you have my respect."

"Thank you," returned the paladin.

"What is the plan?" asked Azrael, looking then to all of the magi present.

"Arlas and I have kept watch of these caves for the last week," began Zadkiel. "Occultists come and go frequently, some of whom we have recognised as known members of the Dark Sisterhood. Not only that, but we have sighted Eryn Caddick herself enter and leave through this very entrance. Without a doubt, this is Caddick's main hideout. From here, we suspect she orchestrates her plans and conducts the majority of her dark rituals. This place is so well hidden that, had Arlas not captured the witch Syvil Laveau, I suspect we would never have discovered it."

"The Cor Valley is remote," agreed Arabis, "and these woodlands are so ancient and difficult to move through that I doubt any of us would have even thought to search them."

"There are at least a half dozen ways in and out of these caves," explained Zadkiel, "and possibly more that we have not discovered. Once we head inside, we will need to move quickly and silently. If they are alerted to our presence too early, then they will flee from the many exits, like rabbits smoked from the warren. They will lose us in these woods and scatter to the winds. This is our best chance to strike and bring an end to the Dark Sisterhood once and for all. Otherwise, they will go into hiding, and it may be years before they resurface again."

"We won't be able to get them all," warned Azrael.

"We won't have to," insisted Arlas. "So

long as we can take out Caddick and destroy her grimoire, then the Dark Sisterhood will be finished. She is the source of necromancy and blood magic within the Occult. When she is done, the Dark Sisterhood will steadily crumble away."

"Do we have an idea on numbers?"

"We suspect there are as many as thirty witches inside," replied Zadkiel. "But the number is hopefully much lower."

"And you are certain that Caddick is in there?"

"Nothing is certain," replied Zadkiel.

"It is possible she might have slipped away through one of the other exits without us noticing," conceded Arlas. "But this is the entrance she most frequently uses, and she is seldom away for more than a few hours at a time."

"Very well," nodded Azrael.

"The three of you will head half a mile south of here," Zadkiel instructed the magistrates. "Arabis knows the location. There, you will find the second major entrance to this cave system. Meanwhile, Arlas and I will make our way in from here. If we move quickly and quietly, we can pincer those inside, trapping them in the heart of the lair before they realise what has happened. If we can manage just such, we should be able to finish them."

"Remember though," insisted Arlas, "Eryn Caddick is the target. Everyone else is secondary. If she does not die tonight, then we have failed."

"What about their defences?" asked Flamel. "Surely they won't just leave the entrances exposed without any form of safeguard?"

"Indeed," agreed Zadkiel. "Expect glyphs,

and other forms of rudimentary warding around the entrances. But remember that this is their base of operation, and a secret one at that. The interior is unlikely to have much in the way of arcane entrapments. And given that this place is so well-hidden and so far out of the way, I doubt any defences you will encounter will be substantial."

"Regardless," warned Arabis, "some of these women are powerful witches. Anything set against intruders will likely be lethal."

"Vigilance is key," nodded Zadkiel. "But I *expect* vigilance from magistrates of the Order. You are all adept in foiling magical wardings, and all of you are keen-eyed and methodical. There is good reason why no lower ranking magi save Arlas are here tonight."

"And you are sure the whole situation isn't a trap?" asked Zadkiel. "We aren't walking into an ambush?"

"They do not know we are coming," reiterated Zadkiel.

"So long as you are sure," replied Azrael.

A period of silence fell before Arabis was the first to speak. "If there is nothing else left to say, then we had better get on with it."

"Good luck my friends," nodded Zadkiel. "We shall see you on the inside."

Azrael and Flamel both issued nods before silently creeping off through the trees.

Arabis loitered for a moment longer. "Be safe, Arlas."

"And you, my friend," returned the young paladin.

Arabis turned and went, following the path of the other two magistrates, leaving Arlas and Zadkiel alone in each other's company.

"How are you feeling?" questioned the archon.

"Somewhat anxious," returned Arlas.

"It is to be expected," nodded Zadkiel. "To be completely at ease would be inhuman. But, this is a good plan."

"I just hope it goes smoothly."

"It will not," assured the head of the Circle. "No plan survives contact with the enemy."

"You say that all the time."

"Because there is great wisdom in it," insisted Zadkiel. "Something will always go wrong. There will always be something that you did not plan for."

"Then what is the purpose of planning in the first place?"

"When constructing this plan, you thought of everything that might go wrong, did you not?" questioned Zadkiel.

"I tried," agreed Arlas. "There are a great many things, it would seem."

"If one of these things were to happen now, it would not be a surprise to you, because you have already considered it a possibility."

"I suppose so," agreed Arlas.

"That is why we plan."

Arlas chuckled at Zadkiel's ceaseless schooling.

"You are right, of course," agreed Zadkiel.

"What do you mean?"

"By now, I have more or less taught you all I can. There is little wisdom that I can offer you which you have not already heard."

"I'm sure that is not true," returned the paladin.

"No, it is," he assured. "You have been a great student, Arlas," insisted the archon. "You are always willing to listen and to learn. You never assume you know better, but are always willing to offer your opinion when you believe your ideas are of value."

"I have merely tried to take the teachings of the Circle to heart," replied Arlas modestly.

"It goes further than that," reiterated Zadkiel. "You are a powerful and talented mage, the likes of which the Circle has not seen for decades. But not only this, you are wise and keen-minded. You are diplomatic and courteous. You are humble and kind. You would offer mercy where others would not, yet you have the conviction to deliver justice when others would fear to."

"You praise me too highly," refused Arlas. "I only do what is expected of me."

"No, you do not. You do more—far more!" emphasised the archon. "What Artemis said… it is true; one day you will make a very wise archon of the Order. Under your leadership, the Circle will prosper. I was going to wait until afterwards to tell you, but now is as good a time as any; when tonight is done, you will be promoted to magistrate."

"You honour me, Archon."

"No," replied Zadkiel. "You honour me. I am proud of you—Son."

Arlas smiled, fighting back a tear.

"I have served you well as an archon," continued Zadkiel. "Of this I am satisfied. But I have failed you as a father—I know this."

"That's not true—" interjected Arlas.

"It is," insisted Zadkiel. "I was not there at your birth, and I barely made but a handful of appearances throughout your childhood. Until your mother died, I was but a stranger, and even then, I was not there when you needed me most."

"You were sworn to the Circle... to protecting Cambria... I understand that, Father!"

"I know you do," agreed Zadkiel. "But even still, that does not excuse my absence. Even after I brought you into the fold and initiated you into the Order, I have been distant. I have served faithfully as your teacher, but not as your father."

"You don't need to apologise," insisted Arlas.

"No. I do," maintained the archon. "Because of your relation to me, you have had to prove yourself more so than any other magi in the Circle. Because of this, I intentionally kept my distance; I did not want it to ever appear that I favoured you above the other members of the Order simply because my blood runs through your veins. I did not wish to make things harder for you than they already were, but I realise now that I was wrong. It is because things were harder for you that you needed me more. I wish I could remake my decisions, but I cannot. That I was not the father you deserved... that is the deepest regret of my life. But, perhaps my absence has in a way been a good thing; were it not for it, you might not have become the paragon that you are."

"Father..."

"No," refused Zadkiel. "You do not need to say anything. I do not wish for your forgiveness. I only wish for you to know the truth—for you to know the reasons for why I have not been the father I should have been."

"I forgive you all the same."

"Thank you, Son."

The two magi sat in silence in each other's company for a few minutes, before finally Zadkiel turned to Arlas and asked, "Ready?"

Arlas nodded, checking the coast was well and truly clear before they crept forwards and emerged from the trees. Swiftly and silently, they moved through the dark, cutting across a sward of grass, closing the distance to the cave mouth in a few short seconds. Staves drawn, the two men hugged the stone walls either side of the entrance, and craning their necks past the edges of the cave aperture, they peered down into the black passageway.

"It seems clear," whispered Arlas, his ears and eyes focussed for any sight or sound that might give away a watchman stood guarding the way in.

"It does," agreed Zadkiel, neither sensing the presence of a nearby occultist.

Together they moved, taking the first steps into the tunnel.

"Watch your footing," warned Zadkiel, indicating to a glyph carved into the floor of the passage, but the paladin had already seen it and was stooping to examine the arcane trap.

"It doesn't appear to be blood-linked," remarked the mage.

"Even still, I wouldn't try to dispel it," cautioned Zadkiel. "It is easy enough to step over; disarming it could alert the caster to our presence."

"Agreed," nodded Arlas.

"It has not been placed here to make the entrance impassable."

"Only to catch out any unsuspecting intruders," finished Arlas.

"Precisely," smiled the archon, reminded once again that there was little he had left to teach his son.

"Come on," beckoned Arlas. "We cannot afford to delay."

The archon nodded, and together they delved deeper into the lair. The natural underground passage twisted and fell beneath the outcrop; looping roots hung across the ceiling and cobwebs matted the walls and floor. The way smelled musty, the air thick and dank. The passage tightened, and more than once the two men had to shimmy through narrow chokepoints in the path. Eventually, a faint glow of candlelight from around a corner ahead told the two men they were nearing the first cavern in the lair.

Stifling their breathing, the two magi inched closer, listening for any indication that there might be witches in the hollow ahead. The resonance of dripping water plopped from behind, whilst up in front, there was a faint susurrus of running water, most likely from some underground spring; otherwise, all was still. Arlas's nostrils flared and a noxious odour of putrefaction filled his nose.

Peering cautiously around the turn in the passage, the mage's pupils constricted in the candlelight. His stomach turned as he looked on, but unable to avert his gaze, he advanced into the grotto. All about the walls hung strings of bones and small animal skulls, interspersed with spiderweb charms woven with feathers. The floor was stained black with dried blood, fresh droplets still trickling down the edges of a sacrificial stone altar cut from the wall of the grotto. Above the altar hung the most macabre sacrifice Arlas had ever laid eyes upon; the body was strung up in a crucifix position and flayed, every inch of skin peeled from his flesh. But the gruesome torture had not finished there; the victim had been blood eagled. The blood eagle ritual was something Arlas had only ever read about; most doubted the authenticity of the torturous form of execution, believing it little more than a literary invention, one never actually performed. Yet here Arlas stood, gazing in cold horror at a man whose ribcage had been splayed from his spine, his lungs lifted from his chest cavity, the maggot-ridden organs now decaying over the cadaver's shoulders.

"Come on," grimaced Zadkiel, putting a hand on his son's arm to pull him away from the traumatising sight. "Let's keep moving."

Steeling his resolve, Arlas pushed the nightmarish vision from his mind and followed his farther deeper into the lair. A short time later, the two magi came to a bend in the tunnel poised before another cavern. Peering around to gaze into the next grotto in the labyrinth of underground passes, Arlas caught sight of a robed woman muttering to herself, back turned. She was stooped over a stone slab on the floor, before her spread a freshly butchered lamb. Clutching a bloodied athame in her hand, the sorceress examined the entrails of the recently sacrificed animal, muttering low incantations under her breath as she did so.

A fire crackled on the far side of the cavern, above which was suspended a bubbling cauldron tended to by a second occultist. The steam and smoke rose upwards through a natural chimney in the grotto, down from which shone the faint gleam of moonlight. Much like the first, the second witch had her back turned, both occultists unaware of the intruders drawing in behind them.

Arlas clutched his staff tightly, creeping closer with the black steel blade of his weapon aimed ahead until it was mere inches from the first occultist's back. He turned to look at Zadkiel. The archon nodded, readying to strike for the other witch the moment his son dispatched the first. After what Arlas had seen moments ago, there was no mercy to be offered to the Dark Sisterhood, and no remorse to be felt.

With a sudden thrust, he impaled his stave through the murmuring sorceress, skewering cleanly into her heart. The witch tending the cauldron turned abruptly, gasping as she prepared to scream, but before the dark sister could emit a wail of terror, Zadkiel had rushed her, opening the crone's throat with a swift slash. She sputtered and retched, hands clutching the deep wound to her neck. Blood spurted from between her fingers, and in a matter of seconds, she collapsed to a heap on the ground.

Without uttering a word between them, the two magi continued towards the heart of the lair. Passing through several more caverns, they struck from the shadows, dispatching another three unsuspecting witches performing various dark blood magic rites along the way. The gushing of running water echoed louder as they approached the main chamber. Above their heads, a fissure opened in the ceiling of the passage granting a slender view of the starry skies, the crack knitted together by a mesh of great tree roots.

The passage widened and the two magi hunkered to the ground. Before them, the tunnel opened to a basin sunk within the centre of the overhead outcrop. The natural rock formation had formed a stone fortress in the heart of the ancient woodland. The walls crowned over the submerged hollow, enclosing to form a natural oculus centred above. Near the entrance where the magi were poised, the ground dropped further away, plummeting into a pit, out from which echoed the babbling of an underground spring.

The massive atrium was where the covens of the Dark Sisterhood had congregated. Together, they moved about beneath the circle of spectral moonlight shimmering through the opening in the cave's roof. More sacrificial victims were strung up and flayed around the centre of the lair, whilst a score of black clad occultists chanted dark hymns to one another, tinkering with blood magic spells in their various gatherings. Hares were being disembowelled, whilst toads and newts were being boiled alive in cauldrons. To what purpose half of the gruesome rituals were being performed, Arlas and Zadkiel could only guess at; regardless, they needed to be stopped.

"What now?" whispered Zadkiel, looking to his son for the next part of the plan.

"We wait another couple of minutes to ensure the others are in position. Then, we strike. We move fast and give them little time to react. So long as we have the element of surprise, we can slay them all before they can escape."

"Agreed," nodded Zadkiel, poking his head up to peer over the verge. "I see two other exits.

If I move fast, I can cover the one from which the others don't emerge."

"And they'll be trapped with no other way out."

"Hopefully," nodded Zadkiel. "Do you have eyes on Caddick?"

"Not yet," conceded Arlas as he scanned the score of witches. As he did so, the gathering of occultists ceased moving about the hollow, each stopping whatever they were doing. All at once, every witch stood eerily still. Then, in unison, they turned, revolving steadily to face the tunnel in which the two magi were hidden. There was a faint series of cackles as several of the witches drew back their hoods.

"Shit," breathed Arlas under his breath. "We need to move now."

"It's too late," returned Zadkiel. "They know we are here now. The element of surprise is gone."

"Then we need to retreat," warned Arlas. "Something is horribly wrong! How could they know?"

"You said it yourself, Son. This is our one chance to finish this once and for all!"

"It's a trap though!?"

"Precisely," nodded Zadkiel gravely. "The only way out now is through."

"You are right," agreed Arlas uneasily, curling his fingers tightly around the dark ebony of his stave.

"On my mark," readied Zadkiel.

Arlas nodded anxiously.

"One... two—"

"No need to make this more difficult then it has to be, Zadkiel Al'Ilha," called out the voice of Eryn Caddick from down in the basin. "Surrender, both you and your son, and I will make your deaths painless."

The two magi remained hidden, both their eyes widening with fear as they looked at one another. Then came a more familiar voice.

"Come out, Arlas," instructed the mage Darren Sayer. "It is over."

"Darren!?" called out Zadkiel, slowly rising to his feet.

"I'm afraid so," returned the mage.

"What are you doing here!?" demanded the archon.

"I've been here for some time," he replied calmly.

"I... I don't understand!?"

Arlas moved to prevent his father from stepping out of the tunnel, but Zadkiel was just beyond his reach. The mage cringed, not knowing what to do. His heart thrummed loudly in his ears as he too rose to his feet. Taking his father's lead, he followed out into the basin.

"It is quite simple, really," remarked Darren Sayer, as the mage stood centred in the throng of witches. "I'm in league with the Dark Sisterhood."

"What!?" cried Zadkiel in disbelief.

Arlas watched as a hooded witch beside Darren drew back her black cowl, revealing herself to be none other than the young raven-haired High Priestess of the Dark Sisterhood. Eryn Caddick entwined her fingers with Darren Sayer's as she took his hand in hers and kissed the mage on the cheek.

"Traitor!" roared Arlas.

"You'll die for this!" threatened Zadkiel,

moving to lunge with his staff. But before the archon let fly a bolt of lightning, he was halted by Sayer's voice.

"Wait!" commanded the mage.

Zadkiel hesitated.

"Do not make another move."

"Or else what!?" spat Zadkiel.

Darren did not need to respond; at that moment, from out of the passage on the far side of the hollow, emerged four more figures: the magi Ramon Rais, Roger Kelly, Michael Bolingbroke, and Edward Scot. Between the four men, they dragged two others. Arabis bled from a gash on his forehead as his feet trailed along the ground behind him; he was dazed and on the verge of unconsciousness, but still alive. Artemis fought and struggled against the two men restraining him as they forced him to kneel; a wet crimson stain was steadily widening around his gut.

"Or else, we will kill Arabis and Flamel," warned Darren.

Zadkiel lowered his staff in horror. "Roger...? Michael...? Ramon!? Ed!?" he stammered in disbelief. "You follow this traitor!?" he pointed at Darren.

"Actually, no," smirked Darren. "Its not me they follow at all."

Fiery agony suddenly tore through Arlas's leg as steel plunged deep into the muscle of his thigh. His knee crumpled. He collapsed to the floor, groaning through gritted teeth, but his own cries of pain were drowned out by the anguished gasp of his father. Arlas peered up to see Zadkiel skewered clean through by Azrael's staff. Planting the sole of his boot on Zadkiel's back, the treacherous mage rent free his weapon from the archon's torso, casting him to the ground.

"No!" screamed Arlas in despair as blood quickly puddled on the stone, trickling across the uneven cave floor.

Arlas grunted in agony as he clawed his way over to Zadkiel. He rolled his father over, dragging his limp body into his arms. Zadkiel's eyes met with his own. His lips quivered, uttering his final words. The mage's teeth were red with blood, and as he tried to speak, more of it merely trickled down his chin.

"Father!" panicked Arlas, clutching the man tightly.

Arlas felt his father's fingers brush gently across his cheek. Then, his arm fell limp. Zadkiel's eyes glazed over and rolled back into his head. The Circle's archon was dead.

"No," whispered Arlas in disbelief. "No." Unfathomable despair coursed through him. The despair turned quickly to rage. His entire body began to quake with fury. He clutched his father's body tighter. Steadily, his burning gaze rose to Azrael; the magistrate strode past him without even glancing his way.

"What have you done!?" demanded Flamel. "You murderer!"

"Kill them both," commanded Azrael.

"No!" roared Artemis as he watched in horror as Ramon Rais drew a dagger across Arabis's throat. Seconds later, Artemis's cries were drowned in blood, his own throat slit open.

The two magi slumped dead on the ground. The air inside the cavern congealed with a smothering unworldly silence.

"What are you doing!?" demanded Eryn

Caddick. "Do you not know the power their blood holds!? A mage in sacrifice... You promised me an offering!"

"And so you'll get one!" snapped Azrael. "The three of them were too dangerous to be left alive. Next to me, they were the three most powerful magi of the Order. They could have killed any number of us if given less than half a chance. Had one of them escaped, they would have led a rebellion against me with half the Circle at their back."

"But you swore to me..." insisted the Dark Priestess.

"And I kept my word," returned Azrael. "I left one of them alive. And he is none other than the son of Zadkiel himself. His blood will have all the power you need!"

"Very well," grumbled Eryn, disappointed but not scorned.

"Azrael!" roared Arlas. To his own amazement, he was stood up, leaning heavily on his staff. Blood was running hot and wet down his leg, and every second that passed sapped more of his strength away. But he refused to die on his knees.

"Well, look at you," remarked Azrael with amusement.

"Why!?" demanded Arlas. "Why betray us? Why side with these fanatics!?"

Azrael chuckled. "The magic you see practised here... It is not new, it is just forgotten. Blood magic and necromancy—they are the first magics that humans ever discovered. It is only through them that everything else has evolved. Only through the power of blood, and control over life did witches and warlocks first discover how to manipulate the Aether! The Binding ritual that turned both you and I into magi... it is a blood magic ritual! Somewhere along the way since the dawn of our order, someone decided that practicing such forms of magic was taboo. They became branded as evil, referred to as *'the dark arts.'* But neither blood magic nor necromancy are evil. They can be *used* for evil, much like any other form of magic, but they are merely tools; tools that can be put towards whatever purpose those with the skill to use them choose.

"The Occult was first founded to accrue arcane knowledge and oversee its practice. Blood magic was restricted—carefully controlled, but not forbidden. Even today, the Occult does not collect tomes and scrolls on dark magic to destroy them; the Occult protects them, from none other than the Circle itself. Even now, after a reformation enforced by none other than our own order, the Occult continues to accrue the teachings and history of blood magic. They may be too afraid to practise the arts under the watchful eye of the Circle of Magi, but they understand that knowledge, no matter how dark or unsavoury, should be preserved.

"Both you and Zadkiel, and countless other magi before you, have sought to destroy the written texts of blood magic. You set out on a fool's crusade to eradicate any alive who have knowledge of how to practise it. And why? All because of some petty preconceived notion that it is inherently wrong! The Dark Sisterhood is not evil; misguided perhaps, but not evil. They have uncovered things, knowledge long forgotten, that holds power you would not believe. If used by the right people, if put to use by the Circle itself... just think what we could accomplish! We could end disease! Cleanse the world of vermin and beasts! Tyrants would fall on our word! All of this can be ours, if we just have the courage to seize it!

"I am willing to do that, Arlas. I am willing to be the villain. I am willing to do the things your father would not. My own life... it doesn't matter. You may condemn what I have done, but in a hundred years, people will look back and say that I only did what was necessary to realise my dream—the very same dream upon which our order was founded! I *will* create a world that is without danger. I *will* create a world that is fair, and good, and kind. But before that can happen, we must discard our restraining senses of morality. What we think is right and wrong—it is all insignificant over the course of a single lifetime. I can see what needs to be done; something Zadkiel never could."

"You are insane!" screamed Arlas. "Look around you! Look at the atrocities these witches have committed! The ends don't justify the means, no matter how much you want them to!"

Azrael sighed laboriously as he moved closer and glanced down at the body of Zadkiel. "I knew you wouldn't understand. You truly are your father's son!"

"Don't touch him!" Arlas snarled.

"I wasn't lying, you know," smirked Azrael. "I meant it when I told you that you have my respect."

"Your respect means nothing to me!" hissed Arlas as his fingers tightened around his staff in preparation.

"Remember what else I said?" chuckled

the mage. "*What happens tonight—it is all because you brought us here.*"

Arlas gritted his teeth in rage.

"I know I shouldn't rub salt in the wound," taunted Azrael. "But I am curious. I want to see what you can do. How powerful really is the mage that slew the chimera?"

Arlas unleashed the tension in his body. With all the speed and might he could muster, he swung his staff. A maroon column of flame erupted from the end of his weapon with a deafening roar. Azrael raised his own staff in anticipation and summoned a bulwark of energy to shield himself, yet the mage had underestimated the strength of Arlas. The ward of force melted away and the blaze of purple lashed across Azrael's side. The mage screamed in agony as his clothes charred and his skin was scorched. But before Arlas could strike again, light-headedness brought on by blood loss overcame him. He stumbled. His knee buckled again.

Azrael thrashed, extinguishing the flames that had enveloped him. Smoke rose from his aketon, the side of his face red and molten. An enraged bloodshot eye looked back at Arlas from beneath a mask of scalded skin. Azrael summoned a retaliatory missile of black kinetic energy. Unable to avoid the strike, Arlas merely raised his staff in defence. The blast of deathly magic drove into Arlas's weapon, hurling him off the ground, sending him tumbling head over heels. His body skidded to a halt. As Arlas regathered his senses, he realised he was teetering on a precipice. Dozens of feet below him, water roared through the darkness. Arlas was dangling half over the edge of a vertical shaft, at the bottom of which rushed an underground spring.

"You'll pay for that, you son of a whore!" cursed Azrael, his fingers gently probing the scorched flesh across his face that would leave him scarred for the rest of his life. The mage began to march towards Arlas, fury raging in his eyes.

"Do not kill him!" warned Eryn Caddick. "You promised me his blood!"

But Azrael did not hear her.

Arlas peered up as death marched his way. This was it. This was the end. He was still reeling from Azrael's last blow, his bleeding leg now devoid of any sensation. He had not the strength to fight. There was no escape. All he could hear was the flowing of water fathoms below. The darkness was coming for him. He could either surrender to it, or face it head on.

Azrael was barely a few yards away. In a second, he would drive his staff through Arlas's heart, killing him the same way he had done his father. But Arlas refused to die that way. He felt his bulk shift as he pushed off with his hands. He rolled over the ledge, becoming momentarily weightless. Darkness swallowed him whole. He dropped down the shaft. In the aperture of light shrinking above, he saw Azrael's burnt and furious face appear over the ledge, the mage crying out in anger.

Suddenly, frigid water clasped hold of him. He seized a single lungful of air. The light above him died. Clutching his staff and protecting his head, Arlas let himself be swept away in the fast-flowing current. He tumbled and rolled, battered time and time again against the sides of the constricting river tunnel.

His lungs screamed out for air, but there was none to be had. Deeper and deeper underground the mage was carried, the waterway twisting along the path it had cut through the rock over the centuries. Arlas grew fainter and fainter. Bubbles streamed from his lips and nose as the very last wisps of air were beaten from his chest. His ribs spasmed, demanding he open his mouth. His entire body began to convulse as he fought every instinct to try and breathe. He knew it was only a matter of seconds before he would no longer be able to resist the commands of his lungs, but the moment he succumbed, his chest would be flooded with icy water and his fate would be sealed.

He clasped a hand over his mouth to buy himself more time, but as he struck another wall of rock in the wending underground river, it was knocked from his face. He prepared to breathe. He prepared to part his lips and let the water flow into his mouth and drown him. He prepared to die. But in that instant, the river spat him out. He was falling again, tumbling weightlessly through the air as a shower of water rained down around him. He managed a single gasp to replenish his air before he broke the water's surface, sinking into the depths of a plunge pool.

His chest was already screaming again, but he could not tell which way was up. He clawed and kicked, fighting against the torrent of water beating down on him. He could see the cold rippling of moonlight through the surface above. He fought and fought against the current, using every ounce of strength his body had left, and as if by some miracle, he broke through the surface.

Arlas coughed, wretched, sputtered, and spat, as he struggled even to stay afloat. Air gushed in and out of his aching chest. His head cleared and he looked around. He struggled his way towards the bank of the plunge pool and heaved his weight up the slope. He lay on his back wheezing. He could still feel unconsciousness creeping up on him. Arlas was bleeding out. He had only moments left. If he lost consciousness, he would die in spite of his escape.

He fumbled with numb fingers for his belt, somehow managing to draw his wand. Groaning as he sat upright, Arlas focussed his mind, trying his best through the grogginess to concentrate. With great difficulty, he managed to close the stab wound to the back of his leg.

He collapsed, panting in the mud. It wasn't over, and he knew it. They would not assume he had died. They would go searching for him. If he delayed, he would be caught. If he were to survive, he needed to fight on. His head was spinning. He was weak and nauseous. He was grieving and betrayed. But despite everything, Arlas clambered to his feet.

He glanced around, studying his surroundings. He was still in Heartwood, somewhere in the Cor Valley, but he appeared to have been carried some way from the outcrop beneath which lay the Dark Sisterhoods liar. If he could make it out of the woods before morning, he might just survive. The Circle's leaders had been murdered, but there were those who would still be loyal. It was not over. Zadkiel would be avenged. And so, leaning heavily on his staff, Arlas limped into the trees.

THIRTY-FIVE

"What do you believe this Anussati means?" questioned Shakyamuni from somewhere behind Rhys.

The mage sat in padmasana, meditating atop the perch on the northern face of Suraksameru. "There are many implications," began Rhys. "It was the Purge... or the beginning of it—that much is clear."

"The Purge?" questioned the guru.

"I'd be lying if I claimed to know much about it... although I suppose now I know more than anyone else alive. It is something Sol told me about, not long after we first met. Our order, the Circle of Magi, was almost wiped out once. Arlas and a few others were all that survived. It was very nearly the end for Magi in Cambria. Purportedly, this is the reason why so much of the Order's history is a mystery; much of it was lost when the senior members of the Circle died in the ordeal."

"And yet, even though you knew little about what came to pass, the events you witnessed through Anussati were not at all what you expected?"

"No," agreed Rhys. "I'm not sure what I expected. It is not something I ever believed I would discover. But a betrayal within the Order... the involvement of disavowed witches of the Occult... Eryn Caddick, no doubt another relation of my own... it is all just so..."

"Familiar?" finished Shakyamuni.

"Yes," nodded Rhys. "The details are different, but everything seems so similar to what is happening now."

"Like different stanzas of a poem; the words are different, yet they still follow the same rhythm and rhyme," suggested the guru.

Rhys chuckled at the analogy. "A rather fitting metaphor."

"Such is the nature of time," explained Shakyamuni. "Time is cyclical. The events of this world repeat again and again. The Dark Age marks neither the beginning nor the end; it is but one part of a great cosmic cycle that is forever destined to repeat itself."

"I figured this conflict was something unprecedented," explained Rhys. "I believed Indus had done something no other mage had done before; but he is merely echoing Azrael's own uprising from a few decades earlier. How many other times have events such as these transpired?"

"The argument over which your Order wages war is not a new one, but has existed since there have been Jhakri in the world. How best can the world be protected? Should Prana be used to rule over those in need of protection, or should those able to manipulate it serve as mere humble guardians?"

"And what do you believe?" questioned Rhys.

"I believe that you are Kalki," responded Shakyamuni. "I believe that you will lead us into the next Golden Age. But first, there is more for you to see."

"I've learnt a lot," agreed Rhys. "This was the longest dream I have had to date. But there must be more."

"Your time in meditation is bringing you closer to Nirvana," insisted Shakyamuni. "Your unconscious mind grows stronger. Whilst resting, you reach samadhi, and whilst woken, through dhyana, you grow closer to it."

"I don't know," doubted Rhys. "What if it was just coincidence? What if it were just another dream?"

"You said yourself, this was the longest Anussati you have experienced to date," replied the guru. "It is because of your training in yoga and gatka. You have gained self-knowledge in the weeks you have spent here. It may take months still, perhaps even years, but day by day you grow closer to Nirvana."

"But I still cannot see these visions at will," responded Rhys frustratedly.

"Even when you reach samadhi, not all will be clear at once. The secrets of the past do not reveal themselves as a flood, but come in waves. Only when you achieve Nirvana will you be able to see the ocean of the past in its entirety."

"You use an awful lot of metaphors," replied Rhys. "You are aware of that, aren't you?"

"They allow concepts to be described that our minds are ill-equipped to understand," explained Shakyamuni. "Once you achieve Nirvana, all will be clear, but until then, there are limits to your understanding."

"I suppose there is truth to that," agreed the mage.

"You are close, Kalki," insisted Shakyamuni. "You have learnt fast. You ask questions, both of me and of yourself. Many who claim to seek Nirvana do not truly desire it; they merely seek the inner peace that comes from it. The daunting realities of Brahman are too much for many to fathom; most prefer to live only within the present, seeking simple lives, not concerning themselves with the greatest concepts of existence. Most who walk upon this world seek comfort and assuredness over all else. For them, the greatest questions of Brahman are to be answered by the teachings of the Brahmin, not by samadhi and Anussati. They claim to seek answers but are not willing to search their inner selves for them, for fear that, if they were to look, they might not find them."

"They accept the teachings of religion as fact over fear of the alternative: admitting ignorance," mused Rhys.

"Yes," agreed Shakyamuni.

"Nirvana is not something that can be taught or gifted by another; it must be sought out by oneself. I can show you the path, but I cannot guide you along it. You must find your own way," explained the sage. "Unlike most who travel here to this temple, Kalki, you already know this. You seek answers where others can give them, and go in search for them yourself when they cannot. Much of what you know and have learnt in your time as Jhakri, you have discovered for yourself. There are many more things you must learn. Only you can truly understand your role in the war to come. Do not be afraid to seek the answers you need."

"I won't," promised the mage.

"Dhyana, Kalki," instructed his teacher. "Breathe in. Breathe out."

Rhys inhaled and exhaled. He cleared his mind and allowed his body to relax. He felt the tension ease out of his muscles. His senses dulled to the world around him. The wind lulled. The rain faded away. The frigid air of the mountain mingled with the gentle warmth of the brazier. Breath filled his lungs and flowed out of his chest. Rhys continued to focus. All of his thoughts died away. All was still.

"Prana flows from and through Brahman," spoke Shakyamuni, his voice echoing from far away, yet the words were clear in Rhys's mind. "It flows through the ground. It flows through the wind. It flows in flames. It flows through the oceans. It flows through you. Do you feel it?"

"No," Rhys answered honestly.

"Dhyana," reiterated the guru. "The power you wield: it is your control of Prana. Your body and mind can change the flow of Prana into any of the elements of your choosing. For you, the element that comes most naturally is Wind. You have power over the Air.

"Your enemy, Indus Mark, like the Vitra the rakshasa revere, and Mahakala himself, has power over Fire. Fire is the most devastating of elements; it is pure destructive power. All fear Fire, for it is indiscriminate in its wrath; a flame that rages uncontrolled purges all in its path and spreads without mercy or thought. It is with fire that Mahakala will destroy the world.

"Water, though life-giving in the form of rain, is a terrible force to be reckoned with in the might of the seas and waves. It drowns men, floods shores, and crumbles cliffs. Over time it carves out valleys and sheers mountains apart. To those ignorant of its destructive power, it may seem harmless, but to those wise to its power, it is every bit as fearsome as Fire.

"Earth may seem the most stable of elements, but Sumeru is testament against this. Any who has felt the ground quake or crumble beneath their feet, or watched the sides of mountains fall away after little more than a whisper has grown into an echo, knows that it's stability is often an illusion. From the Earth comes gravity, Sakti, as prana flows through it; this force alone can prove deadly, and every creature that walks upon this world is beholden to it. Not many truly understand its destructive power, yet to those who have seen it, Earth is as deadly as both Fire and Water.

"To many, Wind seems innocuous. Only when the air is in motion can it even be felt. It is life-giving, more so than Water, as it fills our lungs with breath. When gales rage, they topple trees, ripping their roots from the ground; to many, this is the worst level of destruction that they will ever see wrought by Wind. But in many ways, Wind is the deadliest of all the elements. Any who has witnessed a truly devastating storm knows that Wind can shatter glass, shred cloth, and even rip buildings from their very foundations. When conditions are right, Wind can swirl tightly in on itself and form raging columns that flatten everything in their wake; but even still, this is but a fraction of the power of Wind. It can spread Fire, feeding it and carrying it faster than the flames can otherwise travel. It brings the storm clouds of the monsoon, it stokes the waves that batter shores, and it sweeps floodwaters over fields and up hills. Over time, it carves valleys and mountains, smoothing rugged faces and rounding peaks, in much the way Water shapes Earth. Unlike the other elements, it can act both directly and in directly. It has dominion over Fire, Earth, and Water. It is this power that you wield, Kalki."

Rhys nodded, though the action seemed somehow disembodied in his distant state.

"Prana has dominion over all the other four elements. Though unlike Wind, it can only act indirectly, your power over Wind comes only from your control of Prana. The energy that moves through your body when you manipulate Wind, Fire, Earth, and Water—that energy is Prana. You feel it, do you not? When you control the Wind, you feel Prana flowing through you."

"Yes," confirmed Rhys, his own voice sounding as distant as Shakyamuni's.

"Then feel it now!" commanded Shakyamuni. "It flows through you now, just as it does when you control the elements. It is always flowing. It is always in motion. The reason why you feel it when you summon the Wind is because your mind is focussed. Dhyana now, and you will feel that it is always there. Reach samadhi, and you will see that Prana flows through the world."

Rhys sucked in, flooding his chest with air. His mind slipped deeper into concentration, and the outside world faded altogether. All was still. All was quiet. He was there. He had finally reached samadhi. All awareness of his surroundings had vanished, replaced now with something deeper, something almost ethereal in nature. He could feel a tingling in his fingers. The breath flowing in and out of his lungs seemed alive. Energy strummed from his mind, down his spine, resonating through his chest and limbs, trickling out through the surface of his skin, reaching into the void that surrounded him. Through this reach, Rhys became aware once more; but this awareness, this *surti,* came not from the five senses of his body. It was as if within himself he had awoken another sense altogether, one that stemmed entirely from within his mind.

He had been blind all of his life, and now, for the first time, Rhys could see. No; he had not been blind, he had merely never opened his eyes before. It was not that this sense had been absent until now, it had always been there; he had felt it dozens of times before. Though this was the first time he had opened his eyes, he had always been aware that he could see. Even with his eyes firmly shut, lights bright enough could still penetrate through the darkness of closed eyelids. He had the ability to sense other magi, the ability to sense the conduits; there were stimuli so potent that Rhys could still detect them, even before. But now, Rhys had learnt to open his eyes. He could feel energy moving through him and around him.

Rhys could feel the burning brazier beside him, not by its warmth, but by the energy radiating from it. He could feel the wind swelling around him, not by the chill of the air currents, but by the flow of the Aether. He could feel the effects of the storm, not by the flashing of lightning, the tolling of thunder, or the splattering of raindrops, but by the power stored in the clouds above him. He could feel the ground beneath himself, not by the coldness of the stone, or the sense of weight his body perceived from pressing down on it, but by the energy held within the rock, the flow of gravity drawing both himself towards the stone and the stone upwards towards him.

"Do you feel it?" repeated Shakyamuni, his voice no longer distant, but seemingly sounding from within Rhys's own thoughts.

"Yes," replied Rhys, his own voice echoing both from within and without.

"Then open your eyes."

Rhys's eyelids parted and light spilled in. His mind rushed back to the present moment and all other sensations flooded his body. But the return of his five other senses did not drown out the sixth; he could feel, smell, taste, hear, and see all that was happening around him, all whilst aware of the Aether.

Rhys peered at his surroundings, mesmerised by what he could see. Droplets of rain hovered in the air surrounding him, refusing to either fall or rise as they gently quivered in Rhys's presence. The wind had fallen still in a sphere centred on him, yet beyond the bubble of energy, Rhys could see the lashing downpours being swept sideways in the howling gales. Specks of dust and tiny fragments of stone had risen from the ground, tumbling gently in the suspension of energy, floating preternaturally in the air, whilst embers evaporating from the flames of the brazier took flight and began to slowly encircle Rhys, intermingling with the other four elements.

In that moment, Rhys felt as if the elements had surrendered entirely to his will. He gazed upwards, into the skies. Through the black storm clouds, Rhys could see the Rift; it was a rupture in the fabric of the Aether, visible not through sight, but through his connexion to the flow of energy around himself. He could see the shimmering colours rippling across the sky that formed the scar of light visible to all, yet extending beyond this primary wound to the Aether, Rhys could make out the fragmenting ripples of energy streaking through the atmosphere. These tears were invisible to the naked eye, perceptible only through his mind. They spread across Sumeru, penetrating the mountains and the sea, disrupting the flow of Prana and perturbing all of the other elements. These tears from the Rift were what suspended the mountains in the sky, they lifted water upwards from the sea, and smashed together a violent churning maelstrom of air currents that powered the eternal tempest that engulfed the Stormy Isles.

"I see everything," breathed Rhys.

"Then look further," instructed Shakyamuni. "Search for what you seek. Look into the past. Read the ripples of Prana and find the answers to your questions."

Rhys attempted to cast his gaze further. The sights and sounds and sensations of the present moment faded away. He felt his mind drawn to images flickering faintly beyond his view. He saw through Arlas's eyes, but the images quickly grew blurry. He listened through Arlas's ears, but the sounds grew muffled. Darkness enveloped him, and suddenly all was still once more.

Rhys opened his eyes as rain soaked his hair and streaked across his skin. The wind was raging, and thunder and lightning were in conflict in the skies above. The flames of the brazier flickered violently in the raging wind and the ground seemed once more cold and lifeless underneath him. Above, the Rift was no longer visible through the dark obscuring ceiling of the storm.

"I lost it," sighed Rhys, his mind and body now feeling devastatingly weary.

"For now," nodded Shakyamuni with a gentle smile across his face. "But you held it for longer than I could ever have imagined."

"What do you mean?" questioned Rhys as he began to shiver in his sodden clothes.

"Few can achieve samadhi with their minds open to the world around them. You were able to see both with your eyes and with your mind, both what is visible and what is not, all at once. Very few ever manage this, even after a lifetime of yoga. That you managed to do so on your first attempt…"

"What?" questioned Rhys. "What does it mean?"

"That you truly must be Kalki."

Rhys stared at Shakyamuni. He could see in his eyes the conviction with which the elf held this belief. For a brief moment, Rhys was open to the possibility that the guru could be right.

"If it is as difficult as you say, then why did you tell me to open my eyes?" questioned Rhys, scepticism returning to him once more.

"I sought to return you from samadhi, to break your dhyana."

"Why?"

"It is taxing on the mind. Especially to those new to yoga. But you showed the strength of your dhyana. You remained within samadhi, even with all of the distractions of the world around you; not only this, but through your dhyana, you conquered them."

Rhys nodded, contemplating everything he had seen and felt in a long moment of reverie. "What is next?"

"We try again," responded the guru calmly.

"Okay," nodded Rhys exhaling deeply.

"But not today," replied Shakyamuni.

"Why not?"

"Your mind is tired and fatigued. You will not achieve Anussati today. It is unlikely you will achieve samadhi again. You must rest now. Tomorrow we will try once more—once you have recovered."

"Okay," agreed Rhys, somewhat relieved by the guru's decision.

"For now, continue your learnings in gatka," instructed the sadhu. "You must train your body alongside your mind, for each is only as strong as the other."

THIRTY-SIX

Rhys planted his feet in the sand, watching as his three opponents advanced. His heels were backed right against the rim of the fighting pit, halting his retreat. The trio of kshatriya continued their march towards him, each brandishing an ebony otta stick. Rhys focussed, glancing at them each in turn, keeping all three within the periphery of his vision as they fanned out. His foes halted their advance, turning to look at one another, silently coordinating their attack with little more than a series of subtle expressions. They nodded one by one in agreement, once more turning their attention on the mage before them.

Rhys wriggled his toes. His footing was sure, his balance poised. In less than a second, they would strike all at once. He was ready. Rhys caught the first sign of motion before the elf had truly even begun to move. In a splintered second, the first of the kshatriya lunged forwards, his legs exploding with impossible speed, launching him into a rapid bound. The elf evaporated in an orange blur of energy and hurtled towards Rhys. Hot on his heels, the two remaining elves pounced, likewise disintegrating as they blinked out of material existence, their bodies taking form as energy searing through the Aether.

Pushing his mind into samadhi, Rhys felt their ripples through Prana like the bow waves of oncoming ships. The undulations gave away their movements, and as Rhys's rapidly whirring mind calculated each of their trajectories, his own body began to move. The elastic force stowed in his muscles snapped taught his legs, and as the three streaks of ethereal energy hurtled towards him, Rhys spurted off the mark.

The mage leant back, allowing his momentum to topple him. He hit the sand and slid as the first of the kshatriya rematerialized overhead. The elf lunged for where Rhys had been an instant before, but the mage skidded clean beneath the blow, out of his foe's reach. The elf stumbled over Rhys's sliding body. A slight lift of the mage's staff snagged the kshatriya's flailing ankles, taking the elf's legs entirely out from under him.

Leaping out of the slide, Rhys thrust his quarterstaff forwards the moment the next elf reappeared out of her blink. The tip of his sparring weapon struck the warrior square in the chest, the mage's momentum driving her back with force. Taking the blow in stride, she swung her ebony practice weapon wildly, but driven away hard, her otta flailed helplessly short of the mage.

As the second elf plunged backwards off balance, Rhys maintained his forward impetus, leaping into the air. He tumbled, turning his body sideways, rolling as he careened above the sand. The final elf took form from out of the Aether, mightily lashing with his otta; but the strike had been judged from before the kshatriya had blinked. The swing cleft too low, sweeping beneath Rhys's airborne body.

Rhys touched back down on the sand and rolled gracefully to his feet. He pivoted, allowing his quarterstaff to slide through his fingers, retightening his grip around the stave's very tip. He swung the full length of the weapon in a wide swooping arc, throwing all his body's momentum into the blow. Before the third elf had regained his balance, the length of bamboo whipped powerfully across the kshatriya's back. The staff cracked loudly in the impact and the elf was sent sprawling off his feet.

In the chaos, Rhys backpedalled swiftly away, putting himself beyond the reach of several retaliatory strikes from the first elf. The second leapt back to her feet, likewise resuming her pursuit of the mage. Rhys clashed weapons with the two, dodging and parrying their rapid advances. His feet moved faster than he'd have thought possible weeks earlier, his hands flurrying faster still. Dancing his way around the circumference of the arena, Rhys exchanged blow after blow with his two remaining assailants, but despite his speed and fervour, fatigue was sneaking up on the mage. One elf was difficult enough to keep pace with; two seemed near enough impossible; yet still the mage proved their match.

On the back foot, Rhys changed tact, transitioning into the yak yudhan. A sudden drive of brute force broke through the guard of one of the elves, sending her reeling backwards, causing a momentary interruption in the tempo of the fight. He'd created an opening; one that following a month spent training with Maadurga, Rhys would not fail to capitalise.

Reversing his momentum, the mage dove headfirst towards the sand. An otta skimmed barely an inch above his back. Rhys reached the peak of his parabola. He dropped to the ground. Rolling instinctively, he lashed sideways. The bamboo staff snapped forcefully against the inside of the first elf's knees, buckling his legs, knocking the kshatriya groundward. Twirling his staff, remaining in motion, Rhys spun the weapon around his back, switching hands, sweeping the stave into an upward strike.

The kshatriya planted her feet in anticipation, raising her otta in stationary defence. Bamboo and ebony clacked together as Rhys's blow collided with her block, but the impetus of the mage's stave was too great, breaking through his opponent's static guard. The otta raised in defence was batted aside, the bamboo stave continuing its upward arc, the steel cap clouting the kshatriya across her brow. Her head thrashed backwards, hands rushing to clasp her forehead as she was launched off her feet into the sand.

Rhys spun, turning back towards his remaining undefeated foe. The elf scrambled through the sand, recovering his dropped otta, preparing to leap back to his feet to resume the fight, but before he could stand, Rhys lowered the length of his practise weapon gently across the back of the kshatriya's neck. Feeling the touch of the bamboo, the elf submitted, lowering his head in defeat.

With the fight at an end, Rhys lowered his staff and turned to the elf behind him. Exhaustedly, the mage hoisted her back to her feet as she shook her head, dazedly rubbing her brow where she'd sustained the blow from Rhys. Both her and her partner exited the ring, joining their other defeated ally outside the pit, leaving Rhys, the victor alone in the sand.

The mage panted, recovering his breath as the adrenaline of the fight wore away. With the heat of battle fading, realisation hit him. He had won. For the first time since Maadurga had begun pitting the mage against multiple opponents, he had emerged the champion. He had come close before, but until now he had never succeeded. He was exhausted, drained of all energy, but as he glanced in his opponents' direction, the three elves stood nursing their bruises, Rhys realised he had managed to emerge from the fight unscathed.

Maadurga began to slowly applaud as she stepped into the sparring pit and moved to embrace Rhys. "You did it!" she beamed.

"It nearly killed me," puffed Rhys, hunching to rest his hands on his knees. "But, yeah... I guess I did."

"You are nearly ready," declared Maadurga.

"Ready for what?"

"To face me," she replied.

"I've already faced you," wheezed Rhys, still struggling for breath.

"Not properly," replied the elf. "Not me at my best. And not in front of an audience."

"An audience?" questioned Rhys.

"Yes," nodded Maadurga with a smile. "It is the Khel."

"The Khel?"

"A performance," explained the elf. "A competition between student and teacher; one to prove the student's skill. Every student of gatka must pass the Khel to become a kshatriya."

"Pitting student against teacher...?" began Rhys. "That hardly seems fair."

"The student is not expected to win," explained Maadurga. "Only to demonstrate that they have become a worthy opponent."

"Do they ever win?" questioned Rhys.

"Sometimes," nodded the elf. "I defeated my own teacher during the Khel."

"Who are the audience?"

"The family and friends of the student," she began. "And members of the Kshatriya including the Rajanya."

"The Rajanya Kshatriya?" questioned the mage. "The First Warrior?"

"Yes," nodded Maadurga.

"Isn't that you?"

"Yes."

"I take it then, that it is not common for a student to be fighting the First Warrior in the Khel?"

Maadurga laughed. "No. You are right. It is most uncommon."

"Well, that hardly seems fair," returned Rhys.

"It is also most uncommon for the student to be Kalki himself," replied Maadurga smiling.

"I see your point," conceded Rhys

"Some would say the fight is unfair for *me*," added Maadurga.

"Well, I guess we won't find out until the Khel," repeated Rhys. "When will it be?"

"Tomorrow."

"Tomorrow!?" repeated Rhys. "I thought

you said I was *nearly* ready? Doesn't that imply that there is more I need to learn beforehand?"

"There is much for you still to learn," agreed Maadurga. "But to be ready, all you can do now is rest before tomorrow."

Rhys sighed heavily and gazed past the elf to the three kshatriya stood watching the two of them from outside the ring. "You knew it would be today, didn't you?" questioned the mage. "You knew today would be the day I would finally beat the three of them."

"It was time," Maadurga nodded. "You learn quickly. You have grown faster each day. I could see that you were close. If it were not today, it would be tomorrow, or perhaps the day after. But I knew it would not be long."

"Well," pondered Rhys, "I'm glad I'm at least reaching your expectations."

Maadurga laid a hand gently on Rhys's shoulder. "You have made me proud ," she beamed.

"Thank you," smiled Rhys. "You are an excellent teacher."

"Maadurga, ke tapa insam ga hamro kunai atiriktaka avasya kata cha?" called out Nuraj, one of the three elves with whom Rhys had spent the last week sparring.

"Tapa ilai kreja gari eko cha, Nuraj," replied Maadurga.

The three elves smiled, each bowing respectfully, issuing Rhys and Maadurga a farewell before exiting the pagoda's akhara.

"Any final advice for tomorrow?"

"Pravaha," responded Maadurga.

"Move," translated Rhys.

Maadurga nodded, smiling warmly before

leaving Rhys alone in the akhara.

THIRTY-SEVEN

Rhys took a deep breath in the dim quietude of the antechamber. He tightened the leather wraps around his wrists and clenched his bare toes against the cold stone floor of the pagoda. It was unsettlingly quiet, no noise whatsoever coming from beyond the set of doors separating him from the akhara. Rhys's prediction was that the audience for the Khel would be small; perhaps merely Shakyamuni and a few of the kshatriya would be present. He imagined Sol and Thia would be there, but hoped otherwise. Rhys had been in countless fights, both in training and in combat, but he had never fought in front of an audience before. This seemed less like a rite of passage or test of skill, and more like a stage performance. Supposedly, the Khel was something of a formal affair, one to be judged by all bearing witness. Rhys was dreading it. He had no desire to become one of the elven kshatriya; he was a mage. What purpose did this pageantry serve? If Maadurga believed him a worthy opponent already, then why did he need to prove himself to others? After all, Maadurga was the First Warrior of her people; surely, her judgement alone was sufficient to satisfy the rest of the elves?

The hinges groaned as the enormous set of doors before Rhys began to swing open. He gripped his bamboo stave tightly. Light filled the antechamber, and as the mage's eyes adjusted, he realised he had been way out in his estimates for the size of his audience. The training hall of the akhara was packed to bursting. Seemingly every sadhu, pilgrim, and kshatriya in the Temple of Kalki had turned out to watch Rhys take on Maadurga. In hindsight, Rhys should have expected nothing less; they believed he was none other than the reincarnation of Kalki himself after all. Instead of the dozen odd spectators he'd been hoping for, the mage found himself staring out at an audience numbering in their hundreds. Together, they were stood in near total silence, the monks utterly soundless, with only a few of the kshatriya and pilgrims quietly murmuring amongst themselves. As the doors opened in full, even the hushed whispers died away. Rhys anxiously emerged from the vestibule, all eyes fixed on him.

The mage strode forwards, stepping into the centre of the akhara. The crowd parted, forming a corridor of spectators to the fighting pit, stood centred in which was Maadurga and Shakyamuni. From within the audience, Rhys spotted Thia and Sol. Sol issued Rhys a nod and mouthed a few words of encouragement; Thia meanwhile smiled teasingly, offering a subtle wink that only Rhys picked up on. The mage smiled back their way before turning his attention ahead, stepping into the ring.

"How are you feeling?" asked Maadurga warmly.

"Like you are about to lose," taunted Rhys with feigned arrogance.

"Really?" smiled the kshatriya, raising an eyebrow.

"I should probably tell you something—before this all begins," offered Rhys.

"What is that?" enquired the elf.

"I've been holding back on you up until now," lied the mage with an obvious smile. "Everything until this point... it has all been a ruse."

"A ruse?"

"An act. A trick. All so that you would underestimate me."

"Oh yes?" returned Maadurga amusedly.

"All this time, I've been pretending to be worse than I am, so that I'd catch you off guard today."

Maadurga leant closer to Rhys, smiling broadly as she did so. "I don't believe you."

"Well, you should," warned Rhys jokingly.

"We shall see," replied Maadurga.

"That we shall," agreed Rhys.

"Are you both ready?" asked Shakyamuni patiently, after the two of them had finished their exchange.

They both nodded.

"Very well," concluded the sadhu, switching to Elvish to address the audience. Shakyamuni spoke briefly, his voice raised so that all within the packed training hall could hear. He introduced both Rhys and Maadurga, though neither of them really needed any introduction, before presumably explaining the rules of the contest.

Maadurga had already described to Rhys what to expect: three rounds, the best of which would determine the overall victor. A clean blow dealt by a weapon to the torso, neck, or head ended the round. If either of them stepped outside, or was forced beyond the edge of the ring, they forfeited the round. Otherwise, each fight would continue until either Rhys or Maadurga submitted. It was simple enough, and more often than not, each round lasted barely a minute. When Shakyamuni finished addressing the audience, he bowed to both Rhys and Maadurga and stepped out of the fighting pit, taking his place amongst the crowd to watch the Khel.

Together, Rhys and Maadurga bowed to the audience, before turning to face one another and offering the same gesture of respect. Backing steadily apart, they paced a dozen feet between themselves and awaited the signal for the fight to begin. Rhys sucked in a deep lungful of air. He focussed his mind. Maadurga closed her eyes and took her two ebony rods in each hand.

Rhys studied his opponent as she started her ritualistic mental preparations for the fight. He knew what her opening move would be, he was sure of it. The instant the gong rang, Maadurga would blink. She would close the distance between them in a fraction of a second and strike. Weeks ago, Rhys would never have been able to react fast enough to avoid the blow, but Maadurga had helped train his body and mind to move quicker than ever before. Now, with a small amount of luck, the mage might just be able to avoid her first attack.

Rhys exhaled and took another lungful of air. Maadurga stood calm and still. Her eyes slowly opened. Rhys curled all ten fingers gently around the length of bamboo in his hands and adopted a low guard. The gong sounded.

Maadurga vanished, disintegrating into a streak of energy. Rhys dropped to his knees. He lunged. A blur of light surged into the air. Immediately, the mage realised he had miscalculated. He felt a polished otta brush against his neck as Maadurga reappeared in flight above him. The gong tolled again, Maadurga acrobatically touching down behind Rhys. The first round was over. He had lost in less than a second.

Rhys cursed under his breath as he stood back up. A series of mutterings sounded from amongst the crowd, but Rhys ignored them. He had expected Maadurga to dart low; instead, she'd gone high. The attack had caught him entirely off-guard. Having already committed to protecting against a ground assault, he had been left defenceless. Rhys paced around the pit, meeting Maadurga's eyes as she encircled the far side. She offered him an apologetic look, but Rhys turned away. He took up his starting position once more and awaited the sounding of the next gong.

If he lost this next round as quickly as the last, that would be it; the third round would still be fought, but he would likely have failed to impress any of the kshatriya, let alone Maadurga. With few worse ways to begin the Khel, he was heading into the second round with a mountain to climb; but there was still hope to be had. It would be several minutes before Maadurga could blink again; she had to wait for the Aether to resettle, her Prana to recharge. With a little luck, that gave Rhys perhaps the whole of the next two rounds. She had used up her biggest advantage in her opening play; the next round would be fairer, though by Rhys's reckoning, the odds were still in Maadurga's favour.

Rhys took another deep breath and prepared for the second round. The gong sounded, and without delay, Maadurga was in motion again. The elf sped with light-footed swiftness across the sand, barely leaving an impression with each step she took. Rhys rushed up to meet her, veering left at the last possible moment. He dodged beyond Maadurga's reach, her weapons arcing short of his torso, swinging low with his stave to take out her legs. The steel tip of Rhys's quarterstaff skimmed through the sand. Maadurga flipped, summersaulting clean over Rhys's strike. She landed, carrying her momentum straight into her next advance. Rhys skipped backwards, deflecting a pair of incoming blows. Two loud clacks sounded again as their weapons clashed once more and Rhys was driven on to the backfoot.

Maadurga lurched, closing the distance between them. A twirl of Rhys's bamboo kept her next advances at bay, but the elf pressed in even tighter. At this range, the length of Rhys's quarterstaff quickly became a disadvantage. Maadurga stooped. She thrust for him, but Rhys manage to tumble away, rolling backwards in the sand as he narrowly avoided the strike. Regaining his footing, he felt his heels touch the limits of the pit. He had retreated as far as he could. Another half-step and it would all be over.

Maadurga sensed the end was near. She hurtled forwards, knowing that even if Rhys managed to block her strikes, her momentum would likely force him beyond the bounds of the arena. Rhys knew this as well as her. He needed to act fast.

The mage spurted sideways, Maadurga rushing his way, otta outreached in front of her. Palming his staff around his back, reversing his grip, Rhys brought the weapon spinning around his body. Maadurga dug her feet into the sand as she skidded to a halt and struck for Rhys, but the mage's deft manoeuvre had brought his weapon arcing around Maadurga's back, bypassing her guard, exploiting her lack of defence to the rear.

Exposed from behind, Rhys forced Maadurga's hand. With no other option, she abandoned her lunge for Rhys, pivoting in defence to counter the mage's attack, and in doing so, turned her back to the edge of the ring. Bamboo and ebony clashed, Maadurga successfully blocking the mage's strike. The elf stood her ground, bracing against the impact from Rhys's blow, retaining her balance as she fought to keep her feet planted inside the pit. But now, Rhys had her exactly where he wanted.

All it took was a shove. Their bodies pressed tightly together in contest, weapons locked in a bind, Rhys dropped his shoulder. The mage drove with all his might, breaking Maadurga's guard with the one advantage he had over the elf: brute force. Maadurga flailed as she tried to jink clear, but when rushing the mage, doing everything in her power to push in close past his defences, she had sealed her own fate. Rhys's shoulder made contact and he delivered a strong shunt. Maadurga braced again, standing her ground against the shove, but in doing so, she stepped back to adjust her stance, planting a foot momentarily beyond the limits of the ring.

The gong sounded. Maadurga peered down in surprise to see her foot outside the bounds of the arena. She glanced up at Rhys, flashing him a quick smile, the mage's ploy having clearly impressed her. The two warriors exchanged a nod of admiration, padding the perimeter of the pit as they encircled each other once more, resuming their starting positions.

This was it. The final round. What happened now mattered little. Having defeated Maadurga in even a single round would be enough to impress any of the kshatriya, especially given the brevity of Rhys's training. But Rhys was not finished; he now knew it was possible for him to beat Maadurga. He just had to fight at his best.

Rhys exhaled, focussing his mind, pushing deeper into samadhi. He examined his opponent. Maadurga gazed back at him, analysing Rhys now every bit as intently as he was her. The mage had surprised her, perhaps even knocking her confidence slightly. But now, Maadurga would be twice as wary, and twice as formidable. His fingers locked tightly around the bamboo of his staff. He could feel the energy of the Aether flowing through him. The air hummed. The sand tingled beneath his bare soles. Rhys blanked out the audience from his perception, blinding himself to everything outside the edges of the ring.

The gong sounded and the third round began. Both Rhys and Maadurga waited, rooted in position, each pausing to see who would make the first move. Initiating the exchange, Rhys was the first to lift a foot from the sand, planting it outwards as he began to prowl the ring's circumference. Maadurga mirrored the mage, and for a short time, the two of them merely stalked one another around the perimeter of the pit. Then, without warning, Maadurga spurted towards Rhys, traversing the centre of the ring with a single bound. Rhys lanced with his staff. Maadurga slid beneath his thrust. The mage darted backwards, spearing for the elf again with the tip of his weapon. Maadurga batted away his advance and lunged. Rhys sidestepped. He swung. She parried. Ebony and bamboo clacked. The bout ended. They broke apart.

 Circling the pit for a second time, the two opponents continued to size one another up. Suddenly they were both in motion again, darting back towards the heart of the ring for another clash. Spinning his quarterstaff in a wide overhead arc, Rhys clove downward. Maadurga ducked, deflecting the blow with a glancing parry. Rhys's stave rebounded, curling back around for a second assault, this time directed low. Maadurga leapt, twirling in the air as the sweep blurred under her.

 Still airborne, Maadurga jabbed, the two tips of her otta thrusting at Rhys. Twisting his staff, pirouetting clear, Rhys narrowly parried, stumbling awkwardly as he backed out of the botched counter. Pressing the advantage, Maadurga pursued, dealing another succession of blows as she drove Rhys towards the edge of the ring. Stealing the move that had won her opponent the last round, Maadurga threw her weight into a shoulder charge, connecting with Rhys, shoving the mage off balance, sending him lumbering backwards, his feet skidding to a halt, heels coming to rest as they touched the lip of the ring behind.

Sensing Rhys's vulnerability, Maadurga charged, but wary of what had transpired before, she held back, maintaining her distance, lunging from the limits of her range. Lancing forward, Rhys met her head on, the length of his staff halting her advance and keeping her at bay. Jinking clear of the edge of the ring, Rhys spun, spinning his bamboo weapon around, clashing against the ebony of Maadurga's otta sticks once again. The elf darted inward, pressing in tight to regain the upper hand.

The mage and elf exchanged a flurry of blows, both transitioning from eagle to jaguar, then rapidly dropping into the monkey yudhan. Binding weapons, their bodies locked tightly together, they grappled and counter-grappled, hands, elbows, and knees flurrying as both Rhys and Maadurga wrestled to free themselves from one another's hold. Rhys felt Maadurga's leg snake under his, hooking his ankles as she took his feet out from under him. The mage toppled, but tightening his grip of Maadurga, he heaved powerfully, dragging her over with him. Together they struck the sand, flipping over, instantly landing back on their feet, weapons disentangling as they separated.

Flung apart, skidding towards opposite ends of the arena, Rhys and Maadurga locked eyes. Something was wrong. Rhys could feel it. He'd taken too long. The end of the fight had come. He imminently knew what was going to happen. He was about to lose. The Aether had resettled; Maadurga's prana recharged. She was about to blink.

Maadurga pounced. Her body evaporated, blazing in a streak of light as she arced down at Rhys. Lurching backwards with all his strength, Rhys hurled himself towards the edge of the ring. He lunged, thrusting his staff to full reach in front of him. He planted his feet, heels skidding right up to the rim of the pit. Maadurga snapped back into existence, her body condensing out of the Aether, ebony otta driving at Rhys. The gong sounded.

The akhara erupted into whispers, and together, both Maadurga and Rhys glanced down. Rhys gazed along the length of his bamboo training staff to its tip: it was touching Maadurga's collar bone. Maadurga's arms were outstretched, but the length of her weapons had failed her, her strikes landing short of their mark. Rhys peered rapidly over his shoulder to his footing. His feet were forced right up against the very rim of the pit, but even by his most pessimistic reckoning, they were still within the limits of the arena. Maadurga and Rhys exchanged looks of bewilderment as they both arrived at the same conclusion: Rhys had won.

The akhara fell into silence, broken barely a few seconds later as Thia roared in enthusiasm. "Yes!"

All heads turned to look at the witch. She embarrassedly clasped a hand over her mouth, quelling her excited outburst. But immediately afterwards, a slow clap began from elsewhere in the audience. Shakyamuni was applauding, and in the moments that followed, every sadhu, kshatriya, and pilgrim joined the clapping.

Maadurga beamed proudly at Rhys and squeezed his shoulder. "How did you know I would jhalaka?" questioned the elf.

"I felt it," replied Rhys. "In the Aether."

Maadurga nodded in surprise. "Then Shakyamuni has taught you well."

The guru stood amidst the crowd, smiling approvingly, issuing a single nod of admiration the mage's way.

"That he has," agreed Rhys as he gazed in the sadhu's direction, before turning back to Maadurga. "And so have you!"

THIRTY-EIGHT

The wind billowed about atop the peak of Suraksameru as Rhys sat once more in the padmasana pose.

"You fought well today," remarked Shakyamuni. "You surprised even Maadurga."

"I surprised *myself*," replied Rhys. "I won through luck."

"There is a fine line between luck and fate," returned the guru.

"And what if I don't believe in fate?"

"If you do not believe in fate by now, after all you have seen, all that has happened, and all I have taught you, then perhaps you never will," remarked the sadhu. "But whether you believe in fate or not does not change the path you are destined to tread. Unlike deities or religions, fate does not require your belief in it to make it true. It is merely a part of time, a fundamental truth in the fabric of Brahman."

"I just think the idea that we are all imprisoned along a predetermined path, heading toward an inevitable destiny... it's all just a bit depressing."

"That you do not like an idea does not make it any less true," responded Shakyamuni.

"You have me there," conceded Rhys. "Fine, let me rephrase: It seems unlikely."

"Surely, the idea that an individual can move against the will of Brahman seems more so?" argued the guru.

"You are assuming that the world has its own will," riposted Rhys.

"Brahman does have its own will. It is like the tide. For a time, it is possible to swim against it. When moving against the will of Brahman, the actions you take are adharma. But inevitably, the tide wins out, and those who fight it are swept away. The chaos created by adharma will always be overpowered. Therefore, we are left with a choice: stand against the will of Brahman, and be drowned, or follow our dharma and accept the fates we are dealt."

"That doesn't sound like much of a choice."

"It is the only choice," insisted Shakyamuni.

"I'm not convinced."

"Perhaps one day you will be," mused Shakyamuni. "Or not. What truly matters is that you follow your dharma, as you have done, and as you continue to do."

"I'll do what I think is right," offered Rhys.

"That is what is important," insisted the guru. "Now, dhyana. Samadhi."

Rhys concentrated, taking his mind into a state of deep meditative focus with ease. Once again, his mind became aware to the flow and energies of the Aether. The Rift became visible overhead, along with the web of tears that fractured outward from the main aurora in the sky, the elements surrounding him bowing to his will.

"Look back," echoed Shakyamuni. "Think of the time you wish to see. Trace the memories you have already witnessed and follow them to the next moment."

Rhys visualised Arlas, allowing his mind to drift in search of his dreams.

"Surrender to the will of Brahman. Let your mind be guided along the path."

A myriad of sights and sounds suddenly flooded Rhys's senses. The memories moved so quickly he could not make them out. An overwhelming array of stimuli drowned his mind, and suddenly all went dark.

Arlas stood atop the hill, the fiery sunset burning across the tawny grasses of the Dessex savannah. His eyes scanned the ridge across the valley, the crimson light casting the world in a sinister incarnadine hue. His heart beat nervously in his chest, his palms and brow sweating in the humid evening heat. He continued to survey the hills ahead, biting his lip in anticipation.

"There!" exclaimed Michael Hemsworth, as together they sighted the figures emerge from over the brow of the hill.

"That's all of them," confirmed Ross Baines, counting the dozen men as they took up position across the gulf of the valley.

"This is it," declared Arlas, turning to the score of mages at his back to address them. "This is the end. Twelve years of war have led us to this moment! The Circle is but a shadow of what it once was. Our order has been purged of its greatest magi. But it is not yet over. By the time today is done, there will be fewer still. Perhaps, there may even be none. But across that valley, atop that hill, stands the traitor Azrael Ibn'Israfil, and all that remain of those who sided with him: those who conspired to kill our archon, my father, and the magistrates of our order, butchering them in cold blood in their fanatical pursuit of power.

"They betrayed the Circle and all it stood for. They have employed blood magic and necromancy, using the dark arts to murder countless innocents. They tortured and mutilated your brothers for their cause, brutally executing any who did not bow before them. They sent entire armies to their deaths to fight the battles they refused to themselves. They have schemed and plotted without honour or shame to usurp the rightful leaders of this world.

"But we have defeated their armies. We cleansed the Dark Sisterhood from the Occult. Eryn Caddick is dead, and soon, her lover Darren Sayer will be too. Now there is no one left to stand between us and them. We have made great sacrifices for this cause. We have lost many good men along the way. But we have won this war. We have driven them back—beaten them time and time again. There is nowhere left for them to run. There is nowhere left for them to hide. Today they face justice. Today it ends!"

A fearsome roar erupted from the magi under Arlas's command, each raising their staff above their head.

"Today it is just *us* against *them*. Fight for what we have lost. Fight for what we might rebuilt. Fight for what is right!"

The chorus of men screamed with deafening intensity.

"Follow me," rallied Arlas, raising his own staff high into the air, "and let us finish this once and for all!"

Arlas turned, beginning his march down into the dale. The dozen magi under his command followed, and as he gazed across the valley, he watched their enemy start their advance down the slopes to meet them. Arlas and his men hastened their pace; across the gulf their enemies did the same. Reaching the bottom of the slope, Arlas broke into a jog, his magi fanning out on his flanks. Soon the two lines of men had drawn to within a furlong of each other. In a matter of seconds, they would all be within range.

"Prepare to charge!" commanded Arlas.

"Prepare to charge!" boomed the preternatural voice of Azrael in the distance.

Arlas's heart throbbed. His body quivered with barely contained fury. This was it. Everything he had endured over the last decade had led him to this very moment. Every sacrifice he had made had brought him to this point. In the next few moments, the Magi War would end. He would have justice. He would have revenge. All that was left to be decided was who would remain standing when all was said and done.

"Charge!" roared Arlas, accelerating into a sprint.

The same order reverberated across the battlefield from Azrael as the enemy line began to storm towards them. A sudden fusillade of elements took to the air as both sides unleashed their full arsenal of attacks. Fire, lightning, and ice streaked across the battlefield whilst missiles of stone, flying razors of metal, and scything blades of necrotic energy rained down from the sky. The ground exploded beneath the unrelenting bombardment, soil and dust spouting around Arlas as he hurtled into the fray. Spinning his staff as he charged forth, he unleashed a beam of mauve fire. He watched as the javelin of flame met its mark, impaling Ramon Rais, detonating on impact to immolate the traitor.

Thunderous explosions shook the ground. Arlas hurtled closer to his foes. He shielded his face as a geyser of rock erupted barely a yard ahead of him, a bolt of lightning aimed his way smashing into the ground. Ploughing through the airborne cloud of dirt and pebbles, Arlas emerged from out of the smoke to sight the mage firing at him. Halting for a brief instant, he pivoted, swinging his staff with all his might. Another missile of purple fire seared from the tip of his ebony stave, taking to the air, arcing down out of the sky to engulf Roger Kelly in a scorching inferno.

Arlas stormed on, his enemies now within closing distance. Agonising screams pierced through the deafening cannonade. Magi on both sides of the affray were struck down in the maelstrom of death. Smoke and dust smothered the field of battle, swirling around Arlas as he charged blindly on. He sprinted for the silhouette rushing his way, lunging with his blade outstretched. His staff skewered through the gut of Michael Bolingbroke as they collided. Clashing heads, the two men thumped together. A slash seared across Arlas's ribs, his foe's weapon puncturing his mail, the blade glancing across his flank. Crashing to a halt, Arlas and his adversary toppled over, Bolingbroke's final breath wheezing from his chest.

Rolling the dead body off himself, Arlas clambered to his knees. Wrenching free his stave, the mage probed the tear in his hauberk. His fingertips returned soaked in blood, but it was just a flesh wound. Climbing back to his feet, Arlas revolved on the spot, trying to regain his bearings in the shroud of smoke and ash. His ears were ringing. His eyes stung. Screams shrieked as men were blown apart and cut to pieces in the chaos. He gazed on in horror as his ally Nicholas Cooper stumbled past him, his entire body aflame. Arlas moved to try and extinguish the man, yet before he could barely take a step, Cooper's gargled screams whimpered out, the immolated corpse of his friend continuing to crackle as it smouldered on the ground.

Stumbling through the boiling air, Arlas caught sight of another of his men; Guy Dupuis screamed in despair as he lay in the grass being stabbed repeatedly in the chest. Arlas rushed the mage atop of him, but before he could get there, a stray bolt of lightning zapped out of the smoke, taking the villain's head clean off his shoulders. The decapitated corpse keeled over, dropping off Dupuis. The dying mage met Arlas's gaze, blood vomiting from between his lips, before finally, his eyes rolled back in their sockets.

Mortified, Arlas stumbled away, revolving clumsily, all sense of direction lost in the billowing vortex of ash. Bodies were strewn in every direction he looked. Wherever Arlas turned his gaze, men from both sides were dismembered and disembowelled, beheaded and blown apart.

Torturous screams shrieked from out of sight, some cut short by quick deaths, others lingering harrowingly prolonged. Fire crackled across the brown grass as the final bloody rays of daylight streaked through a rain of cinders. Arlas winced at the horror of it all.

A shadow charged from out of the black haze. Arlas clashed weapons with Daren Sayer.

"You murdered the mother of my child, you fucking coward!" spat Sayer, his eyes bloodshot with the same rage Arlas felt over his father's murder.

"She was responsible for all of this!" hissed Arlas as he knocked Sayer back, dealing the man a kick to the gut. "You have only yourself to blame!"

"You didn't have to kill her!" snarled Sayer as he recovered out of his stumble, thrusting once again for Arlas.

"She was a murderous hag!" roared Arlas through gritted teeth as they clashed again in a brutal exchange of blows. "She skinned men and women alive! The things she did were unforgivable! Killing her was the only way to prevent her corrupting influence from engulfing the entire Occult!"

"I'm going to cut you into fucking pieces!" screamed Sayer, swinging his staff wildly for Arlas.

Capitalising on his foe's rage, Arlas ducked beneath the cleaving lunge, stepping nimbly around to his adversary's flank. With a swift riposte, Arlas thrust his blade between Daren's ribs, impaling him, driving him off his feet and pinning him to the ground. Sayer's staff flung out of his hands. He clasped hold of the weapon skewering him.

"You think you are so much better than us!" gasped Sayer from the grass, his punctured lung steadily collapsing. "You think you are good, and righteous... but how many men have you killed for your revenge!? How many women?"

"Only those who deserved to die," returned Arlas, coldly inching his weapon deeper into Sayer's torso.

Sayer let out a wet cackle as blood speckled his teeth. "Don't you see... we all deserve to die! You especially! The things you've done... they are as bad as any of my crimes!"

"You betrayed your oaths! You murdered your archon and magistrates!"

"All for a cause I believed in!" insisted Sayer. "I wanted to change the world!"

"With blood magic!? With necromancy!?"

"In all the millennia our Order has existed, nothing has changed!" wheezed Sayer. "We still fight the same monsters as we did thousands of years ago. It is a war we cannot win... not unless we are willing to do what is necessary to end all this misery and suffering you see around you now!"

"It's not worth the cost!" insisted Arlas. "How many must die for it to happen?"

"How many have died in this war you have waged to prevent us?" smiled Darren through crimson lips. "How many will die now that we have failed?"

Arlas remained silent.

Sayer let out another laboured sputtering chuckle. "Just as I thought. You aren't fighting to save the world as it is; you are fighting because you are afraid... afraid of what might happen if the world were to change."

"You are wrong!" growled Arlas.

"Am I?" questioned the mage, his final words barely more than a whisper.

Arlas watched as Sayer's eyes rolled back into his head, his eyelids lulling shut. Freeing his staff from his enemy's chest, he turned to gaze about the fiery madness. Finally, he caught glimpse up ahead of the man he had been looking for. Azrael had his back turned. The necromancer cut down one of Arlas's allies, unaware that his archnemesis was making his way across the battlefield towards him. Azrael advanced, moving to engage another of Arlas's men, still ignorant to the encroaching mage's presence. Arlas readied to strike. If he landed this blow, it would end the war. Any of his enemies left standing would throw down their weapons the moment they knew their leader was dead. He drew back his staff, tensioning his body as he prepared to summon one final bolt of flame. He began to swing, unleashing the energy in his torso and arms. Heat flowed through his fingers, down into his weapon. But suddenly, the ground exploded under him.

Grass and sky inverted in a swirling blur of smoke. Arlas tumbled, launched into the air, spinning dizzyingly as he flailed helplessly upside down. Gravity seized hold, and suddenly he was falling, plummeting head-first into a smouldering crater below. When he struck the ground, everything faded to black.

A muffled cackle echoed through the dark. Fire crackled all around. The sickly stench of burning flesh wafted in the toxic breeze. Time had passed, of that Arlas was sure. Perhaps it had been mere seconds, several minutes, or possibly even hours. His mouth was dry. His head was spinning. His brow throbbed. His leg was aflame with agony, his femur broken. Judging from the wet heat trickling across his thigh, he suspected the bone was poking through the skin. Everything was still dark. He was face down. He tried to move, but his entire body was reeling with pain.

A sharp kick dug into his side, and suddenly, he was rolled over onto his back. Arlas screamed, the splintered bone in his thigh tearing the wound wider as it twisted. His vision blurred into focus. Smoke and fire swirled around him. He craned his head as the piercing shrill continued to echo through his ears. Then he saw the melted skin of Azrael's face pinned taught into a crooked smile.

"Well, well, well," chortled the mage. "What have we here?"

Arlas gazed groggily about. He could hear a distant whimper, then a scream cut short as it died. All fell quiet aside from the popping of flames. There was no one else but Arlas and Azrael to be seen.

"I was hoping I would get to finish you myself," smirked the necromancer. "You have cost me everything! You have cost this world its salvation!"

"I did what I thought was right," coughed Arlas.

"You didn't care about what was right. You only wanted vengeance!" hissed Azrael.

"No," refused Arlas weakly. "The power

you have... it is wrong! It's unnatural. The dead should remain dead!"

"Why should they!?" questioned Azrael. "Because you say so?"

"No," gasped Arlas, delirious with pain. "Because it is the way of the world."

"I could have changed that!" roared Azrael. "I could have made it so that none need ever suffer death! I could have put an end to the injustices of this world. I could have saved everyone!"

"How could you save everyone, when you cannot even save yourself?"

Azrael stooped, leaning closer in towards the mage. "I do not need saving."

"Look at yourself," wheezed Arlas. "Look at what you have become. Look at the atrocities you committed in the name of your cause. There is no salvation to be had. Even if you could do the things you claimed... it wouldn't be worth what you have done to achieve them!"

"You are small minded," scorned Azrael.

"And you are condemned and deluded!"

"I'm going to enjoy ending your wretched life," the necromancer smiled, his scars contorting across the tight skin of his face.

"Then what are you waiting for?" demanded Arlas.

"Oh, it's not going to be that easy for you," cackled Azrael, lifting his boot and hovering it above Arlas's thigh. "First I am going to make you suffer."

Azrael slowly pressed his toe down on the shard of bone protruding through Arlas's leg. Arlas howled in anguish. Nausea spread through his gut as he convulsed, but Azrael only continued to press down harder. Tears streaked down his cheeks and blackness swelled around the periphery of his vision. Arlas felt himself about to pass out, when Azrael lifted his boot, causing the darkness to recede.

"I am going to make you beg. I am going to torture you until there is nothing left!" snarled Azrael as he pressed down again.

Arlas felt the splintering bone fracture and grind. Azrael twisted his boot. He screamed and wept. Vomit rose in his throat. He gagged for air.

"I will never offer you mercy. I am going to keep you alive as long as I possibly can. And when you finally die—when your heart finally gives out from all the pain I am going to inflict on you… then," he cackled with deranged glee, "then, I am going to bring you back and start all over again!"

"You are a monster," spat Arlas.

"Perhaps you are right," agreed Azrael, stomping again on Arlas's leg as the mage squealed and writhed. "But that is only what you have turned me into. You have made me what I am. By taking everything else away, you have twisted me into the very thing I sought to destroy once and for all!"

"Please!" begged Arlas as Azrael lifted his foot again. "Please, just kill me!"

"No," smiled Azrael. "It's just you and me now."

Arlas shut his eyes, swallowing down a mouthful of bile.

"Now, where should we begin?" he asked, hovering the jagged blade of his staff above Arlas's face, tracing it down over the mage's chest and abdomen, towards his groin, where it came to rest. "I know," grinned Azrael sadistically. "How about here?"

Arlas closed his eyes, paralysed with agony. He readied for the gruesome blow Azrael was about to deal him. He prayed for salvation. He prayed for death. But he could feel his heart throbbing fiercely in his chest, unwilling to cease beating.

A searing flash exploded behind Arlas's eyelids. A wave of pain shot through him. He opened his gaze. Azrael was no longer stood over him. Another bolt of lightning peeled from out of the smoke, deflecting off the black metal of Azrael's staff as he staggered backwards. A third fork sparked out of the murk; this time followed by a ray of white flame. The two arcane projectiles narrowly missed Azrael but forced the necromancer back in retreat. More spells hurtled after them. Azrael turned to flee.

Arlas turned his aching head to the source of incoming attacks. From out of the smoke rushed Michael Hemsworth and Ross Baines.

"Arlas!" cried Michael, hurrying to his wounded friend's side. "Shit!" he cried, seeing the extent of the mage's injuries.

"Michael, he is running!" warned Ross, beginning to give chase to Azrael. "We need to go after him."

"No!" refused Michael. "Look at Arlas's leg!"

"Oh, fuck!" cried Ross, his eyes widening as he saw the bloodied mess of flesh and bone.

"No!" wheezed Arlas. "You have to go after him!"

"If we leave him, he'll die," insisted Michael, talking over Arlas.

"One of us stay here…" insisted Ross. "The other can go after Azrael."

"No," refused Michael. "One of us alone won't stand a chance against him."

"Shit, you are right!" agreed Ross Baines, clutching at his hair in frustration.

"Leave me!" croaked Arlas. "You can't let him get away!"

"We can't leave him here," insisted Michael. "Not to die like this…"

"God damn it!" shouted Ross in frustration. "You are always fucking right."

"Come on," beckoned Michael as he drew his wand and knelt down beside Arlas.

"Here," offered Ross, unbuckling his belt and folding it over. "Bite down on this."

Arlas felt the leather forced between his teeth.

"Hold him down," instructed Michael.

"Don't you bloody dare die on us now!" warned Ross, pressing his weight down on Arlas's shoulders.

"This is going to hurt," warned Michael as his fingers probed the shard of bone poking through the skin.

Suddenly, excruciating agony surged upwards through Arlas's thigh. His teeth bit deep into the belt in his mouth as he screamed. Darkness swelled around him, and in the seconds that followed, he lost consciousness.

Rhys opened his eyes, gasping for breath. His mind had snapped suddenly out of the past, returning jarringly back to the present. He felt weak and tired. Cold sweat soaked his body as stormy winds howled across the mountaintop.

Lightning forked in the clouds above and the drumming of thunder tolled. He panted, still unable to catch his breath as he looked frantically around. A hand fell reassuringly on his shoulder as Shakyamuni moved in front of him. He began to slowly calm as he met the elf's warming eyes.

"Tell me," pressed the sadhu gently, "what did you see?"

THIRTY-NINE

Rhys awoke in the dead of night. Something had stirred his mind from slumber. He shook his head, disorientated, trying to recollect his dream, but his mind was blank. He had not been dreaming. But what had awoken him?

He sat up, letting the knitted blankets fall away from his bare chest. The air was cool, a light breeze flowing in through the shutter-less windows of the pagoda's top tier. Rhys rubbed his eyes, rising from the bed of goat hides and cushions spread across the floor. The mage rifled through his clothes, drawing the wand from his belt. The obsidian edge turned jade, casting a gentle ethereal glow around him as he made for the candle atop the table in the corner. Igniting the wick, Rhys let the flickering light dispel the gloomy shadows of the room.

He felt inexplicably ill at ease. Something was not quite right, yet he couldn't for the life of him think what. Throwing on his undershirt, Rhys made his way out onto the balcony, gazing out from the pagoda's highest tier. The sky was unusually clear, granting a view of both the moon and stars as they glistered beyond the veils of rippling light forming the Rift.

Rhys tightened the drawstring of his shirt and hugged the loose fabric around his body as a shiver swept across his skin. A single bead of sweat trickled down the run of his spine. Something was definitely wrong. The Aether was whispering to him, but it was too subtle to make out.

He took a deep breath and prepared to enter a meditative state, but before he closed his eyes, something scudded across the periphery of his vision. Rhys peered around, hoping to catch glimpse of what it was that had caught his attention. A shadow had clipped across the edge of the moon, he was sure of it, but as he scanned the skies, there was nothing to be seen.

A sudden thud startled Rhys. It had come from the roof above. Dust trickled down from the eaves covering the balcony. Something was moving about atop the pagoda. Something big. Rhys peered up at the overhanging cornices, listening to whatever was up there pad across the stone. Rhys watched in horror as six hooked talons curled under the eaves. The mage's heart leapt as he realised what was happening. He turned, darting back into the room to make for his staff, but the second he dashed inside, he felt the Aether quake.

A dark streak bled past him, and an assassin clad head to toe in black materialised ahead of Rhys. The rakshasa swung his kukri for the mage, cleaving for his neck. Reacting fast, Rhys raised his wand, catching the assassin's knife against his wand's ethereal guard. The weight of the kukri won out, the arcane implement deflected by the incoming blow. The mage skipped back, avoiding another advance from the hound as he slashed once more for him. Raising his wand again, Rhys took aim for his assailant's eyes, shutting his own tightly in anticipation.

A dazzling flare flashed out of the wand, blinding the rakshasa just as he prepared to deal another strike. Rhys opened his eyes; despite them having been shut to protect his vision against the flare, they were still blighted by blurry glowing artefacts. Squinting through the dark, Rhys made out the assassin stumbling around blindly, clutching his face in his hands. The mage dashed towards him, slashing with the blade of his wand. The edge of the arcane implement bit into the assassin's throat, carving it open, spilling blood across the stone floor of the chamber.

The assassin dropped dead, but out of the corner of his eye, Rhys glimpsed a set of enormous black wings swooping towards the balcony. Swivelling his head, the mage glanced at his staff leant in the corner of the room beside the door. Out of his grip, the weapon's crystalline shaft was dull and lifeless, but even still, Rhys could feel it calling out to him. He dashed towards it, his bare feet slapping across the stone, bloody footprints trailing behind. The Aether trembled with shockwaves, another assassin momentarily shedding his worldly elements as he blinked into the room, followed an instant later by a second of his kin, then a third.

Rhys clasped hands on his staff. His ethereal blade shrieked from out of the air, the emerald veins within fizzling to life. He spun to face the elven cutthroats sent to murder him in his sleep. Three masked rakshasa stood in his chamber, each brandishing a kukri with menace as they slowly encroached closer to Rhys. The mage eyed them in turn, flourishing his stave as they inched towards him. Exploding from the mark, Rhys struck. The air ruptured, a blast of force careening through the chambre and crushing the first of the three, sending the nearest assassin hurling through the window and over the balcony.

The other two hounds sped into motion, flinging themselves kukris first at the mage. Carrying his momentum through from his first attack, Rhys lanced, skewering his ethereal blade through the black mask of the second rakshasa. Jinking aside as the third of his foes sliced towards him, Rhys rent his blade free, snaring the assassin by the hamstring with his hook when the elf lunged past. Tugging sharply, Rhys tore the rakshasa's leg out from beneath him, running the fiend through with a second jab the moment he struck the floor.

Twirling on the spot, Rhys scanned his surroundings for any additional foes. The room was clear, but outside, the knell of gongs began to clang in alarm throughout the lower tiers of the Temple. Rhys rushed back to the window, peering once more out from the balcony. Black wings scudded through the night, the Wild Hunt's cavalcade flocking beneath the light of the Rift. The Temple of Kalki was under attack.

Rhys twisted back towards the door at the sound of the latch lifting. He gripped his staff, preparing to charge the rakasa entering the room, but when the door swung open, it was Shakyamuni stood in the threshold. His eyes moved first to Rhys's staff, then to the three assailants sprawled out dead on the floor.

"Come with me," he uttered calmly, turning to descend the spiral staircase.

"What is happening!?" questioned Rhys, pursuing the guru into the stairwell.

"The Temple is under attack."

"But why?"

"My guess," began Shakyamuni, pausing to face Rhys momentarily, "they have come to assassinate Kalki."

Rhys nodded silently, the answer being what he had expected.

"That they would dare to enter the Sacred Valley... attack the Temple of Kalki itself..." mused Shakyamuni, continuing his descent ahead of Rhys. "It is most troubling."

"Surely it makes sense?" shrugged Rhys. "They knew I'd come here."

"You don't understand," returned the guru. "Though the rakshasa are followers of Mahakala, the entire Trimurti are holy to all elves. They may not worship you directly, Kalki, but to them, you are still one of their gods. To enter the Sacred Valley without invitation is a grievous crime. To spill blood within the Temple of Kalki... it is unforgivable. Those who have trespassed here tonight to come kill you have committed the highest form of blasphemy. Their Atman will be forever branded with the mark of condemnation; they will never escape Samsara! They will never see the Golden Age!"

"Then why would they come at all!?"

"I cannot say," confessed the guru, halting momentarily to gaze through an open doorway. A half dozen sadhu lay butchered on the other side. "No doubt this is Rudra's influence."

"Rudra?" questioned Rhys.

"The leader of the followers of Mahakala," explained Shakyamuni as they continued their descent. "He is a fanatic. He believes the Vritra that has laired atop Kalapa is the reincarnation of Mahakala. But this is not important. Right now, we must get you to safety."

"Where are we going?"

"The akhara," explained the guru. "It is the safest place. Maadurga and the other kshatriya will know to fight their way there. They will protect you."

"What about everyone else!?"

"You are all that is important," returned Shakyamuni.

"I won't hide away in the pagoda whilst others are being slaughtered in a hunt for me!"

"If you are killed, or captured, all of their sacrifices become meaningless. All the training you have undergone in gatka and yoga will be for nothing."

"No," refused Rhys as they reached the lowest tier of the pagoda. "I won't let the sadhu and pilgrims be killed in my name!"

"Please!" insisted Shakyamuni, his hand gesturing to the set of doors to the akhara left slightly ajar.

"You head inside," instructed Rhys. "I know what I have to do."

"You must *wait* to face the forces of Mahakala. The war is here. It cannot be lost—not when it has only just begun! Without you, there will be no Golden Age!"

"I'm sorry," refused Rhys, glancing out the open doors of the tower to the terrace beyond.

"It is not your dharma to fight now," insisted Shakyamuni, pulling wider the doors to the akhara.

"No," agreed Rhys, making for the exit. "But it *is* the right thing to do!"

Rhys gazed out across the upper terrace of the Temple. Gryphons swooped out of the sky, rakshasa leaping from their saddles onto the paved plateau. Lightning flashed from down the steps, thunderbolts surging upwards into the heavens, striking riders and their mounts as the Cŵn Annwn bore down out of the darkness. A rain of arrows clattered across the stone, arcing upwards from the level below as the first vanguard of kshatriya began to emerge atop the steps, Sol leading the head of the charge. Rhys darted out of the pagoda, eager to join the fray, when from behind, Rhys heard a cry of anguish back inside.

"Kalki!" wailed the voice of Shakyamuni.

Rhys turned back in horror as the guru was stabbed through the chest, an assassin emerging from out of the shadows of the akhara.

"No!" screamed the mage, watching helplessly as the rakasa tore his blade from Shakyamuni's heart, the sadhu collapsing to the floor.

Rhys roared. Blind rage consumed him. A torrent of energy surged through the mage, an echoing tide of kinesis charging through the darkness, ploughing into the assassin. The rakasa's body crunched against the doors of the akhara as the fist of impetus flung him from his feet. Rhys stormed into the tower, cutting down a second hound rematerializing from the shadows as he blinked out of the training hall. A third emerged, struck dead by the mage the moment he appeared.

Reaching Shakyamuni's side, Rhys dropped to his knees. He lifted the guru from the widening pool of blood, cradling him in his arms. He was still alive, though only just. The white coating of ash was being washed from his skin by the heavy flow of blood oozing from his wound. Rhys pressed his fingers over the hole, hoping to stem the bleed as he rummaged for his wand, but it was no use, the wound was a mortal one.

"Remember what I have taught you, Kalki," choked the guru.

Rhys nodded, tears burning behind his eyes.

"You are right..." he struggled. "Your place is out there... defending your followers."

Rhys shook his head. "If I'd have gone inside with you this wouldn't have happened."

"No," Shakyamuni rasped. "You did what was right. That is your dharma. Follow it."

Shakyamuni's head lulled backwards, one last breath peacefully exhaling from his lungs. Rhys lifted his hand as he felt the bleeding subside, gazing down in despair at the teacher in his arms. Gently lowering the guru's body to the ground, he closed Shakyamuni's vacant eyes. Sighing in defeat, Rhys took a long cold breath before reaching for his staff.

He rose to his feet, turning back towards the battle outside, but the fight had already come to him. Out of the shadows, a rakshasa lunged for Rhys. The mage tried to dodge, but catching his foot on one of the assassins' bodies behind, he stumbled, tripping back onto the stone. The hound of Annwn leapt for him, arcing down at the defenceless mage with his knife, but before the rakshasa closed in, he was grappled from behind.

The assassin spasmed, flailing suddenly limp as a blade sank into his back. The rakshasa flopped dead in front of Rhys. Slowly, the mage raised his gaze from the body at his feet. There in front, stood Rhys's saviour, kukri tightly gripped as she offered her other hand to Rhys.

"Thia!?" Rhys stammered in astonishment.

"You okay!?" she gasped, helping him up.

Rhys nodded, his gaze lowering to his slain mentor.

"Oh no," Thia whispered despairingly, sighting Shakyamuni's body for the first time.

Footsteps clattered through the atrium as Sol and several kshatriya rushed inside.

"The rakshasa are fleeing!" called the voice of Maadurga as she emerged at their head. "We have fought them off!" the elf celebrated, approaching Thia and Rhys, but as she drew nearer, seeing the expressions across their faces, she slowly turned her gaze to the floor. "No!" she gasped in disbelief. "No. No!" she wept, collapsing in despair beside the body, her hands trembling over the kukri wound to the sadhu's chest. "What happened?"

"It's my fault," croaked Rhys. "They were waiting for us in the hall—I should have been with him but... I..."

"No," sighed Maadurga. "It is not your fault. What happened here today is the fault of only one person."

"Rudra," growled Rhys.

Maadurga nodded.

"Rudra?" repeated Sol.

"He is the Rajanya Kshatriya of the followers of Mahakala," explained Maadurga. "Head of the Rakshasa."

"Head of the Wild Hunt," uttered Sol.

"He's a dead man," declared Rhys.

FORTY

Rounding a turn in the path, Suraksa finally emerged out of the dale below, nestled peacefully between the foothills of the Sacred Valley. Daylight was beginning to fade. The sun struck long shadows down the steep-sided vale, its amber disc sinking beneath the western peaks. Having begun their descent of Suraksameru at first light that morning, their return journey from the Temple of Kalki was drawing to an end. The Temple's sadhu were no doubt still mourning the loss of Shakyamuni, and their countless other brethren who had been butchered during the midnight massacre, but with Rhys now gone, the Temple was hopefully safe from another attack.

"What is the plan?" inquired Sol, taking up position alongside Rhys.

"I'm not entirely sure," the mage shook his head. "We'll spend the night in Suraksa, but after that, I don't think we should linger in the Sacred Valley."

"It's probably for the best," agreed Sol.

They continued on, nearing the outskirts of the village, but before they had arrived, Rhys heard footsteps rushing to meet them. Moments later, he saw both Nathaniel and Alkis racing up the path, Cetan and Shankha close behind.

"Rhys!" cried Nathaniel. "Maadurga!"

The welcome was not one of excitement or surprise; it was one of dread.

"What is it?" pressed Rhys, realising something was awry.

"The Wild Hunt," warned Alkis.

"They are here!?" gasped Maadurga, scanning the skies for gryphons in flight. "The rakshasa are attacking!?"

"No," assured Alkis. "But we've already heard what happened at the Temple."

"Then what!?" demanded the elf impatiently.

"Maadurga," began Cetan. "Tinihar'ule eka dutan patha eka chan."

Maadurga's expression turned cold. "Usale ki bhan yo?"

"Uham kevala Kalki bolnuhuncha," replied Shankha gravely.

"What is it?" pressed Thia.

"There is a messenger at the gates of the Sacred Valley," replied Maadurga solemnly.

"What is the message?" questioned Rhys.

"He will speak only to you," replied the kshatriya.

Rhys nodded, seeing the concern on his friends' faces. "Let's go."

They made haste down the path, entering the village to find it altogether vacant. Marching through the streets, they quickly passed through the settlement, exiting the village at the foot of a broad staircase that climbed towards the valley gateway. Congregated on the steps was every elf in Suraksa, all gazing upwards at the torana stood between the high-rising cliffs of the pass, awaiting word of the messenger outside the gates. Rhys and the others began the climb, approaching the village from behind, when a few elves at the rear spotted the mage's coming; whispers spread suddenly throughout the throng and the crowd yielded at Rhys's approach, elves quickly bowing out of his way. Many of the villagers outstretched hands, brushing their fingers over the mage's clothing as he passed.

"Rhys!" called out Cade, his voice sounding from amidst the masses. Waving his hand, the huntsman drew Rhys's attention, Ulfgar at his side.

Rhys nodded stoically their way in acknowledgement, but under the circumstances, it was no time to exchange pleasantries; instead, he passed them by, continuing the climb. Reaching the top, Sol, Thia, and Maadurga at his back, the mage arrived behind a line of kshatriya archers, bows drawn, arrows aiming out across the chasm ahead. When he drew near, the two central bowmen released the tension in their strings, parting to allow the mage through.

Stepping between them, passing beneath the torana, Rhys sighted the lone rakshasa stood across the bridge. Like the rest of his ilk, the follower of Mahakala was clad in black mirror armour, but unlike any other rakshasa the mage had come across to date, he had removed his mask as he awaited Rhys. His dark mount stood behind him, the enormous gryphon grooming its black plumage. Rhys and the messenger locked eyes across the chasm. Seeking reassurance, the mage glimpsed back over his shoulder; both Maadurga and Sol returned him solemn nods.

Marching out from the rank of archers, Rhys stepped out onto the hanging rope bridge, crossing the gulf to the other side. Dismounting the lines, he approached the rakshasa. The elf eyed him warily, trying to hide his unease as Rhys drew closer, but as the mage halted a dozen yards away, the messenger relaxed, satisfied he would come no further.

"Pransa Mahakala," he began. "Rudra sends his greetings, Kalki."

"Greetings?" Rhys repeated coldly. "Is that what last night was about?"

The elf stared expressionlessly back at him.

"To what do I owe the pleasure?" the mage growled derisively.

"I bring a message from Rudra," he declared, turning to open one of the saddlebags on his mount.

Rhys watched as he reached inside the bulging leather satchel. He produced a severed head. Gripping the macabre offering by the hair, the elf swung it underarm, tossing it to the ground at Rhys's feet. It bounced once, rolling across the stone thereafter, trailing a line of blood behind it, coming to rest in front of the mage. The face turned slowly over and a pair of glassy eyes gazed hauntingly up at Rhys. It was Vihaan, the kshatriya who had volunteered to protect Arne, Vidar, and Eirik down on the Marlin. Rhys's eyes widened in despair.

"Where are they!?" the mage snarled, his hand twitching as he refrained from drawing his staff.

"Rudra has them," responded the messenger. "They are in Mahakaleshwar."

"What does Rudra want!?"

"For you to come to him," smirked the rakshasa. "Come to Mahakaleshwar. Bring those that travelled to Sumeru with you by sea. The elves of Suraksa are not to follow."

"Why?" demanded Rhys. "So that he can try and kill me again?"

"Rudra wishes to talk," insisted the messenger, as he climbed into his saddle. "You have one day. If you do not come, your friends will die."

With its rider astride, the gryphon reared, pouncing into the air. Its pinions spread on the wind, and with a few wingbeats, it was soaring towards the oncoming storm clouds. Thick rain began to splatter across the plateau. Rhys turned away, lowering his head as he made his way back across the rope bridge, avoiding the gaze of his audience.

"Rhys!?" came Sol's panicked voice. "What did he say!? Whose head was that!?"

"It was Vihaan," breathed Maadurga as the mage stepped off the lines.

"Vihaan?" repeated Sol, his worst fears realised. "Rhys, what did he say?"

The mage remained silent, his gaze lowered to the ground as he marched back through the gateway to the Sacred Valley, the crowd parting around him.

"Rhys!" screamed Sol after him. "What did he say!?"

"He has them," he offered finally in defeat.
"What do they want?"
Thunder rumbled through the skies.
"Me."

FORTY-ONE

"How could they know?" panicked Sol, pacing the room, torrential rain lashing down outside. "How did they know who they were? That they mattered to us?"

"If they saw Vihaan, or any of the other kshatriya guarding the Marlin..." replied Thia. "It's a fairly easy assumption to make."

"Fuck!" swore Sol, crossing his arms tightly and covering his mouth with a balled fist.

"How do we know they are even still alive?" asked Ulfgar coldly.

"Ulfgar! Don't even go there!" threatened Sol.

"No," insisted Nathaniel. "Ulfgar has a point. If we head to the Temple of Mahakala and the three of them are already dead, then the risk is for nothing."

"We don't know anything for sure," admitted Rhys. "But what reason would Mahakala have for killing them? They are his main bargaining chip."

"Rhys is right," nodded Thia. "The rakshasa have already tried to kill Rhys—they failed. Rudra needs him outside the Sacred Valley, beyond the protection of Maadurga and the rest of the kshatriya. By killing any of them, he puts his plan at risk. If we had any reason to suspect they were dead, Rudra knows we wouldn't risk going to him."

"And if he had killed any of them, why send the head of Vihaan?" Ulfgar reasoned. "Surely it would've made more of a point sending one of their heads instead!"

"Ulfgar, shut up!" warned Sol.

"He is right," agreed Rhys. "Rudra wants us to believe that there is a chance to rescue Arne, Vidar, and Eirik. Killing them would jeopardise his chance to draw us out. If we somehow found out any of them were dead, we wouldn't go to Mahakaleshwar—he blows his opportunity at getting to me."

"But we *are* going to Mahakaleshwar," pressed Sol. "Aren't we?"

"I don't see what other choice we have," replied Rhys.

"No!" refused Maadurga, rising to her feet in protest. "Kalki, you cannot go! It is a trap! The moment you step through the gates of Mahakaleshwar, Rudra will kill you."

"I know," agreed Rhys. "There is no way this isn't a trap. But I can't let him kill my friends! Arne is practically Sol's father; Eirik and Vidar, his brothers. If anything were to happen to them because of me, I would never be able to forgive myself."

"You cannot!" refused Maadurga. "If you hand yourself over, all of my people who have died to protect you did so for nothing!"

"I know," conceded Rhys, bowing his head as he struggled with the impossible choice.

"They are dead already, Kalki," sighed the

elf. "You cannot save them."

"You don't know that!" shouted Sol.

"I am sorry," apologised Maadurga. "But it is true."

"It might not be," suggested Rhys, the beginnings of an idea seeding in his mind.

"What do you mean?" questioned Thia.

"Maadurga, what do you know about Mahakaleshwar?"

"It is the Temple of Mahakala, the home of the Rakshasa, ruled by Rudra."

"Have you ever seen it? Have you ever been there?" pressed Rhys.

"From afar," replied the elf. "I have never been inside. It is strongly guarded."

"How far is it from here?"

"On gryphon, it is not far," she explained. "But to walk the path... several days."

"So, they are expecting us to fly there," realised Rhys. "Otherwise, there's no way we could get there in time."

"Yes," nodded Maadurga, slightly confused at the connexion Rhys seemed to be making.

"The messenger said that the elves of Suraksa were not to follow—but if we cannot get there in under a day, they expect you and other kshatriya to at least fly us to within a reasonable distance," explained Rhys.

"Yes," nodded Maadurga, still not entirely following the mage.

"Rhys, what are you getting at?" questioned Thia.

"What is the Temple itself like?"

"Not like Suraksameru," replied Maadurga. "It is..." she mused for a moment, searching her vocabulary. "Kila," she came out with before arriving on the Common translation. "A fortress."

"Fortress?" questioned Rhys. "Like a castle?"

"Yes."

Rhys hesitated. If Mahakaleshwar were indeed a castle, his plan would be all the more difficult; but castles, at least those back on the mainland, were built mostly on the assumption that they would only ever be attacked from the ground. High walls, towers, and battlements were all designed to grant protection against invaders attacking from below, not above; though Rhys had not seen Mahakaleshwar, he was willing to bet that it followed a similar architecture.

"Would it be possible to fly into Mahakaleshwar?" he asked.

"They have a great many archers..."

"Forget the archers," interrupted the mage impatiently. "They must fly in and out of there themselves?"

"Yes," agreed Maadurga. "The Temple can be entered from the air... if there are no archers, or gryphons."

"Okay," nodded Rhys, dry running his preliminary plan through his mind.

"Whatever you are thinking Rhys, it is a terrible idea," warned Thia.

"You are right there," agreed the mage, "but it might just be crazy enough to work."

"Please enlighten the rest of us," urged Sol impatiently.

"I'm assuming that Rudra actually wants to speak to me—face to face," began Rhys.

"I thought he wanted to kill you?" interrupted Sol sardonically.

"Of course he does," agreed the mage, "But surely if he has gone to all this trouble to trap me, you'd have thought he might want a word or two with one of the Trimurti before he orders my execution."

"What are you getting at?" asked Thia, the witch clearly pessimistic about his plan.

"We are being invited inside the castle. Rudra is meeting us himself. He already knows I am dangerous; we have killed enough of his kshatriya for him to know that. Therefore, it stands to reason that he will have taken suitable measures to protect himself from me... from us."

"You think he will pull away some of his forces from the walls of the castle?" asked Sol.

"Possibly," Rhys shrugged. "He probably has enough elves to man all the walls, to protect him, and then some. But if something were to happen..." suggested the mage. "If some commotion, or fighting broke out inside the castle—"

"Then it might pull some men away from the defences," suggested Sol.

"This is a terrible idea," declared Alkis.

"I've already said that," retorted Rhys. "Rudra himself probably would agree. That's why he wouldn't expect it!"

"How do you know what he would or would not expect?" asked Thia. "You only heard his name for the first time last night. You know nothing about him!"

Rhys looked to Maadurga.

Maadurga pondered Rhys's silent question for a long moment. "I have never met Rudra," she clarified. "But I have spent my life defending against his rakshasa. He is dangerous, and he is a smart commander. But he is arrogant. He makes mistakes. I have defeated his rakshasa several times by striking when he would not expect. He has underestimated me. He might underestimate *you*, Kalki."

"I still don't understand what your plan is, Rhys?" piped up Nathaniel, no longer able to keep quiet.

"We accept his invitation," explained Rhys. "All of us here, except for Maadurga, enter Mahakaleshwar. I'm making the assumption that our weapons won't be taken from us when we step through the gates."

"Why would he let us keep our weapons?" questioned Sol sceptically.

"Because he knows we would refuse to give them up," replied Rhys. "Because we *will* refuse to give them up! Think about it—*he* knows that *we* know we're walking into a trap, and he knows we don't have a choice; but even still, we won't walk through those gates if its obvious we'll be taken prisoner the moment we do! That's why he'll act like it isn't a trap. He'll let us keep our weapons, because otherwise, it's too obvious!"

"But it *is* a trap, and it *is* obvious," insisted Sol. "Even if they let us enter with our weapons, they'll probably take them from us as soon as we're inside."

"But they'd have to fight us to take them," returned Rhys.

"So?" shrugged Sol. "They'd win!"

"Exactly!"

"Okay... now you've lost me!"

"They know that when it comes to it, we don't stand much hope in a fight against them once we're inside their walls," reiterated Rhys. "So why bother trying to take our weapons at all?"

"Are you listening to yourself!?" puzzled Sol.

"If they're going to kill us anyway, why bother? They'll wait. Rudra wants to speak with us. Trying to take our weapons will just start a fight—they'll wait until after Rudra has spoken with me."

"You are overthinking this Rhys," insisted Sol. "Rudra wants you dead. That's all. He's not bothered about having a chitchat beforehand."

"I know Rudra wants me dead," returned Rhys. "But the messenger did not say that he wanted me to surrender—he said that Rudra wanted to talk. If I believe that I'll be taken prisoner the moment I arrive, then why ask me to come? Why ask for the rest of you?

"Rudra does not believe that Arne, Vidar, and Eirik are enough to persuade me to surrender unconditionally. If such were the case, the messenger might as well have handed me a set of manacles for me to slap around my wrists; he might as well have pointed at the back of his gryphon and told me to hop on there and there so he could take me to my own execution! There is something else he wants," insisted Rhys.

"You know," pondered Thia, "I think he might be right!"

"Thank you!" exclaimed Rhys.

"But I still think this plan is terrible," she added.

"You've still not explained what the actual plan is!" huffed Nathaniel impatiently.

"Sorry," apologised Rhys, beginning again.

"We arrive near Mahakaleshwar, flown there by Maadurga and her kshatriya. They will be expecting gryphons, so if our enemy sees any of Maadurga's riders, then they hopefully won't suspect anything is awry. We head inside to meet with Rudra. Meanwhile, Maadurga and every other kshatriya willing to join us, takes up position, using the mountains and cloud cover for concealment, ready to strike.

"Inside, we speak with Rudra; he no doubt attacks or tries to imprison us—but as he'll probably expect, we fight. This pulls rakshasa away from the walls, assuming they've not already been called away in anticipation, leaving the battlements at less than full strength. If we can get a signal to Maadurga, then she will know to strike. They raid the walls from the skies, and hopefully, provided a hundred odd things go our way, we rescue Arne, Vidar, and Eirik, somehow make a daring escape, and arrive back here in time for dinner!"

Everyone glanced about the room in a long moment of silence.

"Thia is right," declared Nathaniel. "This is a terrible plan!"

"I'm afraid I agree," sighed Alkis.

"I know it is," nodded Rhys, having hoped the others would show at least a little more optimism. "But it's the *only* plan. It is the only way we can save our friends."

"It *is* terrible," conceded Sol, "but I don't think it is impossible."

"Thank you," beamed Rhys.

"Maadurga, how many kshatriya are there in the Sacred Valley?" asked Sol.

"Just over a hundred."

"And how many do you think would go ahead with Rhys's plan?"

"For Kalki? For Shakyamuni?" she mused. "All of them."

"And how many rakshasa does Rudra have?" asked Alkis.

The elf shrugged and plucked a number off the top of her head, "Three hundred... maybe more, maybe less. His numbers are strong—but he has lost many recently."

"Since *we* arrived in Sumeru?" Rhys raised an eyebrow.

Maadurga nodded.

"Those are terrible odds!" declared Ulfgar. "Fuck it. I'm in!"

Sol sighed heavily. "I suppose there is no other choice."

"Yeah, me too, I guess," added Cade unenthusiastically.

"Before we agree to go on another suicide mission," began Alkis. "What is this signal you hope to get to Maadurga and the kshatriya from inside the walls?"

"Well, that's where the plan breaks down slightly," admitted Rhys.

"No," disagreed Thia, "that happens a lot earlier."

"Fine," agreed Rhys. "I figured it was something I could improvise."

"Mm hmm," muttered Alkis, clearly displeased by the response. "I suppose if the rest of you are heading to your deaths, I might as well join."

"You can't be serious about this?" questioned Nathaniel. "So many things could go wrong!"

"So many things already have," argued Rhys.

"Fine," replied Nathaniel begrudgingly. "I'll come too. But if this plan gets us killed..."

"You'll kill me?"

"Yes!" replied Nathaniel sharply.

"Excellent," smiled Rhys. "Thia?"

She sighed. "I don't want to be left behind."

"Then that just leaves Maadurga?" Rhys turned to the elf.

She gazed back warily at Rhys. "To attack the Temple of Mahakala... normally I would refuse. The Sadhu would forbid it. Shakyamuni would have forbidden it. But after last night..."

"Is that a yes?" asked Rhys.

"I will follow you anywhere, Kalki, as will the rest of my people."

"Then that settles it."

"You will need armour and weapons," insisted Maadurga. "And we will need to find kshatriya whose mounts will let you ride with them—all of you."

"I've got a terrible feeling about this," muttered Thia.

"We've survived everything that has been thrown at us so far," assured Rhys. "Let us hope our luck continues."

FORTY-TWO

Rhys slid off the back of Dawon's saddle and gazed across the chasm of sky to the barren mountain peak before him. Atop the summit of Mount Kailasa sat a vast expansive fort that rivalled the greatest castles built by humanity. Sheer-sided walls topped by arched parapets rose upwards from the rugged cliffsides. Octagonal towers intersected the curtain enceinte as it circled the peak, each capped with a dome that apexed in a decorative finial. Inside the walls, several additional towers rose amidst a large keep. Stood central in the fortification, rising as the highest point on the summit, was a vast pagoda.

Despite Mahakaleshwar's imposing height and impressive expanse, and irrespective of all the decorative carvings and detailing, it was clear that the temple of Mahakala was a shadow of its former glory. The reliefs and statues were weatherworn, eroded by centuries of exposure to the tempest; the walls were in varying stages of disrepair, and the towers cracked and crumbling. The Dark Age had caused the great keep to decay; it was vulnerable.

"Behold, Mahakaleshwar," announced

Maadurga.

"It's bigger than I thought it would be," revealed Sol.

"It was once the greatest fortress of our people," replied Maadurga. "It still is," she added.

Rhys peered into the sky above the mountain; storm clouds were brewing, their great black anvils hammering with thunder. They'd ventured several hundred fathoms above the highest point on Suraksameru; up here the mountains were bleak and barren, mostly faced with rugged stone and scree. Rhys focussed his mind, attuning to the Aether, and through his newfound sense of magic, beheld the Rift in the sky above. He glimpsed around at the tears streaking outwards from the wound in the heavens, tracing one such fracture in the Aether's fabric down a flowing scar that seemed to bisect the pagoda of Mahakaleshwar itself.

"There is a tear from the Rift that passes straight through the pagoda," declared Rhys as he exited samadhi.

"What does that mean?" questioned Thia, sidling up beside him.

"I'm not sure," conceded the mage. "It could affect our magic though."

"Right!" Alkis rallied, psyching himself up as he joined the rest of them atop the slope. The knight rolled his shoulders, still growing accustomed to the Elven mirror armour they had each been outfitted with. "Are we ready to go through with this?"

"I suppose there is no sense in delaying," admitted Rhys. "No doubt they will know we are here by now."

"Are you sure you want to do this, Kalki?"

questioned Maadurga.

"No, I'm not," admitted the mage. "But I don't see what choice we have really."

"Very well," sighed the elf. "The rest of my kshatriya are not far away. They are hidden across the mountainsides—out of sight as you said."

"They've done a good job of it too," remarked Sol, gazing around, unable to see a single one of Maadurga's hundred odd warriors lurking amidst the floating masses of rock and swirling mists surrounding the area.

"You need to join them now," insisted Rhys. "Make sure you are seen leaving. We don't want them to suspect for a moment that any of you are nearby."

Maadurga nodded and mounted Dawon. "What sort of signal should we expect?"

"I'm not sure yet, but I'll think of something," he assured her. "You'll know it when you see it."

Maadurga offered Rhys an uneasy smile from her saddle. "Good luck, Kalki."

"We are going to need it," agreed Rhys, bidding her farewell.

Dawon flared out his enormous wings and leapt off the precipice. The six other gryphons and their riders that had flown Rhys and his companions out of the Sacred Valley likewise took to the air, falling swiftly into a vee formation behind their leader. Together, they climbed into the skies, for a time remaining clearly visible against the backdrop of the oncoming storm; moments later, they vanished into the wall of haze gathering before the range, leaving Rhys and the others seemingly alone in the heart of enemy territory.

"Come on," beckoned Rhys, leading the party down the slope.

After a few minutes of descent, they came to a final rope bridge on the path to Mahakaleshwar. Crossing the lines, they arrived on the slopes of Mount Kailasa, beginning the climb to the ominous fortress above. Archers amassed atop the ramparts, arrows nocked on their recurve bows as they aimed down through the crenulations at the encroaching party making the ascent. Black riders took to the skies, some circling above the fortress itself, others gliding hundreds of fathoms overhead, surveying Rhys and his companions from up on high.

Finally, following the trail to its end, Rhys and the others halted before the enormous barbican marking the entrance to Mahakaleshwar. The wooden gates remained sealed for a time, Rhys and the others forced to wait as more and more archers gathered atop the battlements. Then, the sound of a ratchet began to clang, the portcullis rising as the doors slowly opened. Out poured a contingent of black-clad rakshasa, the elves rapidly filing into rank before the gates, each aiming an arrow at full draw. Rhys watched as they fanned outwards, quickly manoeuvring to flank them from both sides. When surrounded, two guards armed with spears emerged from the barbican. Drawing back the veils shrouding their faces, they halted to attention in front of the party, spears held rigidly at their sides.

"Pransa Mahakala!" they uttered in unison.

The phrase was immediately repeated by

the surrounding contingent of archers.

"Greetings Kalki," welcomed the first of the guardsmen. "Rudra has awaited your arrival."

"Well..." hesitated Rhys, not entirely sure what to say in response. "I have arrived."

An uncomfortable silence descended as Rhys and his companions exchanged glances.

"Where are they!?" demanded Sol. "Where are the three men you abducted from our ship?"

"They are safe," assured the second of the rakshasa spearmen.

"That doesn't answer his question!" rebuked Rhys sternly.

"They are inside," he explained, "with Rudra."

"Then I suggest you hand them over to us," insisted Sol.

Another long silence elapsed.

"First, Kalki must speak with Rudra."

"Where is he then?" questioned Rhys. "Tell him I am waiting."

"We will take you to him," returned the other.

"Very well," begrudged Rhys. "Lead the way."

The elves hesitated anxiously.

"Please," one of the spearman gestured diplomatically, "lay down your weapons and we will lead you inside."

Rhys cringed; he had hoped it wouldn't come to this.

Sol turned to the mage at his side, shooting him a nervous glance.

"You expect us to lay down our arms and walk unprotected into your stronghold!?" Rhys scoffed.

"It is a reasonable request," insisted one of the elves.

"Is it?" examined Rhys sharply. "By confiscating our arms, you give us no assurances to our safety. There'll be nothing stopping you from cutting us down the moment we step through your gates!"

"You will not be harmed," insisted the first of the rakshasa.

"And you expect me to simply take you on your word?" Rhys laughed.

"Rudra assures no harm will come to you."

"No," refused Rhys, shaking his head. "I was told by the messenger Rudra sent for me that he wanted to speak. I was not told that I needed to surrender to him unconditionally."

"Rudra does wish to speak," insisted the other elf.

"Rudra doesn't want to speak," retorted Rhys sharply. "Clearly, all he wants is my head mounted above these gates." The mage turned from the elves and began to walk away. "Come on," he muttered, bidding his friends follow.

After a rapid exchange of nervous looks between them, the others took Rhys's lead, following the mage as he started to march off down the path, hoping against all hope that the surrounding archers wouldn't simply be commanded to shoot.

"Wait!" called one of the elven guards after him.

Rhys paused, his bluff seemingly having paid off. He slowly turned to look back at the two rakshasa.

The elves communicated silently, the uncertainty visible in their eyes. Finally, they both nodded in agreement.

"I am waiting!?" declared Rhys with feigned impatience. His nervous heart thrummed loudly in his ears. He doubted his confident demeanour was actually fooling anyone. Twenty arrows were trained on him. With a single order, the rakshasa could loose everything they had. There would be no escape; Rhys and the others would all be killed without ever getting a chance to draw the very weapons they were fighting to keep hold of.

"As a gesture of good will…" began one of the elves, "you may keep your weapons."

Numbing relief flowed through Rhys's entire body, but he dared not show it. "Good," he replied calmly. "I suppose you had better lead the way to Rudra then."

The two elves bowed humbly. With a gesture from one of them, the score of surrounding bowstrings slackened. The archers didn't lower their aim; at any moment the arrows could have been redrawn and loosed, but the gesture meant something at the very least. The pair of spearmen turned and marched back inside through the barbican, signalling Rhys and the others to follow. The mage complied, striding after the two elves, his friends falling into rank behind him. Sol sidled up alongside Rhys momentarily, issuing a subtle expression of disbelief, his friend clearly dumbfounded as to how Rhys had managed to negotiate their way inside whilst fully armed. Rhys offered him a gentle shrug accompanied by a smile, before proceeding through the barbican after their escort.

Stepping through the gate into the fortress's inner bailey, Rhys was reminded that despite Mahakaleshwar's militaristic appearance, it was still a temple of worship. Various stupas and shrines were erected around the complex, each with fresh offerings laid at their feet and across their altars. Dozens of rakshasa stood dispersed throughout the courtyard and atop the surrounding battlements, all watching as Rhys and the others were led through the temple complex towards the towering pagoda at the very heart of Mahakaleshwar.

Mahakala's pagoda was starkly different to the one Rhys had spent the last month living in. Though still constructed of stone, it was free standing, unlike the pagoda of Kalki which had been carved out of the peak of Suraksameru. Mahakaleshwar's tower stood far taller and narrower, rising thirteen stories, each tier tapering sharply into the one above, the whole structure rising from the heart of the Temple as an enormous octagonal spire.

Ascending several flights of steps, Rhys and the others followed their escort up a number of terraces, arriving at the base of the pagoda. The tower was surrounded by a dozen guardsman adorned in silvered mirror armour, each elf armed with a ceremonial spear. When the two rakshasa gatekeepers approached with Rhys and the others at their backs, the ranks of pagoda guardians marched to intercept them.

Quickly shuffling into an obstructive line, the argent rakshasa blocked the way, their commander emerging from the formation to address the two gatekeepers in their native tongue, eyeing the party's assortment of unconfiscated weapons with ire. Though Rhys couldn't understand the exchange, the discourse was easy enough to follow. The two gatekeepers were scolded furiously for having allowed Rhys and the others to retain their arms. One of the gatekeepers attempted to offer an explanation, but the commander seemed indifferent. Regardless, the elven officer appeared forced to accept the situation as it was; with a begrudging curt gesture, he dismissed the gatekeepers.

"The Pavitra Kshatriya will lead you inside," one offered in explanation. "They will take you to Rudra."

"And what about our friends?" questioned Rhys. "You've given us no proof that they are safe —or even here for that matter!"

"You will see your friends in time," assured the rakshasa.

"First you must speak with Rudra," insisted the other.

"Apparently so," Rhys disheartened.

The two gatekeepers bowed and excused themselves from their presence, making their way back towards the barbican.

Rhys turned to the grim-faced pagoda guardsmen.

"Follow," the commander instructed through a thick accent. He turned, marching towards the entrance.

Rhys compliantly took after the rakshasa, his companions following close in file. The silver contingent moved with them, reorganising into a tight formation around Rhys and the others as they were escorted to the doors. Up close, Rhys could sense the fissure in the Aether carving through the tower, the distortions to the fabric of reality potent enough that he could detect them without needing to push his mind into samadhi.

The iron doors drew ominously open ahead. Like much of the rest of the Temple, the pagoda was in a state of disrepair; the once grand carvings stretching across the outer surface faded, the decorative reliefs crumbling from the faces. Portions of the eaves had fallen away, and in sections, the walls of the structure were scarred with cracks.

Entering the pagoda, they stepped through into a lofty atrium that occupied the spire's first four stories. A staircase spiralled around the octagonal interior, hugging the eight walls each in turn as it ascended to the levels above. Continuing to follow the rakshasa commander, they marched up the steps, two abreast, the guards taking up positions between them, circumambulating the atrium as they climbed, shortly arriving on the floor above.

Emerging into the next room, they were met with an eight-armed stone statue of Mahakala sat in the padmasana pose. The effigy rose in height across three full tiers of the pagoda, around it the stairs continuing to ascend. The numerous limbs were splayed at various angles, the upper-two-most pressed palms together above the deity's head. The remaining six extended outwards, each hand raised in a unique gesture, the statue seemingly poised in meditation. Offerings of flowers, spices, oils, and prayer beads were laden around its plinth, incense and candles flickering about the smoky room. Several rakshasa were prostrate in worship, but as Rhys's party and their accompanying contingent of guards marched through, they reared their heads, standing as they watched Rhys make the climb to the level above.

The next floor spanned two tiers, and like the room below, was home to another statue of Mahakala. The four-armed bronze depiction balanced on one leg, the other raised and crossed over the first. The two lower arms clutched a bow and arrow, the right upper hand holding a kukri aloft. The Destroyer's final limb was extended ahead, palm upraised, the flame from an oil lamp concealed inside the hand burning brightly. More offering surrounded the effigy, and just as had happened on the level below, the gathering of worshippers ceased praying to ogle Rhys.

Another statue awaited them above, this time spanning only a single tier. Carved from wood and leafed in gold, this third idol depicted Mahakala with only two arms, both gripping a trident held in front. The largest congregation so far amassed in this room, each member stirring from their prostration, watching silently as the mage passed through, ascending the steps to the upper tiers.

The next floor was lacking the full-sized central effigy like those housed on the levels below. Instead, various smaller shrines and altars were erected against the eight surrounding walls, several topped with small copper and gold Mahakala idols. More rakshasa roused with Rhys's arrival, like their brethren, they too watched in silence as the mage continued his ascent.

The penultimate level was unusually empty. A single bas-relief was set against one of the walls, depicting Mahakala striking down Kalki with his trident. Most of the remaining sides of the room stood open as arched windows, the natural light absent from the floors below streaming in. The tear in the Aether raged turbulently across this level, Rhys's arcane senses flaring alight at the flow of power surging around him. The mage had expected to feel weakened, his powers diminished by the rupture carved through the fabric of magic, but instead, the very opposite was true. The wound in the void was open and raw, erupting with surges of visceral uncapped energy. The very air was alive, charged with static, the sensation bleeding across to his other five senses. Rhys could feel the surrounding power channelling through him, reacting to his body, changed by it.

The mage exhaled, pausing for a moment to regather himself. The entire world seemed out of kilter, the balance of power grossly redirected by the unworldly phenomenon. Stepping briefly into samadhi, he refocussed his senses, tuning out the background noise churning from the Rift, drawing his concentration back to the present, to the here and now.

The rakshasa commander glared back at Rhys in his moment of pause, but as the mage continued to follow him, beginning his climb up the final flight of steps, the elf led on, escorting Rhys out onto the final level of the pagoda of Mahakala. Emerging on the top tier, the mage gazed around at the eight surrounding archways opening out onto the encircling balustrade-less balcony. Above, the ceiling domed beneath the hemispherical roof of the pagoda, atop of which spired the decorative iron finial Rhys had sighted from outside.

A dark figure stood out on the balcony

running his fingers through the feathers of a black and white striped gryphon. Two demonic horns curled out of the helm atop his head, a black gryphon-hide cape of feathers and fur cascading from his armoured shoulders. Slanted in the rakshasa's grip was a gilded three-pronged trident, not unlike the very weapon arming the statue of Mahakala several floors down.

As the others filed into the room beside Rhys, the dozen guards that had escorted them up the tower moved to surround them, closing off any form of escape, flanking them from all sides. Rhys gazed warily at the encirclement of rakshasa. All in unison, they lowered their spears inwards at Rhys.

"Pransa Mahakala," praised the darkly armoured elf, continuing to stroke the beast at his side.

"Pransa Mahakala," repeated the spearmen.

"It is a great honour to finally meet you, Kalki," Rudra smiled as he turned to face Rhys, his voice devoid of all but the slightest hint of an accent.

"You gave me little choice in the matter."

"I needed to get your attention," replied the head of the Cŵn of Annwn. "Let me introduce myself—"

"Let's skip the pleasantries," Rhys cut him off. "I know who you are, Rudra."

"You use my true name?" remarked the rakshasa in surprise. "You are the first of your kin to do so. Most refer to me as Arawn, or Woden; they say that your kind tell stories of me back in your homelands."

"Where are our friends!?" demanded

Rhys, eager to move past the topic of Cambrian legends.

"Straight to the point," mused the elf.

"I'd rather not waste time talking about *you* of all things," sneered Rhys.

"They are not here," smiled Rudra coldly.

"What do you mean!?" demanded Sol.

Rudra turned to leer at Sol, daunting the mage into silence. Redirecting his attention Rhys's way, the elf's demeanour dissolved back into an amiable countenance.

Sol scowled in frustration, but the message had been received by him loud and clear: Rudra would speak only with Kalki.

"Were they ever here?" questioned Rhys.

"No," replied the elf honestly. "I needed you to believe that they were, so that you would come here."

"Then where are they?" pressed Rhys impatiently, each words sounding in staccato.

"They are elsewhere," uttered the elf aloofly. "Once we are finished here, they are to be taken to Kalapa."

"You are taking them to the dragon!?"

"They are to be sacrificed to Mahakala," Rudra nodded in confirmation. "As are you—and the rest of your followers."

"I trust that is the reason you brought me here then, rather than killing me the moment I arrived at your gates?" surmised Rhys. "You wanted me a prisoner—so you could sacrifice me to the leviathan?"

Rudra nodded. "It is not *my* place, nor the place of Mahakala's followers, to slay you. Only Mahakala himself can slay Kalki. Only then can the Dark Age end. And only then can the Golden

Age begin."

"I hate to tell you this," began Rhys, "but that dragon is not Mahakala, and I'm definitely not Kalki."

Rudra's mouth curved into an unnerving smile. "If you are not Kalki, then why do you carry his staff?"

"You are carrying a trident," argued Rhys. "That doesn't make you Mahakala."

"Mahakala's weapon is a *flaming* trident," replied the elf. "That is the power of the Vritra. The Vritra that lairs atop Kalapa is the mightiest of its kin to ever grace the skies of Sumeru. It is Mahakala reborn into his final avatar."

"That is ridiculous," mocked Rhys. "Why would Mahakala return as a dragon? Surely he'd appear the spitting image of all those statues you have below?"

"What better form to face you? What better form to take to bring an end to the Dark Age?" returned Rudra. "You yourself have chosen the human form for your final avatar. Why should Mahakala not choose a different embodiment himself?"

"You are insane," chided Rhys. "You are just spouting nonsense, indoctrinating the rest of Mahakala's worshippers into doing your bidding! You are nothing more than a deluded zealot!"

"I am firm in my beliefs," insisted Rudra. "They are not merely interpretations of the poems my people tell of the Trimurti and Brahman; they do not come from visions of the past like the beliefs of Shakyamuni. The will of Brahman speaks to me *directly*!"

"What do you mean!?"

"I can hear the whispers of Brahman," explained Rudra. "They are difficult to understand at times, but I have come to understand them all the same."

"You hear voices in your head?" questioned Rhys. "You really are insane!"

"No," assured the elf. "They come not from my head—but from this."

Rudra's fingers slid inside a pocket and Rhys immediately felt shockwaves reverberate through the Aether. As Rudra drew out his hand, he presented a black metallic stone in his palm. A portion of the rock was polished smooth, as if melted by extreme heat, pitted with hundreds of tiny indentations; the remainder of the rock was roughhewn, evidently marking a fracture line where the fragment had been cracked off from a larger section. The glossy portion of the stone was etched across its surface, carved with an array of arcane runes, the very same runes Rhys had seen numerous times before, on each occasion cut into the sarsen standing stones of the conduits throughout Cambria.

"This here is just a piece," explained Rudra. "It is all that remains of—"

"The Cintamani Stone!" breathed Rhys as he beheld the fragment of the legendary artefact.

"Yes!" nodded Rudra with surprise.

"Where did you get that?" questioned Rhys warily, feeling the distortions in the Aether that the mythical item was radiating.

"I found it," replied Rudra, "long ago atop Kalapa, the first time I stood in the presence of the Vritra. The creature appeared before me and stayed its hand. It allowed me to live... *Mahakala* allowed me to live—to take with me the final piece of the weapon that cast the world into the Dark Age. I came to understand that it was a gift—from Mahakala himself. He speaks to me—through the Cintamani Stone. It is my dharma to deliver you to him; the stone commands it.

"In the months since Lohri, the Long Night, the Akasa, the wound of Brahman, has begun to fester. The eternal storm of the Dark Age has grown violent and restless in ways that have never been seen before. Above, near Kalapa and Shambhala, the peaks are in motion and Prana is in upheaval. Sumeru has entered a state of chaos that has not been seen since the Cintamani Stone was used to rent it from the sea.

"Throughout the Dark Age, for thousands of years, Sumeru has remained in an unchanging state, but in recent months, the forces of Brahman have begun to move. The end is near. I interpreted the omens of your arrival Kalki, and hear you stand. Now you are at my mercy, and soon you will become an offering for Mahakala himself. Then Kalki, when you are finally defeated, I am to take this piece of the Cintamani Stone to the Chaitya at the heart of Shambala, and finish what my people long ago tried to do: to fulfil the will of Mahakala, to bring an end to the Dark Age, and free us all from Samsara!"

"If you do that you'll destroy Sumeru for good!" Rhys warned. "There won't be a Golden Age to follow. You won't achieve Nirvana and you won't be reincarnated. You'll just die! You and everyone here... the followers of Mahakala... of Kalki... everyone!"

"I am not afraid of what I must do, Kalki," returned Rudra. "It is your dharma to protect Brahman. But it is Mahakala's to bring about its end. Without the end, there can be no beginning."

"You can't actually believe that!" refused Rhys. "That dragon is not Mahakala, and I am not Kalki! This is insane!"

"Please," hushed Rudra gently. "It is nearly over. Soon we all will have escaped the cycle. Lay down your staff, and I will take you to Mahakala."

"No!" refused Rhys, reaching for the weapon across his back and drawing it.

The instant Rhys's fingers closed around the staff, a low thrum echoed throughout the Aether. In a whirl of jade, Rhys's ethereal blades unfurled, the stave spinning as Rhys pulled it from around his back. A circle of spearheads reared upwards, the ring of silverplated rakshasa tightening their formation around Rhys and the others, ready to strike him down if he made any other sudden movements.

"Lay down your weapon," threatened Rudra, this time with malice. "Or I will order my rakshasa to kill each of your friends one by one. Their sacrifice is unimportant; it is only you that matters. I will not hesitate to slay each of them in turn whilst you are forced to watch! Surrender. Now!"

Rhys scowled at the zealot, his fingers turning white with fury as he watched the surrounding spears move steadily inwards.

"Now would be a great time for that signal," whispered Ulfgar as they huddled tightly in together.

"I bloody hope this works," breathed Rhys under his breath.

Rhys pushed his mind into samadhi. Every thread in the fabric of the Aether seemed to be fraying around him in a constant state of flux. Focussing with every ounce of might his body and mind possessed, Rhys forced all the energy stored throughout his corporeal form into his staff. Suddenly, the surrounding Aether imploded. Energy detonated, cascading between the different elements in a chain reaction, a tidal wave of force rupturing outwards in a deafening explosion that tore into the world. A thunderous boom quaked the air, shockwaves surging in every direction. As if struck by a war hammer, Rhys was instantly floored. His knees buckled and the air shot out of his lungs. His head rang, his ears shrilled, and his vision momentarily blacked out.

When Rhys came to in the seconds that followed, he realised everyone else atop the tower had been struck by the same force, all now dazedly coming around on the floor. The first to recover, Rhys heaved himself from the ground and leapt into action. Pouncing on the nearest rakshasa, Rhys skewered his ethereal blade into the elf's back as he lay helplessly prone. Renting his stave free, the mage lashed sideways, opening the neck of his next adjacent foe before the spearmen could clamber to his feet.

Twirling on the spot in search of his next target, Rhys stumbled, the stone underfoot shuddering violently. Skipping over Ulfgar's supine body, Rhys felt the energy reserves rebalance throughout his body. Thrusting with his stave, he fired off a blast of kinetic energy, the missile punching square into the chest of a rakasa guard fighting to get upright. The elf screamed as he was launched from the balcony, but to Rhys's surprise, instead of plummeting over the ledge, his body hurtled upward, his cries fading as he vanished into the skies above.

Rhys cocked his head in momentary confusion, the ground continuing to tremor underfoot. Out of the corner of his eye, the mage caught sight of Rudra pulling himself up off the floor. Rhys span, lightning forking from his staff as he lunged for the head of the Wild Hunt. But as the bolt of electricity arced through the air, a rakshasa guard recently risen back to his feet threw himself in front of the strike. The elf convulsed, lightning zapping through his body, electrocuting him in a shower of sparks, before finally he dropped dead. The corpse flopped aside, regranting Rhys a line of sight ahead, but the mage watched on in frustration as a set of black and white pinions swooped out of sight, Rudra's gryphon diving from the balcony with his master in the saddle.

The whole pagoda was quaking now. Dust rained down from the ceiling and large fissures were cracking open through the rumbling stone. By this stage, everyone gathered on the pagoda's upper tier had overcome the shock of the explosion. A frantic skirmish had broken out between Rhys's companions and the remaining rakshasa spearman. Hooking a guardsman's legs out from under him, Rhys ran him through on the ground, lunging away with a spinning counter just as a spearhead thrust at him from behind. Riposting with a circular cut, Rhys clove through the shaft of the spear, the fluke of his ethereal blade puncturing the rakshasa's silvered mail.

His foe's numbers rapidly thinning, Rhys took aim for an elf up ahead. Before a fist of energy could fire from the end of his weapon, the ceiling above rent open, crushing his intended target beneath a fallen pile of stone.

"Rhys! What did you do!?" cried Sol, cutting down an enemy with a decisive blow.

"I improvised!" shouted back the mage in return.

"That doesn't explain what in the world is happening!"

"I don't know!" roared Rhys over the thunder of splitting stone.

"The tower is being ripped apart," yelled Thia, looking down as a great fissure snaked its way across the floor.

Rhys peered out beyond the balcony. The skies outside were flocking with gryphons, rakshasa and kshatriya alike, the two forces swarming together in aerial battle. "I think Maadurga got my signal!"

"I think the whole of Cambria got your signal!" quipped Nathaniel

"Look out!" warned Cade. "We've got more incoming!"

Dark wings flared out of the heavens all around as the Wild Hunt plunged down from above. Rhys watched the archer at his side rapidly notch a succession of arrows on his Elven bow, loosing each within an instant of the other as he took aim at the skies through the surrounding octagon of archways. Several hounds tumbled from the saddle, skewered by the arrows loosed their way, but as the flock converged on the pagoda, Rhys felt the Aether shudder in a series of compressions, numerous rakshasa riders blinking from aback their mounts to land across the surrounding balcony.

"You're kidding me!?" cried Alkis, finally

dispatching the last remaining spearman, only to see the new wave of enemies appear.

"These bastards really want you dead, Rhys!" shouted Ulfgar as he finished loading a new quarrel onto the runs of his crossbow, taking aim for the incoming reinforcements.

The ceiling overhead continued to disintegrate and more rubble began to rain down, great chunks of stone crashing into the floor surrounding Rhys and the others. The pillars supporting the archway cracked and buckled, the floor of the balcony crumbling, soaring skyward in large sections as the whole tower started to give way.

Rushed by a charging rakshasa, Rhys swivelled, his stave glaring crimson, a great gout of flames spewing from its end. The hound screamed as he was engulfed in fire and ash, flailing his arms as he stumbled backwards, vanishing suddenly in a trail of smoke as the churning gravity well seized hold of him, ripping him away from the disintegrating floor and hurling him into the heavens. Pivoting to meet his next oncoming foe, Rhys clashed blades with a cleaving kukri. He parried, countered, stepped away, disengaged, lunging back for a second strike. His ethereal blade blurred in a jade whirlwind, colliding in a staccato of blows with the elf, before a swift circular riposte sliced through his opponent's guard, opening the rakshasa's mail from nave to chin, eviscerating his torso beneath.

Revolving on the spot, the remaining Cŵn Annwn locked in a mêlée with his allies, Rhys watched the chaos unfurling around him. Debris churned and flaked away from the tower, swirling up from the floor and ceiling in a vortex of dust. Stone sheered in vast chunks, flying upwards as it disintegrated in the rip current of gravity. Suddenly, the remaining intact pillars supporting the domed ceiling overhead gave out in a series of loud cracks. The pagoda roof lifted away, hurtling heavenward as the Rift seized hold of it, the great dome tumbling, the iron finial spinning end over end as it vanished into the storm above.

"We need to get out of here!" warned Rhys, crossing blades with another rakshasa.

"You think!?" screamed Sol with bitter sarcasm as he fought back another advancing foe.

"Quick!" urged Thia, freeing Alkis from a frantic exchange with a deadly lash of her kukri. "The steps!" Darting out of the fray, she scrambled across the buckling floor, hurling herself down the stairwell, as it too began to crumble away.

Rhys carved through the final rakshasa and frenetically began ushering the others after her. "Go! Go! Go!" he hurried, shoving Nathaniel down the helical stairway as large chunks of the floor began flying away. A deluge surged out of the storm, rain spraying from every which way as Rhys charged after him

Hot on Nathaniel's heels, Rhys bounded down the steps in pursuit of the guardsman, but as he gave chase, the mage felt his footfalls begin to lighten. Suddenly, his stomach lurched in his gut, his feet flipping out from under him as gravity inverted entirely. Rhys yelped as the Rift hoisted him off the steps, the mage caught in a momentary stalemate between opposing gravitational pulls.

A hand clasped hold of the end of his staff as he felt the upward tug begin to win out. Rhys peered down to see both Alkis and Nathaniel hanging from the end of his weapon, anchoring him groundwards as he dangled into the sky above.

"Pull me in!" Rhys pleaded, his feet flailing helplessly in the air above as the Rift's gravity tightened its grip.

The two men strained, heaving down with all their might, Ulfgar grappling them both to lend his weight to the contest when it looked as if Alkis and Nathaniel might also lift from the stairs. Together, the two soldiers began to reel the mage in, Rhys climbing hand over hand back towards the ground as they hoisted him down.

Without warning, Rhys's stomach performed a second somersault and the mage tumbled out of the air, piling into the three men below.

"Thanks!" Rhys puffed as the four of them clambered back to their feet, resuming their flight down the tower.

"Don't mention it," groaned Ulfgar, rubbing the small of his back as he hurried after the mage.

"Look out!" warned Nathaniel, as from out of nowhere, another rakshasa blinked through a widening fissure in the wall.

The guardsman raised his shield, catching the cleaving blow of a kukri across the rim just in the nick of time. Alkis lunged from behind Nathaniel's defences, driving his bastard sword through the hound's gut on the stairs below.

The Aether thrummed repeatedly and

Rhys gazed down from the stairwell to see more of the Cŵn Annwn materialise throughout the room, charging to engage Rhys's companions at the head of the party. The way ahead blocked by Nathaniel and Alkis, Rhys hurled himself from the steps. Dropping several feet, he landed hard beside the golden effigy of Mahakala, catching a hound by surprise as he touched down behind him. Running him through, Rhys charged for Thia, hooking the rakshasa harrying her around the neck, nearly decapitating the elf as he yanked back on his staff.

"What's with these guys!" demanded Sol as both he and Rhys worked together to cut down the last of Mahakala's followers in their way. "This whole pagoda is coming apart, and all their concerned with is getting to you!"

"Yeah," derided Rhys. "It's almost as if they are some kind of fanatics!"

At that moment, an almighty crack sounded above as the entire roof was sundered from the walls, shrinking rapidly overhead as it plunged into the heavens. Lightning snaked across the open sky and rain lashed throughout the room. The gilded effigy of the Destroyer began to rock on its plinth, seconds later lifting from the floor as it soared heavenward.

Wings spread out of the glare of the storm and a pair of gryphons touched down in the heart of the collapsing room.

"Kalki!" Maadurga cried in amazement from aback Dawon, Shankha at her side astride his own mount.

"Where have you been!?" demanded Rhys unfairly.

"There is no time," replied the elf, extending Rhys a hand. "Come on!"

"No," refused Rhys, snatching hold of Thia and dragging her over to Maadurga and Dawon. "Everyone else first!" he insisted as he helped Thia into the saddle, hoping the surrounding chaos would be enough to distract Dawon from his uninvited rider.

Maadurga stammered, clearly wanting to protest, but she knew better than to argue with the mage. She nodded, and the moment Thia was securely aback Dawon, she heaved on the gryphon's reins, launching him vertically back into the tempest.

"Cade, get out of here!" ordered Rhys, shoving the archer in the direction of Shankha. "The rest of you, keep moving!"

Without needing to be told, the others piled down the next flight of steps, Rhys tailing close behind. Emerging into the room below, the mage cursed in frustration as they were greeted by more of the Wild Hunt, the riders diving from their saddles through a wide opening gouged out the side of the pagoda.

The head of the first snapped back the instant Ulfgar's crossbow string twanged taught, a quarrel sinking between the gap in the hound's tagelmust. Still halfway up the steps, Rhys launched a javelin of energy, the shell smashing into a rakshasa the moment he landed in the room, hurling him back out the same opening through which he'd entered, the elf disappearing with a fading howl.

Sol, Alkis, and Nathaniel charged down the foot of the stairs, engaging a trio of rakshasa at the base of the four-armed Mahakala. Rhys skipped after them, leaping off the spiral stairwell early so he could rush in to flank. Carving open the skirmish from the rear, Rhys brought the frantic scuffle to a head, he and the others clearing the room just in time for Cetan and Ehani to touch down, their gryphons skating briefly across the stone floor before scrabbling to a halt.

Already familiar with the gryphons of their two mentors, Nathaniel and Alkis jogged over, preparing to mount up. But with the whole pagoda starting to sway, the room disintegrating faster by the second, in a moment of selfish desperation, Ulfgar shoved Alkis aside.

"Out of the way! Me first!" demanded the dwarf unapologetically as he heaved himself ungraciously onto the back of Ehani's mount, despite the beast's angry protests.

Ehani shot Alkis an inquisitive look, hesitant to take off with the dwarf in the saddle, leaving the knight behind. But with a long exhale, Alkis shrugged, graciously conceding his own evacuation, nodding back at the elf, giving him his blessing to take off without him.

"Wow!" remarked Sol, as Cetan and Ehani took to the wind, bounding out through the hole in the wall, carrying both Nathaniel and Alkis to safety. "What a c—"

A crash of splitting stone cut the mage off.

"Yep," Alkis nodded in agreement.

"Move!" urged Rhys, hurrying the two men back towards the stairs.

"You don't have to tell me twice!" returned Sol, rushing ahead.

Rhys charged after his two friends, but with a pulse through the Aether, a rakshasa blinked in front of the mage, blocking his path.

Rhys locked blades with the hound, twisting his stave to counter-parry, when abruptly, he felt the soles of his feet begin to slip across the stone. Suddenly, both Rhys and the elf were on the floor, sliding out of control as they skidded across the smooth surface. Rhys's knees flexed, his boots slamming down hard as he landed somehow back on his feet. Raising his staff, he blocked a strike from his foe's kukri, jinking backwards as they resumed their bout stood horizontally on one of the walls of the eight-sided room.

Rhys deflected a flurry of strikes from the incoming kukri. Using his hook, he locked both their weapons in a bind. Manipulating his foe's knife with the length advantage of his stave, Rhys jerked the rakshasa's blade aside, renting it from his grip with a swift disarm. The kukri flung out of the hound's palm, flying sideways before arcing away through the hole in the wall.

Rhys struck at the defenceless elf, but in the instant before he landed the blow, the wall underfoot cracked and gave way, the elf plummeting sideways out of the room, vanishing into the storm. Rhys stumbled, the section of stonework under his own feet about to shake loose, but seconds beforehand, Rhys felt his weight beginning to shift once again.

The wall rushed away from the mage's boots, his head spinning dizzyingly as he tumbled onto the ceiling. Thumping hard into the roof, Rhys groaned, heaving himself up off his aching shoulder to fight back to his feet. Momentarily struggling to orientate himself as he stood upside down at the top of the room, the mage shambled across the ceiling, great chunks of it crumbling away around his feet, opening to the chasm of the sky above.

The section of stone beneath Rhys cracked loudly. He leapt, just as the ceiling underfoot ripped away into the sky. Reaching with outstretched fingertips, Rhys snagged hold of the bronze headpiece atop the bronze Mahakala effigy. Heaving himself groundward, Rhys shouldered his stave an seized hold of Mahakala's upraised kukri. Clambering down the assortment of limbs, Rhys leapt from the Destroyer's bow arm, just as he felt the statue itself begin to lift from its plinth.

Stretching for the floor, Rhys plunged back into gravity's normal orientation, slamming into the ground as the four-armed Mahakala sailed away above.

Panting through exertion, Rhys staggered back onto the staircase, already feeling his footfalls beginning to lighten again. Fighting to keep his feet on the ground, Rhys raced down into the room below, catching up to Sol and Alkis, the two men paused waiting to see if he was behind them. Rushing down the three tiers of the meditating Mahakala, the trio hurried across the room towards a pair of kshatriya as they touched down through an opening in the wall.

"You next!" insisted Sol, shoving Rhys towards the nearest gryphon. "No arguing!"

Rhys issued a dazed nod of agreement back towards the mage, staggering over to accept the kshatriya's outstretched hand. Eager to seize his second chance of escape, Alkis bounded agilely aback the other gryphon, the rider tugging on the reins and launching from the pagoda without delay.

Rhys gripped the elven rider's palm

tightly, grappling the cantle with his other hand, when suddenly a cry sounded from behind. The mage spun his head back around, watching as Sol lifted into the air. Rhys leapt, brushing fingertips with the mage, but Sol slipped from his grasp, plummeting upwards towards the open sky above. Sol flailed his arms, snatching hold of one of the stone limbs of Mahakala, his legs left dangling above him as he struggled to keep his grip.

Rains swirled around the room and great forks of electricity peeled through the vortex of black cloud above. Rhys glanced back at the mounted kshatriya beside him, his hand shooting upwards to point at his friend desperately clinging to the stone idol.

"Save him!"

The elf hesitated, anxious not to leave Rhys alone in the disintegrating pagoda, but compelled to follow the mage's command, the rider issued a gentle tug of the reins. The gryphon spread its pinions, lifting from the floor without any requirement to beat its wings. Floating up the height of the statue, the kshatriya inverted his mount in the upturned gravity, manoeuvring up alongside Sol, grappling the mage and swinging him into the saddle. Both Sol and the rider glanced back in concern as they glided away on the surging wind.

The giant Mahakala began to tilt, one of its arms snapping clean off as it plummeted skyward. Rhys broke into a sprint, making for the stairs once again, the ground crumbling to dust around him. Fissures snaked beneath Rhys's feet, fragments of stone clouting his body as debris rained up in a constant stream into the sky. Rhys could feel his weight beginning to fail again, his boots slapping faintly across the floor as he fought to keep them planted.

A streak of thunder carved suddenly down in front of Rhys, a span of feathers swooping out of the glare.

"Kalki!" Maadurga shouted, Dawon bounding across the disintegrating floor in the mage's direction.

The elf stretched out her hand, reaching for him. Rhys felt his feet lose traction, and in one last ditch effort to reach her, he dove, lunging with his arms outstretched. For a moment it looked as if he was going to make it, but inches from clasping hands with Maadurga, the upward force of gravity seized him, wrenching him skyward in a sickening somersault.

Rhys flailed his arms, stretching his fingertips for the stone limbs of Mahakala, but the statue was out of reach and Rhys flew clean past. Flipping and tumbling in a ripping torrent of air, Rhys thrashed, fighting the winds, somehow killing his spin as he plummeted faster and faster up towards the storm.

Down below, Dawon was in flight, Maadurga pressed flat to the gryphon's back as he powered through the gales, racing up to meet him. Rhys continued to fall, lightning bolts arcing in jagged beams around him. Dawon was gaining, Maadurga driving her mount upwards with everything she had. The gryphon drew close, fighting to within a few fathoms of Rhys. Maadurga rose from the saddle, extending an outstretched hand as Rhys reached back. A sudden fork of electricity clove narrowly past, forcing Dawon to veer evasively. He dropped away, losing precious feet, but banking back into a climb, the gryphon began to narrow the gap once more.

Mist started to stream past, condensing rapidly as Rhys broke through the cloud ceiling. He momentarily lost sight of Maadurga, Dawon vanishing in the sea of haze. But as a flash of light glared through the thundercloud, Rhys caught sight of a spread of wings climbing out of the murk below. Seconds later, Maadurga and Dawon re-emerged, slicing through the gloom as they closed back in.

The elf and mage stretched for one another again, but in the glare of another lightning strike, Rhys caught sight of a shadow hurtling their way. A sprawl of tangled limbs spun closer and closer, the eight arms of Mahakala careening through the storm straight for Rhys.

"Look out!" screamed Rhys over the toll of thunder, jabbing a finger in the direction of the incoming Destroyer.

Maadurga glanced back over her shoulder, yanking sharply at the reins as she foresaw the impending collision. Dawon tucked in his wings, veering away, narrowly avoiding the colossal idol as it hurtled past.

Rhys flinched, unable to move out of the statue's path, bracing for impact. Mahakala careened through the storm, spinning chaotically as he ploughed towards Rhys, but by some miracle, Rhys glided through the eye of a needle, slipping unscathed between a gap in the statue's flailing arms.

His eyes opening back wide, heart drumming through cold thick adrenaline, Rhys watched the stone effigy vanish somewhere above, wind and rain continuing to rip past. Swivelling his head all around, he scanned the skies, searching once more for Maadurga.

He saw her. Dawon's shadow flapped furiously through the haze, the gryphon fighting against the storm with everything he had. They emerged from out of the gloom once again. For what surely would be the final time, Rhys reached for Maadurga's outstretched hand. The gap closed to a few fathoms, then a few feet. She was only inches away.

Rhys strained his shoulder, stretching his fingertips to the limit, when suddenly he was struck in the gut. A chunk of wayward rubble flew out of the clouds, colliding with Rhys, sending him spinning head over heels. The wind knocked out of his lungs, Rhys thrashed, fighting his rotation.

He'd been batted clear once again, but Maadurga and Dawon were swiftly narrowing the gap. Maadurga reached. Rhys reached back. But in the glare of the storm, Rhys saw a cloud of rubble hurtling his way.

"Watch out!" he gasped through burning lungs.

An instant later, Rhys was hit. A boulder of rock struck the mage's head. Everything went black. As he lost consciousness, his hearing was the last thing to go. A single despairing cry wailed from Maadurga as she lost sight of him in the storm.

"Kalki!"

FORTY-THREE

Rhys gasped suddenly awake. His brow throbbed. His face was heavy. His eyes felt as if they were bulging in their sockets. Rhys's leg was dead, a tight knot choked around his ankle, cutting the circulation. His arms were dangling limply above his head. Freezing breath plumed from between his lips in icy wisps. He shivered, his whole body numb from the cold.

Groggily regaining his senses, the mage peered around. At first, he believed he was hanging upside down, but as he examined his surroundings, he quickly realised he was suspended upright; it was the pull of gravity that was inverted. Flakes of snow were drifting in the air. Dusk was beginning to draw inwards.

Rhys was hung suspended between two floating masses of rock. Above his head, mist swirled, partially obscuring a further grouping of hillocks and boulders locked weightlessly in the air. Peering down past his midriff, Rhys realised one of his legs was ensnared by a length of prayer flags wrapped around his boot. The tether extended below him, to a web of tangled bunting knotted around the four-armed bronze statue of Mahakala. The statue was wedged between the two hills, its head-piece and feet jammed into the stone.

Through providence, Rhys had somehow become entangled with the Destroyer's effigy whilst unconscious. Had he not, he doubted he would have survived the immense upward fall from Mahakaleshwar. Now he hung lifelessly from a single strand, swaying in the gales as they buffeted him left and right.

Craning his neck, Rhys continued to gaze around from his noose, blood pooling dazedly inside his head. More of his senses returned to him. He was alive, miraculously, but alone, suspended above another upwards fall that could soon kill him were the fraying strand of rope attached precariously around his boot to snap. His staff was gone, nowhere to be seen, and far enough away that the mage could not immediately sense its presence. No one, neither friend nor foe, was nearby. He considered calling out, but decided against it for fear that an enemy might hear, discovering the mage dangling helplessly above a precipice. Rhys had no idea where he was, nor how far he had fallen. Furthermore, neither did any of his friends; they more than likely believed him dead, and with good reason.

Rhys fumbled with benumbed fingers along his forehead. A swollen lump had risen across his brow, the skin split painfully open where the rock had struck him. His foot tingled with pins and needles, his ankle feeling bruised where the line of prayer flags had strangled his boot. His entire body ached, twinging from the strain of spending hours hanging inverted.

Rolling his shoulders, Rhys groaned in discomfort. He lifted his arms below his chest and drunkenly examined his torso for any other undiscovered wounds; to his relief, he was already aware of the worst of his injuries. Taking into consideration what had happened to him, Rhys figured he had probably escaped from the fall quite lightly. Fumbling around his belt and pouch, he discovered much to his relief that his wand and codex were still on his person. As he inspected his free-hanging leg, he realised his father's knife had stayed in the scabbard fixed to his boot.

Rhys contracted his abdomen and tried to reach for the prayer flags ensnaring his foot. His core strained, his fatigued muscles struggling against the weight of the mail and plates of his Elven mirror armour. His torso was too heavy. In this weakened state, he could reach neither the line of prayer flags, nor the knife on his boot. If Rhys was going to escape, he needed to somehow doff the hauberk.

Groping for the buckle of his belt, Rhys fumbled with cold fingers at the clasp. After several minutes of clumsy probing, he managed to undo it. Ensuring his wand did not slide out of its holster, Rhys swung the belt over his groin and held it between his thighs. With the girdle removed, the mass of chainmail and plate had come to slump around Rhys's armpits, but despite his wriggling, the hauberk would not pass over his head. Fighting with his elbows to keep the mail at bay, Rhys spent several more minutes strapping his belt back around his waist before reaching to unfasten the leather drawstrings around his collar. Eventually, he managed to pass the mass of steel rings and plates over his head. Thrashing his arms, the mage fought free of the mirror armour and watched as it tumbled away, vanishing in the mist above.

Exhausted now, and short of breath, Rhys rested for a good moment before launching another attempt to reach for the line. Having finally recovered his breath, Rhys once again contracted his abdominal muscles, fighting to raise his chest towards his waist. Flailing with a hand, the mage managed to lock his fingers around the cord of prayer flags coiled about his boot. Swinging his other hand above the first, Rhys heaved himself up the line until he felt the tension loosen around his foot.

Rhys reached down and unsheathed his father's dagger. Gripping the blade momentarily between his teeth, the mage took several turns of the prayer flags, winding the cord tightly around his forearm. Letting himself dangle one-handedly, he took the dagger back out of his teeth and began sawing at the knot fettering his ankle. The edge sliced through the line with little trouble, quickly freeing the mage's leg, but as he raised his foot to resheath the dagger in its scabbard, a sudden gust of wind caught hold of him. Gripping the line even tighter, Rhys swung out like a pendulum. Suddenly, the knotted mass of bunting tangled around the statue of Mahakala unravelled. Rhys lurched downward. He dropped a dozen feet before the line snapped abruptly taught. As the cord retensioned, his shoulder locked jarringly under the strain and the dagger in his hand slipped from his fingers.

"No!" Rhys cried out with despair, watching as the knife, the one remaining possession he had of his father's, slid from his grip. The dagger tumbled, blade over hilt, silently vanishing as it sliced into the gloom above.

It was gone. He would never recover it. There went the last thing he had to remember the man who had raised him: the last possession of Stanley North lost beyond the brink of the world.

Rhys screamed at the top of his lungs, venting his fury, his despair, his trauma, no longer caring who or what heard his cries. He dangled there, swaying back and forth, the occasional gust of icy air billowing him about, until, unable to hang any longer, he started to climb.

He made it barely a dozen feet up the line, when suddenly the web of cord above unknotted further. The rope slipped again. He dropped, falling even farther this time, his arms straining painfully in their sockets as the rope lashed taught. Waiting once more for the swaying to subside, Rhys began to climb again, but after ascending little more than a few inches, his heart sank at the sound of ripping.

Rhys anxiously peered up the line. Several fathoms overhead, the rope was fraying, the snapped plies steadily uncoiling under the mage's weight. Exhaling nervously, Rhys began ascending again, halting suddenly when he realised he was causing the line to fray faster.

Cursing in frustration, Rhys merely dangled for a moment, watching the damaged line sway in the wind. Sighing with dread, as smoothly as possible, Rhys resumed the climb. He watched in horror as the rope steadily unravelled, each foot he rose bringing the line ever closer to breaking point.

He gritted his teeth, continuing to ascend hand over hand. The rope creaked and strained, yarns spinning outwards as they snapped and unravelled. The mage closed the distance, climbing to within a few fathoms of the fraying section. Moments later, he'd drawn to within feet, until finally it was mere inches above his head. Rhys reached upwards, ready to grasp hold above the damaged cord, when suddenly, as if by some cruel joke, he felt the line snap.

The tension twanged slack in Rhys's palm, the final ply giving out under the strain. Rhys lunged with his leading hand, but his fingertips merely brushed at the frayed yarns.

Rhys dropped, swiftly plummeting, the bronze statue of Mahakala watching him fall. He slipped through the mist, accelerating into the sky, but as he fell, the forces acting on him began to shift and turn. He slowed, changing direction, looping along an arcing trajectory, ploughing suddenly into a blanket of snow, skidding to a halt halfway up an icy slope.

Winds blustered around the mage as he heaved himself up out of the snow drift, dusting off his clothes as he gazed around. Flakes swirled amidst the seething fog, ice crystals glistening in the frigid air currents. Through the movement of the haze, another series of floating hillocks unveiled themselves above. Across the surrounding slopes of the range, several dismembered stone arms angled out of the snowbanks, the eight limbs of Mahakala scattered in pieces, dispersed throughout the ruinous remains of Mahakaleshwar's pagoda. Gazing upwards, Rhys sensed his staff speaking to him through the Aether; his weapon was somewhere in the heaps of rubble overhead. But lost in the floating stone islands suspended in the clouds above, the stave was well beyond his reach; it would have to wait for now. Continuing to study his surroundings, Rhys caught glimpse of a rope bridge some way above, and higher still, several lines of prayer flags were tethered between the various floating peaks.

Hugging his arms around himself against the cold, Rhys sunk his chin into the collar of his gambeson and began staggering uphill. A short while later, the mage crested the brow, sighing with relief upon discovering the first in a series of cairns. The trailmarkers led Rhys along the length of the ridge, ending in a drooping rope bridge that rose to the next airborne landmass.

Following a natural set of steps up the hummock, Rhys drew level with the group of snow-capped hills he had sighted from below, across which he could make out a few fragments of the statue of Mahakala. But there was no way across, the path instead continuing on in a different direction, numerous stacks of balanced stone guiding the way. Rhys was faced with only one option; he abandoned the path, cautiously descending a steep bank until he came to a wooden stake driven into the rock. Strung from the post, vanishing into the swirling mist ahead, was a run of prayer flags.

Clutching the pole, Rhys stretched outwards from the precipice, reaching for the rope. He warily tested the strength of the line with a few sharp tugs. When satisfied it would hold his weight, the mage released his grip of the post and took hold of the rope in both hands. Lifting his legs out from the ledge, he heaved them up over the line of prayer flags, hooking the rope into the crooks of his knees. Hanging upside down, Rhys began pulling himself along the line, shimmying out from the ledge and into the mist.

After several moments, the next hill in the chain loomed out of the fog. At the line's end, Rhys dismounted onto a steep rockface. Scampering up the wall via the crags and crimps, the mage pulled himself up onto another snowy slope. Continuing to amble on, ascending to the next hilltop, Rhys traversed another line of prayer flags in the same manner as the first. The second crossing was much longer than the previous, and halfway along, a sudden upsurge in the winds whipped the line of flags violently back and forth. Tucking himself tightly into the rope, his hands contracting hard around the cord, Rhys clung for dear life. When the gales momentarily subsided, the mage quickly shuffled across the final stretch and climbed another wall of stone.

Lumbering up the slope that followed, Rhys watched in awe as two enormous stone arms loomed out of the murk. Anchored into the snow by a fractured chunk of Mahakala's torso, the forearms angled outwards with palms extended, fingers flared and pinched together in a pair of meditative hand gestures. Tangled between the fingers and limbs were more reels of knotted prayer flags, a section of the religious bunting hung taught over the cliffside.

Peering down over the precipice, Rhys investigated further. Strung from the line down below dangled the body of a rakshasa. Like Rhys, the Cŵn Annwn rider had become entangled during the fall, but whereas the flags had left Rhys suspended by the ankle, the noose ensnaring the ill-fated rider had choked around the elf's neck, hanging him from the hand of the very god he worshiped.

Taking a moment, Rhys pondered the symbolism, unsure weather it was one of bitter irony or instead poetic justice. Whichever the case, it made little difference to the mage now, stranded and alone somewhere in the upper peaks of Sumeru. He prepared to carry on, before realising that the elf dangling below was in possession of a kukri.

Without his own knife, the only weapon Rhys was left with was the blade on his wand, and that was more decorative than functional. Resting a palm on the cold stone of Mahakala's forearm, Rhys leant out beyond the ledge, reaching as far as he dared, finally curling his fingers around the length of prayer flags. Shifting his weight rearward, Rhys planted his backside in the snow and dug in his heels.

Astounded once more by the lightness of elves, Rhys hoisted the cadaver upwards, reeling in the line until the corpse dragged up over the ledge. Removing the rakshasa's scabbard from his belt, Rhys drew the blade and inspected it. As far as kukris went, the knife was relatively plain, devoid of the detailed etchings and gilded patterns more decorative blades possessed; irrespective, the damasked steel's surface was mottled and fluid, the metal both hard and flexible, curving along the inward edge and tapering to a polished ivory hilt. Rhys sheath the blade back in its black leather scabbard, affixing it to his own belt around his back. The mage took a moment to search the Wild Hunt rider's pockets, but finding nothing of use, he finally set off again on his way.

Crossing another short line of prayer flags, Rhys began another lengthy climb to the top of the next mountain. Arriving atop the summit some time later, the mage was forced to leap across a short chasm, dropping several fathoms, a snowdrift on the adjacent hillock cushioning his landing. He peered back up to the ledge he'd jumped from; there was no way back now. All he could do from here on was push forth.

Following the whispers of his staff, Rhys was finally led to the top of a gorge. Gazing down from the verge, the mage peered into a narrow and bottomless canyon. Strung between the two walls was a tangled mess of ropes, seemingly a combination of matted prayer flags and the remnants of an old rope bridge that had once spanned the chasm.

Further down, Rhys spied a section of debris that had been strewn skyward in the destruction of Mahakaleshwar's pagoda. The piece of rubble was unmistakably the domed roof of the tower, the stone bowl wedged upside-down between the two walls of the ravine, the distinctive iron finial bent wonky. Cupped inside the roof was Rhys's stave. Sensing the mage's proximity, the weapon momentarily awoke with a flash of verdant energy, fading once again in the seconds that followed.

Rhys examined the walls of the ravine, searching for a way to climb down. Provided the lines could hold his weight, the descent appeared feasible. After a long moment of mental preparation, the mage slowly lowered himself from the precipice, beginning his treacherous descent. Utilising the sparse array of crimps and crags, Rhys steadily clambered down the sheet of stone, always taking his time to select the next handhold in his descent.

By the time he'd reached the halfway point, his forearms were cramping, his hands benumbed by the freezing rock. Wedging his foot in a fissure in the cliffside and resting his other boot on a length of rope, Rhys took a short respite, waiting to catch his breath. Up this high, the air was noticeably thinner, and though it had made little difference whilst the mage had been walking about, climbing a sheer face of stone was taking its toll.

Fully recovered, Rhys resumed his descent, but not much further down, he momentarily glanced upwards at the strip of clouds visible above. A chill ran down his spine. A set of dark wings scudded across the chasm: a rakshasa. Rhys had sighted the rider perched in the saddle as he had glided over, but hidden deep down inside the gorge, he was relatively sure the rider had not spotted him. He stayed silent, clinging to the wall for a long moment, praying that would be the end of it. But moments later, the shadowy mask of a rakshasa peered down from the ledge above.

Rhys swore aloud, there now being no doubt; he had been spotted. Hastily resuming his descent, Rhys began clambering down the rockface as fast as he could. He glanced upwards: no sign of the elf. His foot slipped from its perch. Snatching an overhead line, Rhys caught himself from falling, his feet left dangling momentarily above the void below.

Planting his boots back on the rock, the mage once more upturned his gaze. The dark raptorial head of a gryphon emerged from the precipice overhead. Rhys's heart sank in horror as the creature's hooked talons affixed themselves to the vertical face of stone. The beast flared its wings, slowing its fall, as in a succession of short quick bounds, the gryphon leapt between the two cliffs, descending into the gorge for Rhys.

Talons and padded paws scrabbled at the rock, the monstrous hybrid attempting to find purchase as it darted between the two faces, the rider in the saddle driving his mount deeper, the mage locked in his sights. Rhys threw all caution to the wind, scrambling down the cliff without reservation, his fingers and feet slipping in panic as the beast bore down on him from above.

An arrowhead clattered off the cliffside, narrowly missing Rhys's fingers. The gryphon let out a terrifying screech and the rider nocked another arrow on his bowstring. The hound of Annwn closed in, taking aim for the mage once again as Rhys clung helplessly to the stone. Knowing his foe was unlikely to miss a second time, Rhys hurled himself from the cliffside. The arrow ricocheted off the rock where Rhys had been perched an instant earlier. Air rushed around the mage. Reaching with outstretched fingers, Rhys snagged hold of a rope spanning the chasm.

The line twanged, bouncing Rhys up and down as he clung on for dear life. A piton securing the rope to the cliff face began to jostle free, wiggling in the stone as the line continued to strum. Overhead, the Wild Hunt rider notched another missile. Rhys swung his weight, releasing the line just as the third arrow whistled past his ear.

Catching hold of a ledge, Rhys groaned as his chest and legs slammed back into the cliffside. Above, the gryphon thrashed, snapping its beak as it fought through the web of tangled ropes and prayer flags netted across the gorge. Rhys had made up ground, but the hound was still closing in, the lines entangling him and his mount snapping as the monstrous beast rent them from the cliffs. Rhys hugged the wall tightly, narrowly avoiding another arrow as it skimmed past.

Scaling down the rockface again, Rhys could hear the shrieks of the gryphon as it scrambled after him. The roof of the pagoda was close at hand, Rhys's stave awakening further as the mage nearly drew to within reach, but a quick glance overhead filled him with despair; he wasn't going to make it in time.

Within striking distance, the monstrous hybrid dove for Rhys with outstretched talons. The mage flinched, watching as hooked claws raced towards him. A wayward line snagged around the beast, momentarily stymieing its descent just long enough for Rhys to drop clear. The rope snapped, freeing the gryphon. It lunged again, raking at the air as it went for the mage.

With no other means of escape, Rhys simply let go. He fell. The gryphon's strike missed, its talons scraping across the stone where the mage had been a second earlier. Rhys caught hold of another line, but with both gryphon and rider now level with him, the hound saddled atop the monster swung a kukri Rhys's way.

Rhys released the line with one hand, narrowly avoiding dismemberment, but the Elven blade clove through the rope. The cord slackened. Rhys was falling again. It pinged taught, swinging him sideways as he careened into the cliffside. Smacking hard into the rock, Rhys lost his grip, freefalling down through the middle of the chasm, plummeting into the gulf of sky below.

The wind ejected from Rhys's chest, the rim of the pagoda's dome smashing into his ribs. Clipping the ledge, the mage by some miracle flopped over into the slope of the dome, skating headfirst down the inner surface of the roof, sliding to a halt seconds later beside his staff.

Barely able to wheeze, Rhys felt his fingers close around his weapon, watching in horror as the rakshasa and his gryphon dove for him, claws outstretched. Thrusting upwards, Rhys fired a bolt of force at the hound. The missile struck, crumpling the beast's wing. It overshot its dive, smacking into the edge of the roof. A mass of feathers, talons, and claws scrambled at the rim. Rhys felt the whole dome shift. A section of the roof crumbled away. The structure sharply dropped several feet on one side. The sudden lurch dislodged the beast's purchase, and toppling over the far side of the lip, it vanished, plummeting out the bottom of the canyon.

Rhys let his head fall back. He rested, waiting to catch his breath, but to his dismay, a black glove suddenly appeared over the lip of the bowl, the gryphon's rider heaving himself up.

"Oh, fuck off!" puffed Rhys in both annoyance and disbelief, fighting his way back to his feet.

His foe clambered over the lip of the roof and stood balancing on its edge. Sighting the mage, the rakshasa drew an arrow from his quiver. In the blink of an eye, the rider took aim, but before he could draw, Rhys's hands moved with even greater speed, sending a fist of energy flying from the tip of his weapon. The missile of force tore through the air, colliding with the rakshasa, sending him hurtling from the edge in pursuit of his mount below.

Issuing a long, exasperated exhale, Rhys slumped back into the dome, resting for a while, before finally, scrambling up the smooth inner surface of the pagoda's roof, he started the climb back out of the canyon.

FORTY-FOUR

By the time Rhys heaved himself back up over the top of the cliff edge, darkness had descended across Sumeru. The winds had picked up into howling gales and thunder rumbled through the tumultuous skies overhead. Rhys shuddered, hunching his shoulders and tucking his hands beneath his armpits. His gambeson and breeches did little to stave off the freezing temperatures; he could feel the warmth being rapidly sapped from his body by the blistering wind. Cupping his hands in front of his mouth, Rhys momentarily tried to warm them with his breath. Teeth chattering, Rhys spun slowly on the spot, attempting to find his bearings.

He had climbed out of the gorge on the opposite wall, crossing the chasm to an expansive mountainside, the white slopes fading as they swept upwards into the dark. Knowing that he would be dead in a matter of hours if he did not find some form of shelter, Rhys began to stagger uphill, planting his feet heavily on the ice as he fought against the howling squalls.

Snow began to issue from the clouds in great torrents. Whipped up in the gales, the flakes swirled into a blizzard. Visibility fell to nothing in a matter of mere moments. The whiteout swallowed Rhys, chilling him to the bone. His chest quivered. His limbs turned numb. He fought on, eyes watering, tears freezing to his cheeks. Every step became a battle in its own right, and soon Rhys began to feel his body shutting down. Stumbling, Rhys fell to his knees. The winds shrieked preternaturally around him, and for a moment, the mage considered giving up then and there, accepting his fate, lying down in the snow to die. He could keep fighting on, but how much longer could he survive out in the open with the blizzard raging around him?

Lightning forked through the snowstorm, and for a brief moment, Rhys thought he saw a lumbering shadow skulking through the haze. Raising his head, the mage glanced around in the white murk. Ice and snow whirled about. He couldn't see anything. The wind continued to howl.

There it was again! Lost in the din of the roaring storm, the mage was certain he had heard something. He continued to listen, straining his ears, trying to discern anything over the shrieking air currents. Once more he thought he heard a ghostly wail, but there was no way he could be sure it was not the wind itself.

Clambering to his feet, Rhys drew his staff, leaning heavily on the weapon as he resumed his uphill battle. Frozen gusts burnt his face, the wind's icy fingers cutting straight through his clothing, all the while a crust of snow steadily built up across his body. More time passed as he pressed up the slope, the mage becoming wearier and wearier with every step.

Eventually, Rhys collapsed, falling face down into the snow. Darkness welled around him as his body started to give out. As the snow started to bury him, he felt inexplicably warm.

Unable to surrender, Rhys forced his dying mind into samadhi. He became aware of his slowing heartbeat and failing breath, but for a brief moment, his waking mind seemed to be operating outside the confines of his body. Like a puppet master tugging at strings, Rhys instructed his head to lift from the snow. His consciousness snapped back into place.

Rhys gazed around in desperation. In a matter of minutes, he would be dead. His eyes were blurred with tears, but squinting, he managed to clear them, focussing his vision. He glanced ahead, staring at something he could not quite make out. A dark void loomed in the fog not far away.

Shouting orders from mind to muscles, Rhys painfully lifted himself out of his snowy deathbed and stumbled exhaustedly to his feet. He faltered, collapsing back to his knees. His head rolled. He craned his neck and lifted his chin. The shadowy void was closer now. It was an aperture of blackness receding into the mountainside. Battling to his feet once more, he limped closer. A cave mouth appeared from out of the slope before Rhys. Forcing his failing muscles to fight on for the last few yards, the mage staggered through the entrance, into the shelter of the cavern beyond.

Immediately, the intense biting squalls abated, and Rhys regained a portion of his wits. Enwrapping his torso in his arms, the mage blundered deeper into the cave to escape the wrath of the storm. He shuddered, teeth chattering as he stumbled into the darkness, leaning on both his staff and the surrounding walls for support. When he could no longer see the way ahead, Rhys fumbled for his wand, summoning a faint glowing orb that shimmered through the dark.

Delving through the narrow passages, the mage eventually came to a wider cavern. He glanced around in the dim light. Heaps of bones picked clean of flesh were scattered across the floor. Suppressing a gasp, Rhys took a step backwards in dread. A rib snapped under the weight of his heel. The crack echoed throughout the cavern and his pulse skipped a beat. The den was home to a predator, and Rhys had wandered unwittingly straight into its heart. He tarried, eager to retreat. But Rhys could not venture back out into the storm; doing so would mean certain death.

He moved the arcane light about in front of him, shining it to and fro, illuminating the dark recesses of the cave. He was alone. Perhaps the lair was long abandoned. He took a few steps further inside. Fragments of a skull crunched under one of his boots. Rhys cringed. He glanced about, paranoid he was being watched from somewhere inside the cavern, but after a few seconds scanning his surroundings, confident he was indeed alone, his racing heartbeat began to calm.

The relief was short lived. A growl sounded from behind. Rhys spun, realising that the noise had come from up the passage by which he had just entered. Whatever beast made its den here had followed Rhys inside. The mage peered frantically around in search of another route of escape, but the cavern had only one entrance. He was cornered, trapped by whatever monster was now heading his way. Rhys retreated into the shadows, his mind not made up about whether it was even worth trying to hide.

A new snarl rumbled from up the tunnel, this time closer than before, followed by a spectral howl that sounded like a ghostly distortion of the wind. Whatever it was, it could sense Rhys. The beast knew it had an intruder. The mage could hear heavy footfalls reverberating from up the passageway. He stowed his wand and raised his staff in two hands. His ethereal blade chimed, unfolding from nothing to cast an emerald hue about the darkness. Rhys continued to edge back, waiting in terror for the creature to appear.

An eight-foot-tall hulking mass of muscle and white fur loomed ominously out of the shadows. The bipedal creature stooped, only rising fully erect as it emerged from the passage. A set of piercing cold eyes glowed blue in the dim light, its spectral glare swiftly locking on Rhys. A pair of curling bovine horns reared and the beast bared its fangs, spreading its ursine paws in a display of rage. The yeti roared, its ferocious cry quaking the cavern under its tremendous volume. Incensed by the intruder, it charged suddenly for Rhys.

Slowed by his hypothermic state, Rhys flung a wild slash for the yeti. His blade met flesh and the monster thrashed in retaliation. An immense clawed palm collided with the mage, batting him clean off his feet. The yeti let out an anguished roar and Rhys slammed into the wall of the cave. Rhys dazedly clambered to his feet, glancing back at the monster to see it clutching a bloodied arm hanging lifelessly at its side. It was wounded badly, but the yeti was not yet done with Rhys. Seeing the mage back upright, the abominable creature grunted, lowering its horns as it prepared to charge again.

Fuelled by the fight, Rhys felt the chill leave his body. He leapt towards the beast, blade thrust ahead, skewering the yeti clean through the throat. Dropping to its knees, the monster emitted a gurgled growl, before slumping at Rhys's feet. Skipping away, Rhys watched the yeti from a far as blood puddled around its hulking body. His ethereal blade sheathed itself, plunging the cave into sudden darkness. Scrambling for his wand, Rhys summoned another arcane light. He breathed a sigh of relief to see the yeti was still unmoving. Satisfied the beast was dead, he stepped nearer and prodded it with his staff to make doubly sure. When no response came, he finally relaxed.

Rhys shuddered as the numbing cold took hold of him again. It was sheltered inside the cave, but the air was still icy. Shelter from the storm alone would not be enough for Rhys to survive the night. He needed a source of heat.

The mage examined the body of the yeti before him, intrigued by the hybrid of animals that seemed to make up its morphology; it appeared to meet Maadurga's description, being both ursine and primate in nature, though its horns bore a striking resemblance to those of a goat. After studying the beast for a time, Rhys slumped next to the body, nuzzling inside the crook under its enormous arm. The yeti was still hot, its thick fur coat blanketing Rhys as the carcass's residual heat steadily warmed him. Exhausted from his ordeal, Rhys let tiredness wash over him, and after a short time, he began to doze.

The mage fell in and out of sleep for the next few hours, but once the yeti's carcase had finally cooled, Rhys grew too uncomfortable to sleep. He began to shiver, his teeth rattling loudly throughout the cave. Unable to remain still any longer, he rose to his feet and began pacing in an attempt to stir life back into his benumbed muscles. After circling the cavern a good few times, Rhys found himself staring into the corner. Dung was piled up against the wall, shards of bone visibly protruding from the pile of aged muck. Though a few fresh heaps were still pungent, most of the scat was desiccated, months, or perhaps even years old.

An idea sprung into Rhys's mind. Toeing several dried lumps away from the rest of the pile, Rhys nudged it over towards the yeti. Stooping, Rhys drew his wand. To his amazement, with only a little encouragement, the scat began to smoke and smoulder. Within a few moments it was alight. The mage fuelled the flames, kicking more of the yeti's scat into the burning pile, until before long, a modest campfire flickered in the centre of the cavern. Rhys sat back within the crook of the yeti's body, warming his chest and hands by the heat of the flames.

He continued to stoke the fire throughout the night; the dung burned far more efficiently than he would ever have expected. Suitably comfortable, the mage drifted back to sleep, awaking some time after dawn to find the fire before him reduced to embers. Rising to his feet, Rhys stretched out the bruising and strains he'd sustained the previous day. He was incredibly sore, and even wandering back up the passage towards the cave entrance took its toll.

The mage emerged out into the morning light. The sky was partially clear overhead, appearing a darker blue than the mage had expected. The Rift shimmered green and mauve through gaps in the cloud cover, but for the most part, the wound in the Aether was obscured by the storm raging in the distance.

The world around was smothered beneath a fresh blanket of snow, the blizzard having covered all. Setting off across the mountain, Rhys continued the way he'd been going the night before, scaling the alp towards its peak. After an hour of crunching uphill, the mage sighted something glinting in the sunlight atop the peak. Rhys shielded his eyes, squinting against the sun's glare as he drew nearer. Reaching the summit, he finally made out the cairn marking the trail ahead. He had managed to rediscover the path. Up in front, stretching out from the mountain's zenith, the longest rope bridge Rhys had come across to date extended into the sky, vanishing into a cluster of snow-dusted massifs floating amidst the clouds ahead.

Knowing there was no way back, Rhys stepped onto the swaying lines and walked out beyond the brink.

FORTY-FIVE

Rhys hoisted himself up the last few stone rungs of a ladder carved from the cliffside, arriving atop a snowy ledge marked with another cairn. Recovering his breath, the mage peered through the mist, at the enclosing maze of mountains, attempting once more to orientate himself. He had never veered from the trail whilst following the twisting route through the sierra, but even still, he could not help but feel hopelessly lost.

Spotting the highest ridge in the massif, Rhys alleviated his sense of disorientation and continued to follow the narrow ledge as it worked its way around the circumference of the escarpment. Peering over the precipice, Rhys realised now how high he had truly ascended Sumeru; by his reckoning, he was several thousand fathoms above sea level. Feeling momentary vertigo, the mage stepped away from the ledge, hugging the cliff face as he shimmied along the treacherous pass and rounded the mountainside, emerging onto a wider shelf.

The sound of voices sent alarm bells ringing in Rhys's head. He hunkered down behind a snowdrift as a muffled conversation in Elvish grew steadily more audible. Peering up from behind the mound, Rhys caught sight of two rakshasa, the pair emerging in conversation atop a verge on the adjacent hillock. Rhys ducked back out of sight. He couldn't understand what they were saying, but for one reason or another, he got the impression they were searching the area for something. An educated guess led Rhys to the conclusion that that something was him.

The conversation ended abruptly with a hint of frustration in their voices, and as Rhys cautiously raised his eyes back above the top of the snowdrift, his heart relaxed. The two Hounds had turned away, returning back the direction they had come. Rhys waited until the riders were out of sight and crept out from behind the bank.

Snow began to flutter downwards as the mage arrived at a thin wooden bridge; the crossing consisted of little more than a few fixed planks spanning the narrow chasm between the two neighbouring cliffsides. Stretching his arms out for balance, Rhys stepped out onto the boards, cautiously edging across the gulf to the ledge on the far side. Following a precarious path encircling a vast stone column, the mage rounded a turn, immediately catching sight of another follower of Mahakala heading his way.

Rhys darted back into cover, hugging the wall. The rider had been looking in the wrong direction when Rhys had emerged; by sheer luck, the mage hadn't been spotted. His heart throbbed in his chest as he pricked up his ears, listening attentively for the rakshasa's approach. The elf's footfalls were crunching softly his way. In a matter of seconds, the hound would round the corner and find Rhys. He needed to be dealt with, and silently.

Reaching behind his back, Rhys drew the kukri from the scabbard on his belt. Closing his eyes, he pressed his back hard against the cliff face and waited. The footsteps paused momentarily. Rhys held his breath. The rider started to move again. Rhys continued to wait. His timing needed to be impeccable; striking too soon would be as bad as doing so too late.

Suddenly, the mage lurched from out of cover, pivoting sharply around the corner. Grasping hold of the chest plate on the elf's hauberk, he thrust the tip of the kukri at his surprised foe. Sinking the blade through the rakshasa's throat, he silenced the hound before he could even call out. The zealot flopped limp in Rhys's embrace and the mage lowered the body to the snow, wiping his blade on the robes of his slain enemy.

Rhys crept onwards. More voices sounded in conversation ahead. Two riders from the Hunt were just beyond the next turn in the path. Rhys sighed in frustration. There was no other way around. He had to face them. But two elves were one too many to deal with silently. There had to be another way.

Rhys glanced sideways over the precipice of the narrow pathway. The next portion of the trail wound around a mountainside across the gulf. That was where Rhys needed to get to, but the expanse was far too wide to jump. He looked around. A span of prayer flags was strung between the two sections of path. Making his way silently over to the bunting, Rhys reached overhead and grappled the line. Hauling his weight upwards, he hooked his legs over the cord and began shuffling his way down the stretch of rope. Reaching the far cliffside, the mage dropped down a dozen feet, landing in a heap of snow. Not daring to peek back over his shoulder, he crept on past the next turn in the trail.

The voices faded in the wind behind him, and satisfied he had given the rakshasa the slip, Rhys stood upright and continued along the way. Negotiating around the next bend, the mage stepped out past the turn, unsuspectingly walking straight into a rakshasa coming the opposite way. Rhys and the elf both leapt in surprise at the other's appearance. The rakshasa's hand raced suddenly for his scabbard, but Rhys didn't waste time reaching for his own weapon. He rushed his foe, driving a foot square into his chest. The rakshasa screamed as he was launched from the precipice, his cries fading as he plunged into the depths below. Rhys issued a sigh of relief, but his celebration of reprieve came too soon.

"Tayam tala!" roared a rakshasa from above.

Rhys's eyes shot up to a ledge overhead. Three hounds stood staring down at him from across the chasm, their attention drawn by the cry of their plummeting ally.

"Shit!" the mage cursed, watching as they each drew arrows from their quivers and took aim.

Rhys darted into a sprint. Arrows splintered off the rockface at his back. Dashing around a turn, he skidded to a halt. Hurtling towards Rhys, using the notch of his kukri to zipline down a run of prayer flags, another rakshasa was speeding his way. Drawing his staff, Rhys hurled a javelin of force at the incoming hound, but dematerialising, the elf blinked, narrowly avoiding the mage's missile. The elf snapped back into existence above Rhys, dropping knife-first from the air.

Rhys jabbed upwards, his ethereal blade shrieking in a whirl of jade. The elf slammed into him, immediately skewered by the mage's upturned staff. Knocked off his feet, Rhys tumbled over in the collision. Throwing the impaled elf off himself, Rhys leapt back upright, just as another foe sped from around the corner to engage him. Parrying a blow, Rhys barged a shoulder into the fanatic. Losing his footing, the elf tumbled from the ledge with a cry, but as Rhys turned away, the Aether rippled. Blinking out of his fall, the rakshasa blurred back up towards the shelf.

Pivoting back around, Rhys spun to deal with his foe a second time, only to receive a retaliatory kick to the abdomen as the elf appeared. Grunting, Rhys stumbled back, his heel planting in thin air behind. His stomach lurched as he felt his weight begin to plunge. In a desperate attempt to prevent his fall, Rhys flailed with his staff. His ethereal blade swung around, the hook sinking through the hauberk of the rakshasa that had driven him over the abyss, puncturing the mail, lodging between the elf's ribs. His foe screamed, planting his feet as he resisted Rhys's pull. The staff locked tight in the mage's hands as he balanced over the precipice, one foot perched on the ledge, the other floundering wildly in open air. A sharp tug reversed both his and the elf's fortunes. Switching places, Rhys stepped back onto the shelf, sending the rakshasa flying headfirst over the brink.

More Elvish cries called out from above. Spurting forwards, Rhys dashed along the path. Archers began to appear on the cliffs overhead, lining the ridges as they took aim for Rhys. Arrows dug into the snow and clattered against the bluffs, each missing the mage by mere inches. Stooping beneath a natural stone archway, Rhys darted into a short trench, emerging atop a ledge on the far side. He glanced around, realising he had taken a wrong turn and veered off the trail. He cursed, scanning the imposing cliffs for any sign of where to go next.

More shouting erupted behind. The deluge of arrows resumed. Rhys rushed towards the precipice. Locking his staff in the crook of his arm, he drew his kukri. He leapt, reaching above his head with the blade, hooking the notch of the weapon over a cord of prayer flags, grasping hold of the kukri's spine with the other hand. Rapidly accelerating, Rhys felt a rush of exhilaration as he slid down the line. Open sky blurred beneath him before the shadow of another landmass surged up from below.

Arrows hurtled past him in the air. Still careening down the line, he scanned the trail ahead, judging when to dismount from the rope. Below, a rakshasa emerged from out of a gorge and took aim. Releasing his grip, Rhys dropped from the zipline. Air rushed past as he plunged from the sky. The arrow loosed from below sailed clean overhead. Rhys landed, planting both his boots into the rakshasa's chest. The elf crumpled, pinned to the ground in the impact.

Rhys rolled off his feet, his momentum sending him toppling forwards. Clumsily leaping out of the snow, the mage spun, stowing his kukri in its sheath and grappling his staff in both hands. The crushed rakshasa managed to pull himself up from the ground, but before he could react, Rhys cut him down with a sweeping arc of his blade. Glancing back up the line, the mage sighted another of the Wild Hunt pursuing him down the run of prayer flags. The hound dove from the rope, lunging for the mage, blade outstretched. But before the rakshasa landed, a tine of lightning forked through the air, connecting from Rhys's stave with the elf in mid-flight.

Rhys stepped narrowly aside as the dead body bounced past, ducking into the gorge to avoid another hail of arrows. He sped down the pass, now back on the trail, emerging at the base of a cliff, a steep staircase cut from the stone. The mage raced upwards, climbing almost on hands and knees as the commotion of his pursuers drew near.

Cresting the bluff, Rhys pulled himself over the lip as an arrowhead glanced the back of his neck. Palming away the blood, he set off sprinting, dashing downhill with his foes hot in pursuit. The slope rapidly steepened ahead, and without warning, the fresh snow gave out underfoot. Tumbling head-first, Rhys hurtled down the bank. He thrashed, stopping himself from rolling out of control, stabilising his descent into a measured slide. Skating ever faster across the ice, he peered ahead; another precipice was rapidly approaching.

Unable to slow himself enough to avoid plummeting over the edge, Rhys instead tucked in his limbs in an attempt to gather speed. As the abyss raced up to meet him, he kicked off from the slope, launching his body out from the cliff edge. He arced into the sky, his gut twisting as he flew across the chasm, outreaching with flailing arms for the ledge ahead. He began to drop, plummeting ever faster. A moment of terrifying realisation took hold; he was going to fall short.

Rhys cried out, thrashing his hands ahead of him as he reached for the precipice. Colliding with the ledge at chest-height, Rhys slammed against the cliff. He scrabbled in futility at the ground atop the bluff, digging his fingers into the ice, but the loose snow gave way beneath his hands and he slipped from the ledge. Plummeting once again out of the sky, Rhys felt gravity take another unusual turn. He veered back towards the cliffside, smacking against the wall of stone before finally grinding to a halt. Disorientated, the mage clambered to his feet. He was stood upright on a vertical surface, the cliff face flipped gravitationally to act as the ground.

Rubbing his throbbing flank, Rhys glanced back upwards across the chasm. An avalanche of snow churned from the clifftop, followed swiftly by a series of dark blurs, the pursuing rakshasa launching themselves across the gulf in pursuit of Rhys.

Rhys took aim, sending a fist of energy skyward at the first descending hound. The shell of force crunched into the falling rakshasa, launching him back across the chasm, smashing the elf into the far cliff face, his crippled body dropping out of the air as it vanished below. Swivelling to target the next inbound fiend, Rhys fired a surge of lightning towards a hound skating down the wall of the bluff towards him. The bolt of plasma arced through the air, but with a thrum of the Aether, the rakshasa dodged clear, blinking to close in on Rhys.

Snapping into existence directly in front of the mage, the elf launched a flurry of blows.

Dancing backwards, Rhys dealt a chain of parries as the Aether shook again and again in succession, a band of rakshasa taking form to surround the mage. Suddenly flanked on all sides, Rhys struck at the cliffside beneath his feet. A shockwave ripped outwards, quaking the face of the bluff, sending the enclosing hounds reeling backwards. Rhys swiftly followed up with another blow to the stone, the outpouring surge of energy this time inverting the flow of gravity.

All at once, the surrounding rakshasa lost their purchase, floating suddenly away from the cliffside, thrashing their arms as they tumbled helplessly in weightlessness. Rhys prepared to strike them from the air one by one, but before he did so, the first drifted out beyond the threshold of the cliff's gravity distortion. Without warning, the rakshasa dropped, plummeting groundward with a fading yelp as he vanished into the clouds. One after another, the others each followed, a series of drowning cries streaking away as they tumbled out of the heavens.

Rhys craned his head to glance back up towards the clifftops. Angry orders were being barked in Elvish above, bowstrings drawing taught as a line of archers took aim at him over the precipice. Rhys took off, sprinting horizontally across the plane of the bluff as another fusillade of arrows clattered past. He veered downward, hoping to narrow their line of sight, but as he accelerated towards the base of the cliff, he felt his feet beginning to slip.

Rhys stumbled, catching himself just in time before the forces pressing him onto the cliffside gave out. He dropped to his knees, scrambling back up the escarpment on hands and feet to surer footing. Looking back up at his foes, he realised the rain of arrows had ceased, the rakshasa opting instead to give chase down the cliff face after him.

Hauling himself up off the wall, Rhys sped onwards, making now for a curve in the cliffside. Several pursuing arrows whistled narrowly passed his ears as he descended over the brow, but as the far end of the cliffs drew towards him, Rhys felt his footing beginning to go again. This time, the mage was unable to save himself. Gravity flipped and suddenly Rhys was snatched up into the air, thrown back out across the chasm, sent flying towards the far side of the canyon.

Rhys cried out as he spun uncontrollably in the wind, losing all sense of direction as he was then launched skyward. Sailing out through the top of the gorge, he veered laterally, sucked into a twisting current of gravity that meandered this way and that. Finally, the mage touched down, skidding across ice as he was dragged up a slope of hoarfrost, eventually sliding to a stop near a mountain summit. Heaving his aching body out of the rime, he looked around. His head was spinning, and for a long moment, he was unsure which way was truly down. He was stood atop a peak, the sky above him and the sea below, but the pull of the mountainside was askew, his body planted perpendicular to the incline so that it felt to Rhys as if he were stood on flat ground. Picking his staff out of the snow, the mage gazed back down the slope to see his assailants still giving chase, each of them gracefully skating on their feet up the frozen incline in Rhys's direction.

Picking one of the elves off with a slug

of air, Rhys took off across the flat slope, racing his way towards a vertical cairn stacked atop the peak ahead. With every yard the mage charged uphill, he felt the angle of gravity revolve steadily beneath him, granting him the odd sensation of running up an ever-steepening hill on an otherwise constant gradient.

Puffing loudly in the thin air, Rhys sped over the summit, storming down the bank on the far side, following the row of trail markers ahead. Darting onto a rope bridge, Rhys raced along the lines to a free-floating hillock over the gulf. Once across, he spun back around, slashing at the ropes with his ethereal blade. The two handrails twanged as they were severed by the first blow, the bridge kinking sharply as it lost tension. One of Rhys's pursuers screamed as he was flung from the lines, sent plummeting from the bridge into the open skies underneath. But the others somehow kept balance, continuing to charge for Rhys as they sped with death-defying agility across the tightropes.

Rhys slashed at the cords again, this time chopping through the remaining lines. The Aether shuddered, the pursuing rakshasa all disintegrating as they shot toward Rhys. The three rearmost reappeared short of the precipice, howling in terror as they plunged to their deaths, but those ahead successfully made the crossing, touching down on the stone stairs above.

Spinning to engage, Rhys bounded up the steps, locking blades with the first rakshasa blocking his path. A forward shunt sent the hound stumbling, followed up by a circular cut that clove past the elf's defences, striking the rakshasa to the ground. Bounding over his defeated foe, Rhys sent a gout of flames licking up the stairs, immolating the next villain ahead.

Narrowly dodging a blurring arrow, the mage lanced up the stairway, driving the point of his stave at the third hound dogging him. An exchange of parries and ripostes ended when Rhys parted the elf from his hand. A kick sent the dismembered fiend tumbling from the precipice, and the way ahead opened up.

Dashing around a turn in the climb, Rhys ducked back into cover as a volley of arrows rained down from above. Atop the flight, a group of archers were lying in wait, arrows nocked on tensioned bowstrings as they readied for Rhys to re-emerge. Pointing his stave around the corner, Rhys fired blindly in their direction, a bulwark of kinetic energy surging up the stairs towards them. Leaping for cover themselves, the archers dodged clear of Rhys's attack, hunkering down momentarily behind a turn in the path. Reappearing seconds later, once more ready to shoot, they unleashed the tension in their bows, sending another hail at the mage as he darted over the landing below, throwing himself from the ledge.

Stave stowed behind his head and kukri drawn, Rhys hooked the notch of his Elven blade over a run of prayer flags and accelerated down the ropeway. Arrows whizzed after him as he zipped down the line, one scratching a deep gouge through the leather of his boot, the others missing as he hurtled out of range. The mage peered back over his shoulder, expecting to see the elves following suit, but instead, the line behind him was clear. A horrific realisation came to Rhys an instant before it became reality. The line of prayer flags went suddenly slack as it was cut loose by the elves behind him. Rhys was falling again, plunging out of the sky with no ground beneath him in sight.

Releasing his kukri in freefall, Rhys snatched hold of the trailing string of flags. Abruptly the rope drew taught, the line lurching forward in Rhys's grip. His shoulders and arms tightened under strain and suddenly Rhys was swinging from the line. He looked up to see the underside of a hill racing overhead. The mage slowed, coming to the end of his arc, before accelerating back in the opposite direction like a pendulum. Swaying back and forth several times, Rhys's body finally came to rest as he hung suspended in the swirling clouds.

His heart ready to burst with terror, Rhys took a long moment to calm himself as he dangled in the mist. Then steadily, he climbed hand over hand, hauling his weight up the length of rope until the base of the hillock loomed into view, the lip of a walkway appearing shortly afterwards. Kicking his legs, swinging on the line, Rhys built up enough momentum and threw himself towards the ledge.

Landing hard against the base of the cliff, Rhys paused, taking a moment to listen for the Hounds of Annwn hunting him across the sky. But as the mage peered about the thick swirling mist, he could only hear the wind whistling between the rock features. Wiping the sweat from his brow, Rhys stowed his staff, marching on along the trail, wondering what next awaited him.

FORTY-SIX

Back pressed firmly against the scarp, Rhys shimmied sideways, his toes pointing over the edge of the narrow lip. His eyes peered momentarily downwards, and vertigo overcame him. The fall seemed unending; nothing but murky clouds were visible below. Swallowing a lump in his throat, he continued to edge along the slender precipice, finally stepping down onto a wider shelf.

Hearing voices carried on the wind, Rhys instinctively ducked behind a pile of rock and waited for those nearby to pass him by. But as the mage hunkered down, he realised the voices were speaking Common; not only that, but he recognised them. Thia and Cade were nearby.

Rhys stepped out from his hiding place to see his friends emerge on the neighbouring mountain. They caught sight of him immediately.

"Rhys!" Thia cried out.

"Thia!" called Rhys back, never having been as relieved to see anyone as he was to see her now.

"You are alive!?" she shouted with disbelief, her voice on the verge of breaking.

"Barely," nodded the mage.

"I... no... Impossible!" stammered Cade. "I saw you fall!"

"You would not believe the day I've had!" joked the mage exasperatedly.

Suddenly, another two figures emerged from around the pass.

"Kalki!" yelled Maadurga with incredulity.

"Bloody heck," grumbled Ulfgar as he beheld the mage, equally gobsmacked as any of the others. "We thought you were dead!" he called across the chasm.

Rhys nodded, looking around at his surroundings. "I can see why you might have come to that conclusion."

"Hang on!" instructed Cade. "There must be some way to get to you."

"No, you stay there," assured Rhys. "I'll come to you!"

Rhys jogged along the shelf towards the ledge, easing himself over the verge towards a run of prayer flags that stretched the expanse.

"Rhys, be careful!" warned Thia.

Grabbing hold of the rope, the mage hooked his legs up over the line and steadily shifted himself along its length. Reaching the other side, he dismounted the cord and lowered himself onto the cliff face. Climbing via the pits and jugs in the rock, Rhys quickly ascended to the plateau, hoisted up over the ledge by Ulfgar and Cade.

Before he was even stood properly upright, Thia clasped her arms tightly around his chest. Rhys winced as all of his cuts and bruises ached in her embrace, but wrapped his arms back around her regardless. The two stood silently for several moments, locked in each other's arms.

When Thia pulled gently away, Rhys brushed one of her platinum tresses aside, peering deep into her eyes. Tears welled in the witch's gaze, the pain lifting as she realised she hadn't yet lost him. Her lips quivered, curving into a smile, teardrops now flowing down her cheeks. Rhys lent closer, cradling her tight. He felt her breath on his neck. Their lips came together, and they kissed.

When they parted, Rhys realised their relationship was now out in the open. Ulfgar cleared his throat chaffingly. Cade meanwhile tried to look anywhere but their direction. But Rhys no longer cared.

"How are you alive?" questioned Thia.

"I honestly don't know," Rhys shrugged. "Luck mostly."

"You are a ruddy tough bastard to kill," remarked Ulfgar with admiration in his voice. "I'll give you that!"

"I don't understand," breathed Cade in wonder. "We saw you vanish in the storm…"

"Kalki," beamed Maadurga in amazement, embracing the mage tightly.

As Maadurga released him, Rhys let out a groan of pain.

"What in the world happened?" pressed Thia, now assuming the role of physician as she gently ran a finger along the split on Rhys's forehead. "You look like—"

"Like I fell a hundred fathoms and lived to tell the tale?" quipped Rhys with a wry grin.

"That just about describes it," nodded Thia with worried amusement.

"I don't think you'd believe me if I told you."

"I want to hear it anyway," insisted the witch.

"I bet it will make a bloody good story," added Ulfgar.

"What are you guys doing out here, anyway?" questioned Rhys.

"We were looking for you," replied Maadurga.

"If we are honest," began Cade gravely, "we were expecting to find a body... if anything at all."

"I don't blame you," responded Rhys with an equally sombre tone. "Where are the others?" he questioned, taking note of Sol, Alkis, and Nathaniel's absence.

"They are with my kshatriya," explained Maadurga.

"They went in search of Arne and his sons," elaborated Cade.

Rhys nodded; he had been so preoccupied with surviving the last day and night that he had almost forgotten about Rudra's prisoners completely. "Have they had any luck in finding them?"

Maadurga nodded.

"Where!?" pressed Rhys with a sudden spark of hope.

"We can speak elsewhere," insisted Maadurga, gazing at their surroundings.

"We need to get you out of here and patched up," insisted Thia.

"There is an outpost not far from here," explained Maadurga. "An old shrine to Brahma—long ago abandoned."

"We're hauled up there," explained Cade

"We?" questioned the mage.

"The main force of the kshatriya," explained Thia.

Rhys nodded. "Lead the way."

Following the group along several miles of trail, Rhys was led across the chain of mountains and out passed the floating valley beyond. Finally, they ascended a series of rope bridges that crossed a cluster of suspended boulders, arriving in a tightly knit collection of hills. In the heart of the vale was nestled a shrine and chapel originally devoted to the creator god of the Trimurti.

Gathered out across the steps of the sanctuary were a score of kshatriya and their mounts. Upon noticing the party return, all of the elves stopped and gazed Rhys's way in amazement. As the mage ascended the stairs, dozens of eyes transfixed on him, the kshatriya knelt one by one, lowering their heads in reverence as he passed. The reincarnation of their god had risen from the dead; their saviour had returned. Merely glad to be alive and safe, Rhys lacked the capacity to be agitated by the veneration. Silently, he followed his friends up the steps and was led into the chapel.

Once inside, Rhys was quickly stripped of his tattered clothes and his various wounds were tended to by Thia. Hot tea was brewed and given to the mage as he sat by the warmth of a brazier, and a new gambeson and set of breeches were presented to him, this time accompanied with a set of leather gloves and furs to fend against the freezing temperatures of upper Sumeru. Once bandaged, clothed, and fed, Rhys was joined by his companions and Maadurga, and the explanations of all that had transpired began.

"Mahakaleshwar was destroyed," began Maadurga. "Now there are only ruins left."

"Rudra's forces were scattered in the aftermath, but they regathered themselves not long afterwards and have taken refuge in the Temple of Brahma above here," elaborated Cade.

"The Temple of Brahma?" questioned Rhys. "Why there?"

"Raraprambanan has been abandoned since the beginning of the Dark Age," explained Maadurga. "To steal the Cintamani Stone, the rakshasa attacked the Temple and butchered the followers of Brahma. The Temple is mostly in ruin, but Rudra and the rakshasa have used it for several years."

"It is an outpost," explained Thia. "One they use as a station on the way to the leviathan's lair on Kalapa."

"And that is where they are now?" questioned Rhys.

"Yes," nodded Maadurga. "With Mahakaleshwar destroyed, Rudra and the rakshasa fled to Raraprambanan."

"And are Arne, Vidar, and Eirik there?"

"We don't know," confessed Thia. "That's where the others have gone: to find out."

"If they are there, they will not be for long," explained Maadurga. "Rudra will soon order them to be taken to the Vritra."

Rhys nodded. "He will assume I am dead. He sent dozens of his scouts out looking for me—I don't think they expected to find me alive."

"None of us did," replied Cade.

"We believe Rudra is planning an attack on Suraksa," continued Maadurga. "My kshatriya tell me that the rakshasa have salvaged as many weapons and supplies as possible from the ruins of Mahakaleshwar. They are preparing for something."

"No," Rhys shook his head. "Not Suraksa. They are preparing an attack on Shambhala!"

"What do you mean?" questioned Maadurga.

"Rudra has a piece of the Cintamani Stone. His plan is to take it to the conduit in the heart of Shambhala and destroy it!"

"Of course!" gasped the elf in realisation. "He plans to attack the Amara."

"He wants to finish what his people started. He thinks that by obliterating whatever is left of Sumeru, that he will herald in a new Golden Age."

"We have to stop him!"

"But what about the Amara?" questioned Thia. "You say they are undying? If they guard Shambhala, then surely they will prevent Rudra from reaching the conduit?"

"The Amara have escaped Samsara," explained Maadurga. "They have achieved Nirvana and their bodies no longer age, like all of our kin in the first Golden Age. But they can still be killed."

"Even still," began Cade, "they might be enough to stop Rudra."

"Maybe," nodded Maadurga. "But if not, then all of Brahman will come to an end."

"Maadurga is right," agreed Rhys. "We can't leave it to chance that Rudra will succeed."

"Do you have any idea of their numbers?" questioned Thia. "How many of the Ascendant are there?"

"We do not know," replied Maadurga.

"Rudra will have a better understanding. He and his rakshasa have long ventured to the higher peaks of Sumeru. Until now, the followers of Kalki rarely flew into or above the realm of Mahakaleshwar; it was very dangerous, and many would never return."

"He must think the odds are in his favour," insisted Rhys, "otherwise he wouldn't be preparing for the attack."

"We must help balance the fight," replied Maadurga, before hesitating. "But—the Amara attack all who journey near the Golden City. If we choose to fight against Rudra…"

"You are saying the Amara won't discriminate between us and them?" questioned Rhys.

Maadurga shook her head.

"What if we struck before they left Raraprambanan?" questioned Rhys. "They are weakened and not expecting it."

"They are many," replied Maadurga. "More than I thought before we attacked Mahakaleshwar. And we are few."

"Damn it," cursed Ulfgar.

"There is more," warned Maadurga. "Rudra knows the way to Kalapa, and from Kalapa, the distance is not far to Shambhala. But the followers of Kalki… we do not know which way it is safe to fly. The Wind and Sakti move in chaos with the storm this high up Sumeru; closer towards the Akasa, the effects are greater still."

"I understand," nodded Rhys sombrely.

"There has to be a way," insisted Cade.

"Your friends will return soon with Cetan, Shankha, and Ehani," replied Maadurga. "Perhaps they will bring good news with them."

"Maybe," nodded Rhys pessimistically.

"Get some rest, Rhys," insisted Thia. "It might still be a few hours before they get back."

FORTY-SEVEN

Azrael fled across the desert, and Arlas followed. For months the mage had pursued his archnemesis. For months he had been eluded. But with each passing day, the mage had drawn nearer to his quarry. Now, chased into the barren wastes of the southern regions of the continent, Azrael had marched into the scorching planes of the Sunbleak in a final attempt to lose the mage hunting him; but Arlas had followed.

Taking a swig of water from his skin, Arlas knelt to study a faint disturbance in the sand; it was a footprint. Ahead was another, and further ahead there were more, each rapidly being eroded by the desert wind, filled by the baking sands as the grains steadily swept across the colossal dunes. He was close. But Arlas did not need footprints to tell him that; for the past day, he had sensed his foe. The time was drawing near. The end would finally come. Pulling his hood lower to shade his eyes, Arlas continued on, following the fading boot marks across the dunes, in pursuit of the man who had murdered his father and brought the collapse of the Order of Magi.

Hours later, cresting the ridge of a giant

dune, Arlas caught sight of a dark figure moving on the horizon. This was the first glimpse the mage had caught of Azrael since the battle in the savannah. Arlas knew then and there that before the day was out, either he or Azrael would be dead. The necromancer would not be allowed to escape again, no matter the cost.

On he marched, the blistering sun beating down on him punishingly. He was short of water; only a few mouthfuls were left in his skin. It had been days since he had replenished, and now, the last of his reserves were running dry. It did not matter. He had known that venturing this far into the Sunbleak could be his undoing; but it would also be Azrael's. If he was low on water, then the chances were, so was his foe.

Hours passed. Noon came and went. The footprints grew deeper and fresher, and as Arlas continued to pursue his quarry, he spotted divots in the sand where the dark mage ahead had stumbled and faltered. Azrael was growing weaker. Unfortunately, so was he.

Finally, Arlas spotted the necromancer again. Rising to the top of another dune, he saw Azrael awaiting him in the plane of sand below. The dark mage stood silent and still, his scarred face turned to watch Arlas as he descended the sandbank towards him. Finally, they stood face to face beneath the desert sun, little more than a dozen yards between them. They waited in loathing silence, each mage standing off against the other. Minutes passed as neither moved nor said a word.

War had been waged between the two men for the better part of thirteen years. It had begun with Zadkiel's murder. It would end here.

"Where are they?" croaked Azrael finally. "Baines and Hemsworth?"

"Dead," replied Arlas coldly.

Azrael's lips curled into a twisted grin as the news brought him genuine pleasure. "So, it's just you and me then?"

"Just you and me," nodded the mage.

"It's what you've always wanted, Arlas."

"This was never what I wanted."

"But now you'll have your revenge," he replied. "Or at least, a chance at it."

Arlas maintained his glare without responding.

"I should have finished you back on that battlefield," spoke Azrael. "But I let my hubris get in the way—I won't make that mistake a second time."

"Your actions have finally caught up with you," warned Arlas. "This is the end."

"We both know you can't defeat me," chided Azrael.

"How long ago did you run out of water?"

Azrael paused, maintaining his wicked grin.

"Was it today? Or have you been without a drink since last night?"

"It matters not," replied Azrael dismissively. "I can take yours from your corpse. But judging by the state of you, you are nearing the end of your supply as well."

A lengthy silence drew out.

"Lay down your staff," insisted Arlas. "I will give you a clean death."

Azrael chuckled. "I doubt that. Not after the pain I've caused you. No! You would torture me as I did you. I bet you've been dreaming of the things you want to do to me for the last decade."

"I have," nodded Arlas bitterly in agreement. "But I assure you, if you surrender, I will make sure you do not suffer."

Azrael gripped his staff, lifting it from the sand. "I fancy my chances better this way."

"You will not win," Arlas assured him.

"I've told you before, Al'Asim, I have conquered death," responded the necromancer. "Even if you could strike me down, that would not be the end. I would rise again. You cannot comprehend the power I possess."

"This is your last chance," warned Arlas.

"Quit stalling and fight me you bloody coward!" snarled Azrael impatiently.

Arlas lifted his staff and looked up into the glaring sunlight descending from atop the dune behind his enemy. He nodded.

Azrael began to swing, preparing to launch a ray of necrotic energy at Arlas, when down from above, a bolt of red lightning crackled from the dune at his rear. The fork of electricity struck Azrael in the back. Sand cascaded from the ground and the necromancer was launched upside down, the staff flying from his grip.

As the dust settled, Arlas slowly approached Azrael. The mage was sprawled on his back, one hand clutched over the deep smouldering wound in his side. The necromancer scowled as he gasped in agony, looking up into Arlas's eyes.

"Nice shot," remarked Michael Hemsworth appearing at Arlas's side.

"I couldn't really afford to miss," replied Ross Baines as he too arrived to stand over Azrael.

The necromancer gritted his teeth in fury at the subterfuge. "I knew you wouldn't have the gall to face me alone!" he spat.

"That's pretty rich coming from you of all people," remarked Michael.

"Come on," beckoned Ross, putting a hand on Michael's shoulder to pull his friend away. "Our part in this is done."

Azrael wheezed as he let out a grimacing chuckle. "Well done. I should have seen that coming."

"It's over," declared Arlas.

"It will never be over," refused the dying mage. "Even if I've failed, someone after me will succeed. Magi have tried before—they will try again. Eventually, my side will win out."

"No," proclaimed Arlas definitively.

"You know it as well as I," insisted Azrael. "Our powers are a gift; we are destined to change the world in which we live. So long as we exist, this fight will never end."

"It will," replied Arlas. "It already has."

"Then you are lying to yourself!"

"No," Arlas shook his head. "The Circle is done."

"You know how to bind men to the Aether. You know how to rebuild," replied Azrael. "It is not over."

"You are wrong," replied Arlas. "There are only three of us left. In time there will be none."

"You would let the Order die?" questioned Azrael. "You would end our legacy?"

Arlas nodded.

"But what of this world?" replied the mage in disbelief. "Who will defend mankind from the darkness?"

"Mankind will have to defend itself."

"No!" Azrael panicked, now finally believing Arlas's intentions. "No, you cannot! Without our order, chaos will consume Cambria. We are all that stands in the way!"

"You are wrong," replied Arlas. "I believe in the strength of people. Mankind will prevail. To say that they need us to protect them is arrogance. The reality is, we pose the greatest threat to their existence."

"Arlas, don't do this!" warned Azrael. "You may hate me. You may hate everything I have done. But do not leave our people unguarded against the perils of this world!"

"I am sorry," replied Arlas, raising his staff above the heart of his archnemesis. "But I will ensure that our order dies with me."

Arlas thrust down, and with a single blow, it all ended.

FORTY-EIGHT

Rhys walked out of the chapel and stood atop the steps. He had been given word that the kshatriya scouts were seen approaching, and sure enough, from out of the valley, Sol, Alkis, and Nathaniel appeared at the base of the steps with Ehani, Shankha, and Cetan close behind. The group of six began their ascent, and as they neared the top, Sol looked up, catching sight of Rhys. The mage halted. Alkis and Nathaniel stopped beside him, peering up at the mage in astonishment.

Rhys and Sol swiftly strode towards each other and locked in a firm embrace.

"I thought you were dead!"

"By all accounts I should be!"

The two magi released one another, and Rhys was suddenly flanked by both Nathaniel and Alkis, the two soldiers nearly crushing him between them.

"How in the world are you alive?" demanded Alkis.

"And how did you end up here?" added Nathaniel.

"Long story short," began Rhys, "I survived the fall and was found by Thia and the others."

"I don't understand," exclaimed Sol. "Maadurga said you were lost in the storm!"

"I got lucky," shrugged Rhys. "I'll tell you all about it. But first we need to hear what *you* have to say."

"Right," nodded Sol.

"Come on," gestured Rhys, "let's go inside."

"They are alive Rhys!" replied Sol. "We saw them!"

"That's great news!" sighed Rhys with relief.

"We might just have a chance to save them."

Together, they headed inside and were swiftly greeted by the others. Cetan spoke briefly in Elvish with Maadurga before everyone gathered around the brazier in the centre of the chapel to hear Sol and the others' report.

"We were right," began Sol. "Rudra was holding Arne, Eirik, and Vidar at Raraprambanan. They are still there; we saw them moved between two of the structures before we left. But I doubt they will remain put for long. Rudra and the entirety of his forces are readying to move. They are loading up their gryphons and readying their arms."

"They are preparing to attack Shambhala," declared Maadurga.

"Precisely," agreed Sol.

"We reckon Rudra and the bulk of his force will make for Shambhala," explained Alkis. "But at least some of his rakshasa will first head to Kalapa with Arne and his sons."

"It makes sense," nodded Rhys. "It's on route, and they wouldn't just leave them in Raraprambanan."

Sol nodded. "We figured they will head out together, or at least, they will travel in units at short intervals."

"I sense you have some semblance of a plan for a rescue?" asked Rhys

"We have more than that," replied Sol. "I'm not going to pretend that I know what the Cintamani Stone is, or what it is capable of, but I could feel the power radiating off of it, and I know that the conduits channel magical energy. Whatever happens, we cannot let Rudra make it to the conduit in Shambhala."

Everyone spoke up in agreement.

"We have already discussed this," explained Maadurga. "But we do not know how to get to Shambhala."

"That is why we let Rudra show us the way," announced Sol.

"Huh," mused Rhys.

"Here me out," began Sol, already justifying his idea against criticism. "We know that Rudra will be heading to Shambhala. We know that we don't have the numbers to face him on our own. So, we wait. We hide amongst the mountains and the clouds around the Temple of Brahma, much like the kshatriya did at Mahakaleshwar, and we wait for Rudra and his forces to leave. Then, we follow, staying far enough behind so that we don't alert them to our presence. We let them show us the safe way up to Kalapa and Shambhala. We wait for them to attack the city. That's when we rescue Arne, Vidar, and Eirik—whilst the Wild Hunt thin out their numbers against the Ascendant. If Rudra and his elves manage to break through the city's outer defences, then we engage; we strike when they are no longer at full strength. And maybe... just maybe, if the Ascendant see that we have come to their aid, they might refrain from attacking us as well."

When Sol finished speaking, silence fell amongst the others.

"Well, come on then?" pressed Sol. "Out with it. What's the big thing I've overlooked?"

The others exchanged a series of looks between them.

"Nothing," shrugged Rhys. "I don't think you've overlooked anything. It's so brilliantly simple. I think it will work."

"Oh?" responded Sol, somewhat taken back.

"This is a good plan," declared Maadurga.

"I agree," added Thia. "We can rescue Arne, Vidar, and Eirik and make our move against Rudra at the same time."

"And if we wait until after the rakshasa have engaged with the Ascendant, we might just have a chance at this," insisted Alkis.

"So, we are all in agreement then?" asked Rhys looking around the circle.

Everybody nodded.

"Then what are we waiting for?" questioned Maadurga, before rapidly giving Ehani, Shankha, and Cetan a series of orders in Elvish.

The three elven kshatriya nodded and hastily exited the chapel to begin preparations for the attack.

"That went better than I expected," Sol mumbled quietly to Rhys as a bustle of action began to occur throughout the sanctuary.

"It's a good plan," insisted Rhys, patting his friend on the back. "Certainly better than *my* last one!"

"Hey," argued Sol, "that plan got us all out of that pagoda alive and dealt the Wild Hunt a serious blow. They must have lost a third of their forces during the attack."

"No," refused Rhys, "the whole of Mahakaleshwar being ripped apart—that wasn't part of my plan. If anything, that was an accident."

"You mean you didn't mean to do that?"

"No."

"Oh," mused Sol. "I thought you were joking when you said you improvised. I was wondering why you didn't give the rest of us any warning."

"All a happy accident I am afraid," smiled Rhys. "Or an unhappy one perhaps, given that it nearly got me killed."

"Yeah. No, you are right," agreed Sol smiling. "Your plan was terrible!"

"Come on," beckoned Rhys, shaking his head. "We don't want everyone to leave without us."

"Right," agreed Sol, leaving to go make his preparations.

As Rhys turned to do the same, he found himself faced with Maadurga.

"You are going to ride on Dawon with me."

"I wouldn't have it any other way," replied the mage with a smile.

"After what happened last time, I am not letting you out of my sight!"

"All things considered, I think that is quite wise."

"And no *'improvising,'* this time!" she warned.

"Fair enough," agreed the mage.

"Now come," she insisted. "We must be quick, or we will miss the rakshasa when they leave."

FORTY-NINE

Rhys gripped the cantle of the double-seated saddle, his thighs clutched around Dawon, feet wedged tightly in the stirrups. Hanging off the rugged mountainside with his raptor talons and feline claws, the gryphon was perched on an almost sheer face. Rhys and Maadurga leant back in the saddle, as upright as possible, both sat in silence, waiting. Snowflakes drifted through the breeze, swells of mist flowing between the floating alps.

"There," breathed Rhys, releasing the cantle with one of his hands to point below.

Maadurga nodded.

From out of the clouds a hundred fathoms down emerged the first span of dark wings. The rakshasa was swiftly followed by dozens more, and suddenly, the sky below was swarming with the entire cavalcade of Rudra's army. Nearly two hundred gryphons were inflight, swooping and soaring between the maze of stone, clouds, and swirling gravity currents. The Wild Hunt meandered silently through the sky, their numbers thinning as one by one they vanished into the gloom, until finally, the last trailing riders had passed under Rhys and Maadurga.

"Now," whispered the mage.

Maadurga gently spurred her mount and the monstrous gryphon took his cue. Releasing his grip of the cliffside, Dawon tucked in his legs and pinned back his wings, dropping from the precipice, diving into the sea of clouds below. Adrenaline shot through Rhys's veins; he wrapped his arms tightly around Maadurga's waist, clinging on to the elf and gryphon for dear life. Dawon continued to pick up speed as they plunged groundward; Rhys fought back the urge to scream in terror.

Continuing to dive, the mage peered around. Issuing from the concealment of countless crooks and crannies of the surrounding cliffs, the rest of the kshatriya began to take flight, diving into the skies as they followed Maadurga's lead. Suddenly the air flocked with a second army, the cavalcade of Kalki plummeting into the clouds in pursuit of the Cŵn Annwn.

Maadurga tugged back on the reins. The enormous creature beneath her spread his feathers, pitching his beak back upwards. Rhys strained against the downforces pressing him into the saddle, Dawon swooping from out of the nosedive, levelling off to a sustained altitude. Gliding momentarily on the momentum garnered from the descent, Dawon then began to beat his wings powerfully, fighting against the oncoming wind.

Mist and snow streamed towards them and the sky started to darken. Lightning flashed as they raced to catch up with the rakshasa ahead. Boulders and cliffs emerged from out of the murk, silhouetted against the fog with the glare of each lightning fork. Maadurga twisted and turned, subtly offering her mount guidance with the stirrups and reins; Dawon followed her lead, banking left and then sharply right to narrowly sail between the gaps in the stone.

"Hold on," warned Maadurga as they sighted the next cluster of rocks suspended in the clouds ahead.

Rhys gripped tighter, gritting his teeth in preparation. Dawon swooped beneath the underside of a hillock, fanning his pinions to brake, before veering sideways, banking sharply on the air currents. The giant mount briefly planted his feet on a boulder and pounced from its surface, using the rock to change direction sharply in time to avoid colliding with the hillside ahead. A thrum of his wings gave him a quick burst of uplift, carrying himself and his two riders upwards again as they cleared the floating rock formation and drove higher into the sky.

Emerging from out of the cloud, Rhys caught sight of the last few rakshasa at the rear of their enormous convoy. He glanced sideways to see Shankha pull alongside them, Sol in the rear seat of his double saddle.

"We need to get closer," urged Sol, shouting over the volume of the ripping wind, "or we'll lose them!"

"If we get too close they will see us!" warned Maadurga.

"We have to risk it!" insisted Rhys. "If we lose them, it is all over."

Maadurga nodded and Shankha pulled away. Kicking her feet in the stirrups, the elf urged Dawon on. Beating his giant wings, the gryphon drove against the air, forcing harder into the wind. The rear of the rakshasa flock drew closer, just as the next oncoming cloud swallowed them. Snow and hail streaked past. They continued to climb higher and higher, ascending towards the upper skies of Sumeru. Dawon dipped and swerved to avoid more onrushing hills, soaring ever faster into the tempest, until up ahead, the silhouette of flared wings re-emerged through the storm.

"Keep on his tail," insisted Rhys.

The rakshasa in front lunged suddenly upwards, narrowly clearing a peak as it rushed out of the haze. Dawon spread his feathers, delivering a tremendous downward thrust. Clawing at the hill's crown with his rear feet, the beast sprung off the snow, launching himself and his riders clear, continuing to give chase.

For several minutes, they maintained their pursuit of the rakshasa army, hanging back to remain undetected. Dawon banked and wove between stacks and boulders, swooping and diving under archways and over mounds, veering this way and that in a helter-skelter run through the air. At several points, gravity took full hold of their ascent, Dawon tucking in his wings as if he were diving, allowing the warped drag of gravity to send him and his riders swirling along the path.

Emerging suddenly through the cloud tops into blue skies, Rhys realised they were out in the open. The rearmost rider of the rakshasa horde peered back over his shoulder and caught sight of the vanguard of kshatriya in pursuit. He shouted to the nearest of his brethren, and a dozen rakshasa peeled off from the Wild Hunt, dropping back to assail those giving chase.

"We've got incoming," warned Rhys, drawing his staff from the strappings on Dawon's rump.

Dropping several feet, Maadurga directed Dawon back into the cloud cover racing underneath, vanishing from sight as the rakshasa fell back to engage them. Lightning glared as the murk recondensed around them, the sky darkening as they sank deeper into the cover of the storm. A shadow of a gryphon rider loomed from out of the fog on their flank and Maadurga released her grip of the reins to reach for the bow stowed across the horn of her saddle.

"Hold him steady," commanded Rhys, taking aim.

The closing rakshasa suddenly veered out of the haze towards them, kukri drawn, mount lunging for Rhys and Maadurga with talons outstretched. Maadurga shifted her legs, instructing Dawon to roll, and Rhys felt his stomach invert. Tucking his wings in tight, Dawon twirled in the air, flipping upside-down, his riders kept in the saddle by the momentum of the corkscrew, all three righted again as the gryphon swivelled back around.

Turning his head in dizzying confusion, Rhys realised their enemy was now on the opposite side. Thrusting his staff at the rakshasa, Rhys let loose a fist of force energy. The bolt crunched into the gryphon's wing as it recovered from its swoop, feathers crumpling in the impact. The rakshasa cried out as his mount suddenly plunged out of the sky with him still in the saddle.

"Ahead!" cautioned Maadurga.

More wings flared through the glare of the storm, another gryphon swooping down talons-first from directly in front. Dawon dove and Maadurga reclined, Rhys pressed back into the saddle behind her. Threading an arrow onto her string, the elf loosed her bow, the missile zipping out of sight the instant the gryphon streaked narrowly overhead. Maadurga righted herself and Rhys craned his head rearward. Expecting to see the winged mount curving back around for another attack, instead Rhys watched the hound plummet from the air, Maadurga having pulled off a seemingly impossible shot.

"On our left!" called Rhys, as from out of the murk, another rider drew level with them.

The rakshasa nocked an arrow and began to draw. But before he could get his shot off, Rhys unleashed a gout of fire. The elf's mount veered away to avoid being roasted, the rakshasa's arrow sailing wide. The hound drew from his quiver again. Rhys readied to return another attack, yet before he could do so, a streak of lightning arced sideways out of the cloud, electrocuting both gryphon and rider. The rakshasa slumped forwards in the saddle, the gryphon hanging momentarily aloft, suspended on outstretched wings. But as the dead beast's pinions slackened, it slowed, dipping out of sight, vanishing in the gloom below.

Sol, the origin of the thunderbolt, drew parallel with Rhys on the rear of Shankha's saddle. "We are falling behind!" the mage warned. "We'll lose them in the storm if we aren't careful!"

Maadurga looked the mage's way and issued a nod of acknowledgement. Gliding clear of Shankha's mount, she willed Dawon to fight back upwards. Dawon powered higher and higher until the wisps of mist forming the upper ceiling of the cloud receded beneath them. With the rest of Kalki's cavalcade close behind, Rhys and Maadurga erupted through the ocean of storm clouds, emerging back into open skies once more. Above, the Rift burned lilac and green in the deep blue heavens. The sun glared through the parting tempest and Rhys caught sight of a lone cluster of islands suspended aloft in the highest reaches of the sky. From atop the airborne isles, the sunshine glimmered in a reflective glare. Shielding his eyes from the dazzling sheen, Rhys realised he was looking at nothing less than the Golden City itself.

"There it is!" gasped Rhys, pointing above his head as the clouds moved swiftly to obscure his view. "Shambhala!"

"We must be close," declared Maadurga, continuing to spur Dawon on after the fading shadows of Rakshasa ahead.

Suddenly, Rhys felt blood rushing to his head. Dawon accelerated, not of his own doing, and they were lifted rapidly skyward. The gryphon folded in his pinions, flipping upside down to account for the inversion of gravity, following the invisible flow of air launching them upwards towards their destination. Thunder drummed and electricity glared. Dawon dove higher in a twirling helix, letting only the pull of the Rift drive him. Hale and snow whirled in the icy winds and Rhys's eyes began to water as they accelerated faster than they had ever flown before. In a dizzying moment of deceleration, they erupted through the top of the clouds into another expanse of clear blue.

Dawon rolled upright and stretched out his wingspan, levelling his flight into a steady glide. Rhys overcame his vertigo and glanced ahead. A rugged horn of stone and ice rose starkly above an expansive plateau. Around the peak, the great horde of the Cŵn Annwn pitched upward into the sky, banking in a wide arc as they encircled the horn, turning back in ascent as they continued on towards Shambhala.

"That's it," declared Maadurga, pointing to the peak ahead. "Kalapa!"

"The leviathan's lair," breathed Rhys in dread as he watched numerous rakshasa peel away from the main flock to descend towards the plateau. "I don't see the dragon," he announced with relief.

"It will be in the depths below," shouted Maadurga.

"Then we might just be able to do this," replied Rhys. "Take us in!"

Maadurga kicked her feet in the stirrups and Dawon resumed the beating of his wings, accelerating on the sweeping airflows towards the foot of the horn. Watching the rakshasa land on the plateau ahead, Rhys caught sight of Arne, Vidar, and Eirik fighting against their restraints as they were dragged from the saddles to which they'd been hogtied. The bindings around their ankles were cut, and each of the three sailors were hauled to their feet with blades at their throats, dragged over the icy plateau to several upright steaks driven into the ground. The rakshasa swiftly clapped manacles around their prisoners' wrists, chaining their hands above their heads and securing them to the posts.

Dawon descended, touching down into a sprint across the snow, the elastic muscles of his feline haunches propelling him and his riders at full pelt towards the rakshasa ahead. The riders of the Wild Hunt shouted in alarm as the army of kshatriya descended upon them. A hailstorm of arrows took flight, and chaos ensued. Dawon skidded to a halt and Rhys and Maadurga both leapt from the saddle. Maadurga began loosing a fusillade at the surrounding rakshasa whilst Rhys charged headlong into the skirmish ahead. He veered left and right, nimbly avoiding arrows and kukris alike as his ethereal blade whirled in cleaving arcs, cutting down any rakshasa in his way.

The Aether shook with violent waves as dozens of elves, both kshatriya and rakshasa, were struck out of existence to reshape back in material form, each blinking towards and away from their opponents in the frantic ambush. An explosive cannonade of lightning shocked through the remaining hounds in Rhys's path as Sol appeared at his side, discharging the build-up of electricity his staff had conducted during his flight through the storm.

"Sol! Rhys!" Arne and his sons called out in near unison as the two mages rushed over to aid them.

"You came for us!" cried Vidar with amazement, jostling the chains attaching him to the post.

"Of course we did!" scorned Sol, driving the point of his blade through one of the links of the sailor's restraints to prise it apart.

"After all," began Rhys, sundering Eirik's chains with his ethereal blade in a single cleave, "without you, who will sail us back home on the Marlin?"

"Thank you," issued Arne, as Rhys made

his way over to the sea captain. His face was black with bruising.

"This should never have happened," apologised Rhys, breaking the man's restraints.

"Where even are we?" asked Vidar as the link Sol had been working on sprang open and his hands were freed. "Why are we here?"

"Perhaps its best you don't know," suggested Rhys.

"We'll tell you later," promised Sol. "Right now, you need to get out of here!"

"Maadurga!" Rhys called out as the elf cut down a rakshasa.

She peered Rhys's way to see that the prisoners had been freed. Sticking her fingers in her mouth, the elf whistled loudly, and from out of the sky landed a trio of kshatriya.

"Come on," urged Sol, gesturing for Arne and the others towards the three gryphons.

"Tin harula Suraksa dinohosa!" ordered Maadurga.

The elves nodded in agreement as Sol and Rhys guided the three sailors through how to approach the beasts. After a hasty greeting that seemed only to perturb the three gryphons, Arne, Vidar, and Eirik managed to gently place their hands on their feathers. Once their respective riders were content their mounts would allow the seamen to climb onto their backs, they each helped their respective passenger clamber up into the saddle.

"Don't worry," assured Sol. "They will take you to safety."

"You aren't coming with us?" questioned Vidar in confusion.

"No," Sol shook his head gravely, looking

up into the sky where the city of Shambala sparkled beneath the brewing tempest that had begun to swirl around the Rift. "There is something we have to do first."

"You can't be going up there!?" cried Eirik in horror.

"They have to," uttered Arne, the wise captain clearly understanding that whatever their task, it was of great importance.

"Be safe," offered Rhys, issuing the three of them a goodbye.

"Don't let go!" instructed Sol, nodding to the beasts on which they were mounted.

The two magi gave the three gryphons a wide berth, and one by one, they each spread their wings and took to the air, gliding over towards the edge of the plateau. Rhys and Sol moved closer towards the clifftops and watched as the three sailors vanished into the cloud cover. When their friends finally faded from view, Rhys felt a panicked elbow suddenly jabbing him in the ribs.

"Rhys!" blubbered Sol in alarm as he pointed to a floor of white cloud spread out from the eastern fringes of the horn.

The mage watched as the smoky veil began to bulge and mound. Seconds later, the vapour started to evaporate away, finally ripping open in the moments that followed. An albino draconic head reared from out of the cloud, followed swiftly by a spiny neck and colossal wingspan. The leviathan erupted from the storm, swooping straight upwards into the air, soaring high above the horn of Kalapa. Its immense wings unfolded overhead, briefly blotting out the sun, casting a gigantic shadow across the plateau.

"I think, Sol, that might be the part of the plan that you overlooked," mumbled Rhys as he stared wide-eyed at the dragon banking on the winds, the great wyrm turning in a vast circle to descend towards the mountain.

"Shit!" cried Sol in alarm as the colossal monster straightened its run and began to swoop their way.

The gryphons circling in the sky above scattered, kshatriya and rakshasa caught in mêlées atop the plateau disengaging from one another to leap back into their saddles and take flight. Cries rang out and panic ensued as all began to flee in terror at the sight of the leviathan.

"Come on!" urged Sol as they began to run back towards Maadurga and Shankha.

"Maadurga!" Rhys shouted, waving his arms above his head to signal his position to the elf stood scanning the chaos.

Maadurga whistled and Dawon swooped down to land beside her. The kshatriya leapt into the saddle of her mount and Shankha did the same, but as Rhys glanced up past them both, he watched in horror as the dragon descended towards them. The leviathan parted its enormous maw, and from down its gullet, an amber blaze surged.

"Oh no," breathed Rhys, skidding to a halt across the rime.

Sol slowed as he too realised what was about to happen. Together, the two magi turned and began running back the direction they had come. Peering back over his shoulder, Rhys watched as Maadurga and Shankha spotted the impending doom and spurred their mounts into the air. A column of fire erupted from the dragon's jaws as it strafed the ground. An inferno scorched over the plateau, consuming all beneath it caught in the blaze. Maadurga and Shankha managed to narrowly escape immolation as they veered away from the pillar of fire. But as the dragon glided Rhys and Sol's way, the incinerating cone swept towards them.

    Looking ahead, Rhys realised both he and Sol had unsuspectingly charged right to the very edge of the plateau. They were trapped with no means of escape. Sol ground to a halt and looked back as the column of fire raced towards them. Rhys continued on. Shoving Sol square in the chest, Rhys pushed the mage over the cliff, and in a terrifying moment of nausea, he dove after him.

FIFTY

Fire surged above as Rhys plunged over the edge. The blistering heat of the blaze seared around him, dissipating as the leviathan scudded across the sun. Rhys was plummeting, Sol tumbling a few fathoms ahead. Wind whipped across the mage's face. The cliffsides vanished, the floor of clouds quickly approaching. Wings swept underneath as Shankha and his mount snatched Sol from out of the air. Rhys frantically scanned his surroundings, hoping that Maadurga was close behind.

Slowly, Dawon's hulking form emerged under Rhys's feet as the gryphon descended in a nosedive to draw level with him. Maadurga clasped her fingers around Rhys's gambeson, dragging him out of the air and into the saddle. Wrapping his arms around his saviour, the mage threaded his boots into the stirrups as Maadurga yanked back on the reins.

Dawon pulled up, abandoning the dive, swooping back skyward. Beating his wings mightily, the gryphon powered upwards, racing to draw clear of Kalapa. Rhys peered back at the dragons' lair and watched as the leviathan lined up for another strafing run, the elves still trespassing atop the plateau locked in its sights.

"That was close," wheezed Rhys, his heart beating so furiously he felt he could barely breathe.

"You are telling me!" returned Maadurga.

Rhys gazed around as the cavalcade of kshatriya steadily flocked around him and Maadurga in formation, Sol and Shankha taking up position just behind Dawon at the head of the pack. Cade, aback Ehani's mount, and Alkis in the saddle with Cetan, drew in on Rhys's left. Finally, Thia riding with Tilak, followed closely by Cade and Ulfgar, glided over to the right. Looking back, it seemed the majority of those caught in the inferno of the leviathan's wrath were mostly those who revered the wyrm as an incarnation of their god.

Rhys peered ahead, towards the glimmering sight of Shambhala. The Golden City spread across the floating archipelago, rising as the highest peak of Sumeru. Shining finials peaked amongst the glinting buildings, countless stupas scattered over a half dozen isles separated at different heights. The Rift raged above, swirling black clouds taking form around it as plumes of fog were drawn upwards from the lower sea of cloud to feed the tempest. Lightning flashed, thunder rumbled, and the sky darkened as they approached. Rhys made out the occasional rider of the Wild Hunt flying through the drowning air currents of the storm, but the skies above Shambhala were emptier than he would have thought them to be.

"The Chaitya is at the heart of the city," explained Maadurga, as they began to draw near enough that Rhys could make out parts of the city in more detail. "If Rudra has made it past the

Amara, he will be there."

"If you take us in low, I should be able to guide us to the conduit," explained Rhys, concentrating in an attempt to sense the presence of the standing stones.

The Aether raged with turbulence this close to the Rift. What he had heard as mere whispers on the mountainsides below now roared in tumultuous wails through the mage's awoken mind. He focussed, pushing himself into samadhi to make sense of the violent waves ebbing from the Rift, but Rhys's concentration was suddenly broken. A missile streaked through the air, narrowly missing his brow. Rhys glanced around as a hail of arrows rained up at them from the edges of the city below. Elves cried out and gryphons shrieked as several mounts and riders were struck by the oncoming barrage.

The flock of kshatriya scattered in the chaos. Maadurga drove Dawon low as they swooped towards the outskirts of Shambhala. Dawon let out a sudden harrowing screech. Rhys peered down to see the fletchings of an arrow wedged between his feathers, the shaft protruding from just beneath the gryphon's wing.

"Dawon!" cried Maadurga in despair, her mount quickly losing altitude.

Dawon ceased beating his wings, outstretching his pinions to prevent them from tumbling straight out of the air. His feathers splayed as the ground rushed up to meet them, but as he glided for a wide street on the outskirts of the city, his injured wing faltered. Together, the three of them dropped out of the sky.

Dawon's legs crumpled beneath him as they landed hard. Rhys was thrown from the saddle, slamming into the white setts as he tumbled end over end before rolling to a stop. The gryphon ground to a halt with Maadurga still clutching to his back, and as Rhys struggled painfully to his feet, he breathed a sigh of relief to see the elf clamber out of the saddle. Rhys rushed over to the elf as she inspected the arrow sunken into the base of Dawon's wing. The enormous hybrid huffed, keeling his head aside as his master nursed him. Grabbing the arrow shaft, Maadurga ripped the head free with a sharp tug. Dawon whined, clacking his beak in annoyance before lying back again as Maadurga pressed her palms over the bleed.

"Maadurga..." began Rhys unsure what to say or do.

"I cannot leave him," apologised the elf, bowing her head in shame. "Not out in the open like this. I need to get him inside—somewhere safe!"

"I understand," nodded Rhys.

Maadurga moved to put her hands under Dawon's body, encouraging him to stand. The gryphon groaned as he attempted to lift his weight up from the paving, but he slumped back to the ground, one of his legs giving way, the hindlimb injured in the crash.

"Here," offered Rhys moving to assist the elf, "let me help you!"

"No!" refused Maadurga. "There is no time!"

Rhys nodded, taking a step back.

"Rudra cannot reach the Chaitya with the Cintamani Stone. If he does, Sumeru will be destroyed. Head to the heart of the city and stop him. I will follow. I just need to get Dawon off the streets first!"

"Okay," Rhys agreed, clutching his staff. "Be safe."

"And you," she returned, firmly embracing him. "Now go!"

Rhys took one last look at Maadurga and Dawon and took off sprinting down the white street. He ran to its end and studied his surroundings, figuring out which way would lead him deeper into the heart of the sacred lost city. Spotting a higher islet floating ahead, Rhys knew which way to turn. He darted up a set of cracked steps and rushed past a stupa into a narrow side street.

Surveying the buildings as he raced past, Rhys realised the state of decrepitude Shambhala had fallen into. From afar, the buildings appeared like shining beacons of solid gold, but up close, Rhys could see now that they were merely painted. Furthermore, the gilded finish of the surrounding structures was cracked and peeling, in some cases almost entirely stripped away. Half the houses were in total ruin, and many of the stupas and shrines were crumbling to dust. The snowy roads were cracked and buckled from where the city had long ago been rent from the ground. Shambhala was more of a set of ancient ruins than a sacred paradise watched over by immortal guardians.

Rounding a corner, Rhys saw the alley open up to another wider throughway leading toward the city's centre. He dashed on, skidding to a halt an instant later as several dark clad rakshasa rushed past the entrance of the alleyway. None of them had caught sight of him. Rhys began to move again, but he could not help but feel troubled. He had only caught a short glimpse of the followers of Mahakala, yet it hardly appeared as if they were charging towards the conduit. If Rhys had to guess, he might have thought they were instead fleeing in terror.

Arriving at the threshold of the alleyway, Rhys poked his head out and peered warily both up and down the main thoroughfare. A few rakshasa bodies lay face down amongst the rubble, but the concourse was otherwise empty. Rhys stepped out of the shelter of the backstreet and hurried along the road ahead, but movement on the fringes of his vision caused him to stop and turn.

A mounted rakshasa descended from the sky and landed in the road beside Rhys, the archer aiming a fully drawn arrow at the mage. Rhys swung his staff to cast a blast of force at his foe, but before Rhys could attack, the rakshasa was unseated. A streak of violet hurtled out of the Aether and a dagger sank into the neck of the rider, toppling him from out of his saddle. The same blur lurched again, this time driving its blade into the top of the gryphon's head, slaying both rider and beast in one fell swoop.

Moving with supernatural haste, the creature that had slaughtered the hound and his mount dropped to the street and darted for Rhys, lunging with a horizontal-gripped push dagger. The triangular blade extended outwards from the creature's knuckles, the point spearing straight for Rhys. The mage leapt back, narrowly avoiding the swing, his heel snagging on a pile of rubble behind, toppling him off his feet.

Lying helpless on the ground, Rhys raised his staff in defence as the creature pounced at him with his katar. The elven shape descended on him, punch dagger lunging for the mage's throat, when suddenly, his head snapped sideways. The creature collapsed limp atop of Rhys, the katar clattering out of his grip. Rhys shoved the body aside, noting the arrow sunken through the creature's temple. Leaping to his feet, blade raised, Rhys gazed swiftly back up the road. The mage sighed, lowering his staff as Cade came jogging towards him, bow at his side, Thia close behind, armed with a kukri in one hand and wand in the other.

"Thank goodness it's you," breathed Rhys with relief, turning his attention back to the body of his slain attacker.

The creature was elven, but he resembled no elf Rhys had seen before. His eyes glowed supernaturally as two mauve orbs, the light rapidly fading now in death. The grey skin around his sunken eye sockets was cracked and darkened, the rest of his face stark and gaunt. Beneath his set of tarnished gilded armour was a wiry frame. Whilst alive, the guardian of the city had moved faster than any other elf Rhys had seen to date.

"I take it these are the Amara?" mused Rhys as he knelt to inspect the elf closer.

"Are you okay Rhys?" asked Cade. "We saw you and Maadurga go down."

"I'm fine, and so is Maadurga," insisted the mage. "What about you two?"

"A little rattled," replied Thia. "We didn't exactly have the softest landing either."

"I don't think anyone did," added Cade. "We got separated from the others when we were ambushed by the rakshasa. Ehani..." he trailed off.

"Damn it," breathed Rhys, sensing the anguish in Cade's voice.

"Tilak was killed as well," sighed Thia. "Cade and I were forced to retreat."

"Maadurga could use your help," announced Rhys, looking suddenly to Thia.

"Of course," nodded the witch eagerly.

"Well, technically, it is Dawon that needs help," elucidated the mage.

"Right," nodded Thia understanding Rhys's inference. "Where is she?"

"Down that alleyway there. Follow it to its end—head down the steps past the stupa; if she hasn't yet gotten Dawon off the street, you should find her easily enough."

"Got it," nodded the witch, visualising Rhys's directions.

Rhys turned to Cade. "Make sure she gets there safely."

"What about you?"

"I need to get to the conduit," replied Rhys solemnly. "Rudra cannot get there ahead of me."

"Rhys, you can't go alone!" refused Thia.

"I'm sure I'll find some of the others along the way," assured the mage.

"Alright," agreed the two of them reluctantly.

Cade patted him firmly on the shoulder and Thia embraced him tightly before the two of them kissed.

"Be careful!" she insisted.

"You know I won't be," smiled Rhys in return.

"I know," Thia groaned with annoyance. "I love you."

"I love you too."

"Go!" she insisted.

Rhys nodded, lingering for one last look at her before turning to dash off along the road once more. Speeding between the ruined houses, he passed a small temple, its finial laying on the ground at its feet beside the smashed dome of its gilded roof. On the mage hurried, swiftly crossing a court of decrepit shrines and broken altars before clambering up the remains of a staircase to the top terrace of the island. Reaching a gulf flooded with fog, Rhys traversed out onto a rope bridge suspended between the two isles, ascending to the next landmass in the tightly clustered chain.

Charging around a bend in the road, Rhys stumbled upon a skirmish between rakshasa and the Amara. The Ascendant rapidly slaughtered the outnumbering riders of the Wild Hunt, and as Rhys skidded to a halt on the fringes of the square, the immortal guardians turned to look at him with their violet glowing eyes.

Before Rhys knew what was happening, the three Ascendant before him were hurtling across the square with staggering speed. They lunged for him, katars pointed his way as they closed the distance in a matter of seconds. Rhys swung his staff, striking the ground, sending a shockwave of force at his charging foes. To his astonishment, a colossal tide of wind rent the paving from the ground, obliterating the enemies in his path.

When the dust settled, Rhys peered down at the emerald veins throbbing through his staff, surging brighter now than they had ever done before. In the same way Sol's weapon was overcharged by the lightning from the tempest, Rhys's staff was absorbing the turbulent energies of the Rift around him.

"Well, that's bound to be useful," Rhys muttered to himself, taking a moment to observe the mangled bodies of the Ascendant buried beneath the stone and soil.

Glancing around to ensure the square was clear, Rhys jogged across and climbed another set of broken steps to a stupa. He found himself perched on the edge of the isle. From this vantage point, he could spot most of the other surrounding islands. Scanning them each in turn, he watched several skirmishes unfold between amara, rakshasa, and kshatriya alike. The Ascendant seemed fewer in number than the other two sides, but as Rhys had just witnessed, the speed with which they moved seemed to easily overcome that disadvantage. Whether the Ascendant were actually immortal protectors who had achieved Nirvana, it was anyone's guess. But what seemed more likely to Rhys, was that the elven guardians had somehow been changed by the Rift itself. The distortions in the Aether were so chaotic this close to the rupture that Rhys could not begin to imagine what the long-term effects of exposure might be.

After spending several minutes reconnoitring the islands, Rhys realised the conduit was nowhere to be seen. He attempted to sense its presence amongst the ruins, but he gave up after a few seconds of trying; the conduit was definitely out there, he could feel it as clear as day, but trying to discern its location in the maelstrom of arcane energy swirling about the Rift was futile.

Returning to the search with his corporeal

senses, Rhys glanced above the isle on which he was stood. Several portions of the city were raised above his current altitude, but one island was suspended above the rest. If the Cintamani Stone being detonated within the conduit had truly created the Rift and brought about the sundering of Sumeru, then Rhys suspected the standing stones would be the closest thing to it. That was where he needed to go: towards the Rift, to Sumeru's highest peak.

Studying the way ahead, Rhys plotted his route. He would need to circumnavigate the city to the far side; there a single rope bridge ascended to the uppermost island. Rhys stepped back from the ledge and began making his way towards the bridge nearest to him. It was going to be a long and gruelling fight across Shambhala, but this was what he had been training for.

Suddenly overhead, a deafening roar drowned out the thunder peeling through the heavens. Rhys peered around, looking for its source, when from out of the storm, the leviathan descended. The draconic beast swooped down through the tempest, soaring over Rhys's head, gliding towards the lower regions of the city on its immense wingspan. Banking on a vortex of wind, the wyrm rained fire down on the ruins, immolating all that its infernal breath touched.

"No!" despaired Rhys as he watched an entire thoroughfare consumed in flame.

Whether the beast was retaliating for the invasion of its lair, or if it had simply pursued those fleeing up to the city from Kalapa, it was unclear. Rhys was certain the dragon was anything but the incarnation of Mahakala bent on foiling his attempts to stop Rudra, but he suspected many of the elves fighting throughout the ruins would not share his conviction. Whatever the case, the leviathan's assault on Shambhala was a complication he could never have accounted for; one that could spell doom for the whole of Sumeru.

FIFTY-ONE

Rhys clambered over the remnants of a collapsed stupa and emerged into another crumbling street. Fires raged amidst the ruin, whilst ash and snow swirled in the howling winds. The dragon continued its assault upon Shambhala, the din of fighting echoing through the thundering storm. The mage had made it halfway around the city's circumference. Several ambuscades launched by rakshasa and amara alike had ended abruptly, each sortie decisively won with a few overcharged blasts from Rhys's fizzling staff; but for the most part, the mage had managed to avoid the main bulk of the fighting.

Ducking under a partially collapsed torana, Rhys emerged upon a road littered with bodies. Kshatriya and rakshasa lay slaughtered side by side in the rubble, their corpses interspersed with the occasional dead amara. Steeling his resolve, Rhys jogged past the massacre and continued to make his way towards the next bridge on his way up to the conduit. Nearing the edge of the island, he heard a distant voice calling out his name over the clamour of battle.

"Rhys!" cried Sol again from afar.

Striding towards the ledge, Rhys scanned the battle, finally spotting his friend waving some way below. "Sol!" Rhys shouted in return.

Alkis and Ulfgar were stood beside the mage, along with a group of kshatriya. The isle on which they were gathered wasn't one Rhys had crossed. It floated only a furlong away, but was suspended nearly twenty fathoms down. There was no way for Rhys to reach it from where he was now.

"Stay there!" insisted Sol, shouting up to him. "We're going to try and find a way up to you!"

Rhys scanned the city below and identified the various bridges needed to be crossed for them to reconvene. Sol and the others could not have been in a worse position from Rhys. The only way they could reach him would be to skirt around the fringes of Shambhala, circumnavigating half the city in the process.

"I don't think you can!" lamented Rhys in frustration.

"Come back this way," replied Sol. "We'll meet you halfway."

"There's no time!" refused Rhys. "Head north from here. It will take you up towards the conduit. I'll meet you there."

Sol turned to the others beside him and had a brief inaudible conversation with them. "You're right," he finally agreed with reluctance. "Someone needs to get to the conduit before Rudra."

"Have you seen any of the others?" called out Alkis.

"Yes," Rhys shouted down. "I found Cade and Thia. They are safe!"

"We've not seen Nathaniel," warned Alkis.

"I'll look for him along the way."

A silence elapsed as Rhys peered down at his friends and them back at him.

"I'll meet you at the top," yelled Rhys, knowing that time was running out.

"Rhys," Sol called up to him one last time. "Don't do anything foolish!"

"This is me we are talking about—I always do something foolish!"

Though it was difficult to make out from this distance, Rhys believed he saw Sol issue him a weak smile. He returned his friend the same expression and turned away to make for the rope bridge. Dismounting the lines on the far side, Rhys sighted a skirmish ongoing between rakshasa and the Ascendant. Swerving into a backstreet, Rhys skirted a series of tight alleys, making his way around the conflict as the two opposing sides slaughtered one another. Emerging clear of the fray, Rhys dashed warily across a disintegrating temple complex and arrived at the next crossing.

Rhys stopped in his tracks. Far ahead, Rudra and his hounds were cutting their way through both amara and kshatriya. The First Warrior of the followers of Mahakala led their charge. Storming the lines of his enemies, the elf flourished his trident, cutting down any who dared stand in his path. The rakshasa pressed their advance, butchering the immortal guardians rushing to meet them in battle. Rudra fought out front, leading by example as he drove the tines of his weapon through the heart of the last amara standing. With the fight at an end, the head of the Wild Hunt paused, glancing suddenly back across the ruined cityscape in Rhys's direction.

The two adversaries locked eyes across the battlefield, before both took a moment to gauge their position in relation to the other. Rudra was ahead; only one last bridge stood between the elf and the highest island of Sumeru. Seeing that Rhys was trailing behind, he issued the mage a mocking smile and drew the fragment of Cintamani Stone from his pocket as he prepared to make the crossing

The deafening roar of the leviathan thundered from above. Rudra stooped, scanning the skies in terror as he searched for the incoming wyrm. Rhys dashed across the hanging bridge in front of him, traversing onto the next island. He caught sight of Rudra again as the rakshasa and his forces began the climb to the zenith of Shambhala. From out of the storm above, descended the white wings of the dragon. The beast swooped over the bridge on which Rudra was balanced and glided down towards the ground. Rhys felt the road quake underfoot as the leviathan landed in the centre of the island.

Flames tore out of the wyrm's gullet, a dozen agonised screams snuffed out in the raging firestorm ahead. The run of spines down the leviathan's back thrashed above the rooftops, buildings crumbling in great plumes of dust as the dragon wreaked havoc through the streets ahead, decimating any and all elves caught in its wrath.

Rhys gazed back up to Rudra in horror as he realised the beast of legend now lay between him and the conduit. Rudra quickly arrived at the same conclusion, no doubt seeing the event as an act of divine intervention. From the zealot's perspective, Mahakala had joined the battle to face Kalki himself, providing Rudra, his most loyal follower, with a clear path to the conduit at the heart of the Golden City. Now Rudra was free to fulfil his dharma, delivering the Cintamani Stone to the conduit where he would lay waste to the world, enacting the Destroyer's will and heralding in a new Golden Age. Rudra took one final glance at the leviathan in Rhys's path and issued the mage a smug grin from afar, before turning on his way, ascending the rope bridge towards his destiny above.

Rhys cursed, watching as the wyrm flattened the buildings in front of him. Though both rakshasa and kshatriya were fleeing in terror from the colossal reptile, the Amara rushed to engage the beast. They leapt and blinked to within range, some even succeeding in climbing atop the creature's back. They assailed the beast with katar, driving their punch daggers into its scaly hide, but the Amara's short blades seemed almost incapable of puncturing the dragon's armoured skin, most blows failing to even draw blood.

Despite its flesh being seemingly impregnable, the monster was enraged by the assault upon it nonetheless. It whipped its tail, crushing those behind it, simultaneously thrashing its wings in a series of downbeats; great currents of air swept outwards, blasting several nearby amara off their feet. Some of those knocked to the ground met their end beneath the dragon's gargantuan feet, whilst another torrent of fire erupting from down the wyrm's throat immolated any that remained.

The Amara were thinning fast, the surrounding rakshasa and kshatriya continuing to flee. The leviathan was a force to be reckoned with, decimating anything in its path, but for the next few seconds at least, it was distracted. If ever Rhys was going to have an opportunity to make it past the dragon, it was now.

Dashing into a side street, Rhys sprinted as fast as his legs would carry him. He vaulted over a heap of debris and darted around the rugged fringe of the isle. More screams sounded from the chaotic affray between the Amara and the leviathan, and as Rhys swivelled his head to look, he saw the dragon snatch one of the Ascendant from the ground and thrash it about in its enormous jaw. Tossing the elf's limp body aside, the beast locked its blood red eyes on Rhys.

The mage skidded to a halt, watching in horror as the jaws of death parted. The glow of a furnace burned down the wyrm's gullet, spewing from the beast's mouth in a torrent of fire and smoke. The street ahead vanished, swallowed in a sudden blistering inferno. Rhys felt his body crumple, a shoulder thumping hard into his gut as he was tackled to the ground. Flames licked narrowly past, the heat scorching around the cover of the low wall shielding Rhys

Nathaniel offered the mage a hand, helping his friend up off the ground, the two men rising to kneel in the concealment of a crumbling building.

"That was close," breathed Nathaniel with relief.

"Thank you," gasped Rhys.

Nathaniel peered through a crack in the wall and watched as the leviathan resumed its massacre of the Amara. "I don't think there is any way through this," he sighed. "We'll have to wait—hope it takes off again when it is finally done with whatever those things are."

Rhys peered up over the sill of a ruined window frame. More amara were arriving at the scene, assailing the colossal reptile with vehemence. They streaked around the creature in blurs of purple, sinking their blades into its scales in futility as it immolated and obliterated them with its terrible might. Rhys sat back, resting his head against the cold stone as snow and ash fluttered down around him. The eye of the tempest had opened above the uppermost island, the Rift's ribbons of lilac and verdant light burning at the heart of the vortex.

A distant screech sounded from amongst the tumult, and as Rhys peered into the sky, he saw a flight of gryphons soaring above the battle, up towards the peak of Sumeru. At the head of the vee, Rhys made out the orange and black markings of Dawon, upon his back rode Maadurga. Thia had managed to find the elf and heal Dawon enough to get them back into the air. Now they ascended towards the heart of the storm, avoiding the hails of arrows being fired at them from below as they made for the conduit. There was hope. But as Rhys watched several gryphons drop from the sky, he realised there were too few of them to stand a chance at stopping Rudra.

Rhys peered back over the window ledge at the battle raging between the Amara and the leviathan. A scorching wave of flame erupted from the wyrm's mouth, and the last few ascendant guardians of Shambhala were scoured from the street. The beast fell still, swivelling its head as it searched for more prey.

"Come on," whispered Nathaniel. "Just go! Leave! Fly away you dumb beast!"

Rhys continued to watch the colossal monster as it let its maw hang open. Its forked serpentine tongue wafted the wind, and the wyrm sucked in great swathes of air through its nostrils. Its head turned towards Rhys and Nathaniel's hiding place. The mage ducked back into cover, Nathaniel continuing to tentatively peer through the thin cracks in the wall.

"Shit!" whispered the guardsman. "It can smell us."

Rhys felt vibrations judder through the ruined house as the creature took several slow steps across the island.

"It's coming this way!" breathed Nathaniel in despair as he ducked beside the mage. "We need to make a run for it!"

"No," Rhys mumbled.

"What do you mean!?"

"You need to go," insisted the mage. "Maadurga is up there. She'll need your help stopping Rudra."

"And what are *you* going to do!?" demanded the guardsman, fearing he already knew the answer.

Rhys issued his friend a grave look.

"No," Nathaniel shook his head. "No, you can't!"

"I have to," insisted Rhys. "If I don't give you this chance—it will kill us both."

"No!" refused Nathaniel. "There has to be another way!"

"No, there isn't," insisted Rhys. "There isn't enough time."

Nathaniel looked back in despair at the mage.

"Besides," grinned Rhys weakly, "it's my destiny, isn't it?"

"But you don't even believe in any of that!"

"Maybe I should," Rhys shrugged, issuing another feeble smile.

"Rhys, I can't let you do this. *You* need to be up there—not me! Let me distract it. Let me draw it off so you can make it up there yourself."

"No," Rhys shook his head. "You won't stand a chance. It has to be me."

"Rhys, *you* won't stand a chance against that thing! It's too powerful... even for you."

"Please," insisted Rhys, resting a hand on his friend's shoulder. "Just do this."

Nathaniel bowed his head and pressed shut his eyes. He nodded.

"Thank you," smiled the mage.

"You are a good man, Rhys," offered the guardsman, clasping a hand firmly on the back of Rhys's neck and butting their foreheads together. "Best I've ever known!"

Nathaniel released the mage from his embrace.

"Thia..." began Rhys.

Nathaniel nodded. "I'll know what to say."

Rhys beamed at his friend one last time and climbed to his feet. "I'll draw its attention. The moment I do, you run, and don't look back!"

With that, Rhys stepped out of the ruins, into the scorched street where the leviathan lay in wait. The dragon locked eyes on him and snorted loudly as it beheld the mage steadily striding his way. Its leathery lips lifted and the monstrosity bared several rows of fangs. Slowly, its maw parted to reveal the fire burning deep inside its throat. Smoke issued from its nostrils, and as Rhys drew closer, a sea of flames erupted from its mouth, flooding down the street to engulf the mage.

Rhys drove his staff at the ground, feeling the surging power flowing down its length. The butt of the weapon cracked into the white sets, and as the inferno swallowed him, a bulwark of force ripped outwards from the ground. A crater was torn into the rock, and a shield of energy swept in front of Rhys, a protective ward forming between him and the maelstrom of fire raging beyond. Even inside the bubble of sheltering magic, Rhys could feel the searing heat, everything outside consumed in the firestorm. The conflagration raged for several seconds, before finally, the dragon's breath ran out and Rhys's shield of magic collapsed inward.

Rhys stood panting amidst a charred street of embers. The smoke and ash steadily lifted, revealing to the dragon that its quarry had survived unscathed. Though little more than a bestial intellect existed behind the wyrm's gaze, when Rhys peered into the leviathan's slitted eyes, he saw fear.

The dragon bellowed another ear shattering roar, revealing that the fire burning down its gullet had gone cold, the fuel of the beast's inner furnace temporarily exhausted. Serpentining its incredible hulking mass, the wyrm clawed at the street and rushed towards Rhys. Buildings toppled as its spiney tail thrashed in its wake. It gnashed its rows of teeth, rearing its head as it darted for the mage. Rhys stood his ground.

Sweeping his weapon in a powerful arc,

Rhys unleashed a torrent of wind and force that condensed into a tidal wave of kinetic energy. The swell of destruction hurtled down the road, churning up ash, ice, and stone as it ripped through the air towards the leviathan. The battering ram of magic collided with the charging beast, smashing square into the wyrm's nose. The monstrous fiend shrieked as its head was hammered aside, its neck coiling as the blow knocked the dragon from its feet. Careening sideways, the wyrm crashed into the buildings lining the road, smashing through the walls of stone as it tumbled helplessly over.

Rearing its bloodied head, Rhys saw the wyrm was missing half its teeth, its jaw shattered by the immense blow the mage had dealt it. It roared, clawing at the rubble as it fought back to its feet. Rhys marched forward. Gritting his teeth in fury, he charged, screaming as he stormed towards the beast. The leviathan parted its broken maw, the furnace inside its belly aflame once again. It roared, preparing to exhale another spout of fire.

Rhys lunged, launching an unrelenting salvo of attacks as he raced towards the dragon. A deafening cannonade thundered through the street, shockwave after shockwave ripping outwards. Buildings crumbled. The ground quaked. And shell upon shell of kinetic force bombarded the leviathan. The wyrm's wings folded, its legs buckled, its teeth shattered, and its neck flailed. The dragon collapsed, thrashing back into the rubble around it. Wisps of fire sputtered from between its fractured jaws, as grunting and whining, it struggled to heave its broken body back upright.

Still rushing towards his foe, Rhys lunged, leaping through the air in a soaring arc, staff raised high overhead. Streaking down through the fire and smoke, blade unfurling with a spectral howl, Rhys descended, spearing the jade point of his ethereal weapon through the slitted eye of the Leviathan. Rhys felt his staff drive into the soft flesh of the dragon's eyeball, rupturing through the rear of the socket, lancing deep into the grey matter beyond. The flailing tail of the wyrm spasmed and coiled, and billows of black smoke gushed from between the monster's lips. In a final contortion of muscle, the leviathan's colossal body fell dead.

Wheezing to catch his breath, Rhys staggered back, leaving his staff embedded in the eye socket of the dragon. He dropped to his knees in exhaustion. His chin sank against his chest as he felt the energy of the Aether steadily recharge his body. Slowly, he climbed back to his feet and peered into the sky above.

Rudra was on the precipice overhead. The rakshasa gazed down, his face horror-stricken as he peered at Rhys. The mage was still stood beside the corpse of the leviathan, the embodiment of his god. It was obvious the head of the Wild Hunt had watched the fight, witnessing Kalki slay Mahakala firsthand, spitting in the face of the prophecy upon which he and all who followed him had built their fanatical faith. Rhys had defied Brahman. In spite of everything Mahakala's most zealous follower believed, the mage had survived the battle with his god's final avatar, emerging the victor.

Enjoying the brief moment of satisfaction, Rhys cocked his head, issuing the fanatical leader of the rakshasa the same derisive grin that Rudra had given him minutes earlier. Rudra's horrified expression hardened to one of bitter resolve. He turned away from the precipice and vanished from sight.

Gripping the shaft of his bloodied staff in two hands, Rhys rent the weapon out of the dragon's eye. Leaping down from atop the rubble, Rhys watched, as from out of the shelter of the surrounding ruins, numerous survivors of the leviathan's wrath began to emerge. Both rakshasa and kshatriya appeared throughout the desolated streets, gazing at Rhys in awe as he stood beside the slain dragon.

The kshatriya all dropped to their knees, stretching their bodies prostrate across the ground in reverence of the mage. Glancing about at the followers of Kalki lying in prayer, one by one, the followers of Mahakala threw down their bows and kukris, kneeling beside their elven brethren to pay homage to Kalki.

FIFTY-TWO

Rhys leapt off the hanging bridge and rushed to the top of the steps. He gazed around the crumbling stupas and pagodas rising from the summit of Sumeru, searching frantically for the conduit. He climbed over a mound of debris and sighted both Maadurga and Rudra some way ahead. The two elves, both First Warriors of their people, were in a duel of blades as they danced gracefully through the ruins of Shambhala, dodging and countering each other's advances as Maadurga's kukris clashed against Rudra's trident.

Rhys descended the slope of rubble and began to race towards them. Sprinting through the ruin, he watched as they exchanged blows, countering and riposting in a tightly bound mêlée. Suddenly their weapons locked, the three prongs of Rudra's trident pincering Maadurga's crossed kukris. The rakshasa dealt a knee to Maadurga's gut. She recoiled, staggering back. Rudra thrust again, lunging with his trident. Recovering her footing, the kshatriya twirled clear in a pirouette, narrowly parrying away her foe's strike, deflecting the blow groundward. She swung to counterattack, but Rudra rent back his weapon and the barbed tines sliced across the back of Maadurga's calf.

Maadurga screamed as the leather of her boot splayed open, blood issuing from the wound beneath. She dropped to one knee, raising a kukri above her head in defence as Rudra swung down at her. Her blade clattered to the ground, spinning out of her fingers as the trident struck it from her grip. Lunging with her other weapon, she slashed desperately for the rakshasa, but reversing his trident, Rudra blocked the slash, knocking the kukri aside and sending it flying.

Disarmed and helpless, Maadurga tilted back her head, glaring up at Rudra as the zealot stood over her. Raising the barbed prongs to the kshatriya's throat, Rudra drew back his trident and thrust.

"No!" Rhys roared in terror, too far away to intervene.

The three tines speared down at Maadurga, sinking into the wooden bulwark of a heater shield. Charging out of the ruins, Nathaniel had darted between the two elves just in time to intercept Rudra's killing strike. Driving with his full might, Nathaniel shoved the rakshasa back, ramming the elf with the face of his shield, sending Rudra stumbling away. Pressing the advantage, Nathaniel swung his axe in a series of cleaves. The rakshasa staggered left and right, clumsily dodging the incoming barrage of axe blows.

Rhys hurtled through the ruins, weaving between pillars and vaulting piles of rubble as he made for the two men locked in battle.

Finally regathering himself, Rudra parried, skipping gracefully away from the next incoming strike. Throwing himself headlong after his foe, Nathaniel continued to hack at the elf with unreserved aggression. Backpedalling, Rudra span, knocking Nathaniel's weapon aside with a circular counter. Nathaniel followed up the strike, lunging with all of his might, throwing his entire weight into the blow. Rudra jinked aside, capitalising as Nathaniel overcommitted to the swing.

His axe sailing through nothing but thin air, Nathaniel stumbled. He raised his shield in desperate defence to block an incoming strike, but the rakshasa was too fast for him. Rudra's trident clove down on Nathaniel's elbow, rending the limb clean at the joint. Nathaniel let out a harrowing scream as his severed forearm dropped to the ground, his axe clattering across the stone. The guardsman dropped to his knees, blood spurting from his dismembered limb. His shield slumped to his side as he looked up at Rudra. Offering no mercy, the rakshasa speared down at his foe, driving the three points of his trident into Nathaniel's chest.

Rhys screamed in despair.

Nathaniel let out a final gasp as he was impaled by the trident.

Rudra span to Rhys's haunting cries. Seeing the mage draw near, he turned, fleeing off through the temple complex.

Rhys dropped, sliding on his shins through the snowy rubble. He clasped hold of Nathaniel, catching the guardsman as he slumped to the ground. Nathaniel's eyes rolled upwards, his gaze locking with Rhys's for a brief instant. He blinked, his lips quivering into one last pained smile. Then, without warning, the light faded from his gaze.

"No... No... No, no, no!" pleaded Rhys as his friend's head slumped backward, the guardsman's eyes lulling shut. "No. Please!" he begged as tears burnt hot and fierce in his eyes. He pressed his palm against Nathaniel's cheek. He looked down to see himself covered in his friend's blood. His hand moved to the wound, still oozing hot and incarnadine. Nathaniel was dead.

"Kalki..." winced Maadurga, clutching her leg as she dragged herself over towards Rhys.

Rhys reared his head, awaking from a stupor, suddenly feeling cold and alone.

"Kalki..." Maadurga struggled again. "Rudra... you have to stop him!"

Rhys raised his gaze. Across the complex of ruined shrines, he caught his first glimpse of the conduit: eleven sarsen stones seated in the very heart of the Golden City. Fleeing across the broken remains was Rudra, making straight towards the stone circle.

"I'll watch him," offered Maadurga, placing a hand gently on Nathaniel's brow.

Rhys gritted his teeth and relinquished his grip of Nathaniel. He clasped his staff up from the ground, rising to his feet. His body shook with rage, his hands trembling in blind fury. Locking the rakshasa in his sights, Rhys broke into a sprint, giving chase to the man who had murdered his friend.

Thunder drummed and lightning surged through the raging tempest. Snow, hail, and ash rained down across Shambhala. Rhys hurtled through the ruin, weaving between stupas and the crumbling foundations of a gilded pagoda.

On he charged, chasing down the servant of the Destroyer, through the desolate remains of the Golden City, closing the gap as the stone circle rushed towards him. Sliding to a halt through the rime, he arrived at the bottom of the steps leading to the conduit. There, stood in the heart of the stone circle before the altar, was Rudra. In his hand he clutched the fragment of the Cintamani Stone, but to both his and Rhys's confusion, it was not the only piece of the cataclysmic artefact present. Orbiting above the altar were several other shards of dark burnished stone, each etched with the same runes that inscribed the standing stones surrounding them, floating in the air as they encircled one another.

"It's over, Rudra!" Rhys screamed over the raging storm. "Your god is dead! I killed it!"

"This world has to end!" roared Rudra in fury. "Only then can we be reborn!"

"This is madness!" boomed Rhys. "You don't know what will happen! No one does! If you go through with this... the world could just end! There might not be a Golden Age! You were wrong about the leviathan. You were wrong about me! What makes you think you aren't wrong about this!?"

"I know what I have to do," insisted the elf, studying the chunks of the ancient weapon swirling in the air before him, weighing the piece in his own hand. "If Mahakala cannot kill you, then I will do it myself!"

Rudra thrust the fragment of the Cintamani Stone above the altar and drew back his empty hand. The black shard began to revolve, the other pieces suddenly reacting to its presence. Together, the remnants of the Stone began to spin faster and faster, their orbits drawing tighter upon themselves as the ancient doomsday weapon prepared to reform.

Rudra darted out from the circle and down the steps, lunging at Rhys with his trident. Rhys's ethereal blade uncurled from the air and the two of them clashed weapons. Rhys leapt back, avoiding a twirl from Rudra's trident, stepping away a second time as the bladed prongs cut an inch short of his face. Rudra thrust low. Rhys struck the trident with the edge of his blade, sending it lurching wide.

The rakshasa lunged again, driving at Rhys with his triple-pronged spear. Rhys parried and their weapons locked together. Blades entangled, both mage and rakshasa swivelled their grips, manipulating one another's weapon through the bind. The staff and trident looped and curved in a quick bout of arcs, before finally Rhys's fluke dislodged from Rudra's tines and their weapons parted.

Exchanging blows back and forth, they dodged and countered in a dizzying bout of ripostes and parries. Rudra dealt a kick into the mage's knee, sending him staggering back, but as the rakshasa darted after Rhys, the mage struck the floor with his weapon, launching a shockwave rippling outwards.

The storm swelled to a crescendo overhead. Lightning began forking down from the Rift, striking the sarsen of the conduit as the orbiting pieces of the Cintamani Stone drew tighter and tighter together. The runes etched into the fragments started to glow with white heat, those cut into the standing stones mirroring the effect. Wind gushed outwards from the conduit, sweeping snow and dust into the air as powerful gales surged away from the reforming weapon.

Rhys felt the Aether distort as Rudra blinked, but with the fabric of reality so turbulent this close to the churning Rift, the elf snapped suddenly back into existence, expelled from the Aether in the opposite direction, cast off his feet. Rhys rushed his foe. Rudra nimbly flipped back upright. The mage leapt off the ground, swinging his staff down overhead with all his might. Rudra raised his trident horizontally in defence.

Arcing for his foe, Rhys's ethereal blade ignited, the jade weapon surging with light as it fizzled and sparked, cutting through the air on its downward trajectory. The spectral edge struck the gilded shaft of the rakshasa's weapon, hewing clean through the metal, slicing into Rudra's neck, carving through to his torso.

Rudra's trident parted, its two halves clanging against the stone as his arms slumped at his sides. Blood spurted from the rakshasa's cloven chest, his eyes locking with Rhys's. The mage rent his staff free, and Rudra collapsed dead in the snow.

Shielding his eyes against the blistering winds and radiating light erupting from the Cintamani Stone, Rhys fought against the gales and ascended the steps to the conduit. Grasping hold of one of the sarsen stones, Rhys drove his weight forwards, leaning into the torrent of air and energy being expelled from the ancient weapon. He battled up the last few steps and dropped to his knees at the altar. Raising his hand, he slid it across the stone and felt the grooves of the Atlas under his fingers.

The stone awakened under his palm, and as Rhys focussed his mind, he felt the raging power of the Rift channelling through the Cintamani Stone and into the conduit. The fragments were pulling together in a maelstrom of energy, the forces of magnetic attraction overcoming those of repulsion. The Cintamani Stone was forcing itself together, being forged anew by the energies of the Aether. If it recombined, Rhys could not fathom what would happen, but as he felt his own will and control over the Aether being concentrated and focussed by the conduit, he sensed he had the power to stop it.

Pushing his mind into a state of powerful focus, Rhys felt the pieces orbiting chaotically above his hand through the violent churning it exerted on the Aether. Driving with his thoughts, he fought against the imploding stones, lending his own strength to the repulsive energies battling the reforging. His mind cried out in agony. His body contorted. Converging his thoughts, using every technique of mental fortitude Shakyamuni had taught him, he compelled the shards, prising the fragments back apart. But it wasn't enough. Rhys could not simply prevent the Cintamani Stone from being remade. If it remained in pieces, in time it could once again be reforged. No. It had to be destroyed, utterly and completely.

Rhys focussed harder, channelling his mind more powerfully than he had ever done before. His senses began to blur, both corporeal and ethereal, as he concentrated on every particle within the revolving shards. The fragments of the Cintamani Stone began to glow in their entirety, each piece of iron radiating heat from its shimmering surface. Darkness began to press down on Rhys as he willed the stones into oblivion. He was growing weak. He was growing faint. The energies of the Aether were flowing through his body faster than either the Rift or the conduit could recharge them.

He pushed harder, fighting with every morsel of willpower his mind could summon, expelling one last bout of energy out of his body into the altar. An immense shockwave ruptured outwards, quaking every mountain, boulder, and mote of dust across the entirety of Sumeru. Lightning surged down from the Rift and struck the Cintamani Stone. The fragments were flung apart, each obliterating in a searing explosion. Darkness swallowed Rhys. All went silent.

FIFTY-THREE

Taking a deep breath, Arlas rapped his knuckles against the cottage door. A moment later, it creaked open, and Arlas was faced with the dark eyes of a beautiful young woman. She narrowed her gaze as she studied the stranger before her, but before Arlas could introduce himself, she turned to look back inside the door.

"Mother?" she called out.

A second later, an older woman, almost identical to her daughter save the years that had aged her, appeared in the doorway. Her eyes warmed at seeing the mage and she issued a gentle smile. "Arlas," she greeted him.

"Hello Linda," croaked Arlas.

"He'll be so glad you are here. He was afraid you would not come in time."

"I made my way here the moment I heard," replied the mage hoarsely.

Linda smiled again, yet this time doing so only with her lips. "Come," she gestured, drawing open the door wider and beckoning him inside. "I'll take you to him."

Arlas nodded, stepping anxiously over the threshold. He looked around the interior of the quaint little cottage; a fire crackled in the hearth with a few old chairs arranged around it. A kettle hung above the flames, faint wisps of steam beginning to issue from the spout. Linda's daughter kneaded dough in the kitchen as she resumed preparing the evening meal. Arlas closed the door behind him and wiped his tattered boots on the mat. Unfastening his travelling cloak, the mage draped it over a hook on the wall and smiled at the sight of a tarnished staff resting in the corner.

Following Linda's lead, Arlas passed the hearth and stepped through another doorway into a dimly lit bedroom. A silver-haired man coughed beneath the blankets. Linda moved to his side and handed her husband an earthen mug of water. With trembling fingers, the man took hold of it, taking a laboured sip, before Linda relieved him of the cup.

Placing it back on his bedside table, Linda whispered in her husband's ear. "Look who's come to see you."

The elderly man gazed up at the mage stood lingering in the threshold and his aging face gurned into a smile. "Arlas!" he wheezed.

"Hello, Michael," beamed Arlas weakly.

"I'll leave the two of you alone," smiled Linda as she made her way back towards the door. Before she exited the room, she laid a hand on Arlas's arm and whispered, "If he needs me, I am just outside."

Arlas nodded as Linda stepped out of the room and closed the door.

"Come in, come in, old friend!" rasped Michael Hemsworth with glee.

Arlas smiled at his lifelong friend, making for the chair beside the old man's bed.

"How are things?" asked the mage. "Still looking after everything out there in the world?"

"I am," nodded Arlas.

"You know, I didn't think you'd come," stammered Michael. "I didn't think you'd want to see an old man on his deathbed."

"Of course I came," croaked Arlas. "I couldn't let you die having the last word, could I?"

"I just wanted to see you one last time," replied Michael. "Before the end."

"There must be something that can be done," suggested Arlas.

"I'm not sick, Arlas," assured Michael. "I'm just old."

"Even still..." mused the mage.

"It happens to us all," chuckled Michael. "Well... all of us except you."

Arlas nodded.

"How old *are* you now?" asked Michael, studying his friends face.

"Sixty-four," replied Arlas.

"Sixty-four," murmured Michael in repetition. "And yet you've barely aged a day since I first met you. Incredible!"

Arlas nodded silently again.

"You know what this means... don't you?"

"What do you mean?"

"You know what you are?"

"No?" Arlas shook his head.

"Did Arabas never tell you the stories?" smiled Michael. "The legends of the Archmagi?"

"Archmagi?"

"Do you really not know?" coughed Michael in amazement.

"Know what?"

"I never believed the stories of course... well, not at first..."

"Please," smiled Arlas, resting a hand gently over Michael's trembling fingers.

"Yes, yes of course," agreed the elderly mage. "Well, supposedly they existed in days of old... in the early days of the Circle. The Archmagi... the most powerful of our kind. The Aether bent to their will; they could do anything. Magic ran so potently through their blood... like the first men... the Prime."

"Please," urged Arlas, "continue."

"Well... I can't remember most of it," apologised Michael. "But Arabas used to tell such great stories. That's what I thought they were... stories." Michael issued a laboured smile and studied Arlas's face with his swirling arcane eyes. "I don't remember a great many things... so much has been lost in the dark..." he continued, his eyes wandering about the room in his muddled reverie. "Arabas used to say their connexion to the Aether was stronger than other magi; an Archmage not only had power over it, but could read it... see things written in its echoes. He could control the conduits, the Nexus... like the Prime who built them."

"What else?"

"There's not much more I can recall..." apologised the old man. "There is one thing... Arabas used to say that the Aether flowed through them differently... like the elves... The Archmagi grow old, but over hundreds of years. Ross..." chuckled the mage, smiling as another memory came to him. "We couldn't agree—I thought it would be great... to go on living for hundreds of years. But Ross, he thought differently. He thought it was a sad thing... to go on living, watching all those you love grow old and die... long before your time. I never really thought about it." He suddenly began sputtering, his chest convulsing as he coughed.

"Here," offered Arlas, refilling the man's mug from the ewer on the nightstand and raising it to his lips.

Michael sipped at the water and his coughing steadily subsided. "It's not something I'd ever wish on anyone... especially not you of all people, old friend."

The two men locked eyes with each other and Arlas felt himself being studied by Michael. His face and body had withered and wrinkled over the decades, but his eyes, the eyes of a mage, had never changed in all this time.

"You've suffered so much, Arlas. You've lived through things that will haunt you for all your years..."

Arlas continued to stare into the man's gaze.

"The nightmares will end for me soon... I will take them to my grave. But you..." he trailed off, his head nodding steadily back as he began to doze.

Arlas sat silently beside his friend for a long while, watching him sleep.

After a time, Michael awoke abruptly, his eyes darting about the room frantically. "Linda!" he croaked. "Linda!"

"She's just outside," soothed Arlas, resting a hand on Michael's to calm him. "Do you want me to get her?"

"Arlas...?" beamed Michael, comforted by the sight of him. "I thought you'd left without saying goodbye!"

"I'm not going anywhere," the mage assured him.

"Good," smiled Michael, leaning his head back in the pillow. "Linda is such a good wife..." he muttered sleepily. "She looks after me."

"She does," agreed Arlas.

"Why have you never married, old friend?"

"You know I can't," replied the mage amusedly.

"Oh yes... of course," he wheezed. "You are still out there... protecting the world."

"Well, someone has to," replied Arlas warmly.

"Yes..." agreed Michael. "I supposed they do."

Arlas sat in silence once again as Michael began to slip back into sleep, but just as he was ready to drift off, the mage spoke out again.

"Do you ever regret the decision we three made, all those years ago?" whispered Michael with his eyes closed. "To let the Circle die with us?"

Arlas stayed quiet for a long moment before answering. "It was the right decision—it still is."

"I don't for a moment regret fighting the war... we did what we had to do... we stopped Azrael! We lost so many friends... But... when it was all said and done..." Michael's voice trailed away.

"What is it my friend?" asked Arlas.

"If there was one thing I could change— one regret I have... it is the Circle... If I could go back and change my mind."

"We did what we thought was right," insisted Arlas.

"I know," agreed Michael. "But it was not what was best," replied the dying man.

"What do you mean?" questioned Arlas.

"We should have tried again. Begun the Circle anew; but this time, made it better."

Arlas sat in silence, listening as his friend's breath died to a whisper.

"My only regret, Arlas, is that we didn't try."

Rhys opened his eyes. His body ached and his vision was spinning. As his vision drew into focus, he saw Maadurga peering down at him. She was cradling his head.

"Kalki," she breathed with a sigh of relief.

Rhys gazed up past her. The storm was dying in the sky above, the clouds slowly evaporating away, letting through thin beams of sunlight. The Rift had closed; all that remained were a few faint veins of emerald light gently gleaming across a scar that might never heal.

Snowflakes were fluttering softly down in the still air. Rhys strained his muscles, sitting upright on the icy ground. He was some way from the conduit, his body having been blasted clear in the explosion. The Cintamani Stone was gone; all that was left of it were tiny fragments of metallic dust peppered across the snow. Rhys rubbed his eyes and gazed around. He heard footsteps rushing towards him.

"Rhys!" gasped Sol. "What happened!?"

Rhys peered ahead at the slain corpse of Rudra, turning then to peer back at Nathaniel, the guardsman's body laying not far away.

More footsteps followed as Alkis rushed

over. He was the first to see Nathaniel lying dead in the snow. "No," he whispered, staggering to kneel at the guardsman's side.

"Nathaniel?" croaked Cade, arriving at the scene with Thia and Ulfgar beside him.

"Rhys… what happened?" Sol repeated in despair.

Rhys shook his head, fighting back tears, lowering his head in shame.

FIFTY-FOUR

Rhys stood on the beach as the waves rolled up the sand. Foam seethed around his feet, the tide on the verge of turning. He watched, tears stinging his eyes, as Alkis and Sol gently pushed the boat out from the shore. The tiny vessel bobbed on the ebbing sea as it drifted away, Nathaniel lain atop a bed of straw, his arms crossed over his chest beneath his shield, axe laid at his side. His pale skin gleamed in the faint sunlight as he floated outwards on the receding waves.

Together, Rhys and his companions watched in silence as the rowboat receded into the bay. After a short while, Cade stepped forwards, lighting the arrow nocked on his bow in the bonfire flickering on the beach. Aiming the Elven bow skyward, he drew back the string and released. The smouldering arrow sailed high into the air, arcing out over the bay, descending true and landing in the boat.

In the minutes that followed, Rhys watched as fire consumed the oil-soaked straw, the flames rising to cremate Nathaniel. The boat drifted out of the cove and eventually faded from sight as it was carried off by the currents of Thule. Rhys continued to watch a while longer, staring onwards at the horizon as rain started to drizzle out of the dreary skies. The eternal tempest had been quelled when Rhys reactivated the conduit and destroyed the Cintamani Stone, but this far out from the mainland, in the ragged archipelagos of the Wyrm's Triangle, there would always be rough waters and raging winds.

A hand came to rest on Rhys's shoulder. "Come on," beckoned Sol gently. "It is time."

Rhys stooped and picked his pack up from the sand. Arne and Vidar were loading the last few supplies into the rowboat. Eirik and the others were already onboard the Marlin, the white sun-bleached caravel anchored out in the bay.

"You are sure the seas will be safer now?" questioned Vidar, still unconvinced.

"I believe so," nodded the mage.

"Even if they aren't," replied Sol, "the three of you managed to get us here in the first place. The journey back can't be any more difficult."

"We'll be fine," assured Arne, resting a hand on his son's shoulder. "Come on," he added, gesturing for Vidar to climb into the boat.

Rhys stowed his pack in the bow and prepared to clamber in, but as he did so he heard a faint screech carry over the winds.

"Hang on," paused Rhys, stepping away and turning to look up at the skies.

Dawon's striped wings descended from out of the clouds above, Maadurga on his back. The majestic beast descended steadily towards the bay, swooping to land on the sand ahead of Rhys. Maadurga stepped out of the saddle and turned to face her mount. She cradled Dawon's head, running her slender fingers through his feathers. She spoke to the gryphon in Elvish as Rhys steadily made his way over. Stepping back from her mount, she gave him a wide berth. Dawon spread his wings and leapt into the air above Maadurga's head, taking to the sky and soaring away, vanishing high above the island.

Maadurga revolved to face Rhys, a single tear beading in her eye which she swiftly brushed away. "Kalki," she beamed, shouldering Dawon's saddlebags.

"Maadurga," Rhys greeted her warmly.

"You were going to leave without me?" she smiled.

"Without you?" questioned Rhys in confusion. "You want to come with us?"

"Of course," she nodded. "I am Rajanya Kshatriya, First Warrior of Kalki."

"Maadurga..." beamed Rhys. "You don't have to come with me."

"No," she agreed. "I don't have to. But I do want to."

"But..." began Rhys. "What about your people?"

"My people do not need me anymore," she replied. "My dharma here is complete. Rudra is defeated. The Vritra is destroyed. The Akasa is closed. Those who once worshipped Mahakala now praise your name, Kalki. Suraksa is at peace, and Shambhala is safe once again for my people."

"Couldn't they use your help in rebuilding?"

"Do I look like a builder to you, Kalki?" she asked sharply.

"No, I suppose not," agreed Rhys.

"I am kshatriya: warrior caste," she insisted. "Rudra is defeated, but Indus is not. The war of my people is over, but your war, the war of mankind, has only just begun. I fight for you, Kalki. That is my dharma. Wherever you must go, I will follow. You are the saviour of my people. I will help you now to become the saviour of your own."

"Well," smiled the mage, "when you put it that way…"

She embraced Rhys firmly.

"I think there is one space left," declared the mage, leading Maadurga over to the rowboat.

Arne pushed the boat out from the shore and climbed inside. Gathering up the oars, the sea captain began rowing with his powerful arms. In a short time, they arrived at the Marlin, and clambering up the rigging, they boarded the caravel.

Leaving the others to hoist up the rowboat and the last supplies, Rhys showed Maadurga to the quarters beneath the forecastle where he left her to stow her possessions. Exiting out on deck, Rhys climbed the steps to the prow as Arne and his sons began preparations to set sail. Stood before the bowsprit, Rhys found Thia.

"Hey you," he greeted her.

"Hey yourself," she smiled back, wrinkling her nose before they embraced.

Thia took his hand in hers, interlocking their fingers, resting her head on his shoulder as they gazed out to sea.

"I figured it out, you know," announced the witch after a time.

"Figured what out?" questioned the mage, not at all sure what Thia was talking about.

"The Cintamani Stone," she explained.

"When I saw it, back in Mahakaleshwar, in Rudra's hand, I thought I recognised it."

"You mean the runes on its surface?" questioned Rhys.

"No," she replied. "Although I couldn't help noticing they bore a striking resemblance to those carved on the conduit's standing stones."

"The same runes are on all the conduits," explained Rhys.

"Are they actually?" questioned Thia in surprise.

"Yes," Rhys nodded. "Shakyamuni claimed the conduits were built by the first elves, but the runes carved in their stones don't bear even the slightest resemblance to any Elven Sanskrit I have seen in our time here."

"Then what?" questioned Thia. "Who do you think built them?"

"Something older," replied the mage. "Something more ancient than elves or men. But that is just a hunch."

"I think you might be on to something," agreed Thia.

"What were you saying about the Cintamani Stone?" questioned Rhys. "You recognised it?"

"I did," confirmed Thia. "Though, at the time I couldn't think what. But I remember now. I've read about stones like that; it was dark, and smooth across its surface, almost as if the outside of the stone had been melted."

"What are you thinking?"

"Have you ever heard of a lodestone?"

Rhys shook his head.

"They are stones with unusual arcane properties," she explained. "They attract metals, sticking to them so powerfully that they can even defy gravity. Supposedly, they can channel the Aether and focus it in unusual ways. And, though I can't tell you if this is true, apparently, if you suspend one from a string, or find a way to float it on still water, it will always turn to point north."

"That sounds familiar," nodded Rhys. "Are these lodestones common?"

"No," replied Thia. "Supposedly, they are very rare. No one quite knows where they come from, but there are some unusual ideas suggested by scholars."

"Such as?"

"The craziest one I read was that they are the remains of shooting stars, fallen to the ground after they have burnt up in the sky."

"You are kidding?" chuckled Rhys.

"Why?"

"If you recall, the elves believe that the Cintamani Stone fell from the stars," explained the mage.

"Well," smiled Thia, "I suppose that lends more credit to the idea."

"That it does," nodded Rhys. "And, if those runes were carved by the same people who built the conduits, then we know who weaponised it."

"Perhaps how to do so is one piece of knowledge that is best left forgotten."

"Agreed," nodded Rhys, wrapping his arm around the witch and pulling her in tight.

Arne began to shout orders to Vidar and Eirik, and soon the anchor was raised and the Marlin's sails let out. The sailcloth began to swell with wind and the Marlin cut through the water towards the mouth of the bay.

"What now?" questioned Thia as the two of them stared at the horizon.

"We head home," replied Rhys. "We'll figure out what to do when we get there."

"Something will have happened in the time we were away," warned Thia. "Indus will not have sat still since we've been gone."

"No," agreed Rhys. "He won't have. But we'll be there to foil his plans. I still think the conduits are the answer. We've found four already, and the rest must be out there. But whatever happens, we'll find a way to stop him!"

BOOKS BY THIS AUTHOR

Rise Of The Apostate

Rhys North awakens to find that his village has fallen prey to a dark curse. All life and colour has been sapped from the land and every single inhabitant of Longford has perished during the night; all except Rhys.

Amidst the ruin, Rhys comes upon a mysterious stranger named Arlas, the leader of the Circle of Magi, an ancient order of magical warriors sworn to the protection of the continent of Cambria. Driven by the need to uncover the truth behind the fate of his village, Rhys embarks on a journey to join the Circle of Magi, yet in doing so, he becomes entangled in cataclysmic events that threaten peace across the continent.

Thrust to the forefront of a conflict that has been building for centuries, Rhys is forced to seek out long lost stone circles that reside in every forgotten corner of Cambria, in a desperate attempt to save the world from a fanatical mage of unspeakable power.

Dawn Of Tyranny

Rhys North and his companions find themselves in Orthios, the once capital of the Cambrian Empire, in search of another stone circle to restore the Nexus. But the so called 'City of the Gods,' is a dangerous place. Orthios is on the brink of revolt, and their presence has not gone unnoticed. In his attempts to seek retribution against the traitorous mage Indus Mark, Rhys finds himself caught at the heart of a long-brewing political struggle between the city's Council of High Lords, whilst targeted by a mysterious religious cult known as the Church of Ashes.

With war looming, and Indus's influence growing ever more powerful throughout the continent, Rhys once again finds himself at the heart of world changing events, unsure who to trust, yet determined to stand against the tyranny of his enemies.

Printed in Great Britain
by Amazon